SEASON OF EMBERS

THE BONDED: BOOK ONE

RACHAEL VAUGHN
WENDI WILLIAMS

Wendi: To E., G., and G. My everything, for always.

Rachael: To Trent and Seva.

CHAPTER 1

SOFI

"Sofi, hold *still*."

Arina's voice was shrill as she yanked my head into position. My eyes watered as she tied another ribbon into place around a lock of my pale blonde hair, careful not to displace the bright blue cornflowers that had been tucked through the plaited strands. My mother made a sound of dissatisfaction from behind Arina, and in the mirror, I could see her reach over my oldest sister's shoulder to adjust a stray tendril of hair that had snaked free from one of my elaborate braids.

My mother's reflection disappeared as I caught a flash of flaxen hair out of the corner of my vision.

"Marten, no!"

A crash sounded from the kitchen, and my mother sprinted out of my bedroom after my two-year-old nephew. My middle sister, Hanna, was hot on her heels. The house was filled near to bursting, with my mother, grandmother, two aunts, three cousins, two sisters, and five children between them. It was bedlam.

It was always like this on Spring Day, when all the men of the house disappeared and left the women to prepare for the Ceremony. I capitalized it in my mind, the importance of the event clear even though I knew barely anything about what the night held in store.

A cry came from the kitchen, and my head turned at the sound, but Arina gave my hair a vicious tug and I quickly straightened, stifling a groan.

"Don't pull all my hair out." My voice came out in a whine. My nerves were showing.

I had endless childhood memories of Spring Day preparations—watching my sisters and cousins get ready for their Ceremonies. I'd peeked around doors, watching my mother braid their hair, watching them don their elegant dresses, their faces all calm and composed under flawless makeup. I'd wondered endlessly about the secret ceremony—what did they *do*? And then when they returned the following morning, they always seemed so grown up, so *knowing*. Each time, I'd dreamed about what it would be like on *my* day, when I was finally eighteen and getting ready for my own Ceremony.

I'd never expected to be so *nervous*. My stomach was in knots, my mind spinning. Where would we be going? What was going to happen there? What if I made a fool of myself in front of the whole community? I clenched my hands into fists to keep them from trembling, hoping my sister wouldn't notice. It was a miracle I'd been able to keep from throwing up.

"There." With a final eye-watering twist, Arina fastened the last ribbon into place and turned me to face my reflection in the mirror. "Look, I put great-grandma Lisandra's clip here on the side."

I turned my head, admiring the sparkling blue clip, fashioned in the shape of a tiny cluster of flowers. I had to admit, my sister had done an amazing job. The front part of my hair was caught back in a series of elaborate braids, all twined with satiny white ribbons. The rest was left to fall free in soft white-blonde waves. Cascades of cornflowers, the very first of the season, were also woven through, held in place by tiny clips. Against the dark brown of my eyes and my pale skin, the effect made me feel pretty. I hardly recognized the face in the mirror.

A second shrill cry echoed down the hallway, and Arina glanced up sharply at the sound of her own child, five-year-old Mia. She flashed a quick smile at me in the mirror. "You look beautiful. Don't worry, you'll do fine."

Uh-oh, I must not have hidden my nerves that well after all. Bending forward, she gave me a quick hug from behind. "I wish I could be there with you," she said. Her voice was wistful, but the look in her eyes was unreadable. Worried, maybe? The knot in my stomach twisted tighter, but before I could puzzle it out, she left the room to deal with the escalating cries coming down the hall from the kitchen. Since only women over eighteen were allowed to attend the Ceremony that night, Arina had volunteered to stay at home with the children. Looking at the stranger in the mirror, I half-wished I could take her place.

I was never good at being the center of attention. But despite that, I had to admit I was *curious.* So much of the Ceremony was shrouded in secrecy, I had only been able to glean the basics over the years.

Spring Day itself was a widely cherished event that our town had been celebrating ever since my great-grandfather and the small contingent of other immigrants had left our small, Eastern European homeland in the late 1800s, fleeing foreign occupation and establishing our little community of Vaikesti here in the midwestern U.S. Nearly everyone in town was descended from the immigrant population, and we kept to the old traditions, which included Spring Day. The bulk of the festivities would take place the following morning, on the first of May, including singing, dancing, and plenty of food. And while every child in town looked forward to the carnival-like atmosphere of Spring Day, it was the events of the night before that made my stomach twist with nerves.

I knew the Ceremony took place at midnight. I knew only women were permitted to attend. I knew it would honor every girl who had turned eighteen since last Spring Day. And I knew I had to participate in a secret ritual. But that was all I knew. The women of the community were notoriously tight-lipped, and even my sisters had been unwilling to share more.

My thoughts were interrupted as my mother reentered the room.

Her dark eyes, normally tired, were sparkling in her lined face, and she held in her arms a beautiful white dress I'd never seen before.

"Are you ready?" She laid the dress out on the foot of my bed. I raised an eyebrow as I took in the yards of white fabric woven through with white ribbons and seed pearls, lace netting around the hem and scooped neck. I didn't remember either of my sisters' dresses being this fancy.

"Is it Spring Day or am I getting married?" I asked, half-joking, but my mother didn't smile.

"This is the dress I wore on my Spring Day," she answered, her expression wistful. "It should be just your size. Besides, it's tradition."

I knew better than to argue with that. 'It's tradition,' was the answer to pretty much any question I'd asked since I was old enough to ask questions. Besides, the dress *was* beautiful. Shrugging, I got to my feet and pulled off my t-shirt, then wriggled out of my jeans. My mother helped me step into the dress and maneuver it into place, doing up the hidden zipper in the back. She fluffed my hair out around my shoulders and turned me to face the mirror.

I really *did* look like I was going to a wedding. My own. I sucked in a breath. My mother was getting teary-eyed behind me. My discomfort grew. What exactly was going to happen at the Ceremony?

Hanna stuck her head around the door frame. She gave me an approving smile before addressing my mother. "Arina's getting the kids ready for bed. Then it should be about time to go. Are you two ready?"

I had no idea if I was ready, so I didn't answer, but my mother gave a nod and crossed the room to speak with my sister. I looked toward the mirror again, meeting my own wide-eyed gaze. A lock of hair had come loose near the crown of my head, and I reached up to fasten it down. A stab of pain made me stifle a gasp as my finger caught on my great-grandmother's clip, the edge of the metal digging in deep. I jerked my hand back and stuck the finger in my mouth, but not before a bright drop of blood landed on the shoulder of my dress. The red was vivid against the pristine white fabric, and my stomach sank. Surely that wasn't a good omen.

My mother turned from the doorway, and I quickly pulled some of my hair over my shoulder to hide the spot and pasted on a smile as she joined me by the mirror.

"Make sure your *Vanaemake* is awake and ready," she told my sister. "We'll be there in a minute."

Hanna nodded and left to find my grandmother. My mother turned me to face her.

"Do you remember all your words?"

"I think so," I said nervously. Each of the girls participating in the Ceremony had a series of lines to recite as part of the ritual. I'd been practicing my phrases, and while every kid raised in Vaikesti had more than a passing familiarity with the traditional language of our ancestors, the phrases were meant to be sung, and I'd have been lying if I said I wasn't afraid I'd mess up and make a fool of myself in front of my friends and family.

My mother sat on the edge of my bed and patted the quilt next to her. I joined her, perching awkwardly in my dress. Her face was serious as she looked me over, and my heart sped up. Was I *finally* going to find out what the night had in store for me?

"Sofi," she began. "Tonight is a very special night, you know that."

I didn't know anything, so I kept still and didn't interrupt.

"I don't know what your sisters may have told you, but I don't want you to worry."

What was *that* supposed to mean? They hadn't told me anything. Naturally, I immediately began to worry.

"The rituals are old," she went on, "but the binding is symbolic. Maybe a long time ago the magic really worked, I don't know, but—"

Hanna poked her head around the door again, cutting off my mother's words. I could have strangled my sister. Binding? *Magic?*

"We're ready when you are," my sister announced.

My mother made no effort to finish what she'd been saying; she just leaned in and gave me a quick kiss on the cheek. "I'm proud of you, *kallike*," she whispered, then rose and left the room. I didn't miss the meaningful glance she shared with my sister on her way out.

Hanna must have seen the panicked expression on my face, because she gave me an understanding smile. "Don't worry," she said quietly as she ushered me out of the room, fussing over the trailing ribbons on my dress. Her lips were close to my ear. "The binding isn't real. I think they always hope it will be, but the words never work."

Before I had a chance to react, my aunts and older cousins joined the procession, my grandmother bringing up the rear, and I was herded out the door and into the cool night air. Whatever questions I might have had, it was too late. The Spring Day Ceremony was here.

CHAPTER 2

DARJA

I was floating. Weightless and untethered, blood thrummed in my fingertips and buzzed beneath my lips. My eyes were open, but everything around me was pleasantly out-of-focus. Velvet darkness hovered at the edges of my vision. I blinked, then blinked again, lingering in the darkness, gently coaxed by the siren song of unconsciousness.

But, no. It was important that I stay awake. I couldn't think why, but I knew it mattered. I sucked in a deep breath and felt my lungs fill with cool, antiseptic-scented air. Another breath. This one I held until I saw spots dance in front of my vision.

I turned my attention to my surroundings, curious about what was causing this delicious lightness, like my whole body had been inflated with helium. I looked down my arm and saw something resembling a plastic butterfly perched on the back of my hand, and I smiled, delighted. It occurred to me only in a fleeting moment of clarity that 'delighted' was not a word I would have used to describe my life before this place—this feeling—but I shook it off.

From the butterfly, a plastic tube snaked its way up a crisp white sheet, looped over a bed rail, and then twined around a metal pole before disappearing into a plump bag filled with clear liquid. This, I was mostly sure, was the source of my current state of zen.

"Thank you," I mumbled incoherently in the general direction of the bag. My voice sounded thick and far away, not-quite-connected to the rest of me. The rest of me, meanwhile, pulsed with a thrilling numbness, like a foot fallen asleep, warm and heavy.

"What was that?"

The voice sounded as equally as distant as my own, and for a moment, I thought it must have been me. But then a presence materialized at my side, a slim figure in a red polo and khaki pants. *Ms. Kross.* I tried to smirk, but couldn't get my face to cooperate. I had gotten in trouble for telling her all the *tajas* looked like they ran cash registers at Target. It felt like ages ago, but couldn't have been more than a few weeks.

It had been a sound beating, but nothing less than I'd deserved, as *Mama Taja* had reminded me throughout. I'd laughed at her afterward, was struck again, then sent to Ms. Kross, who'd been stone silent as she'd bandaged my backside. Had I blushed? I couldn't remember at this point, but I didn't think so.

I looked at Ms. Kross, her heart-shaped face stern. She'd told me once that looking mean made her seem older, and that made the girls respect her. I hadn't told her that at night, in our rooms, we frowned as hard as we could, seeing who could come closest to looking like 'Kross the Boss.'

I snorted at the thought, louder than I'd expected in the

quiet room, nearly frightening myself out of my still-tingling skin.

"Is something funny?" she said, moving closer to check the tubing attached to my happy little butterfly. "Does it hurt?"

"Yes," I said, answering the first question. Then, to the second, "And, no. Nothing hurts. Everything feels wonderful."

She cleared her throat. "Yes, well. That's the medication doing its job. It should last until..." She cleared her throat again, then busied herself clicking a small dial near the bag that hung above me.

"Until...?"

"The Ceremony. You remember, of course?"

I did. No amount of happy juice could cloud those memories. Naturally, I'd never attended one, but it was seemingly all we learned about, all we talked about, and sometimes, all we dreamed about. The Ceremony was our reason for existing, or so we were told. We wouldn't all be Chosen, but we were meant to act like we were. Because eventually, when we turned eighteen, one of us would be selected for the honor of representing the *koolis* at the Ceremony. It was a hard path, *Mama Taja* seemed to enjoy telling us, but whoever was Chosen would be rewarded beyond her wildest imaginings.

Was this my wildest imagining? The buzz was great, sure, but the rest of it? I wasn't sure I'd been dreaming of celebrating my eighteenth birthday shivering naked under a sheet in a hospital bed, too stoned to move.

"What's going to happen?" I asked, feeling suddenly breathless. I looked at the plastic butterfly on my hand, and wondered if there were other butterflies inside me, beating their wings and sending my heart pounding into my throat.

"All shall be revealed," Ms. Kross said softly, the tired words sounding even more exhausted than usual.

"And the spirit shall be fulfilled," I responded, as I had done every morning in *eksam*. I used to think if I just moved my lips without vocalizing the words, it wouldn't count. I didn't know why it had even bothered me, but it had, so I'd continued my silent protest until Helena Tamm went to *Mama Taja* and told her I refused to receive the spirit. I couldn't sit for a week.

"Good girl," Ms. Kross said, patting my arm. "Are you able to move?" she asked, crossing to a wardrobe in the corner and opening its doors to peer inside.

I tried to lift my arm, but only managed a couple of fingers. "Not really," I said, attempting a shrug.

Ms. Kross sighed. "I'll need to find someone to help dress you." She turned away from the wardrobe, holding a long white dress over her arm, lace spilling nearly to the ground in a frothy cascade.

I swallowed, hard, feeling some kind of emotion at seeing the dress, but not understanding what any of it meant. It was gorgeous, that much was obvious. The kind of dress I would have said I hated, but would have secretly wanted to crawl into, feeling the soft, handmade lace shift and slide against my skin.

I realized then what Ms. Kross had said. "Not *Mama Taja*," I said, hoping my face looked as pleading as I wanted it to.

"Darja," she said warningly, draping the dress over a chair and walking closer.

"Please," I said, meeting her eyes. Her icy blue gaze was piercing, but I didn't look away. I never had.

Finally, she relented. "Fine," she said tightly. "I'll go find Ms. Luts."

"Thank you," I mumbled, but the door closed on my words, and she was gone.

Alone, I gathered whatever wits the drugs hadn't dulled and tried to think. We were in the *koolis*, I thought, largely due to the drab gray paint on the walls and the chipped tile floor, but it wasn't a room I had ever been in before. Aside from the hospital bed and the wardrobe in the corner, the furnishings were sparse. Two chairs, my white dress draped over one, sat near a shuttered window. Next to the door, a cabinet with a sink was attached to the wall. Above it hung a metal medicine chest. There were no mirrors. No pictures, no linens or curtains anywhere. It may as well have been an actual hospital room, as sterile as it was. The only confirmation that I was, in fact, still in the *koolis* was just over the medicine chest—a tapestry woven with two trees, heavy with spring blooms. Between them, a bonfire burned in red and orange threads. At the bottom, the words *Tasakaalus, harmoonia* were inscribed. In balance, harmony.

I didn't know what was coming. I didn't know if I was afraid, or excited, or just ready to get it over with. There hadn't been a day in the last eighteen years that I hadn't wondered what the hell The Ceremony was all about, and why no one could ever talk about it until they'd been to one. And even then, only to the other women in Vaikesti who'd attended. I'd seen the glances exchanged. The hushed whispers after another one of the *koolis* girls had her ceremony.

I wasn't sure what happened after. The girls were integrated back into Vaikesti when The Ceremony was over. We weren't told more than that; just that the girls had fulfilled their Great Command, and were free to return.

Return to what? I'd often wondered, but even at my most rebellious, I'd never had the courage to ask. I was raised at the *koolis* and though we had one day of classes each week at the county school, and one day a month to shop or socialize in the next town over, we mostly kept to ourselves. The Vaikesti kids all knew us by the blue shift dresses we wore, and largely refused to interact with us. *Mama Taja* said it was because they resented our status, our opportunity to be selected as Chosen, but the looks they gave us didn't convey jealousy; they were fearful, disgusted, even pitying. The county kids just thought we were weirdos and steered clear.

I was pulled from my confused and foggy thoughts by the sound of the door opening. Ms. Kross walked in with Ms. Luts in tow, holding a handful of vivid blue cornflowers. Ms. Luts was all round softness to Ms. Kross' slim compactness, and she was one of the few *tajas* that actually deigned to smile on occasion.

"Well," she said with a forced cheerfulness, bustling over to the bed and fiddling around with the same dial Ms. Kross had adjusted. "Are we ready to begin?"

"Begin wha—" The words were lost in a tidal wave of unimaginable bliss. Heat surged through my hand and up my arm, dispersing a warm glow throughout my extremities. I couldn't breathe, and I didn't much care. My eyelids fluttered, seemingly the only body part still capable of movement.

"That should do it," Ms. Luts said. I felt the bed sink as she sat down at my feet and began pulling off the sheet, exposing my naked body to the chill air. "Let's get her dressed."

"Evelin," Ms. Kross said, sounding chastising, but already, their voices were fading. I didn't care about my nakedness. Didn't care that I was being pulled and tucked into my dress like an uncooperative toddler. Didn't even care when Ms. Luts pulled a brush through my long blonde hair, hitting every snag along the way.

I was floating. Drifting. Disappearing. It was Ceremony

time, and even though I couldn't muster the energy to care, I knew with some sort of sixth sense, ESP bullshit feeling that everything was totally, irrevocably about to change.

CHAPTER 3

SOFI

It was pitch black under the canopy of the forest. We'd parked the cars in the gravel lot at the edge of town behind the Rebane's house, where Merili and Lea Rebane had joined us, and went the rest of the way on foot. The sense of anticipation I'd been feeling all day seemed to blanket our group as soon as we reached the trees, and a hush fell over us, the only sounds the swish of our dresses and the crunch of leaves underfoot. I could scarcely believe I was really *here,* following the narrow trail through the trees, the path lit only by the sweeping beams of the flashlights. It was surreal. The twist of anxiety in my stomach began to loosen, settling into a sort of nervous excitement.

It was finally happening. My mother's and sister's words from the house faded into the background. I was surrounded by women who had participated in this very same ceremony on their own Spring Day, and no matter what the secrets may be or how many cryptic comments were made, each of these women had made it through no worse for wear. I could do this, too. I could become a real member of our community. Someone to be taken seriously, trusted with the secrets of the Vaikesti.

I'd never been to the old country, but I'd been told more than half the land there was blanketed with forests. And so, it was forests the immigrants had sought here as well, looking for any opportunity they could find to hold onto the old traditions. I couldn't imagine the trees here were anything like those back in that place the elders still called *Sünnipaik*, 'home,' but this was the only home I'd ever known. These woods were familiar to me, safe and comforting, the source of a thousand games of hide-and-seek. And after a minute I began to recognize where we were going—the old bonfire grounds, where the whole town would gather to celebrate Midsummer Night and *Jõulud* in the winter.

This was probably just a bonfire and some ceremonial words. Just like all of our rituals. *Don't get so worked up,* I mentally chastised myself. It almost worked.

I caught sight of another cluster of flashlight beams through the trees, and a little further down the path we met up with Marta Kask and her family. Marta had been in my class at school since we were kids. We weren't exactly close, but seeing a familiar face in her own flowing white gown made me blow out a breath I didn't know I'd been holding. She looked like a ghost, her dress glowing pale as it seemed to float above the ground. If I remembered correctly, there should be two more girls here from my class. That is, assuming there weren't any girls from the *koolis* participating as well. There might be a girl or two my age over there, but we only saw them once a week at school, and like everyone else, I tried to steer clear.

Marta met my eyes and I could see my relief reflected back at me. I wondered if her family had told her any more than mine had. I doubted it. I directed what I hoped was a confident smile her way, and was met with a grimace that likely mirrored what was actually on my face.

Our two groups joined seamlessly and silently as we continued on into the woods. It wasn't far, less than a quarter mile, before I saw the flickering light of the fire in the distance. The wind rustled through the trees and I shivered in my thin dress. The weather was still temperamental this early in the spring, and the night air was chilly. Wishing I had a sweater, or at least long sleeves, I stepped faster, eager to feel the warmth of the fire on my skin. I supposed I should at least be glad it wasn't raining.

The trees began to thin gradually before giving way entirely to reveal a large clearing, and then suddenly we were there, the old bonfire grounds, and my heart began to pick up again. The clearing was packed with women. It seemed we were the last ones there, and I didn't know where to look, my eyes jumping from the blinding light of the bonfire to the crowd, lighting on familiar faces and away as I tried to pick out other white dresses.

The crowd parted, making space for our two families. It wasn't just my white dress that made people step aside, nodding in deference—both my parents were on the Town Council and my father was the town's doctor—and I could feel the eyes of the crowd on me from head to toe. My mother's hand landed on my arm, gently guiding me, and then when I didn't respond fast enough, grabbing my hand and dragging me around to the far side of the circle.

There were murmurs of greeting as we took our places, but the crowd was largely quiet, the sound of the crackling fire and thrumming of insects louder than the voices of what seemed to be nearly a hundred women. The night air was thick with anticipation, and I began to feel a bit queasy.

To my relief, we didn't have to wait long. We had just settled into place when the Ceremony began.

I wasn't surprised to see Eliise Tamm step forward. She leaned heavily on her cane as she turned her back to the fire and faced the gathered women. Eliise was the oldest woman in Vaikesti by nearly a decade, and a member of the Town Council. Elders held a place of high esteem in our town, and Eliise often presided over town events.

When she opened her mouth to speak, the already quiet crowd fell still. Her body may have been frail, her spine bent with age, but her voice was clear and strong in the silence of the clearing.

"Welcome to Spring Day." A murmur of response echoed through the clearing. "We gather here tonight to welcome another generation of girls to Vaikesti adulthood. Tomorrow we celebrate the changing of the seasons and the synergy of our relationship with the earth. But tonight..." She glanced around the circle, her eyes lingering as she picked out the white dresses in the crowd. "Tonight we celebrate *you*."

A shiver ran up my spine. Eliise cleared her throat, then raised her voice again. "Marta Kask, please step forward."

Marta's eyes were huge and round, but she joined Eliise by the fire.

"Elisabeth Koppel, please step forward."

Liz's dark head bobbed through the crowd and joined Marta at the front.

"Anna Saar, please step forward."

There was a pause, then another white dress materialized as the crowd across the way parted and let Anna through. She caught my eye as she took her place and winked. I held my breath.

"Sofia Ilves, please step forward."

My breath released in a whoosh. I felt a nudge from Hanna behind me, and then I was moving, my feet carrying me forward to join the row of girls by the fire.

I turned to face the crowd of women, faces I'd known since birth. The dancing flames reflected in their eyes. I cast my eyes down, not wanting to meet all the expectant gazes. Then, softly at first, Eliise began to sing. Her voice was lovely, high and haunting as it spiraled away into the darkness. A moment later, voices from around the circle picked up the song, and soon the whole crowd had joined in, a harmony rising above the main melody in the words of the old country. My chest loosened slightly at the sound, and I joined in. A festival in Vaikesti was never complete without music, and the familiarity was comforting.

The other girls join in as well, and I felt Anna's hand slip into my own. She had linked hands with Liz on the other side as well, and I gave her fingers a squeeze.

The song ended the way it had begun, the voices dropping out one by one, until the chorus came around again and only Eliise was singing, her voice fading softly as the last note stretched out into silence.

We all stood for a moment, quiet and expectant, and then Eliise spoke again. "Darja Kallas, please step forward."

I blinked in surprise, and felt Anna's hand tighten in mine, as the crowd parted and another girl stepped through. I hadn't seen her at first, standing as she was back by the trees. She was wearing the same style of flowing white gown as the rest of us, cornflowers caught up in her dark blonde hair.

Was it her Spring Day Ceremony as well? Were there actually five girls? But if that was the case, why hadn't she been called up here earlier with the rest of us? I slid a confused glance over to Anna, who gave me the briefest shrug.

As the girl moved through the crowd, her face caught the light and I realized I recognized her. She was one of the *koolis* girls. I'd never seen her out of the blue dress she'd worn when she'd joined our class once a week. It made sense, though. The *koolis* girls were kept apart from us in almost everything they did. Why not the Ceremony as well?

The girl—Darja, Eliise had called her—was flanked by two women as she walked, both wearing the recognizable khaki and red uniform of the *tajas*. They each had a shoulder under her arms, guiding her forward, and the crowd shied back as they passed, giving them slightly more room than strictly necessary. I also moved aside without thought, making space for the girl.

Wait—something was wrong. The *tajas* weren't *guiding* the girl, they were *carrying* her. She hung limply between them, her head lolling to the side, her feet dragging in the dust. What—?

The girl's eyes were alert though, and when she drew close her gaze met mine and I stepped back involuntarily, dropping Anna's hand in the process. Darja's pupils were dilated, the black orbs swallowing her eyes, and they locked on mine with an intensity that made me shudder. What was *wrong* with her?

Before I had time to react further, Eliise was speaking again, raising her voice to address the crowd.

"It is time. Time to welcome the Spring. Time to welcome five new members of our community. We have all watched these girls grow from children into women, and today they will earn their place with us as full members of Vaikesti, sworn to uphold the traditions we hold dear. Henceforth they will be bound to us, as we are all bound together, in life as in death, a circle of renewal that has no beginning and no end."

I tried to focus on her words, but I was acutely aware of the girl by my side, propped upright between the two *tajas*.

Eliise turned from the crowd to address the four—now five—of us, pitching her voice so everyone could still hear.

"From the earth we were born, and to it we return. We are bound to the earth in life, as we are bound in death. Tonight, we gather to strengthen those bonds, linking together the new members of our community with an *ohverdus,* so they may experience the bonds that connect us all."

I knew that word. *Ohverdus.* Sacrifice. My breath caught in my throat and I felt suddenly cold, despite the heat from the fire that blazed behind me.

Eliise went on, looking at each of us in turn.

"The bonds we forge here tonight are permanent and real, and will guide you through the rest of your days. Will the *ohverdus* please step forward."

She looked expectantly at Darja, and the two *tajas* moved forward a step, hauling the girl with them. I glanced between Eliise and Darja, the tightness in my throat growing.

The old woman reached a withered hand into the deep pocket of her pants, and came out holding a wickedly-sharp looking pair of scissors, the blades glinting in the firelight. I surreptitiously wiped my damp palms on the skirt of my dress as she leaned on her cane and hobbled a step toward Marta, who was staring with wide eyes.

A whispered word passed between the two, then Marta leaned down, letting Eliise tug a thick lock of her hair from beneath her elaborate styling. Raising the shears, Eliise snipped off a hank of Marta's golden hair, and I heard a muted sound of protest escape Marta before she could stop herself. Eliise had pulled the lock from underneath, where it wouldn't show, but I still winced as Marta raised a hand to touch the blunt ends of her hair.

Without pause, Eliise moved down the line, removing a tress from Liz's dark hair and then one from Anna's loose curls before coming to stand in front of me. Obediently, I lowered my head as the other girls had, and the old woman separated a handful of strands from underneath my loose waves. The metal of the shears was icy cold where it brushed my neck, and I shivered as the blades sliced through.

Holding the four locks of hair deftly between the fingers of her gnarled hand, Eliise turned to stand before Darja, who stared back, unblinking. I expected the woman to remove a lock of Darja's hair as well, but I blinked as she replaced the scissors in her pocket instead. She let her cane fall by her feet and gestured at the *tajas*, who turned the girl around, so her back was to Eliise and the crowd. I watched, fascinated, as Eliise separated out a lock of Darja's dark blonde hair with surprising dexterity and began to weave an intricate five-part braid. I could barely follow as her fingers flew through the strands, weaving us all together.

This must be the binding Mom and Hanna were talking about, I thought, the lump in my throat receding slightly. My mother's words echoed through my head. *"The binding is symbolic."* I shifted my weight from foot to foot. I was starting to get uncomfortable from standing so long. So far, the Ceremony had been rather underwhelming—singing and braiding hair? This is what I'd been so worked up about?

And yet I could still feel the presence of the *koolis* girl next to me, still as a statue. What was *wrong* with her?

Eliise finished her braiding and tied off the ends, then stepped back. "It is time for the *usutalitus* song."

I'd nearly forgotten.

"Marta, you may begin."

There was a long pause before Marta started. Her voice wavered and she took it slowly, carefully pronouncing the words. I glanced down the line and saw her eyes were closed, her cheeks pink as she sang.

In no time at all it was Liz's turn, and she picked up right where Marta had left off, repeating the melody, her voice strong and firm. She looked out over the crowd as she sang, and I envied her poise, wishing I had half the confidence she did.

Anna's voice was soft and slightly off-key when she picked up the refrain from Liz. She stumbled over a few of the trickier words, and I felt a little better.

My heart was beating fast when she neared the end of her lines, but I started in where I was supposed to. My eyes picked out my mom and Hanna in the crowd, and I kept my focus on them, trying to pretend no one else was listening. The relief that washed over me as I ended my refrain was palpable, and I was so glad I'd gotten all my words right I didn't even care how many wrong notes I'd hit.

I trailed off my last note, expecting Darja to pick it up and keep the song going, but my note trailed into silence. I glanced over, and caught the *taja* on the side closest to me shifting under the weight of the girl. My shoulders stiffened, my unease returning. Could the girl even talk?

Eliise stepped forward again, a smile on her lined face. "That was beautiful, girls," she said. Turning to the crowd again, she raised her voice. "It is time for the *sidumine*, the binding, the last part of our ritual." She turned to Darja then, and raised a withered hand to lay against the girl's brow. She spoke rapidly, words in the old language, too fast for me to follow. When she was finished she stepped back and nodded at the two *tajas*. "You may proceed."

The two women hoisted Darja between them with a soft grunt of effort and turned. I hadn't noticed the plank, set into the bonfire at an angle, flames lapping at its base. It happened so fast, I didn't have time to react. The *tajas* moved the girl into position at the base of the plank, then let her arms go. Darja fell back against the thick plank, head cracking against the wood, limbs limp. Flames began licking at the lace of her skirts even before the *tajas* had moved out of the fire's reach.

What?!

I tried to say something, but the words caught in my throat, and before I could move, before I could *think*, Eliise was there, a small container in her hand. She dropped it at the base of the plank. The fire plumed upward, billowing around the girl.

Eliise's voice was loud in my ears, "*Vaim on täidetud.*"

And the voices of the crowd even louder, "*Tasakaalus, harmoonia.*"

But the crowd, the other girls, everything else was muted as my focus narrowed down to Darja, where she lay motionless against the wooden plank, her body consumed by fire. Her eyes, though. They were still alert, dilated but aware, and they locked on mine, horror and agony clear in her gaze even though she was silent and still. My heartbeat thundered in my ears. Was this a trick? It couldn't be real.

Suddenly a flash of light caught my eye and I tore my gaze away from hers. It was her hair, the braid where Eliise had joined our locks together. It gleamed, flaring more brightly than the blinding light of the fire, for just a second, then faded. Had I imagined it? Was I imagining all of this?

That was when the screaming started.

CHAPTER 4

DARJA

I couldn't remember most of the car ride, but when Ms. Kross parked in a darkened field on the edge of Vaikesti, I knew we had arrived for the Ceremony.

The drugs had taken hold of me in a way that was entirely unpleasant. Tremors wracked my body, shuddering through my muscles and leaving me quivering like a twanging bow string. I was freezing beneath the piles of lace, but I couldn't seem to get my limbs to cooperate with my brain long enough to wrap my arms around myself.

My stomach roiled and churned with sharp pangs of nausea. I dry heaved in the backseat, Ms. Luts' hand rubbing circles on my back. By the time I heard Ms. Kross release her seatbelt, I was completely immobile, though my mind raced, thoughts and questions tumbling over one another amidst an internal voice screaming *No! No! NO!*

This wasn't how it was supposed to be. Whatever I'd speculated it meant to be *chosen*, it wasn't this. I'd expected rituals. Singing. Silly prayers disappearing into the unhearing sky. But this...the drugs and the secrecy and the dawning realization that I'd been groomed for the last 18 years for something well beyond my understanding...this felt *wrong*. This felt terrifying.

The back door opened to the sound of crickets chirping the early choruses of a spring night. A chill stole across the backseat, prickling along every inch of exposed skin. I wanted to rub the feeling away, wanted to huddle in on myself and cry all the hot, angry tears I could feel building up behind my eyes, but I was incapable of doing anything but slumping against Ms. Luts, mentally pleading with her to meet my eyes.

She didn't. Instead, she stepped out of the car and stood talking to Ms. Kross in a hushed tone. I strained to hear, but couldn't make out the words. In the distance, I thought I heard singing.

Finally, Ms. Kross leaned through the back door to peer in at me, her pale eyes inscrutable.

"It's time, Darja." Was it just me, or was there a hint of strain in her voice? I met her eyes and hoped she could see my terror. If she could, if it bothered her, she managed to keep her face unreadable.

"We'll need to carry you. I'm going to pull you out of the car, and then Ms. Luts and I will lift you up."

My heart pounded as her cool hands wrapped around my shoulders and pulled me toward the open door and into the night. I couldn't have done anything else if I'd tried, but I willed my body to go heavy and limp nonetheless. No sense making it any easier on them than it needed to be.

I slid out of the car, Ms. Kross' arm beneath my shoulder blades, and felt her stagger backward under my weight. I crumpled to the ground in a heap of lace and useless limbs, my cheek pressed against the damp grass.

"Dammit, Laine," Ms. Luts said. She huffed out a breath and bent over me, taking my arm and heaving me into a sitting position. "She'll be filthy before we get her to the gathering."

"What do you want me to do?" Ms. Kross said. "Carry her there myself?"

"You know my back—"

Ms. Kross let out a sharp exhalation and the older woman faltered.

"I'm going to lift her. Be ready."

I felt Ms. Kross bend down behind me and slide her arms under mine. I looked up at Ms. Luts, searching for some reassurance, but her face was carefully, purposely blank. With a grunt, Ms. Kross shoved her weight against my back and hoisted me up. Immediately, I began to sway, unable to bear any weight on my feet. Ms. Luts yanked my arm up and ducked underneath, pulling my hand around her shoulders. Ms. Kross did the same on my other side and, breathing heavily, they began to inch forward, dragging me like a cross between them.

At the edge of the woods, they paused, adjusting my weight and tightening their grips around my waist. I was pulled past the treeline, the hem of my dress catching on the high grass, and this time, I was sure I heard voices, lifted in song. It was beautiful. Haunting. I let the tears fall, hot and scalding, down my cheeks.

It seemed like they carried me for eternity, harsh, gasping breaths and occasional grunts their only communication. My heart hammered beneath my chest and my breathing went rapid and shallow. I began to feel lightheaded, and a wistful sort of longing for the peace of unconsciousness set in.

When we broke through the trees and into the clearing, the singing abruptly stopped. A few faces turned to look at me, their smiles and fever-bright eyes garish in the flickering light.

The fire light. Ahead, I could see the pyre, and the platform that sat just above the licking flames. I knew then, with a certainty that would have paralyzed me, if the drugs hadn't already done the job, that the platform was for me.

I tried to scream. Tried to gather the strength to move, but I couldn't manage more than a frantic blink. Ms. Kross and Ms. Luts drew me through the crowd, and I heard the approving whispers, the murmurs of excitement as we approached the line of girls—Vaikesti girls—standing in front of the fire.

At their head stood Eliise Tam, who I remembered seeing at the occasional town celebration when the *koolis* girls had been permitted to attend. She drew up her shoulders as we approached, looking regal and mighty and completely at ease. Maybe I was wrong. Maybe I'd misinterpreted the purpose of the pyre. Maybe it was just a bonfire for the women of Vaikesti to gather around. Maybe.

Or maybe not. Eliise said something then, though I couldn't process her words. But as she said them, I was dragged closer to the flames, and I knew I hadn't been wrong. Ms. Kross and Ms. Luts pulled me between two of the girls, and one of them turned to meet my eyes.

I saw my horror reflected in her widening gaze. Had she not known? Didn't they tell them, either, about the rites of spring? Would she help me? Could she?

I tried to hold her eyes, tried to beg her wordlessly to help, to act, but she finally turned away, confusion and fear contorting her features. I knew her, or thought I did, though I couldn't think of her name. The other girls were tense, and kept their eyes locked on the old woman, refusing to glance in my direction.

The rest of the ceremony passed in a sort of blur. I hung between the *tajas* as locks of each girl's hair were braided into my own, songs were sung, and words were chanted in the old language. I couldn't follow any of it. I felt trapped in my own body, like a moth caught in a lantern, beating its wings uselessly until, exhausted, it tumbles into the flame.

I was barely aware we were moving again until I felt the heat of the fire against my face. Ms. Kross and Ms. Luts pulled me towards the flames, turning carefully until I faced the crowd. Slowly, they lowered me onto the plank. My breath rushed in and out of my nose as I hyperventilated. Tears streamed from the corners of my eyes, wetting my hair at the temples.

My eyes went wide as Ms. Kross bent over me, her face an unrecognizable mask. "Darja," she whispered, a crack appearing in her facade. "I'm so—"

"*Laine*," Ms. Luts hissed, and then, both were gone, disappearing like the wraiths of smoke that twined above me.

My dress caught first, the snowy white blossoming into orange and red. It wasn't until it reached my hair, the acrid smell of charred cornflowers, and worse, crawling through my nose and down my throat, that the pain registered. It was consuming. Excruciating. A violent burst of agony that felt never-ending.

Until it did. One moment I was there, ablaze and immobile and helpless against the ravenous flames, and the next, blackness rushed up to meet me.

When I came to, I was standing at the back of the crowd. The women gathered in rows in front of me held hands, some with their faces raised toward the sky, smiling. Some were singing; others hugged, congratulating each other on another blessed Spring Day.

I looked down, my lace dress perfect and pristine all the way to my ankles. As I did so, my hair fell over my shoulder, gleaming honey gold in the flickering light. I looked up again at the fire, still burning, and the figure at its heart, blackened and shriveled.

What was happening? Had I dreamed it all? Was I still dreaming? I turned to the woman nearest me and tried to ask for help, but all that came out was a croaking, gasping breath. She looked ahead, not noticing, and when I stepped closer, she turned to her neighbor and said, "What a lovely night."

I looked to my left, to the next row of women, and finally managed to rasp out a strangled, "Hello?" but no one even glanced at me. They were whispering excitedly, gesturing toward the girls who were still standing in front of the pyre.

I moved slowly down the aisle, the same path I'd taken earlier, dragged between Ms. Kross and Ms. Luts, watching to see if anyone in the crowd was looking at me. They weren't.

When I reached the front of the crowd, I stopped. The old woman's gaze was moving expectantly between the figure in the fire and the row of girls before her. Her pupils were large and her nostrils flared as she searched each of their faces for...something.

The girls were uniformly pale, their faces pinched and somehow older, more world-weary. The girl on the end, the one who'd seen me before, was crying, not bothering to wipe the tears as they dampened the collar of her white dress.

I shifted my focus to the fire, through the flames that still licked hungrily towards the sky. The body on the platform was unrecognizable. And yet I knew, with complete and utter certainty, that the body on the platform was mine. The searing pain that echoed along my arms and legs had been real. The sizzling smell of burnt hair was the smell of my hair. The betrayal of my childhood, my upbringing, the promise of being *Chosen* was real. Total. Complete.

I fell to my knees, a sob ripping from my throat, shattering the buzzing, chittering noise around me. I screamed until I felt empty, hollowed out and dry like a corn husk. Around me, the triumphant conversations continued.

Then, I heard a gasp above me—a shuddering and frightened intake of breath followed by a stifled cry. I looked up and saw her, the last girl, the girl who'd looked at me...

...and saw she was looking at me again.

"Oh, God," she whispered, her eyes darting to the fire, then back to me.

I stood up slowly, shivering, not daring to take my gaze off her. "Can you—?"

She nodded, her lips parting as she sucked in a breath. I could see they were trembling.

"Am I—?" I started to say, just as she whispered, "Are you...?"

The last word hung between us. We didn't need to say it.

I was dead.

CHAPTER 5

SOFI

I felt like I was seeing double.

The girl—Darja—stood in front of me, whole and intact, white dress unmarred, blue cornflowers twined in her hair. Then she stepped toward me and my vision blurred—I could see *through* her. And on the other side was Darja again, the same girl, but this one was a twisted black husk of a body, dress a tattered burnt rag, cornflowers lost in the blaze. But she was still standing there; I could *see* her. Her eyes were huge as they met mine, her gaze beseeching.

"You can see me." It wasn't a question.

Her voice was thin, transparent like her body, and it seemed untethered, as if it came from far away and was whispered in my ear at the same time. A shudder crawled up my spine.

The Ceremony had wrapped up without me as I'd stood, transfixed with horror, wincing at piercing screams no one else seemed to hear, staring at this wraith no one else seemed to see. Voices were raised in song again, and while the other three girls also stood awkwardly in front of the pyre, a little dazed, the rest of the crowd had started to mingle, some still singing while others exchanged hugs and pleasantries, smiles and well-wishes.

Was I losing my mind?

I chanced a glance at the fire, where the plank had collapsed into the inferno and the charred remains of the body—the sacrifice—*Darja*—were no longer visible, swallowed by the flames.

The wraith girl, the other Darja, she was still there, her wild eyes raised as she scanned the crowd as well. As I watched, her outline wavered, fading into mist before solidifying again. I tore my gaze away. Maybe if I didn't look, she would disappear and I could convince myself I had imagined it all.

I closed my eyes and took a deep breath.

When I felt a hand on my arm, I nearly jumped out of my skin. Could I *feel* the girl too?

My eyes flew open to reveal my sister and mother standing before me, and my sister snatched her hand away from my arm.

"I'm sorry, Sofi," she said hastily. "I didn't mean to startle you." When I just stared at her blankly, she grabbed my shoulders and pulled me in for a quick hug. "You did such a great job though. You didn't forget a single word."

Was she *serious?*

My mother gently pulled my sister back. "Give her some space, Hanna." Then she betrayed her words by pulling me into her own arms for a tight squeeze. "I'm sure you have lots of questions, *kallike*," she said, drawing back and holding me by my shoulders.

I sure as hell did, but I still couldn't bring myself to do anything more than stare at her blankly.

"The Ceremony is over, so once the singing and visiting dies down, everyone will head home," my mother explained. "You four girls will stay, as will I and the other mothers, and Eliise. We'll talk for a while, explain everything, answer any questions you girls may have. Then you'll each spend some time alone, holding vigil tonight."

"It's supposed to give you time to get used to the bond," Hanna put in, a bit of a wry twist to her mouth. "You know, commune with the dead? But since it's all symbolic, it's really just boring as hell. Try not to fall asleep."

"Hanna," my mother gave her a quelling look. "It's tradition."

I blinked, trying to keep up, trying to listen, to slow my racing thoughts.

"Anyway," my mother continued, "you'll stay until dawn, then you'll be able to go home and get some sleep. Don't forget the Spring Day festival starts in the afternoon, and you and the other girls will have places of honor at the feast." She paused and looked at me expectantly. I managed a dazed nod.

"Now, everyone wants to congratulate you before they leave."

My mother stepped back, and with a start I realized a group of people had gathered behind her, clamoring in close once she'd moved aside.

I felt my grandmother's bony arms go around me, my aunts and cousins pressing close, kisses on my cheeks, words of praise and congratulations that didn't register. My attention was already gone, skimming over the dwindling crowd.

Darja was nowhere to be seen. Could I have imagined it? A hallucination brought on by the shock? Could I be so lucky?

The other three girls' families had also crowded around them, offering hugs and well-wishes. Marta looked a little blank as well, her eyes glassy in the firelight as her mother gripped her hand. Liz and Anna were pale, but seemed to be at least able to interact with their families.

I searched for Darja again, scared I would find her. Scared I wouldn't. There was no trace of her.

My mother's hand slid into mine, pulling me gently forward, and I realized we were alone. My family had all left, joining the parade of onlookers that were heading back through the trees, bobbing flashlights visible in the distance before they were swallowed by the forest.

I kept my eyes on the ground, studiously avoiding looking at the fire, as my mother led me around to the other side and sat me down on one of the upended stumps positioned in a cluster around the fire. I complied, feeling like a rag doll as I collapsed onto the stump and continued to stare. My mother sat next to me, watching me with a mixture of caution and concern, but I ignored her, my mind still spinning in circles.

Had they really just *murdered* that girl? Burned her in a funeral pyre like some sacrificial animal? And why couldn't she move? What had been wrong with her? *And why the hell could I see her?*

I felt pressure building inside me. Tears maybe, or hysteria, I didn't know, but I tamped it down. My mom had said they would explain. She'd said they would answer all our questions.

———

Fifteen minutes later, the clearing was deserted. The roaring fire and the group of us hunched on logs were the only evidence that anything had happened here at all. At some point my mother had procured a thin blanket, which she'd wrapped around my shoulders, and I found myself gripping the ends tight, trying to ward off the chill.

The four girls and four mothers had each taken a seat on the circle of stumps. Silence had fallen, and they all looked expectantly at Eliise, who was settling herself into position on the last stump, directly across the circle from me, letting her cane fall to the ground next to her.

"Girls, first I want to congratulate you. You all did so well, and I'm so proud to be able to call you all members of our community."

There was a murmur of agreement from the mothers, and Liz's mom put in, "And you all looked so beautiful up there." More agreement.

I tried to keep my focus on Eliise, waiting to hear the explanations, but it was hard to prevent my gaze from sweeping around the clearing, searching.

"In case your mothers haven't yet told you what the rest of the night holds in store," she went on, "we will talk as a group first, answering any questions you may have. And you may ask anything, not only about your Ceremony tonight, but any questions you might have about your roles as women in our community. This is sacred space, and you are safe here. We are here to help you with your transition into adulthood. After that we will separate so you may each have some time alone to adjust to the new bonds that have formed here tonight."

I saw Anna and Liz exchange a glance across the circle.

"So, who wants to start?" Eliise said.

After a beat, Anna hesitantly raised her hand. Eliise gave her an encouraging nod.

"The girl, the...sacrifice. Was she...did she know?"

I leaned forward as Eliise gave Anna an understanding smile.

"Did she know the role she would play tonight, you mean?" Eliise clarified.

Anna nodded.

"Yes, my child. Darja has known for years that she was Chosen. Each member of Vaikesti has a different role that we play in order to serve our community. Many of us have more than one role. Parent. Teacher. Child. Elder. All of us make sacrifices. The Chosen are no different. They serve their community in their own way, and like the rest of us, they take pride in their service."

Darja. Between one heartbeat and the next, she was there again, materialized out of thin air. She stood across the circle with her back to me, hunched forward with her face inches from Eliise.

"LYING BITCH!" Darja screamed.

I nearly fell off my log.

My mother shot me a concerned glance, and I looked wildly to Eliise, but she didn't react at all. No one did.

"Liar," Darja said again, her voice coming in a thick rasp and breaking on the word. "All of you. You never—"

But Eliise had continued on, and with the two speaking over each other, I couldn't concentrate on either of them.

"Stop," I said without thinking, meaning Darja, but they both stopped. Everyone turned to stare at me. I felt my face flush and I shook my head. "Sorry," I mumbled. "Go on."

Eliise gave me a queer look, but continued on, answering a question I hadn't heard. I couldn't focus on her answer though, because Darja had turned at my outburst and was staring at me again. She had a question in her eyes, but she didn't voice it. I could see through her, see Eliise on the other side of Darja's body, and I felt like my eyes didn't know where to focus.

Darja slowly moved to the old woman's side and raised her hand, tentatively reaching out as if to touch Eliise. I held my breath, and I didn't know if the wraith girl had breath to hold, but she seemed to pause as well, anticipation clear in her rigid form before she extended her arm all the way. Her hand passed clear through Eliise's body with no resistance at all.

I let my breath out all at once and saw Darja sag on her feet. She turned again to peer at me, and the expression on her face made me want to look away, but I couldn't seem to bring myself to move.

We stayed that way for a long moment, Eliise's voice reduced to a drone in the background, before Darja straightened and began to move. She walked across the circle toward me, and I shrank back, only relaxing when she sank to her knees in front of me. Slowly, hesitantly, she raised her hand, holding it up in front of me.

I couldn't help it, I raised mine too. We both hovered there, hands in front of our faces, inches apart, breath held again. Her hand, so close, was so pale, so transparent, the flickering light from the fire passing through to cast no shadow on the ground. Mine was solid, real, trembling.

Our hands moved by millimeters, both of us clearly afraid, gazes locked on our outstretched limbs, heartbeats—mine at least—pounding rapidly.

When at last our hands met, it was like stepping into a pond and watching your reflection merge with itself. I don't know which shocked me more, watching her hand disappear as it passed through me, or the shock of the ice cold sensation I felt as it happened. A gasp tore from my throat.

It took me a moment to register that the talking had stopped, another moment to realize that all the eyes in the circle were trained on me. My arm dropped like a lead weight.

"Sofi, are you all right?" It was my mother, concern on her face.

"Yes, I'm sorry, I just—" I cleared my throat, my cheeks flushing hotly. "Can no one else—?"

"Don't!" This time it was Darja, her voice urgent as she

glared at me with wide eyes. "Don't tell them. Don't say anything."

"What? I—"

But she was gone. In the middle of standing up, she wavered and disappeared, and I blinked, trying to focus on something that was no longer there.

"Sofi?"

I pulled myself together with a monumental effort. "I'm okay. I'm sorry. I won't interrupt again."

There was a pause before the conversation resumed, several wary eyes still trained on me. I kept my gaze down, not meeting anyone's eyes.

Eliise continued what she had been saying, answering one of the girls' questions about the festival the following day, before glancing around the circle. "Are there any other questions? Marta? Sofi? You've been quiet."

I shook my head; I didn't know what I could possibly say.

Marta tentatively spoke up. "The bond, between us and…the, uh, *koolis* girl. You keep talking about it. Is it…I mean…" She glanced around the group. "What exactly are we supposed to be feeling?"

Eliise didn't respond right away. The mothers exchanged glances. Eventually Eliise sat back and steepled her fingers, but before she could respond Liz cut in. "It's not real, right? I mean, it's just symbolic."

Anna chimed in as well. "Are we not supposed to talk about it? Because I don't feel anything, either. Were *you* bonded at your ceremony?" She directed the question at her mother, who seemed a little uncomfortable.

They all had my full attention.

Anna's mother didn't get a chance to answer her daughter before Ellise broke in. "The bond between the living and the dead is fundamental to our community," she

39

started, and I ground my teeth in frustration at the vague answer before she went on. "We know the bond is real, that it did exist; we have reports from the old country confirming it. We know at least two of the founding members of our community were bonded when they settled here. But it is true. It has been some time now since a new bond was forged."

"How long?" Marta asked in a quiet voice.

"Generations."

"But why do we keep doing the Ceremony then?" Anna asked.

The mothers looked shocked, and Eliise's face was gentle but as unyielding as stone. "We honor our traditions. We honor our ancestors. We pay homage to the magic that rests silent within us, and pray that someday it will live again, and new bonds will be formed. Vaikesti is nothing without its past, its roots, and the moment we question that, we take the first step toward losing our magic forever."

My mother nodded from her place by my side, and the other girls appeared thoughtful.

A long moment passed as the girls took this in, myself included. "What was the bond like?" Marta finally asked, her voice tinged with wonder.

Eliise's eyes softened, and her voice was reverent and wistful. "I don't know exactly. Our ancestors could communicate with the *ohverdus,* could see them and interact. But so much knowledge has been lost. We all must pray that we live to see another bonded pair in our lifetimes. In the meantime, we treat the bond as the sacred link that it is."

I frowned at the non-answer. A sacred bond it may be, but something didn't add up. I'd seen Darja's eyes, before and after. I yearned to speak up and tell the others, but something stayed my tongue.

The conversation switched to more mundane topics

then, and the mothers chimed in as the girls discussed their plans for the summer. I kept quiet though, avoiding my mother's concerned gaze, and finally, after what seemed like forever, the conversation seemed to wind down.

"Are there any other questions, girls?"

When Eliise's question was met with shaking heads all around, she retrieved her cane from the ground and used it to lever herself to her feet.

"Now is the time for contemplation," she announced, brushing debris off the seat of her pants. "Your mothers will be going, and they'll return to retrieve you when the sun begins to rise. Until then each of you will hold vigil alone, to contemplate your bonds and consider your new roles as adults in our community. I will remain here at the fire in case I am needed."

I glanced around at the dark of the woods outside the circle of firelight and pulled my blanket tighter around my shoulders. I didn't want to stay out here until dawn. I didn't want to stay out here a minute longer than necessary, especially not with the spirit of an *ohverdus* that only I could see. Bonded or not, she horrified me. I wanted to go home, fall into bed, and forget any of this night had ever happened.

But instead I let my mother help me to my feet. Small side paths led away from the clearing like spokes on a wheel, and I followed as my mother clicked on her flashlight and led me down one of the paths, deep into the woods and away from the other girls. The path didn't go far before the trees parted again to reveal a tiny second clearing where another fire had been constructed, this one small and clearly made to provide light and warmth for just one person. The flames crackled merrily, but I still shuddered at the sight of it. A small pile of firewood had been placed off to the side, and I settled myself unceremoniously down into the dirt beside the fire, wanting to avoid the images it brought to mind, but wanting its warmth more.

My mother hesitated before crouching down next to me and laying a hand on my knee.

"Sofi, are you okay?"

I nodded. She began to rise, her eyes still on me, before hesitating and kneeling low again. "I know the Ceremony can be hard sometimes. It's a lot to take in. If you need to talk, or have any questions, you know I'm here for you, right?"

I nodded again. I didn't know what else to do.

Finally she left, casting a worried glance over her shoulder. "I'll be back at dawn."

And then I was alone. I hoped.

The forest was loud in the dark of pre-dawn. Night animals rustled in the trees and insects sang loudly; the fire cracked and popped. The moon was bright overhead, and the stars were visible. I guessed it had to be around two or three in the morning. Hours to go before dawn.

I sat motionless, my eyes searching the perimeter of the clearing. I didn't know what I was supposed to be doing, or thinking, or feeling, so I sat still, trying not to see the burning body, trying not to hear the screams, trying not to think at all.

When Darja phased back into existence, she was sitting by the fire as well. I flinched even though I'd half expected her to turn up at some point. She was huddled in a ball, knees tucked up under her chin, arms wrapped around her shins, and she stared blankly into the flames.

We sat together for a long moment, her staring into the fire, me trying not to look at her, before I gave up and cocked my head to face her.

"Can you feel it?" I asked in a low voice. "The fire?"

She shook her head, not meeting my gaze. "I can't feel anything." Her voice was a whisper.

I was quiet, not sure what to say. Eventually, she turned to look at me. "What do I *do?*"

I raised my shoulders in a helpless shrug, but she shifted her body to face me more fully. "Who *are* you?"

"My name's Sofi," I responded. "Sofia Ilves."

"I know *that*," she snapped. "I've been in your class once a week for years."

I was taken aback. I hadn't known who *she* was aside from one of the *koolis* girls. My face flushed at the realization.

"I meant, why can you see me? What makes you so special? Are we really bonded, like that lady said?"

I shrugged again. "It sure seems like it. Could you hear her? Were you still...there? When I couldn't see you?"

She nodded. "It's...different...like this. Being dead." She seemed like she was trying the words out to see how they sounded. "I can't seem to control my body very well. It comes and goes. But I'm still there, I think. I can hear, anyway."

I took this in. "Why didn't you want me to say anything? In the circle, I mean. You told me not to tell them anything."

Anger darkened her translucent face. "Those liars. *Murderers.* Don't trust them."

"But maybe they can help us," I protested. "Tell us what to do."

"So they can hurt me more?" she bit out.

"They wouldn't—" They would. They *had.*

"Why couldn't you move, when you came in? The *tajas*, they were carrying you." I wasn't sure I wanted to hear the answer. "Why didn't you fight? Or scream?"

Darja's face was unreadable. "They drugged me. Back at

the *koolis*. Held me down and hooked me up to an IV. I couldn't move a muscle."

I sucked in a breath, then sagged a little. "But then you couldn't feel—"

"I felt *everything*."

A chill ran through me, bone deep, and I shuddered despite the warmth of the fire. I didn't know what to say, so I said the only thing I could. "I'm sorry. I'm so sorry."

She didn't respond, just turned to stare into the fire once again. After a minute I turned too, and when I looked into the flames I could see the blackened body on the plank again, agony in her eyes. I didn't try to fight the image this time, and I felt the wetness of tears on my cheeks as the image played over and over in my mind like a movie reel.

She didn't speak again and neither did I. We sat in silent vigil, and waited for dawn.

CHAPTER 6

DARJA

As it turned out, being dead sucked. Like, for real. I could feel a tugging deep within my... soul? It felt like someone had cast a fish hook and caught me under the navel, pulling me toward something unseen. But every time I tried to follow the feeling, I disappeared. Flickered out, as Sofi described it.

I was still there, in those moments...wherever 'there' was. But nothing was the same. The world around me dimmed, like an old Polaroid left in the sun, the image floating distant and blurred beneath the cellulose. A rushing noise filled my ears, a dull roar that felt disorienting and strange. There were voices, carried through the air around me; plaintive sounds that never formed into recognizable words.

I had sat with Sofi in the woods while she struggled to stay awake, blinking in and out of existence seemingly against my will. We hadn't said much, as the other girls, though out of sight, might still have been within earshot. Besides, what was there to say about this messed up situation, other than just that? We didn't know what it meant, or where to go for answers.

So we sat, silent and still, each lost in our own thoughts. I could see Sofi shivering as the deepest dark slowly faded to gray, but I couldn't feel the chill. Eventually, just as the dew began to shimmer along the delicate spider webs spun through the grass, Sofi's mother came to collect her.

They hugged, and Sofi peered at me over her mother's shoulder, her eyes searching and unsure. I didn't know if I should follow her, or even if I could, so I just shrugged. The two began to walk toward the edge of the woods, and as they got farther away, the tugging sensation inside me grew stronger, nearly unbearable. It wasn't a physical pain, but there was an ache—an empty sort of yearning—I couldn't define.

I scrambled to catch up as they moved through the trees, and the longing subsided—though it did not dissipate—the closer I got to Sofi. They walked out into the field where Ms. Kross had driven me the night before, a few tire tracks denting the grass the only indication anything may have happened in the woods beyond. Sofi walked around to the passenger side of a small blue car, and I felt a surge of panic. I didn't know where she lived. Didn't know if I could ride in a car, or how Sofi might feel about a dead girl riding along in the backseat. And very suddenly and very certainly, I didn't want to be left alone.

I silently pleaded with Sofi to look back at me, to see me like no one else could. To tell me what the hell I was supposed to do. But she slid into the car and buckled her seat belt without a backward glance.

"Bitch," I whispered half-heartedly, even knowing it wasn't fair. After all, she was just as freaked out and overwhelmed as I was. *But at least she's not dead*, I thought bitterly. I watched the car move slowly across the field and turn onto the road that ran down to the *koolis*.

Don't panic, I told myself. *Just breathe*.

Except I couldn't breathe. The realization knocked me sideways and sent me reeling. I was dead. I had died. And I had come back. But not back to life.

Back to what?

My mind raced. Was I a ghost? A spirit? Was I *haunting* Sofi?

A hysterical giggle bubbled up in my throat. I flickered then, everything around me going suddenly out-of-focus, those strange noises rushing up to envelope me like a physical presence. I gasped, the ache inside me growing so strong I doubled over, wrapping my arms around my body.

I clamped my eyes shut, humming loudly to cover the sound of the voices pleading, taunting, wailing. I knew I was dead. Knew I had lost my body. But I felt I was losing my mind as well.

When I opened my eyes again, I was in a bedroom. It wasn't my own sparse dorm at the *koolis*, decorated with a cork board full of plaintive song lyrics, less-than-flattering doodles of all the *tajas* and not much more. This room was warm and bright and messy, a dark wooden bed in the corner strewn with cast-off clothing. Situated just under a window outfitted with soft yellow curtains was a squashy armchair covered in floral fabric and mismatched floral pillows, an equally squashy orange cat perched in the middle. I swore loudly, startled by the sudden change of scenery, and the cat flicked his eyes toward me, issuing a sound that could have been a purr or a growl. Then, with a careless yawn, he curled deeper into the cushions and closed his eyes.

I frantically took stock of my surroundings, noting the photos tucked around the vanity mirror, the braided flower crown from some midsummer past slung over the bed rail, and the laptop open to the lyrics of a song in the old language perched on the desk.

Sofi's room. But how—?

My thoughts were cut off by the soft creak of the door handle turning. I didn't know where to go or what to do, so I quickly sat down on the bed, trying to look casual.

The door opened and Sofi entered, her shoulders slumping as she crossed the threshold. She looked up, eyes going wide, and staggered backward into the hall.

"Holy *shit!*" she squealed, palms flat against the wall behind her. I could hear a muffled voice from somewhere else in the house asking if she was okay.

"I'm fine," she called, though her voice wavered. "Just forgot that Sprat was in here."

Sprat, who appeared to be the fat orange cat in the chair, cracked an eye, then swished his tail before resuming his nap.

Sofi inched slowly back into the bedroom and closed the door behind her, staring at me like she'd hoped the whole night before had been some sort of bizarre fever dream.

"What the *hell* are you doing in my room?" she hissed. Her long blonde hair was wild where it had pulled loose from the unity braids, and the cornflowers hung limp and wilted, tangled with dried bits of grass and a few withered leaves. A smudge of soot ran down one cheek, and the hem of her white dress had turned dingy brown.

"You look like shit," I responded. The pain and terror of the night before was written plainly across her face, and a surge of guilt spread through me.

"Well you look like—"

"Like what?" I said, my guilt subsiding.

She looked away. "Like a ghost," she muttered.

Her words lanced through me like needles, and I winced.

We lapsed into silence, though I could feel the unanswered questions hanging between us. I gazed down at the quilt on the bed. It was smooth all around me, no wrinkles or indentations where I sat. The realization that I had no weight, made no impression, unnerved me.

"What now?" I said finally, glancing up to meet her eyes.

She sighed and began to fidget with the ribbon at the end of her braid. "I wish I knew. I mean, it worked, right? For the first time in more than a hundred years. It has to mean something, right?"

I shrugged. "Mean what? That a hundred and fifty years of murdering girls is suddenly fine because the magic works?"

"That's not what I meant," she said softly.

"Because it's not fine."

"I know that."

"They drugged me. They dragged me against my will into a fire and threw me in it *while I was still alive*. There is *nothing* that can justify that."

"I *know that*," she said again, and this time, the firmness in her voice stole whatever fight was left in me. This wasn't her fault, and no matter how much I wanted to throw some blame, she was my only ally in this thing, and I wasn't going to get far without her.

"I'm sorry," I said. "I know you know. I just...I'm just freaking out."

"Same here," she said with a tight, humorless smile. "I just want to go to sleep and pretend it never happened. When I got in the car with my mom, I thought I could. Then you were here, and I just..." she sighed, then glanced down at her dress. "Ugh, I'm disgusting."

I let the abrupt change of subject slide. "You are," I said instead, grinning when she shot me a look.

"I need a shower before we can figure out what to do next."

"Knock yourself out," I said, pretending that I hadn't just realized I'd never again experience a hot shower.

Sofi grabbed a pair of leggings and a t-shirt off the bed, careful to avoid the space I sort-of occupied, then gave me a quick smile before disappearing out the door.

I sat motionless, staring aimlessly for a few minutes, wondering what to do, when I heard Sprat scratching the seat of the chair.

"Bad kitty," I said offhandedly, but to my surprise, he turned and looked directly at me, letting out a curious mewl. I narrowed my eyes. "Can you see me?" Feeling a bit dumb, I waved a hand in the air, then let out a low swear when Sprat's eyes followed the motion.

By the time Sofi returned, wrapped in a towel and a cascade of damp hair trailing down her back, I had a plan.

I waited impatiently while she got ready, rolling my eyes but obliging when she asked me to turn around so she could get dressed.

"So," she said, while I gazed out the window at the late morning sunshine. "You're saying Sprat can *see* you? Just like I can?"

"He knows I'm here," I said with certainty. "I'm sure of it."

"And this means we have to go to the *koolis* because…?"

I sighed, not sure how to explain. In that moment, when I'd realized Sprat knew I was there, I'd remembered something. There'd been a cat at the *koolis*. A slim and standoffish calico that one of the *tajas* had fed once and then never gotten rid of. Sasha, as we'd called her, lived almost exclusively in the library. She was fond of lounging outside the door of the historic section, a small, glassed-in room that held texts, paintings and artifacts from the old country. Every few days, Sasha would emerge from the library and saunter down to the kitchens, where she'd wait at the back door until the egg lady appeared.

The egg lady was an elderly woman who lived alone on the outer edge of Vaikesti. She kept chickens in her backyard, and a few times a week would bring a basket of eggs to the *tajas* who also worked in the kitchens. In a separate basket, she would wrap up several small fish she'd caught in the stream that ran along the outskirts of the town, and these she would leave just outside the door for Sasha.

I was fascinated by the egg lady. She wore odd clothing —heavy skirts draped in scarves and patched in numerous places, and a threadbare velvet coat that looked as if it came from another century. We all knew the egg lady was crazy, as she spent most of her visit muttering incomprehensibly to herself and looking nervously over her shoulder.

I had always thought it was odd that Sasha was the only one with whom she spoke directly, petting and cooing over her while she put out the fish. What was even stranger, I remembered thinking, was that Sasha always seemed to be looking beyond the egg lady, following something just behind her with a careful, curious gaze.

The same gaze Sprat had given me.

"Darja?" Sofi said, interrupting my memory.

"Yeah," I said, turning back to face her. "I'll explain when we get there."

"Speaking of," she said, running a comb through her hair. "How *are* we getting there?"

I shrugged. "You drive. I'll meet you there." I wasn't sure I could replicate whatever had gotten me from the field to Sofi's bedroom, but I was about to find out.

CHAPTER 7

SOFI

I didn't know if Darja had developed some kind of magical ghostly teleportation powers or what, but she had flickered out of existence before I could open my mouth to respond.

"Right," I muttered to myself. "I'll just drive over to the *koolis*. No big deal." I retrieved my car keys from the top drawer of my bureau before grabbing a cardigan I'd left hanging over the desk chair. I pulled it on over my thin t-shirt.

I'd never been to the *koolis*. It wasn't off-limits, exactly. It was just...not a place you wanted to be seen. I didn't know what Darja's story was, why she'd been there or for how long, but I'd heard the rumors at school, the whispers that circulated each week when the *koolis* girls joined our classes for the day. The *koolis* was where they sent the troublemakers. The girls who didn't follow the rules. The girls who needed rehabilitation. It was best to steer clear.

But I'm breaking all the rules today, I thought, warily poking my head out of my room and glancing down the hallway. No one was in sight, and I stepped into the hall and pulled the door to my room shut behind me. I crept as silently as I could down the hall toward the kitchen.

I didn't need to worry, though. The house was empty, the rest of my family having already left to set up the fairgrounds for the festivities that afternoon. Still, I was cautious as I let myself out the kitchen door and made a beeline for the driveway. I felt like a criminal. It wasn't that I wasn't allowed to leave the house, but I didn't want to have to explain to anyone why I wasn't in bed catching up on the missed sleep from the night before.

My car was a much-dented and heavily-abused Honda Accord with well over two hundred thousand miles. It was more rust than paint at this point, and the check-engine light had been on for as long as I'd had it, but it always started right up and never gave me any trouble. And—most importantly—I'd bought it myself, with my own money, after working two summers doing inventory at Kask Family Market.

My eyes were gritty with lack of sleep as I slid into the worn seat and started the engine. I pulled out onto the road and turned north. I may have never been to the *koolis* before, but everyone knew where it was.

Physically, I felt exhausted, like my limbs were too heavy and the morning sun was too bright for my tired eyes. Mentally though, I knew there was no chance I'd be able to sleep. My mind was still spinning, trying to come to terms with everything that had happened. Compared to Darja, I felt like I had no room to complain, but nevertheless, it was as if I were a stranger in my own body, like everything I'd ever known or believed had been turned upside-down, and I didn't know how to make things right again.

I didn't *want* to be bonded to a dead girl. I didn't *want* to be able to see her, or hear her, or know what it was like to be dead. I wanted to go back to when everything was normal, when my biggest worries were if I would be late to school or if my dad would be mad that I forgot to keep the cat out of his office. Barring that, I wanted someone I could talk to about all this. Someone who was alive, and normal, who wouldn't think I was crazy or lying or seeking attention. Someone who didn't think that what had happened the night before was somehow *okay*. Somehow *justified*.

The roads weren't busy at this time of morning, and I passed through a green light and turned east, barely paying attention to my surroundings as I drove, my body on autopilot.

I shook my head, my thoughts still cast back to the night before. Why did no one else seem to have a problem with what had happened? They'd *murdered* a girl, right there in front of half the town, and no one had said a word. No one had seemed even mildly upset. If anything, they treated it as an occasion to celebrate. Was it really just because they believed that Darja had gone willingly, had offered herself as a sacrifice?

I thought of the other three girls around the fire with me. They had seemed to be struggling too, until Eliise had assured them that it was a choice Darja had made. Would I have been so easily convinced if I hadn't known otherwise? Would I have dismissed Darja just as they had? I wasn't sure, and that scared me even more.

But I *did* know otherwise, I reminded myself. Darja had been drugged, and sacrificed unwillingly, and unknowingly, and *awake*. Surely no one would be okay with that if they knew. Surely.

I drew in a sudden breath as a thought crossed my mind, a thought I couldn't believe it had taken me this long to consider. This may be the first time the binding had worked in centuries, but it was certainly not the first time they had tried. Every single adult woman in Vaikesti had been through her own Spring Day Ceremony. That meant a sacrifice every year. What about *those* girls? Had they been unwilling? Had they known their fate? My stomach twisted and I felt sick.

And what about the men? I knew the boys of our community had their own coming-of-age ceremony, but it was just as shrouded in secrecy as that of the women. Did their rites involve a sacrifice, too?

My mind racing with the implications of these realizations, I didn't even register the sound of the siren behind me until the flashing lights strobed through my car, blinding me with their reflection in the rearview mirror.

"Shit," I exclaimed, my hands clenching on the steering wheel as my gaze dropped to the speedometer. I'd been going well over the speed limit.

I quickly braked and pulled over to the side of the road, cursing my luck. I'd only been about a mile from the turnoff to the *koolis*. I was sure that between my lack of sleep and the stress of the past hours I probably looked like hell, but still I tried to smooth my expression into an innocent smile as I rolled down my window.

I'm just a normal teenager on her way to do normal teenager things.

But when the officer reached my window and leaned down, surprise wiped any other expression from my face.

"Jared?" My voice came out in a squeak.

The familiar face peering in at me was young and handsome, only a few years older than me. He had thick dark hair that he'd always worn long and unruly, with a lock in the front that tended to fall in his eyes. Sometime since I'd last seen him he'd had it cut short and styled away from his face. If you'd asked me last year, I would have said that the thought of Jared Braden cutting his hair would be a travesty, but in fact, the cut looked great on him. It made him seem older, more put together. And the uniform didn't hurt either. My face flamed red.

His handsome features were arranged in a quizzical smile.

"I remember you," he said, putting his hands on the door frame and leaning in to peer at me. "Sofia...something. Right?"

I felt my cheeks heat further, torn between whether to be pleased that he remembered me or embarrassed by the whole situation.

"Sofi," I confirmed with a nod. "Sofi Ilves."

"That's right. You were a couple of years behind me. What are you now, a junior?"

"Senior. Well, I mean, I just graduated."

"Oh, congratulations." His smile was warm and seemed genuine, and I was suddenly reminded of why I used to be so smitten with him.

Jared Braden had been three years ahead of me in school, the same age as my brother Henri. Old enough that we hadn't moved in the same circles, but our school was small enough that I'd known of him. But then, everyone had known of Jared. He was the golden student. He was smart and popular; the teachers loved him because he always had the answers and aced the tests—he made them look good. The girls loved him because he was handsome and popular and athletic. And the guys loved him because his dad was the sheriff and he had ways of making small infractions disappear.

But me...I'd always liked him because, despite it all, he'd always seemed genuinely *nice*. Also, he was a townie, not a Vaikesti kid. And while dating outside of the community wasn't exactly forbidden, it was certainly frowned upon, and while I'd never been much of a rule-breaker, it still served to give him an extra level of allure.

"Thanks," I said, then nodded to his uniform. "Congratulations to you, too. I'd wondered what happened to you after high school. I haven't seen you around."

He glanced down at his dark blue uniform and shrugged self-consciously. "Yeah, I took some college classes then went to the Academy in Springfield. You can't join the force here until you're twenty-one."

"Oh, did you just graduate then?"

He nodded. "Last month." He gave a short laugh. "You're actually one of the first people I've pulled over for speeding."

Suddenly I remembered what I'd been doing, where I was going, and the levity of running into an old crush evaporated like it'd never existed.

Jared must have misinterpreted the shift in my demeanor, because he hurried to reassure me. "Don't worry, I'm not going to give you a ticket. Just let me check your license and registration and I'll let you get going. You guys have a festival today, right? I've seen a ton of cars heading to the fairgrounds all morning."

I didn't bother to tell him that wasn't where I was going, just dug my license out of my wallet and retrieved my registration from the glove box. I handed them over. He flashed me a smile that on any other day would have made me swoon, and headed back to his car. I tapped my fingers against the steering wheel as I waited what seemed like forever before he reappeared at my window and handed the papers back to me.

"Just watch your speed," he said with a grin that made him look younger, exactly as I'd remembered him, in spite of the more mature haircut.

"I will," I promised with a weak smile.

"It was good to see you, Sofi."

And then he was gone. I waved with a shaky hand as the cruiser drove by, then took a deep breath, collecting myself before pulling back out onto the road.

―――

All thoughts of Jared had fled my mind by the time I pulled up to the main building of the *koolis* and parked in the small lot in the front. There was no sign of Darja, and I had no idea what to do if she didn't turn up, and fast.

I sat in my car, feeling conspicuous while I waited. There wasn't anyone around for the time being, but there were plenty of other cars parked in the lot. I hunkered down in my seat and cast my curious gaze over the buildings of the *koolis*.

The main building before me was a low one-story structure of brick and glass, well-kept but still slightly rundown somehow. I couldn't put my finger on it exactly, but it had a kind of lonely, neglected feel, even though the pathways were well swept and the landscaping carefully maintained. After a moment of consideration, I realized what it was that seemed off to me. For a place that served as both school and residence for sometimes up to dozens of girls, there was nothing personal about the place. No decorations in the windows, no colorful signs or announcements like the ones that had been plastered all over my own school. Nothing that gave any sense of personality or vitality. It was a perfectly fine building, but it certainly wasn't a *home*.

I was just contemplating what it must be like to live in such a place, let alone grow up there, when I caught a movement out of the corner of my eye and shifted to see Darja skulking in the shadows near the front entryway. I blew out a relieved breath as I climbed out of my car. Even though I hadn't made a sound, her head still swiveled toward me as if the bond between us were a physical thing that alerted her to my presence. Hell, maybe it was.

She was still standing in the shadows by the door as I approached, as though she still hadn't quite come to terms with the fact that no one could see her and she didn't need to hide. I smiled and opened my mouth to speak, but before I could say anything her gaze drifted over my shoulder and the expression on her face changed to one of horror. A car door slammed behind me and I froze. Darja stepped further into the shadows.

"Excuse me, can I help—?"

I turned toward the voice behind me and came face to face with one of the *tajas* I'd seen last night. Immediately my mind flashed back and I could see the woman moving slowly through the crowd, staggering slightly under the weight of Darja's motionless body. My stomach lurched.

The *taja* clearly recognized me as well. There was a moment of uncomfortable silence before the woman cleared her throat.

"Sofia, right? Are you...can I help you?"

I didn't know what to say. I didn't dare look to Darja for help. I could sense her behind me, still as a statue.

"I...um..."

"You're here about Darja, aren't you?"

My eyes went wide, but she continued on.

"Sometimes it can be hard to come to terms with...everything that happens during a Spring Day Ceremony," she started gently, and just for a second something in her eyes made me wonder if maybe I wasn't the only one having trouble accepting what I'd seen. "Sometimes it can help to learn more about the girl who was Chosen for your Ceremony. Is that it?"

I looked into the *taja's* sympathetic face and saw a

pleading expression under the surface, and I felt even more sure in my conviction that I wasn't the only one struggling. This woman clearly had known Darja well. I found myself nodding.

"I'm Ms. Kross." The woman held out her hand. Darja had stepped out from the shadows behind me and come around to the side, where she was glaring daggers at me.

"Sofi," I responded faintly, shaking the woman's outstretched hand, even though she clearly knew who I was.

"We need to *go,*" Darja hissed. It took everything I had not to look her way.

Ms. Kross released my hand, but made no move to leave. "Would you like to see her room?" she asked in a gentle voice.

I could feel the blood drain from my face even as Darja's expression twisted in dismay. No, there was nothing I wanted less than to see Darja's room.

I didn't know what to do. What excuse could I make? I'd only just arrived, and Darja hadn't bothered to tell me what we were here for anyway.

"Okay..." I answered in a weak voice, and it came out more like a question than a statement.

"No!" Darja actually reached out to grab my sleeve, but her hand passed through in an ineffectual brush of icy cold. Without batting an eye, the *taja* turned and headed toward the front door. There was nothing I could do but follow helplessly behind.

———

The experience was just as awful as I thought it would be. The dormitories were attached to the main building by way of a short covered walkway in the back, and as we navigated the long corridors of the main building Ms. Kross kept up a low stream of one-sided conversation, pointing out the library, the cafeteria, the classrooms, all while peppering her tour with information and anecdotes about Darja. Darja, for her part, trudged silently by my side, a look of pure torture contorting her features.

I didn't want to listen. It felt like a betrayal, an invasion, but there was nothing I could do. I kept my eyes on the ground, not making eye contact as I learned that Darja had been raised at the *koolis* since birth, unwittingly born into the scandal of a pregnant teenage mother and an unidentified father. Her mother had, like her daughter, been chosen as *ohverdus* and sacrificed in a bonding ceremony at age eighteen—a fact that Darja's sharp indrawn breath implied she hadn't previously known. My heart ached.

I learned that Darja was smart, and had liked to bake, and had a soft heart hidden under a sharp tongue.

By the time we reached Darja's room at the dormitory, I felt as if a thousand pound weight was crushing down on me. It was mortifying to be there, listening to Ms. Kross strip away Darja's layers even as the girl trudged by my side, her transparent arms wrapped tightly around her middle, her face an unreadable mask.

Her room was even worse. It was practically barren, devoid of color and personality just like the rest of the building. And she had lived here since she was a *child.* The forlorn papers tacked to the walls and the worn quilt on the bed hardly accounted for a lifetime of memories.

I hovered in the doorway, shifting my weight from foot to foot as Ms. Kross smoothed the corner of Darja's quilt in a way that seemed like an invasion of the girl's personal space, and turned to me.

"Does that help at all? Do you have any questions?"

I shook my head, desperately trying to think of a way to excuse myself and run away as fast as my legs could carry me, when a loud chime sounded the hour through the hallway and Ms. Kross looked up sharply.

"Is it that late already? I'm so sorry, Sofi, but I have to get to class. Do you remember the way out?"

I nearly sagged in relief. "Yes, I'll be fine. Thank you."

She gave me a smile. "Come find me any time you have questions or need to talk."

I plastered what I hoped was a convincing smile on my face and mumbled something banal as the *taja* stepped past me and disappeared down the corridor.

I stood there for a long moment before turning to the girl by my side. "Darja, I—"

"*Don't.*" Her voice was a vicious rasp as she rounded on me. I hastily backed up a step.

She glared at me. "If I sense even a *drop* of pity from you, I'll...I'll *haunt* you." She spun on her heel and started stomping up the hallway. "Come on," she shouted over her shoulder when I didn't immediately follow. "We might be too late as it is."

Too late for what, I didn't find out until we had left the dormitory and snuck around the side of the main building toward the back door to the cafeteria. Darja proceeded to pretend the entire fiasco of the past half hour hadn't happened at all—something I was only too eager to go along with—and filled me in on her theory of the egg lady and the *koolis's* resident stray cat.

What began as skepticism on my part began to morph into cautious excitement as she described the cat's reaction to the old crazy woman, and when she explained that the egg lady generally stopped by around this time of morning a couple of days a week, I finally understood why she had dragged me all this way.

"She takes eggs around to some of the local markets too, and this is usually her last stop on her way home," Darja explained, her voice low even though no one could hear her. "She must have, like, a million chickens."

I pressed myself flat against the brick exterior of the cafeteria wall, under an overhang that cast a deep shadow against the sunlit wall, even though Darja assured me that everyone would be in class at this time of morning.

"Won't there be people in the kitchen though, getting ready for lunch?" I hissed at her.

"Not today," she reminded me with a sidelong glance and a raised eyebrow. "Even the *koolis* kids get to go to the Spring Day festival. Classes will end early and they'll all leave before lunch. There's probably only a couple of *tajas* in there right now."

Honestly, I had forgotten all about the festival this afternoon. I shuddered at the reminder, knowing I would have to be there. As one of the Ceremony participants, it would be expected for me to be part of the festivities, honored as a new adult member of the community. I felt sick at the thought, and pushed it from my mind.

"How do you even know she's coming today?" I kept my voice low, trying to stay flat against the wall. I had no idea what I would say if we were caught again.

"I don't," Darja admitted. "But she usually comes on Fridays, and it's better than sitting around in your room wondering what to do. If you have a better idea, I'm all ears."

I didn't, which she knew, so I didn't respond.

Time seemed to slow and stretch as we stood, me shifting from foot to foot as my legs grew sore and restless, Darja motionless as a statue. Finally, I gave up and slid down the wall to sit in the grass, grimacing in relief as the pressure eased off my aching feet. I was about to suggest that we come back another day when I heard a sound from the path that led around the side of the building toward the parking lot. My heart leaping, I scrambled to my feet, afraid it would be another *taja* coming around to the back door.

But Darja had positioned herself to keep watch down the path, and she waved me back as the footsteps grew closer. When the figure rounded the corner and drew into view, I saw the stooped form of an elderly woman, easily in her late sixties or early seventies. Her clothing was decidedly strange, multicolored layers of skirts and scarves, mismatched and well-worn, topped with a heavy velvet coat that seemed too warm for the bright spring morning. Her white hair was surprisingly thick and long, and she wore it tied back in a braid. In her weathered hand she carried a large basket, piled high with eggs ranging in color from white to brown to the palest blue.

The lady stopped when she saw me standing by the door, and I looked hopefully to Darja, unsure of what I should say. But Darja's face had gone quite still, her eyes huge with shock, and when I turned back to the egg lady she wasn't looking at me anymore. Her gaze was fixed to the side, her head cocked as if to listen, and then as I watched, all the blood drained from her face and the basket of eggs slipped from her arm, crashing to the sidewalk and painting the concrete in a mess of broken yolks and shattered shells.

CHAPTER 8

DARJA

The girl standing next to the egg lady was definitely dead. In fact, if I'd ever thought, "Hey, I wonder what a ghost actually looks like," this would be the girl. She looked like she'd stepped right out of some sort of gothic horror movie, high-necked lace gown, brown hair piled on top of her head, and dark, glittering eyes. When our gazes met, she flickered in and out, her whole being turning to static in front of me.

We stared at each other for a long moment, my shock and curiosity reflected in her expression. Finally, I remembered Sofi. I could practically feel her trembling beside me.

"Darja," she whispered, "can she see you?"

The *she*, I realized, was the egg lady, and I shook my head. "But there's a girl," I said quietly. "Like me."

"Oh, God," Sofi said, sinking back against the brick wall of the building behind her. Her eyes moved frantically between us, searching for something I knew she couldn't see.

I looked over to the egg lady, who had gone very pale, beginning to resemble her non-corporeal friend.

The two of them were also conversing quietly, but heatedly, and I realized how she'd gotten the reputation for being the town crazy lady.

"What do we do?" Sofi asked, her voice wobbly and uncertain.

"We go," the egg lady said, though the question had been meant for me. Bending with some effort, she retrieved her basket, looking around surreptitiously as she straightened her back. "We shouldn't draw attention."

I snorted, and the ghost girl shot me a withering glare. I shrugged an apology and turned to Sofi. "Go with her," I said, nodding toward the egg lady. "I'll find you."

"But what do we—?"

"Just *go*," I snapped. Then, softening my tone, "I'll be there. I promise."

Sofi took a deep breath and nodded. The egg lady gestured for her to follow, then hoofed it around the corner, faster than I would have given a woman of her age credit for. Sofi cast one last glance over her shoulder, and I tried to smile encouragingly. It felt more like a grimace.

Once they had disappeared around the side of the building, I turned to the ghost girl. She was still staring at me intently, as if I were a specimen under a microscope.

"So," I said, wondering what kind of etiquette applied when meeting another non-living person for the first time. "I'm Darja. Uh…how are you?"

"Dead. And you?"

"Right. Sorry. Same, I guess."

I thought I could see the start of a smile tug at the corner of her mouth, but it never materialized. "How did this happen?" she said. Her voice was raspy, like sandpaper on metal.

I looked at her carefully. "I think you already know the answer to that," I said. "Big party in the woods? Bonfire? Ritual sacrifice? Any of this ringing a bell?"

"The *bond*," she said sharply. She flickered again, buzzing out then back in before I could blink.

"Isn't the bond the whole point?" I asked, and she gave me an impatient look.

"Aside from Mirtel and I, the bond hasn't worked in generations. I want to know why it worked for *you*." Her face was pinched, but there was something else behind it. Something that may have been...hope?

"Wish I could tell you."

She seemed impatient with my casual tone. In truth, I was about to come out of my skin. Spirit. Whatever. The rush of excitement I felt in knowing there was someone else like me—someone else like *Sofi* and me—was overwhelming. But I didn't want to give too much away. We needed answers, and if they'd been living like this—*existing* like this—since they were 18, they must know something about the bond.

Ghost girl drifted closer to me, and I thought I caught a scent of lilacs drifting on the breeze. I'd only smelled ash and smoke since it had happened, and it caught me off-guard.

"Um... I don't know," I said, hating the uncertainty I could hear in my voice. "I don't know why it worked."

She assessed me for another moment, and apparently finding me lacking, shrugged her shoulders. "We need to hurry," she said. "They'll be almost to the wagon by now."

"The wagon? What—" but before I could finish, she'd flickered out and disappeared.

I sighed. "I really freaking hate this." I closed my eyes, suddenly feeling that almost-painful tug I noticed whenever

Sofi wasn't around. "Fine," I grumbled, following the invisible pull, "*apparate*, or whatever."

I flickered back into existence along the bank of the river that ran the far edge of Vaikesti. It was heavily wooded, but just ahead I could see a small clearing, and perched beyond the trees, an actual wagon. I imagined it had once been painted in bright purple and green, but had faded over time to a dull, chipped patina.

"I'll be damned," I muttered, moving closer. It was an old box wagon, the kind people who pretended to like camping stayed in when they wanted to rough it, but it had seen better days. A *lot* of better days. A tattered awning jutted out above the door in a crazy patchwork of mismatched fabrics, and a set of rickety wooden steps led up to the entrance. Around the side, a large patch of earth sat brown and bare, picked clean by the chickens I could see milling about. On the other side, between two trees, a clothesline was hung with a bizarre array of skirts and scarves.

"Curiouser and curiouser," I said, moving toward the steps. I wasn't sure what to do next, so I closed my eyes again and followed the tug. When I opened them, I was inside. The small space was a crazy jumble of old, broken-down furniture, worn cushions and tatty throws. Every surface was stacked with books, some nearly reaching the ceiling. Against the far wall, Sofi and the egg lady—Mirtel, the ghost girl had called her—sat on a squashy loveseat covered in old quilts. Ghost girl herself hovered nearby, watching the two of them with a guarded expression.

Sofi looked up sharply when I arrived, relief plain on her face. I gave her a small smile and after a moment, she returned it.

"She's here, then?" Mirtel asked, following Sofi's gaze. Sofi nodded. So did ghost girl. A screeching noise pierced the air then, and Mirtel, not seeming phased by it, heaved herself slowly off the sunken cushions.

"Milk and sugar, dear?" she said, moving to a small counter where an old ceramic teapot sat on a single, battery-operated burner.

"Sure," Sofi said, glancing over at me and raising her eyebrows.

"It's goat milk," Mirtel said, bustling around the small kitchenette and pulling a real china teacup from a cupboard mounted to the wall. "Much easier to keep than cows. And healthier, too. Besides, goats are much better company, don't you think?"

Crazy, I mouthed to Sofi.

"*Darja*," she said admonishingly, and Mirtel turned to her, a strange smile tilting her lips.

"Is that what it's like?" she said, turning back to rummage through a drawer, eventually pulling out a small silver spoon. "It's no wonder I've been the town nutcase all these years." She glanced back at ghost girl then, and the two shared a knowing look.

"Well," she said, returning to the loveseat and handing Sofi a cup of steaming tea. "I'm sure we have quite a few questions for one another, don't we? But first, perhaps some introductions are in order? I'm Mirtel. Aforementioned town nutcase. Aggie—Agnes—is the one you can't see. And you are?"

"Sofi. Sofi Ilves. And Darja is my..." She looked at me as if waiting for me to finish the sentence, but I had no idea how. Ghost? Haunt? DFF—dead friend forever?

"Your bonded," Mirtel said gently, and Sofi nodded. "Hello, Darja," Mirtel said in my general direction. "You're welcome here." She looked at Sofi. "Both of you are."

"Thank you," Sofi said, then erupted into a massive yawn. "I'm so sorry," she said, face flushing pink. She took a quick drink of her tea, becoming very interested in the delicate floral pattern on the cup.

"So, it's only just happened then?" Mirtel said knowingly. "At last night's ceremony?"

Sofi nodded.

"You must have so many questions, dear. But, there'll be time for talking later. For now, you need to rest."

"Oh, I don't think I could—" Sofi began, then yawned again.

"You won't make it through the festival otherwise. Just through there," Mirtel said, pointing to the back of the wagon, where two curtains hung over a cord strung between the walls," there's a bed. It's not much, but it's quite comfortable. I'll show you." She got to her feet, and motioned for Sofi to do the same. With an uncertain look back at me, Sofi stood up, swaying with exhaustion. I nodded at her to follow, feeling guilty I'd kept her up for so long.

The two of them disappeared behind the curtain, and I heard Mirtel jabbering about this and that while Sofi mumbled an occasional acknowledgement. I looked over to ghost girl—Aggie—who was studying me unabashedly.

"So, you two have been bonded for…a while," I said, not sure what kind of small talk dead girls were supposed to make.

"Fifty-two years," Aggie said. Her eyes were a striking gray. She was pale, slightly translucent, like me, but I could tell this had been their color in life, like the sheer limestone walls carved out of the hills just south of Vaikesti. Her hair was brown, pulled up in an intricate twist and piled on top of her head. She must have died—been killed—sometime in the 70s, but the dress and the hair looked almost Victorian. It must have been for the ceremony, I thought, glancing down at my own old-fashioned dress. She was petite, shorter and smaller than I was, and her features were delicate. I wondered how she'd wound up with this awful fate. How any of us had.

Mirtel returned then, taking up her spot on the loveseat and looking toward the door. "She'll be able to rest now," she said softly. "Please, make yourself at home."

"Thanks," I said, then realized she couldn't hear me. "Can you tell her?" I said to Aggie, who nodded shortly.

"She says thank you," she said, and Mirtel smiled.

"Well, dear, what a time you've had."

I snorted. "That's an understatement."

Aggie gave me a look that told me she wasn't interested in being my translator, then turned her attention back to the older woman. "Mirtel, how could this have happened? In all these years, there's never been another bond. What changed?"

Mirtel looked troubled. "I don't know," she said. "Darja, I wish we had answers for you. I know you must be frightened and angry—just like we were."

I stared at Aggie, aghast. "It's been decades," I said. "You don't know anything about the bond?"

"I know more than you," she said waspishly.

"Like what?"

"I know that it means my spirit can't move on. To...to whatever is out there. Whatever is supposed to happen... after. I know that no one really believes the magic works anymore, but they keep on performing this... *sacrilege*... year after year. I know that when Mirtel tried to tell the others what had happened—that the bonding had worked—they laughed at her. Mocked her. Made her a pariah."

"What's supposed to happen," I asked, "*after*?"

"Does it matter?" Aggie said with a bitter laugh. "We'll never know."

"But why? Why can't we move on?"

"*Because our spirits are trapped.*" A heavy silence hung in the air between us. Aggie cast her eyes downward. "I'm sorry, Mirtel. I shouldn't—"

But Mirtel waved her off. "We've been through this hurt before," she said. "I would heal it if I could."

"I know," Aggie whispered.

"Perhaps," Mirtel said then, "we should tell Darja what we do know. How we ended up...here."

Aggie nodded. "Yes, of course." She looked at me then, all the previous anger gone, her small frame seeming even smaller, depleted. "I'm sorry, Darja."

"No big deal," I said, even though it was.

Aggie nodded at Mirtel, who seemed to take this as her cue to begin her story.

"I was born in Vaikesti," she said, "to a very poor family. My father was a farmer. His parents had lived in the old country before coming here to start over. My mother was from outside. She was happy to adopt the beliefs of our people, and they allowed her in, but never truly accepted her. They died when I was quite young. I'd likely have been sent to the *koolis* myself, but my father's sister took me in." Her voice was soft and her gaze was far away. "By the time I was seventeen, all I could think about was leaving Vaikesti, finding my mother's family. But my aunt convinced me to stay until my ceremony."

"And you tried to tell them?" I asked, forgetting she couldn't hear me. "They really didn't believe the bonding had worked?"

"They thought she was trying to improve her station," Aggie said, and Mirtel nodded her agreement. "There hadn't been a successful bonding since the town was first settled. No one thought it was real. It was just..."

"For show?" I said, and Aggie nodded. "But they kept murdering girls anyway," I added bitterly.

"Yes," Aggie said, and I could see a fire in her eyes that

reflected the rage I felt. "They called Mirtel crazy. Spread rumors about her. Tried to drive her out of town."

"They only pushed me this far," Mirtel said, sounding a bit triumphant. "This was my father's land. They'd taken most of the farm, but he held onto this parcel. We came here after my aunt died. I was twenty-one."

"You've lived here for fifty years?" I said, staring around at the cramped space. "In a *wagon*?"

Aggie shot me a look. "It's home," she said, and I felt a flush of guilt.

"Better than the *koolis*," I said, and Aggie gave a wry smile.

"That's the truth," she said.

"Did you grow up there?" I asked.

She looked away then, her face going hard again. "No," she said flatly. "I grew up in town. I was moved to the *koolis* when I was sixteen."

"What?" I sputtered. "You were almost to your own ceremony. What happened?"

"It isn't important," she said stiffly.

"Like hell it isn't. Another two years, and you would have survived."

"Sixteen months," she said softly. "But I ended up there, and then I ended up here."

I stared, mouth agape, not knowing what to say. This was all too horrifying to process. I wanted to flee the wagon, screaming about the outrage of it all. I wanted to wake up in my lumpy bed in my barren room in the *koolis*. I wanted Ms. Kross to write me up for disciplinary infraction. But more than anything, I wanted this whole nightmare to be over.

"Well," Mirtel said, breaking the tense silence that had fallen over us. "I don't know about you two, but I feel invigorated."

"*What*?" Aggie and I said simultaneously.

"We gave up on finding answers once it became clear no one in town was going to help us. Perhaps we gave up too soon. If there are others being bonded, there must be something that connects us. Some reason it worked for us, and not the rest."

"And you never found anything about what's supposed to happen?" I asked.

"Nothing," Aggie said. "We scoured the library at the *koolis*, looked through every page in the history section, but never found a word about it."

"But that's not our town's whole history," Mirtel said.

"What does she mean?" I asked Aggie, who looked as confused as I felt.

"Mirtel," she said, "what are you—?"

"There'll be time to talk later," Mirtel said. "Right now, I've got to feed the chickens. And then I suppose we have a Spring Day Festival to attend."

"Mirtel, you haven't been to a Spring Day in fifty years."

Mirtel smiled. "Well then," she said, "it seems I'll need to work on making my entrance."

CHAPTER 9

SOFI

I could hear the low murmur of conversation through the thin curtain that sectioned off the 'bedroom' of the wagon, punctuated by silences when Aggie must have been talking, and I hated that I was missing out on what was hopefully important revelations about our bond. I had half-convinced myself to get up and go join the others, but between the long sleepless night, the surprising softness of the bed, and some sense of self-preservation—my overwhelmed brain must have known I couldn't handle any more—I fell asleep before I could bring myself to move.

I awoke feeling...anxious. I'd half-hoped I would wake up the way people did in stories, having temporarily forgotten whatever recent tragedy they'd endured, treated to a long moment of blissful ignorance before everything came crashing back. Unfortunately, it didn't seem to work that way in real life, and my first thought upon waking was *where's Darja?*

The wagon was quiet as I rose, feeling sweaty and

wobbly, and I ducked through the curtain to find the small space empty. Mirtel was out in the yard, tossing handfuls of what appeared to be food scraps to a tight cluster of voracious chickens. She glanced up when she heard me approach and smiled.

"I was about to come wake you. We need to leave soon if you're going to get to the festival before your family notices you're missing."

"Where's Darja?" I asked, my voice betraying the surprisingly visceral sense of loss I felt at her absence. Mirtel gave me a sympathetic glance.

"It's a strange feeling to be separated from your bonded, isn't it?" Her gaze drifted to the left, toward the empty patch of grass beyond the chickens where the trees closed in thickly and the faint sound of rushing water drifted through the foliage. "It gets a bit easier with time. Well," she amended, "not easier. Maybe just more familiar." She turned back and looked at my face before taking pity on me. "She's with Aggie," she reassured me softly. "Learning more about...her situation."

I nodded, surprised and a little disconcerted at how quickly I'd come to rely on her presence.

"She'll meet you at the festival," Mirtel assured me. "But you really do need to get going before they send out a search party."

My car was right where I'd left it in the long drive that led to Mirtel's wagon, and the uncomfortable feeling in the pit of my stomach stayed with me as I rushed home, changed my clothes, and headed out to the fairgrounds. The parking lot was packed when I arrived, the festivities clearly in full swing.

To my immense relief, Darja was waiting for me by the gate, and despite her protests that we could talk later, I pulled her back to my car and made her fill me in on what she had learned from Mirtel and Aggie while I'd been napping. It was surprisingly little, and my spirits sank.

"What did she mean, your spirit is trapped?" I asked, staring at Darja. She sat in my passenger seat, one leg pulled up under her. Her relaxed posture was incongruous with her transparent skin and flowing white gown.

"I *obviously* don't know," she replied. "I also don't know why they stopped searching for answers. There has to be *something* that can help us."

"Fifty years is a long time to search and come up empty," I said softly, even though I agreed with her. How could you ever stop looking for answers? "They didn't say anything else?"

"No." Darja shook her head. "I *told* you everything. Mirtel said we'd talk more later."

I nodded, then fell silent. Part of me wanted to ask her what she and Aggie had talked about, but I wasn't sure I wanted to know. I also wasn't sure if she would want to share. I hadn't yet figured out what level of openness was appropriate between a person and her dead-slash-bonded, ghost-slash-murder-victim.

Darja interrupted my thoughts before I could make sense of them. "If you're done hiding in the car, you should really get in there."

I shot her a glare and she relented. "You're right. I wouldn't want to go in there either."

Inside the fairgrounds, the festivities were the same as those of every Spring Day festival I'd been to over the course of my life. The bulk of the activity was located inside the largest building, a square brick structure. The words *Cattle Hall* were stamped above the wide doors, which had been flung open as the town took advantage of the warm spring day to overflow out into the yard where picnic tables had been set up and blankets spread out on the lawn. Groups of people filled the tables and milled about, chatting and mingling, while music filled the air and the smells of food wafted out on the warm breeze.

Normally, this was one of my favorite days, second only to the festival at Midsummer, and I would spend the afternoon and long into the evening stuffing my face with food as I laughed with my friends and joined in the singing.

But everything was different this year, and I had an uncomfortable feeling, like all my senses were heightened. The music was too loud, the cacophony of voices a dull roar that seemed to clog my ears. The colors were too bright, the smell of food too strong and slightly nauseating.

I paused in the doorway, and Darja gave me a sympathetic glance as I gathered myself with an effort.

"Sofi!"

Before I could move, my family descended like a tornado. I felt hands grab mine, arms envelop me, and I was half guided, half dragged into the building, voices tumbling over each other to ask questions that no one paused to let me answer. The familiarity was comforting.

"Where have you been?"

"Is *that* really what you chose to wear to your own Spring Day festival?"

"Hush, Hanna, she looks lovely."

"Congratulations, Sof."

I looked up at the deep voice and saw my brothers had joined the fray.

"I got you a plate, honey; you can sit at the table of honor with the other girls." That was my mother, and I could hear the hidden question in her voice, *Are you okay?*

I gave her what I hoped was a reassuring smile. I hadn't

been in any great shape when she'd last seen me, but for all she knew I'd spent the whole morning asleep and had time to recover.

The chaotic whirlwind of my family swept me to the front of the wide open room, deposited me in a chair with a flurry of kisses and ruffled hair, then receded into the crowd as abruptly as they'd come.

I found myself in a folding chair seated before a long table set with a white plastic tablecloth, bunches of blue cornflowers in vases at intervals on the table, and a paper plate piled high with the finest a Vaikesti potluck had to offer steaming in front of me.

Dazed, I looked up and met the eyes of the rest of the table's occupants: Marta, Anna, and Liz. They were all watching me over half-eaten plates, and I stared back, my mind a blank. After a long moment, Darja materialized behind them and raised her eyebrow at me.

"Sofi?"

I jerked my gaze back to the table.

"Uh, hi," I greeted them lamely.

Anna eyed me sympathetically. "You don't look like you got any sleep at all this morning. I had trouble too, I was just so excited."

Excited? My shoulders stiffened, but no one seemed to notice.

The other girls had picked up their conversation where they'd left off.

"I can't believe how nervous I was," Marta said.

"It's because of all the secrecy," Liz agreed sagely. "If they would just *tell* us what was going on beforehand, we wouldn't have been so freaked out."

"I'm just glad I remembered all my words," Anna put in, and the others nodded.

I stared around the table at the other girls' faces as their words faded into the background. They all looked tired, too, but there was no strain on their faces, no shadows behind their eyes.

Darja's voice was bitter in my ear. "It's like they were at a different ceremony."

"They *were* at a different ceremony," I responded under my breath.

"What's that, Sofi?"

"Nothing."

―――

I covered my silence with the excuse that I hadn't had anything to eat since the previous day—which wasn't a lie—and the other girls seemed content to ignore me as I dug into four different versions of 'the best chili in Vaikesti,' along with enormous helpings of Mrs. Tamm's macaroni and cheese and Lea Rebane's fruit salad, which was everyone's favorite because it was liberally studded with marshmallows and drenched in honey.

It took quite an effort not to look at Darja, or respond when she made snide but amusing comments about the people wandering by, and I began to see why Mirtel had quickly gotten a reputation for being the town crazy lady. I focused on my food, shooting withering glares at Darja that she cheerfully ignored, and it wasn't until I caught sight of a face that seemed out of place that I tuned back into the conversation happening around me.

"Who *is* that guy?" Marta asked under her breath, and when the others turned to stare it was clear they were talking about the same person I'd just noticed.

I didn't think there was anything in particular that made a person recognizable as being from Vaikesti, aside from maybe an above average likelihood of blonde hair, but whatever that unidentifiable attribute might be, this guy clearly didn't have it. Everything about him screamed out-of-place, from his dark red hair that curled slightly too long over his ears, to his round glasses that slipped down the bridge of his nose, and his nondescript dark jeans and green hooded sweatshirt.

I watched him for a moment, my brow creased, until I realized that it wasn't the way he looked or the way he acted that made him stand out, but the way everyone *else* looked and acted. People moved out of his way, giving him a wide berth as he wandered through the crowd, eyeing him out of the corners of their eyes before turning to whisper to their friends.

"I don't know," Liz whispered back, "but he looks familiar."

She was right, I realized, he *did* look vaguely familiar. But it wasn't until the crowd in front of him cleared and revealed the large shiny black camera hanging across his body on a thick strap that I realized where I'd seen him before. It was here. Last year, at the Midsummer festival, and again at *Jõulud*. He always hung around the outskirts of our festivals, taking pictures but never interacting, never joining in. He was very clearly not from Vaikesti, but I had no idea who he was.

This was the first time I'd seen him actually moving through the crowd, talking to people, though his conversations were clearly short and met with frowns and narrowed eyes.

The other girls obviously knew more than I did, and I turned my attention back to them, keeping one eye on the stranger.

"My grandmother has talked to him," Anna was saying. "He goes to school in Springfield, at the university there."

"Is he joining Vaikesti?" Liz asked with a sly twist to her mouth. "He's kinda cute."

"I don't think so." Anna rolled her eyes. "He just comes on festival days and asks questions. Takes pictures, too."

"He's coming over here," Darja commented, and I turned to look again, forgetting no one else could hear her. The others followed my gaze though, and the stranger stumbled slightly and flushed under the sudden weight of four—five—sets of eyes.

"Um...hi," he started, then gestured awkwardly at an empty seat between Liz and Anna. "May I join you?"

There was no rule, but traditionally no one sat at the table of honor with the Ceremony participants. Liz leaned over though and pulled the chair back. "Be our guest," she invited with a smile.

He eased into the seat and set his camera on the table. Up close he seemed younger than I'd thought, maybe just a few years older than me. His face was still red, but he didn't act embarrassed when he introduced himself. "My name is Stephen. I'm a graduate student at Springfield University, and I've been doing a little research on c—on the Vaikesti." He corrected himself so fast it was hard to tell if he'd misspoken or simply stumbled on his words. I also noticed his flawless pronunciation of our town's name. No one who didn't live here ever got it right on the first try. I shot a glance at Darja, who met it with a shrug.

"I'm Liz." The dark-haired girl gave a flirtatious smile. Marta and Anna also introduced themselves, if a little more reservedly, and I eventually did as well.

"So, what kind of research are you doing, *Stephen*?" Liz emphasized his name with a giggle, and I rolled my eyes.

But the boy simply turned to her with a friendly smile, pushing his sliding glasses back into place.

"Just on the, ah, dynamics of small communities and

how they function. You know, like social issues, gender relations, history and social events, things like that. I'm looking at a couple of other communities as well, and I hope to include this research in my thesis."

Liz leaned in closer.

"Your *thesis*? Are you going to write a book about us?"

Stephen laughed a little self-consciously. "No, well, probably not. Just a paper."

"That's *fascinating*. So what have you learned about us so far?"

I saw Marta roll her eyes too, but Anna was smiling at Liz's antics.

Stephen pushed his glasses up again, seemingly oblivious to Liz's flirting, if that was possible. "Well, I've learned that you all like your festivals. I got some beautiful pictures at *Jõulud* in the winter."

Another flawless pronunciation.

"I hear you girls are the center of today's celebration though, is that right?"

Anna giggled and Liz smiled broadly. "That's right, today's our Spring Day."

"What does that mean, exactly?" Stephen asked, leaning in.

I exchanged a glance with Darja.

"Wellll," Liz said, "it means we all turned 18 this past year, and the festival celebrates our new roles as adults in the community." She batted her eyes at him and I watched his face light up, though I suspected his excitement was more due to the new information for his project than her suggestion that she was technically legal.

"Really," he said, looking thoughtful, then laid his hand on the camera. "Would you mind if I took your picture?"

I frowned. I didn't like the idea of someone researching Vaikesti. I didn't like the idea of someone prying into our secrets, especially after the revelation that there really were secrets to protect. And I certainly didn't want my image involved, but Liz was already nodding and scooting in close to Marta. Stephen took her assent as agreement from all of us, and stood, stepping back and raising the camera to frame us all in the shot.

"Say cheese!"

"Cheeeeese!"

The shutter clicked, and over his shoulder I saw Eliise Tamm in the distance, watching us with a frown and furrowed brow.

He took a few shots, then settled back into his chair, his smile wide. "So, I understand there's some kind of Ceremony, right? A ritual you girls participate in?"

A hush fell over the table. I felt myself physically lean away in shock, and saw the wide-eyed glance Marta exchanged with Anna. Even Liz had fallen silent, growing rigid in her chair. *How could he possibly know that?*

If Stephen noticed the reaction we'd had to his words, he didn't let on, just pushed his glasses back up his nose and continued. In the heavy silence, his words fell like stones. "What is the ritual like? Singing and dancing, I'll bet. You guys do a lot of that." He grinned, gesturing around, then lowered his voice and leaned in. "Do you still do the old bonding rituals?"

"*What the hell?*" Darja's voice was loud by my shoulder and I started visibly at the same moment that Marta let out an audible gasp.

"Did any of you get bonded?" he continued on, oblivious.

But before anyone could say another word, another figure materialized at our table, and I looked up, not sure what I was more shocked by, Stephen's words or the sudden presence of Jared Braden, who put both hands on the table and leaned over Stephen's shoulder.

Jared was a townie, not a Vaikesti kid, so at first I was confused to see him here at the festival, before I realized he was in uniform again, dark blue shirt and dark pants, gun and handcuffs gleaming on his belt. What the hell was going on?

The answer came in the form of Jared taking Stephen by the arm and guiding him to his feet with the words, "Stephen Jennings? You need to leave now."

I watched as Stephen took in Jared's uniform and the color visibly drained from his face. "What? Why?"

"Please just come quietly. I don't want to have to arrest you."

Stephen jerked his arm out of Jared's grip. "*What?* I haven't done anything."

The other three girls watched with round eyes.

"Public nuisance. Disorderly conduct. We've had some complaints."

Stephen took a step back, his glasses slipping down his nose again. "This is a public festival; I have every right—"

Jared grabbed his arm again and spun him around, then bent him against the table. My mouth fell open as he pulled the handcuffs off his belt.

"*Stop.*" Stephen's voice was strangled. "I'll go willingly. Just stop."

But Jared already had one of his wrists locked in, and with a twist, he locked the other wrist down and yanked Stephen to his feet.

Jared turned, his hard eyes meeting mine for a second, and I saw them soften slightly. "I'm sorry, ladies," he said. "I hope you're enjoying the festival." And then they were gone, the crowd parting around the pair as Jared dragged Stephen toward the exit.

Voices all around us rose in agitation, and the other three girls were still watching the spectacle. Darja's eyes met mine, then she nodded at the table. My gaze followed hers and widened. In the confusion that followed, I covertly grabbed the camera Stephen had left behind and stealthily made my own exit.

CHAPTER 10

DARJA

My conversation with Aggie had been...enlightening, in some ways. Maddening, in others. It seemed that, just like she'd said, I was stuck. Or in her words, *trapped*. Our spirits were meant to cross over to some sort of otherworldly plane, or something. Be one with the earth. Turn into a river, or a rock, or a leaf on a tree, or something. A week ago, the thought of becoming some sort of nature nymph would have been laughable. Now, it felt...right. Which meant that whatever I was now was just...*wrong*.

I'd tried to get Aggie to tell me her story, but she'd been tight-lipped, just saying that it didn't matter anymore. But when I'd asked, her face had gone all pinched and her eyes had gotten even darker, and I could tell it still mattered, a lot. I'd given up on questioning her though, since she was about as open as Fort Knox.

The conversation weighed on me for a long time after that, until all the craziness erupted at the Spring Day festival. But when Sofi had grabbed Stephen's camera and ducked out of the crowd, all thoughts of Aggie and her theories on the afterlife had evaporated.

I met up with Sofi in the cherry orchard on the eastern edge of the fairgrounds. She hadn't told me where to find her, but the bond tugged away at my navel until I flickered my way to where she was. She was sitting under a tree heavy with white blooms, almost as if it had been caught in a sudden blizzard. Petals drifted down around her, collecting in her hair and dotting her dress, but she took no notice.

"Whatcha doing?" I asked, then stifled a laugh when she screamed, dropping Stephen's camera into her lap.

"What the hell is wrong with you?" she hissed, looking up at me with an indignant frown. I dropped down beside her and peeked over at the camera, ignoring the way she pulled back when I leaned in close, as if afraid the whole dead chick thing might be contagious.

"Anything interesting?" I said, nodding at the camera. She turned her attention back to the small screen and frowned even deeper.

"It's weird," she said, tilting the camera so I could see some shots from the start of the festival. "I mean, it's creepy, right? He's just lurking around, photographing our festivals?"

I shrugged. "Maybe he's got a thing for insulated small towns with dark secrets?"

She shot me a look and I rolled my eyes. "Or maybe he's writing his thesis, like he said."

She scrolled backward through the photos, her face darkening with every shot. "I don't like it," she said. "I don't trust him."

"Oh, you mean the interloper who made a scene and got arrested in front of our whole town? What's not to trust?"

"I don't think this is a joke, Darja. Something about this

—about *him*—didn't feel right. And I think we should—"

Sofi sucked in a sharp breath.

"What is it?" I asked, leaning back toward her to look at the camera. This time, she didn't move away.

I cursed under my breath. It was a photo of Mirtel's wagon, overrun with hungry chickens on one side, all faded purple and green in the dappled sunlight.

"Maybe he was out for a walk and stumbled across—"

"I don't think so," Sofi said firmly. She flipped back again. This time, it was a photo of Mirtel, outside the wagon, gesturing intensely at…no one.

"Aggie," I whispered.

Sofi continued scrolling. There were images of Mirtel engaged in lively conversation, seemingly with herself, and then photos of Mirtel ushering a terrified-looking Sofi up the stairs of the wagon. A few pictures later, it was Sofi and Mirtel, each looking away from one another, a dozen shattered eggs at their feet.

"How long has this asshole been following us?" I demanded. Sofi was white as a—well, as me—and looked petrified of clicking to the next image. After a long moment, she did, and both of us gasped.

It didn't look like anything, at first glance. An open field, green and muddy from the spring rains, with a line of emerald forest at the far edge. In the lower corner was a car parked on the grass. I hadn't known the make or model or even the color, but I knew that it was scented with cloying pine from the paper tree dangling off the rearview. I knew the fabric covering the headrests was musty, scratchy and worn. I knew that it needed new shocks, as every bump had nearly sent me sliding into the floorboards.

"Shit," I hissed. "Shit, shit, shit."

Sofi clicked a button and the camera screen went dark. She turned to me with a grim expression. "He knows."

"We don't know that."

"Why the hell else would he follow us?" Sofi said shrilly.

I shook my head, trying to rationalize, but I couldn't. This creep knew more than he was letting on, and he was researching more than a thesis. If he'd seen what had happened...if he'd witnessed what they had done...

I froze. What if he *had*?

"What?" Sofi said, and I realized I'd spoken out loud.

"What if he was there?" I said, a building excitement kindling somewhere within me. "If he saw what happened—if he *photographed* it—there's evidence. There's proof I was murdered. We could take the camera to the police. If he saw it all, he can back us up." I smiled gleefully, feeling like every awful thing that had happened could maybe be made right. That the ones who made it happen would actually pay. I laughed. "Then those bitches are gonna fry."

But Sofi wasn't laughing. She sat, stony-faced, hands gripping the camera like she thought she might be able to strangle the secrets out of it.

"I hope I'm not one of those bitches," she said tightly, and I felt the smile slip from my face.

"Sofi, you know that's not what I—"

"Then *what*?" she said, her breathing coming fast and sharp. "I was a part of it, wasn't I? I didn't stop it...I didn't even *question* it. If I'm in those pictures, I'm as guilty as anyone there." Her voice got higher, more frantic with every word.

"You aren't guilty of anything—"

"I let them murder you!"

"Sofi..." I tried to reach for her, out of some sort of leftover human instinct, tried to comfort her by placing my hand atop hers. But instead, my fingers passed through hers. She jerked her hand away, looking at me as if I'd done something unforgivable. I sat back, feeling stung. I knew she felt guilty, knew she wished she'd done something to help me, but right then, it felt like she was more concerned with covering her own ass than getting me any kind of justice.

"We need to talk to Stephen," I said quietly, afraid to say much else.

Sofi looked at me, aghast. "Sure," she said. "I'll just march into the jail and tell them I brought my dead girl as proof. I can go ahead and turn myself in while we're there. It'll be so convenient."

"I'm sorry," I said, feeling a fight brewing and beginning to warm up to it. "But as the dead girl, I'm having trouble understanding how this is suddenly all about you."

She laughed, humorless and bitter. "As the *alive* girl, I'm the one facing a future in prison if they think I had anything to do with you getting killed."

"I'm already in prison!" I shouted, and immediately flickered out, crackling with static that felt like a lightning storm building up inside me. I flickered back in and saw that Sofi had gotten to her feet, the camera hanging limply from its strap over her shoulder. Her eyes, large and blue and shining with hurt, were filled with tears.

"Is that how it is, then?" she said softly, tucking her hair behind her ear and looking suddenly much younger. "An eye for an eye? A life for a life?" She shook her head, and the tears finally spilled down her cheeks. "Maybe that's what I deserve."

"You let me know when the pity party's over," I said, my anger softening, but only slightly. "Then maybe we can actually get back to figuring out *what the hell is going on around here.*"

She opened her mouth to respond, when a sudden eruption of loud voices interrupted. Shouts, and what sounded like a woman screaming. Sofi and I stared at each other. Finally, I nodded back at the fairgrounds. "*Go.*"

She sprinted off, still keeping the camera clutched close to her side. Feeling rattled, I closed my eyes and let the tug pull me behind her. I flickered out, then back in...in the midst of absolute chaos.

Mirtel, wearing God knew what sort of Rensaissance Festival hodgepodge of skirts, was standing in the middle of a group of townspeople, looking particularly frazzled. Several men and women were circled around her, some sneering, some looking genuinely concerned.

"Oh, so the 'Egg Lady' says the town has secrets?" one of them said, his voice dripping with sarcasm. "Well then, we'd better call in the troops."

"You aren't *listening*," Mirtel said raggedly. There was an ache of desperation in her voice.

"We heard you, Mirtel," said a woman, whose face was carefully schooled into a calm expression, though her voice gave away her frustration. "We've heard you muttering about it for years now."

"Our girls have had *questions*," another one chimed in, looking scandalized. "You can't go around babbling to yourself about secrets and conspiracies in front of such...*impressionable* minds."

"Our girls deserve the truth," Mirtel shouted. By then, everyone in the hall had turned their attention to the unfolding scene.

One of the men stepped closer, and I saw Mirtel shrink away.

"You've made enough trouble around this town," he said, pulling himself up to his full height and staring the older woman down.

Mirtel was silent for a moment, and then she seemed to

steel herself, straightening her shoulders and meeting the man's eyes with a defiant look.

"You haven't seen *half* the trouble I'm about to make," she said.

I caught sight of Sofi on the other side of the hall, where she was watching the scene, transfixed and horrified. Whether she was concerned for the older woman's safety, or the secrets she was preparing to reveal, I didn't know. Maybe it was a mix of both.

She tore her eyes away from Mirtel and searched the crowd until she found me. She let out a breath, and I could see from her expression she felt some small relief knowing that I was there. I felt terrible about what we'd said—about what *I'd* said, and I hoped she could see the apology on my face.

Our tender moment was interrupted though, as the man gripped Mirtel by the wrist and began pulling her toward him.

"That's enough for today," he said, stepping out of the circle and yanking her behind him. "It's time for you to leave."

"I will *not*," she said, digging her heels in. She was significantly slighter than his stocky frame though, and it wasn't difficult for him to pull her along. After a few staggering steps, Mirtel fell to her knees.

I looked at Sofi, panic building inside me. The hold he had on her wrist—it had to hurt. This wasn't okay. We needed to stop this, but—

Suddenly, another man, younger and handsome, yet oozing authority, pushed through the throng, making his way toward Mirtel. I recognized him as the town doctor, though I'd only ever visited the *koolis* nurse

"What's this?" he said, kneeling down beside her and putting a hand gently on her shoulder. "There, there, Mirtel.

You must be feeling ill. Let's get you over to the office and get you checked out."

Mirtel stared up at him with shrewd eyes, but said nothing. The crowd began to relax then, sensing the show was over, and the tension in the room began to fade.

"All right, everybody," the doctor said, smiling genially. "The excitement is over. Mirtel isn't feeling well, but we can right that, can't we, Mirtel?"

She looked up at him then, and something in her face cleared. Her eyes narrowed. She went completely still, her breathing ragged, but steady.

"Yes," she said quietly, and the doctor's smile widened.

"Good girl," he said, patting her again. "Let's get you up—"

Mirtel spit in his face. The crowd, which had been resuming a quieter level of chatter, went utterly silent.

Across the room, I heard a familiar voice yell, "*Dad*."

Sofi? Her dad was the town doctor? I'd never known, but I'd never had a reason to. She pushed her way toward him, until an older girl, maybe her sister, judging by the similarly plaited hair and slightly upturned nose, caught her around the waist and held her back.

Meanwhile, the doctor nodded to the man who'd previously been holding onto Mirtel, and he lunged forward, grabbing her arms and wrapping her long skirts around her ankles like a binding. Mirtel began to struggle, but again, she was no match for the barrel-chested brute. Another man stepped in to help, and they heaved her up and began to carry her toward the rear entrance. A woman—Sofi's mother, perhaps—walked up behind the doctor and put a hand on his shoulder, but he shook her off.

"I'll be at the office," he said shortly, rising to his feet and pulling out a handkerchief to wipe his face.

She nodded and scuttled off in the opposite direction.

The doctor, who was wearing a dark green polo shirt, straightened his collar and turned a sudden smile on the crowd.

"You know, I think this might go down as one of the most exciting Spring Day festivals in Vaikesti history," he said, and the crowd laughed, though somewhat uncertainly. "Well, you won't be disturbed again," he said, his voice warm. His hair was dark blond and his piercing blue eyes crinkled at the corners when he smiled. Sofi had his eyes. "Carry on with the festivities," he said, gesturing encouragingly as a few of the women moved back toward the kitchen area. "Mirtel will be in good hands. And I know she'd want you all to continue celebrating."

She'd want nothing of the sort, I was sure. I didn't know exactly what had happened, but I could guess that the revelation of our bond had driven Mirtel to action. I knew that Sofi and I had to work this out. We had to see the rest of what was on Stephen's camera, and find out if he was on our side or not.

I looked toward Sofi, hoping she'd understand my look, but she was being guided firmly toward the door by her sister. She glanced back once and met my eyes, and I could see she was as confused and overwhelmed as I was.

I gave her a reassuring smile, even though I didn't feel sure about a damn thing, and tried to communicate wordlessly that I'd catch up with her later.

In the blink of an eye, she'd disappeared into the crowd.

CHAPTER 11

SOFI

With no heartbeat and no need to breathe came no need to sleep, and so I'd left Darja curled in the overstuffed armchair nestled under the window of my room when I fell asleep that night, and found her still there when I awoke early the next morning. I couldn't imagine that she'd just sat there all night, but I was afraid to ask. I found her presence in my room both disturbing and comforting. On one hand, having her with me made me feel safe, like I wasn't alone in this mess I'd found myself in, and it was good to have someone to talk to, even if our talking often devolved into arguing. On the other hand, it was profoundly disturbing to consider the fact that she was *dead*.

Some carefully worded and hopefully casual questions directed at my dad the previous night had revealed that he was keeping Mirtel overnight at his office for observation, so the sun was barely up over the trees when my blaring alarm dragged me out of sleep and into my clothes. I avoided looking at the camera perched on my bedside table as I pulled on a hoodie and hurriedly left the house.

I needed to know that Mirtel was okay after what'd happened at the festival. That and figure out what the hell she'd been thinking. I was all for finding answers, but her outburst was only going to cause more harm than good. Surely she could see that.

Dad's office was part of Vaikesti's municipal building, along with the tiny police station, tax offices, library, and post office. I'd been there a million times, but I still nearly made a wrong turn on the way, my mind lost in thoughts of the previous day, before a quick word from Darja brought me back to the present. She'd ridden along with me in the car this time, something I hadn't been sure she was able to do, and she slanted a glance in my direction as I pulled into a parking space and cut the engine.

"You okay?" she asked, an eyebrow raised as she watched me wipe my sweating palms on my jeans.

"Yeah," I assured her, dropping my keys into my purse. "It's just a lot, you know?" I glanced over at her. "Are you *sure* my dad's not here?" I wanted to talk to Mirtel, but I didn't want to involve my dad in any of this. I still didn't see why we couldn't wait until they'd sent her home, but Darja had been insistent. I thought about her recent experience with being sedated though, and couldn't exactly blame her for her concern.

"*Yes,*" she said. "I told you, I checked before we left. He's not even up yet. If anyone's here, it'll just be the nurse. Let's go."

There weren't many cars in the parking lot this early, but I still scanned our surroundings as we made our way to the entrance. My paranoia was uncalled for, after all there was no reason I couldn't be here visiting my dad's office as I had my entire life, but I still felt inexplicably guilty for some reason, and I didn't want to run into anyone.

The heavy glass doors swung open and silently admitted

us into the cold conditioned air of the hallway, a large map and sign on the wall needlessly directing us through to the atrium, a big central space with small hallways extending outward like spokes on a wheel. Across the atrium and down the hallway to the right would take us to my dad's office.

We had just stepped into the wide open space of the atrium, where a ring of benches angled around some brightly colored planters, when I heard heavy footsteps coming toward me and looked up. There wasn't enough time to duck back down the corridor or scurry around the far side of the atrium, so instead I took a deep breath and straightened, meeting Stephen's eyes as he came toward me.

The entrance to the police station was across the atrium to my left, and I realized he must have been held overnight and only just released.

His steps slowed as he approached me, and I hastily sped mine up, praying he wouldn't try to talk to me. I could see Darja eyeing him curiously though, and I chanced a glance as well.

He looked terrible. There were dark circles under his eyes and his hair was mussed and matted, sticking up at odd angles. He walked stiffly and the frames of his glasses appeared to be bent.

"Sofi?"

I froze in my tracks. How did he know my name?

"Sofi." The call came again before I realized it hadn't come from Stephen, who had instead picked up his pace and hurried down the hall away from me. I glanced around in confusion for a moment before I registered Jared, still in uniform, leaning out of the door to the police station and beckoning at me.

I crossed to him.

"I'm glad to see you," he said. "I was actually going to come find you this morning."

He was? I wasn't sure whether to be flattered or confused.

"Do you have a couple of minutes to talk?" he asked, pushing a hand through his hair.

"Who is that?" Darja's voice was loud next to me, and it took an effort not to look her way or reply.

After a long pause I realized I hadn't answered Jared either, and he was staring at me as if unsure whether he should repeat himself.

"Um, sure," I said quickly, face flaming red. "I was just..." I gestured vaguely toward my dad's office, then cleared my throat. "I have time though. I can talk."

"I'm going to see Mirtel," Darja informed me, making no attempt to keep her voice low. "Hopefully Aggie is with her and I can talk to them. I'll catch up with you after."

I nodded at her before I could stop myself, but Jared had already turned away and was holding the door open for me to pass ahead of him.

I glanced back as I went through, but both Stephen and Darja were out of sight. Inside the station, Jared took the lead again, ushering me past the front desk and down a short hallway to a tiny office. I followed, wondering what on earth he wanted to talk to me about.

The plaque on the door read *Charles Braden, County Sheriff*, and Jared held the door open for me again then closed it quietly behind us. He gestured for me to take a seat in one of the two stiff office chairs before sliding behind his father's desk to sit in front of the computer there.

When I finally got a look at him up close, I was surprised to see that he didn't appear to be in much better shape than Stephen. His eyes were also tired-looking, ringed with circles, and his hair and uniform were rumpled. It made him look young, like the shaggy-headed boy I remembered from high school.

"Are you okay?" I asked, gazing at him with concern, and it drew a smile out of him.

"Yeah, I'm okay." He glanced down at his clothes, then back up at me. "I must look terrible, huh? I didn't get a chance to sleep last night. It's good though, actually." He leaned forward and rested his arms on the desk, his eyes warm as his smile deepened, and lowered his voice confidentially. "I just got assigned my first real case."

"Oh." I couldn't help the answering smile that spread across my face at his look of embarrassed pride. "Congratulations."

"Thanks," he said, his ears turning a little pink as he picked up a pencil from the desk and fiddled with it. "I didn't expect them to give me something this early. I was up all night reading through the files and taking notes. I really don't want to mess this up."

"I'm sure you'll do a great job," I said. It was true, I was sure he would, though his insecurity was endearing. I wondered why he'd brought me in though. Surely not just to share this news.

"Did you...am I part of this new case?" I asked, and Jared seemed to refocus, clearing his throat and dragging a hand through his hair again. I remembered the nervous gesture from our time in school together, though his newly-cropped hair didn't give him much to drag through.

"Oh, right. Uh, not exactly. I just need to ask you a few questions." He threw a smile my way before adding, "You're not in trouble or anything. I'm just hoping you can help me out."

He transferred the pencil to his other hand before opening a notebook on the desk in front of him. Bringing the eraser end of the pencil to his mouth, he rested it against his lips as he appeared to skim down whatever was written in the notebook. My eyes followed the trajectory of the pencil, and I swallowed involuntarily. He really was so handsome.

"Do you know a girl named Darja Kallas?"

All thoughts fled from my head as my eyes flew to his.

Crap.

"What?" I asked, stalling for time. How the hell was I supposed to answer that?

He glanced down at his notes, then back up at me. "Darja Kallas," he repeated. "Ever heard the name?"

How on earth was I supposed to answer? I was pretty sure my surprise had betrayed enough that I couldn't just say no. I obviously couldn't tell him the truth. *Uh, yeah, she's just a dead girl I'm bonded with. Did you want to talk to her?* But I couldn't mention the Ceremony either, not to an outsider. I'd have to go with some version of the truth, at least until I figured out what he was looking for.

"I think so," I hedged, trying to sound casual. "She was one of the *koolis* girls that came to our class once a week, right?" I mentally kicked myself for making it sound like I was guessing on a multiple choice test.

But Jared just nodded, making a note in his notebook. "That's right. Did you know her outside of class?"

Committing to this version of my story, I raised an eyebrow. "I don't think anyone really knew the *koolis* girls outside of class. It's not like we hung out with them or anything."

"Have you seen her since school let out?" he asked.

I concentrated on keeping my expression smooth. The others may not have technically been lies, but this one was. "No. I haven't seen her. I don't know what happens to the *koolis* girls after graduation."

Why was he asking this? What did he know—or not know?

But he didn't give anything away, just leaned back in his chair and tapped his pencil against his lips again. He didn't look like he was keeping any big secrets. I decided to take a risk.

"Why?" I asked, watching his face. "Did something happen?"

He looked up at me. "No, it's nothing crazy," he assured me. "She's been reported missing, so I'm following up. Do you know anyone who might have known her?"

I shook my head. "Just the other girls from the *koolis*, I would guess. Maybe...maybe she ran away?" I offered.

"Yeah, that's what I'm guessing too. I just have to follow up with anyone that knew her." For the first time, his expression grew opaque and something I couldn't identify crept into his voice. Obviously, he didn't think that. Besides, he'd told me they'd assigned him to his first real case, and I didn't think he'd have been up all night if he was just following up on a runaway. There was something more going on here. And I needed to know what it was.

But Jared had closed the notebook and was smiling at me again, his expression open and his dark eyes friendly.

"That's all I needed then. Will you let me know if you hear anything?"

"Of course," I said, my concern warring with relief that at least he didn't seem to suspect anything that involved me.

The thought made me feel slightly ashamed. I remembered what Darja had said during our fight at the fairgrounds. She'd been almost excited at the prospect that Stephen might know our secrets, might have evidence of what had happened to her. She wanted justice, and what's more, she deserved it. The instinct to protect our community and keep our secrets was ingrained so deep inside me that it was hard to imagine any alternative, but I wondered for a second how bad it would be if Jared found out what had really happened to her. Stephen—he was a lunatic, a stalker. But Jared, that might be different. If the police got involved, Darja might really get the justice she deserved.

My thoughts were interrupted as Jared pushed his chair away from the desk and stood, coming around to open the door for me. I rose and squeezed past him into the hallway, and we walked together to the entrance, where the door opened back into the atrium. He stopped me there with a warm hand on my arm, a smile, and another pass of his other hand through his hair. "Thanks for your help, Sofi, I really appreciate it."

My stomach fluttered a little at the sound of my name in his deep voice, and for a second I wondered again how it would feel to spill my secrets and let someone else share the burden. Not all the secrets, not the ones that would make him think I was crazy, but just enough to right some of the wrongs.

"And..." he went on after a pause, "it really was good to see you this morning."

"So you could question me about your new case?" I teased him.

He smiled back. "No. It's always good to see you. Maybe I will again soon." He let go of my arm and stepped back through the glass door, letting it swing shut behind him.

My face felt warm, but I didn't have any time to bask in whatever cocktail of emotions I was feeling before Darja was at my side, her voice sharp and urgent.

"There you are. Thank God, I was about to come in after you."

I glanced around quickly, keeping my voice low, but there was no one else in the atrium. "Darja, what—?"

"Come on, hurry. You have to see this." She reached down and grabbed at my hand, then growled when her hand passed through in a wave of cold. I flinched.

"Just come *on*."

Without waiting to see if I was following, she took off across the atrium, passing right through the benches in the center as if they weren't there. I hurried behind, sidestepping the benches as she headed down the hallway to the left, opposite where my father's office was located.

"What's going on?" I hissed, hurrying to keep up, but she didn't answer. She didn't stop until she stood at the very end of the hallway, outside the arched doorway stamped with bold letters that read *Vaikesti Library and Archives*.

She turned to me. "In here. Follow me, but stay back so he doesn't see you."

"What—?" I tried again, but she'd already gone through the closed door, and I almost walked headlong into the glass in an attempt to follow her before stopping and wrenching the door open.

The Vaikesti Library was actually one of my favorite places, and had been since I was a child. I was the youngest of six kids, and by the time I was born my mother had long since mastered the trick of pairing off the older kids with the younger ones to increase the odds that someone would notice if anyone went missing. I was most often left in the care of my middle sister, Hanna, and since much of my childhood coincided with her high school years, which brought with them a lot of time spent in the library—meeting study groups, working on term papers, and also meeting with boys outside of the watchful gazes of our parents—I'd spent a lot of time here as well, curled up in the worn chairs of the reading section, nose buried in a book.

So, when I stepped through the door into the familiar smell of paper and wood-cleaner and saw Darja turn to the left, I knew she was heading to the reference section.

I aimed a quick smile at the librarian on duty, who nodded absently at me as I passed.

The reference section, located in the back corner beyond the media area with its rows of computers, was not one I'd spent much time in. It held all the boring stuff—the books you couldn't check out, the town records, the rare books.

In the center of the space was a series of tables set up for patrons to review the materials since they couldn't be removed from the library. Darja stopped abruptly against the wall just beyond where the tables began, and I nearly walked right through her before I pulled up short.

I didn't need her gesture to direct my gaze; my eyes immediately landed on Stephen where he sat at one of the tables, head bent low over a thick book that lay open in front of him. He was the only figure in the room; even the reference desk was deserted. A stack of other books sat in a haphazard pile to his side, but his full attention was focused on the book before him.

I lowered my voice to a whisper. "So? He's reading a book."

"Go see what it is," she hissed back.

Our position against the wall meant we were behind him and to the side, so he wouldn't see me if he happened to glance up, but it also meant that his body blocked the contents of the book from my view. I edged closer, keeping against the shelves like I was looking for a book as I sidled into viewing range.

I heard before I saw. His voice was low as he read aloud to himself. He stumbled slightly on some of the words, pausing to take notes or sound out a passage, but there was no mistaking it.

"Vaata, maa vaim on tugev ja selle võlakirjaga ma õnnistan seda—"

The old tongue. The language of the old country.

My gasp must have been audible, because the reading broke off abruptly and he turned toward where I was suddenly very preoccupied with the shelves.

There was a pause while I pretended to ignore him, but I clearly wasn't fooling anyone.

"It's Sofi, right?" he said, and his voice was surprisingly different from the day before. At the festival he'd been all obnoxious questions and oblivious cockiness, but this morning he seemed subdued, as if a night spent in jail had at least tempered his exuberance.

I was caught, so I nodded, and at Darja's urging, I went ahead and slid uninvited into a chair across the table from him.

"I didn't know you could read the old language," I said, staring down at the book. It was huge and heavy-looking, bound in dark brown leather with thick cream pages. "Do you actually know what it says?"

He nodded a little, seemingly unbothered by my intrusion. If anything, he looked cautious, as if he was afraid I might yell at him or call the police again. "I've been studying it, as part of my project. I'm not fluent by any stretch, but I can follow the gist."

I wasn't sure how to respond to this. Even in Vaikesti, I didn't think anyone but a small handful of elders could still actually read the old tongue. Darja had circled around behind him, and was peering over his shoulder at the pages, but at this, she too looked up in surprise.

"What is it?" I asked, leaning forward to examine the page he had open.

"It's...uh..." He cleared his throat. "Well, it's a book of spells, actually."

"What?!" Darja and I responded at the same time, but he only looked at me, his eyes wary at my too-loud voice.

"Just...you know, like from the old religion, how to have a good harvest, curing fevers, stuff like that."

"Where did you get it?" I demanded, and he stared at me like I was an idiot, rightly so according to Darja's expression, before gesturing toward the shelves.

"In the stacks," he said slowly. "It looked interesting."

I took a deep breath and tried to smile. "Sorry, yeah, I just meant I've never seen anything like that here before."

"Do you spend a lot of time in the research section of the library?" he asked, and I started to stammer a reply before I caught the teasing glint in his eye. He laughed. "I'm kidding. It was in the back, and covered in dust. The whole stack was," he said, nodding to the pile of books at his side. "I doubt anyone has pulled these out in a while."

It seemed like he was starting to relax, so I leaned closer, pulling the book toward me a bit. The lines of text seemed utterly foreign to me. We still used a lot of words and phrases from the old tongue, but no one my age could actually read it. Stephen seemed bolstered by my interest, and began to flip through the pages, stopping to point things out. "See, there's hundreds of old spells in here, some have drawings, and—"

"Why are so many of those pages empty?" I cut in, gesturing as he flipped. Every few pages there would be a series of blank pages, sometimes one or two, sometimes what seemed like a dozen, before the dark lines of print picked up again.

He paused on one of the blank pages, finger tracing down the edge. "I don't know," he said thoughtfully. "The whole book is like that though. I thought maybe it was for people to take notes, but nobody has written anything there."

"They're not blank." Darja's voice was barely more than a whisper.

"What?" I looked up at where she stood leaning over Stephen's shoulder.

"What?" Stephen looked up at me, but I ignored him.

Darja reached a hand out and traced a finger down the page, her hand passing directly through Stephen's as she did. He didn't react.

"It's not blank," she said again, staring at me with wide eyes under a furrowed brow. "It's full of text."

"What do you mean?" I asked, pulling the book out of Stephen's grasp and flipping to another series of blank pages. "Here, too?"

"Are you okay?" Stephen's voice cut in, but adrenaline was pumping through my system and I didn't spare him a glance.

"Yes," she answered. "I don't see any blank pages at all."

I slammed the book shut and stood, my body on autopilot, overriding my brain.

"Sofi—"

My voice came out hoarsely, cutting him off. "I have to go."

"Sofi—" It was Darja this time, but I ignored them both, heaving the book into my arms and taking off toward the entrance.

"You can't take that out of—" Stephen's voice faded in the distance as I broke into a run. The librarian's desk was thankfully empty as I hurried past, and I was in my car, speeding down the road with the heavy book propped in the passenger seat before I realized I'd left Darja behind as well.

CHAPTER 12

DARJA

I wasn't exactly thrilled with the little stunt Sofi had pulled in the library. Of course, we both knew by this point that our bond meant I'd be able to track her down easily and flicker my way to wherever she was, but still. Rude.

I stood there for a while, watching Stephen scratch his head and stare at the doorway Sofi had charged through during her grand exit. I didn't think he was as nefarious as Sofi was making him out to be. A little too interested in our podunk town and insular way of life, sure, but I didn't think that meant he was out to expose the Vaikesti for its villainous, murderous treachery.

Which was a shame, because villainy, murder and treachery seemed to be A Whole Thing around here.

No, I was pretty sure Stephen wasn't out to get us. I didn't peg him for an undercover cop, or a journalist in the trenches. If anything, he was a harmless, hapless nerd, who had a lot of useless knowledge of our people's history...that suddenly had become very useful. I was going to have to talk Sofi into trusting him, for at least as long as it took to figure out what was in that book. I didn't know what it could be, but I had a feeling it was something important. It seemed to somehow hum with energy, almost as if it were alive. That required some investigating.

But it would have to wait. I could feel the bond tugging away at me as I lingered in the library. It wasn't painful exactly, but it wasn't pleasant, either. I felt a little bit at sea when Sofi wasn't around, unsure how to be in this world in which I no longer really existed. I could mimic sitting, standing, walking, but I had to force it, as if the muscle memory of even the simplest actions had fizzled out at the same time my heartbeat had.

It was...lonely. If I was being honest, it was more than the bond that kept me hovering close to Sofi at all times... even while she slept. The idea of going deeper into...whatever this was, this afterlife...terrified me. Sofi was my only link to the world I'd been taken from, and while it hadn't always done right by me, it was the only world I knew. This new world, this otherworld, with its hushed voices whispering a near-constant stream of gibberish into my ear—I hated it. I didn't belong in it. And when Sofi wasn't around, I could no longer deny what I was.

Dead.

If I let it, if I thought about it, the whirlpool would suck me in, drown me in the unknown. Sofi—the bond we shared—kept me safely in the shallows. As long as she could see me, talk to me and keep me tethered to this life, well, I wouldn't have to face what came after.

But just then, just when she had stormed out and left me without a backward glance, the whirlpool drew me closer. It pulled me toward some sort of realization of my mortality that I knew I wasn't ready to face. This half-life wasn't what I was meant for. This non-existence was not my destiny.

But if not, then what was?

"What the *hell* are you doing here?"

The barking voice jolted me out of my swirling thoughts and I was apologizing before I realized they couldn't have been talking to me.

Stephen, who'd gone back to the stack of books at the table in front of him while I contemplated the meaning of life, jumped at the sound, sending his phone clattering to the floor. He quickly bent to pick it up then stood up, turning toward the officer, Jared, who was standing menacingly in the doorway to the reference section.

"It's a public library, isn't it?" he said, sounding a little braver than he looked. He pushed his glasses up his nose and squared his shoulders.

Jared took a step closer. He was several inches taller and significantly broader, and he must have known how intimidating he could be.

"Yeah, well you aren't a part of this *public*. You've done nothing but cause trouble since you got here, so beat it."

"I haven't caused any trouble," Stephen said, standing his ground. It was admirable, I thought, if a little pitiful.

Jared rolled his eyes. "You're a snoop," he said, "and a creep. Taking pictures of our girls, intruding on the town's festival—"

"*Our* girls?" Stephen said, not bothering to keep the scorn out of his voice. "Talk about a creep—"

"Watch your mouth," Jared growled, leaning closer so his face was only inches away from Stephen's. "And stay the hell away from Sofi."

I wasn't sure who looked more surprised—Stephen or me.

"Uh, what?" Stephen finally said.

Jared ran a hand over his close-cropped hair and seemed

to sag a bit. "Just...leave her alone, okay? I saw you at the head table, chatting up all the girls yesterday."

"I wasn't chatting up anyone," Stephen said. "I was researching—"

"Whatever," Jared said. "Sofi...she's not like the others. They just want attention. They think you're going to write some article and turn them into pop culture celebrities or something. But Sofi's too smart for that shit. So just...back off."

It was Stephen's turn to look agitated. "Look, man," he said, pushing away from the table and picking up his backpack with an angry jerk, "I'd love nothing more than to get in my car and put this godforsaken shithole behind me. But I'm not leaving without my camera."

"And I told you," Jared said, "that no one has seen your camera. If it turns up, I'll be in touch."

Stephen's face was flushed, his freckles standing out starkly across the bridge of his nose. "That camera was a gift," he said in a strained voice. I felt a little guilty, standing there watching the exchange, but I wasn't going anywhere until I knew what happened.

"Well now, that's bad luck," Jared said, schooling his face into a sympathetic expression. "I'll be sure to keep an eye out."

"Screw you," Stephen said, gathering his things and pushing past Jared toward the doorway.

"Come back and see us again soon," Jared called after him. "I'll hold your cell."

Stephen's response was muffled as he was already booking it back through the atrium, but I thought I picked up on a few choice words. I didn't blame him. He hadn't actually done anything wrong while in Vaikesti, but he was being run out of town like a criminal in the old west. Meanwhile, Jared seemed to have a soft spot for Sofi...but that didn't stop him from acting like a real dick.

I watched him turn and stride out of the library, back toward the station, wondering what he and Sofi had been talking about when he'd whisked her away. She'd looked flustered when I caught up with her—maybe he'd asked her out?

Feeling annoyed that I'd wasted my time worrying about Sofi's love life *while I was dead*, I decided to resume my earlier plan to visit Mirtel. I'd gotten waylaid when I saw Stephen creep around the side of the municipal building and re-enter through a side door that led into the library. Sofi could wait. I'd track her down through the bond after I made sure Mirtel was okay.

It was still early, and since it was Saturday, the office seemed deserted. There was a glassed-in booth at the far end of the reception area, containing a small desk and a decades-old filing cabinet that likely held the complete medical histories of every resident of Vaikesti.

There was a solid wooden door leading back to the exam rooms, and since that hadn't seemed to stop me since I'd lost my corporeal solidity, I pushed myself straight through it.

Once I was through, I moved to the rear hallway, where there were a few rooms for extended-stay patients. The county hospital wasn't far, but I knew that every now and then, in the case of a broken bone or non-life-threatening illness (or, as rumored at the *koolis*, an occasional birth), Vaikesti residents could opt to be treated here instead.

I heard muttering from the farthest room at the back of the hall, and followed it to a door that was slightly ajar. I stepped through it and saw Mirtel stretched out on a flat, unmade hospital bed, her wrists bound to either side by leather straps. In the corner, Aggie hovered over a chair as if curled up on the seat, her arms tight around her knees. She looked up sharply when I entered, narrowing her eyes.

"What are you doing here?"

"I just wanted to check on Mirtel." I looked over to where the older woman was tugging helplessly at her restraints, her eyes open but unfocused. "How is she?"

"How do you *think*?" Aggie hissed. She was wearing her standard frown, but I could see the genuine worry in her dark eyes.

"Drugged?" I asked.

"To the gills. What the hell *happened*?"

I moved closer to where she sat. Her white dress looked grayer than it had before. In fact, all of her looked gray—washed out and pale. If it were possible, she looked even more dead than usual.

"You tell me," I said, attempting to lean casually against the wall next to her. I had to stop myself from falling right through it.

"I was mad when she took off for the festival," she said, looking over at Mirtel pitifully.

"There's a surprise."

She turned the full force of her glare on me and I tried to school my face into a contrite expression.

"She was...I don't know. Upset, over what happened to you and Sofi. But she was calm."

"Too calm, sounds like."

Aggie shrugged. "I guess. But I'm not her keeper. I can't stop her when she's got her mind set on something."

"Did she say what these secrets were that she planned to reveal?"

Aggie gave me an inscrutable look. "What do you think?"

I gritted my teeth, trying not to let my frustration take over. Aggie was about as easy to decipher as a sphinx.

"What was she trying to accomplish?"

Aggie sighed. "I have no idea. Revenge? Exposing this community for what it is?"

"And...what is it?" I asked carefully.

Aggie looked at me unflinchingly. "Evil."

I couldn't argue. This town—the town I'd grown up in—had been murdering girls for generations, and for what? A bond they didn't even really believe in anymore? 'Evil' pretty much summed it up.

"What do we do now?" I asked. "We can't leave her here."

"I'm not planning to," Aggie said defensively. I could almost see her hackles rise.

"That's not what I meant," I said, raising my hands in a placating gesture. "We need to get her out before the doctor gets here. Have you...can you...touch anything?"

Aggie shook her head. "I've tried. I can walk and sit, like you, but my body doesn't actually *touch* anything. It's... kind of a pantomime, I guess. But I've never been able to pick up anything, or touch anyone."

I tried not to think about an eternity without any physical contact. I couldn't fathom it anyway, so I shoved it down for another day.

Instead, I shifted my thoughts to how two ghosts were going to be able to move a living person without raising suspicion. Could we have Mirtel rock herself off the hospital bed and maybe snap the restraints? That didn't seem likely to work, and would just attract attention...not to mention possibly injuring her.

While my brain struggled to come up with a solution, I realized I could hear footsteps coming swiftly down the hall. I shot Aggie a look and she got up from her spot in the chair, moving to hover next to me. My instinct was to hide, even though I knew no one would see me.

The door creaked open, and I held my breath. Was it the doctor? Was he going to drug her even more? Would he hurt her? Send her home with a warning? Send her to an institution?

My thoughts were spinning uncontrollably, so fast and furious I almost didn't recognize the figure in the doorway.

It was Sofi. She was clutching the book she'd taken from Stephen protectively against her chest. She looked at Mirtel, then at me, relief flooding her face.

"Is Aggie here?" she whispered, and I nodded to my right. She shot a tired, half-hearted smile into the void and then looked back to me.

"Okay," she said. "My dad is on his way. We have to hurry."

"What are we going to do?"

Sofi placed the book gently on the bed at Mirtel's feet, then fixed me with a steely gaze.

"We're breaking Mirtel out."

CHAPTER 13

SOFI

Getting Mirtel back to her wagon was both easier and more difficult than I'd expected.

Easier, because despite my fears, whatever drugs she'd been given appeared to wear off quickly. Though she seemed a little disoriented when I shook her shoulder, whispering at her to keep quiet while frantically trying to unclasp the leather straps that bound her to the bed, she was perfectly able to walk on her own once I'd freed her.

More difficult, because Darja and Aggie spent the entire time trading barbed comments that seemed to be quickly escalating to a full-on shouting match. And though I could only hear one side of the argument, it was still enough to distract me so that I almost missed my father's car pulling into the parking lot at the same moment we all stumbled out of the front doors of the municipal building. It was Mirtel's sharp indrawn breath that made me look up, and then we were all stumbling to the side, my left hand supporting Mirtel and my right clutched tightly around the book I'd snatched from the library.

Thank God for the overgrown hedges that framed the front of the building, not yet manicured into shape by the landscapers the city kept on contract. That and the fact that my dad was anything but a morning person. I pulled Mirtel behind the tall shrubs, the two of us disappearing into the thick foliage, though I could tell from my father's glazed eyes as he passed by not three feet from us, a cup of coffee gripped in his hand, that he probably wouldn't have noticed us if I'd been waving my arms and shouting. I still held my breath until the door had shut firmly behind him, then gave Darja the darkest glare I could manage before we all scuttled across the lot to my car and piled in.

The drive to Mirtel's was silent and tense. Darja was in the car with us again, but I didn't know if Aggie was there or not and I didn't ask. Mirtel seemed lost in thought, her brow furrowed as she stared out the window, and I left her alone, preoccupied by my own troubled thoughts.

The quiet broke the second we stepped through the brightly painted door of Mirtel's wagon and latched it firmly behind us.

"What were you thinking?!" That came from Darja, directed at Mirtel, who of course couldn't hear her, but Aggie could, and responded with a vicious snap.

I couldn't hear her words, but they must have been harsh, because Darja looked furious.

Mirtel turned at Aggie's words as well, and both she and Darja spoke over each other. I ignored them, moving instead to the tiny kitchen table, where I let the heavy tome I'd been carrying fall with a *thump* on the worn wood. In the brief beat of quiet that followed the noise, I spoke, my voice loud in the small space.

"The police are looking for Darja; someone reported her missing. And this book has pages that can only be seen by dead people."

The silence after that was absolute. Both Mirtel and Darja turned to stare at me, and I could only assume Aggie was quiet too, because their attention didn't waver.

"What do you mean, they're looking for me?" Darja said softly, at the same moment Mirtel said, "What do you mean, seen by the dead?"

Then both of them turned to stare at the empty space between them, and I gave up and sagged down into the plush armchair in the corner.

"This would be a lot easier if we could all *see* each other," I grumbled.

Mirtel shot me an apologetic glance and chose a seat next to me in a rickety-looking rocking chair. "Tell us about Darja."

I quickly filled them in on my conversation with Jared. There wasn't much to tell, but Darja seemed even paler by the time I'd finished.

"Who could possibly have reported her missing?" Mirtel asked, bewilderment on her lined face.

"It would have to be someone outside the town, right?" I asked. "No one from Vaikesti would have. I mean, all the adult women *know* what happened, and no one outside the *koolis* would have known her."

"We did see people outside of the *koolis*, you know," Darja put in acerbically. "It's not like they chained us up in there." Then she fell silent.

No, not chained up maybe. Just drugged and murdered on a bonfire. I didn't say it. I didn't have to.

Mirtel cocked her head to listen for a moment, then turned to me. "Aggie asked why Jared was questioning you, specifically."

I shrugged. "I don't know. I don't think he was looking for me. I just happened to be there outside the station and he knew we were in class together."

Darja shook her head. "No, when we walked up, he said he was glad to see you, and he'd been planning to come find you this morning. I heard him. He would have come looking for you if you hadn't happened to show up there."

I'd forgotten he'd said that. I shook my head. "I don't think he meant he was going to come find me to question me. He might have just wanted..." My face flushed. "...to stop by," I finished lamely.

Darja narrowed her eyes at me. "I don't trust him."

"You don't trust *him?*" My brows shot up. "He's better than that creep following us around town, taking pictures when we're not looking."

"We're the ones that followed *him* to the library," she shot back. "He didn't follow us!"

"Girls," Mirtel cut in mildly. "Remember we can't all hear you."

I took a breath, then apologized, filling her in on everything she and Aggie had missed after the debacle at the festival. Stephen, and his camera, his arrest, and then the events at the library. I retrieved the book from the table and brought it over, sitting and cradling it in my lap. Darja came over to perch on the arm of my chair, and for the first time, I didn't find myself shying away from her at all.

Mirtel's gaze sharpened. "He said it was a book of spells? How could he know that?"

"He could *read* it," I said, flipping through the pages, turning it around in my lap so the text faced her. "He wasn't fluent, but it was obvious he had a lot of experience."

There was a pause, then Mirtel nodded toward where Aggie must have been standing. "No," she answered the girl. "I don't think anyone in Vaikesti is fluent anymore. Some of the elders still can read the words pretty well, but I don't think they know what it all means."

There was another pause, and then she laughed, her eyes crinkling at the corners and making her whole face fold like origami. "Me? You know I was never a very good student. I probably know a few words here and there, but that's about it."

She rocked the chair forward and leaned over the book where it was propped on my knees.

"Here," she said, pointing at a word in the block of text. "*Tulekahju*. That means 'fire.'"

I glanced up at Darja, but she was staring at the book.

Mirtel flipped a couple of pages, then stopped when another word caught her eye. "Here," she said with a laugh, then moved her finger along the text, "and here, and here. *Ja*. That means 'and.'"

Darja snorted.

Mirtel turned the page again then paused. "It's blank," she said unnecessarily. "And you said the book is filled with blank pages?" She flipped further through, answering her own question. She stopped on an empty page near the middle, the weight of the thick tome spread evenly over my lap.

"I don't understand why you can't see them," Darja said softly, and I repeated her words to Mirtel.

The old lady turned to the side, raising an eyebrow.

The silence must have held confirmation, because Darja sucked in a breath. "Aggie and I can both see the words there," she said, leaning close to the page.

"But you can see the words on the other pages, too?" Mirtel asked, directing her question at Aggie, but Darja nodded in response.

"I wonder if it's because they've been alive, but we've never been dead," I mused, staring at the page as if I expected something to appear on the wide swath of blank parchment.

Mirtel tilted her head to the side in a thoughtful gesture that reminded me of her chickens. "That's a good theory."

We all fell silent for a long moment as Mirtel flipped further through the book, skimming her fingertips across the pages as she went.

"Why would Stephen be looking through a book of spells?" I asked, my mistrust of him rising again.

"Maybe he wanted to try one," Darja said lightly.

"Don't be ridiculous," I snapped. "Magic doesn't really work." The second the words left my mouth I could hear how dumb I sounded. I was standing here, surrounded by dead people, claiming magic didn't exist.

Darja raised an incredulous eyebrow at me, but Mirtel didn't seem surprised at all by my outburst.

"Magic has always existed," she said calmly, her attention still on the pages. "We've just forgotten how to use it. The first settlers from the old country still had the use of it." Her gaze softened with what I assumed was memory. "I remember my mother used to talk of it with her sister, my aunt, before she died. They used spells for many things in the old country."

"Did you see them use magic? Your mother and her sister?" Darja asked.

Aggie must have repeated the question, because Mirtel looked up. "No, I was too young. The spells must have stopped working shortly after they settled here. By the time I went through my Ceremony, none of the bondings or other spells were successful anymore." She shared a glance with the space to her right. "Except ours."

Other spells.

Despite the fact that I sat here with a book full of spells on my lap, despite the fact that my bonding ceremony had worked, despite the fact that I had proof of magic right in front of me, in the chaos of the last few days it hadn't really occurred to me that the bonding wasn't a standalone incident. There were *other spells.* Spells to do all sorts of things. And they probably *worked.*

My breath caught as the weight of the realization settled over me. I could see Darja watching me out of the corner of my eye, but I carefully kept my gaze down, refusing to meet her eyes.

Mirtel turned another page, tracing her finger down the lines, and I frowned, trying to work through everything in my mind. "But why do you think they work sometimes and not at other times? Or is the binding spell the only one that works at all anymore? You never hear of other magic. And do you think it just *doesn't work* or do you think we're doing something wrong, and that's why?"

Mirtel looked thoughtful. "I think it's because something...maybe more than one something, has been lost over time. It's like we're trying to make a cake, but we don't have the whole recipe anymore."

"And maybe sometimes we stumble across the ingredients by accident?" Darja put in.

I repeated her words and Mirtel nodded. "Maybe. That's just my theory."

I was quiet for a moment, turning this over in my head, before frowning and returning to my original point. "But still, whether the spells could work or not, why would Stephen be looking at them?"

"God, Sofi," Darja exclaimed. "Give him a break. He had a whole stack of books to look through. He's not the devil."

I scowled at her, but let it drop. I didn't trust him. I'd seen his camera.

Leaning back in my chair, I stretched my arms over my head, careful not to jostle the book on my lap that Mirtel was still flipping through.

"I think so," Mirtel said, clearly in response to something

Aggie had asked. "I just don't know what they mean, but it's not hard to sound out the words. Honestly, you probably know more than I do. You were always a good student." She laughed.

Part of me envied the two of them, how easily they spoke to each other and interacted. I wondered if Darja and I would ever have the ease and familiarity that Mirtel and Aggie had. What must it be like, to be bound together for so long, over fifty years? My mind shied away from the thought.

Mirtel had flipped to a new spot near the back of the book. The left page had three words at the top, clearly the title, then a small paragraph of text. There was a drawing of a candle below the text, and then another larger block of text took up the bottom half of the page, this one broken up into numbered sections. The facing page was blank. It must have been a short spell.

Mirtel was leaning far forward over my lap, one finger tracing the words in the title.

"*Eemaldus,*" she sounded the word out, then paused. "No," she answered, "I have no idea what that means, do you? *Valgus.* Yes, that one's 'light.'"

She paused again as Aggie answered, and I tuned them out, turning to Darja.

"Can you read it at all?" I asked, keeping my voice low so as not to interrupt Mirtel.

Darja laughed. "Not a word. I wasn't exactly a model student. Well," she amended, "I mean, I can probably sound out the words. But I don't know what any of them mean. You?"

I shrugged. "Probably about the same. We'd get in trouble if we messed up the prayers and stuff. I probably know like ten words."

She nodded, glancing over at Mirtel and Aggie. "They

must have taught a lot more back when they were in school. They're sounding those words out much faster than I could."

"Does Aggie know any of it?" I asked, looking curiously into the empty air to Mirtel's right.

"She's not doing bad," Darja said, leaning over the book.

Mirtel was talking again, working her way through the top paragraph on the page. She was reading faster than I could stumble over the unfamiliar words, and I gave up trying to keep up. I leaned forward, following Darja's gaze down to the blank page.

"What do you think it means?" I asked. "That you can see words where we can't?"

"Well, I—"

It was so obvious, in hindsight, I couldn't understand how we hadn't connected the dots that were right in front of our faces.

Because when Mirtel stopped reading, and raised her finger triumphantly from where she'd been tracing the letters on the page, there was a long moment of silence, when surely Aggie was sounding out the words on her side. And then, without any warning, every light in the small wagon went out and we were swallowed by darkness.

CHAPTER 14

DARJA

"Well that's...inconvenient," Aggie said. I could barely see her silhouette in the darkness, an eerie sort of glow at her edges, the same color as a rainy spring dawn.

"And interesting," I said, wondering what the hell had actually just happened. I could feel an energy thrumming inside me, tingling through my fingers. Was that what magic felt like?

"That, too."

"So," I said, leaning over Sofi and Mirtel to squint at the shadowed pages, trying to swallow down the wild sort of excitement that had begun to well up inside me, "is there, like, an off switch?"

Aggie shrugged. "Mirtel?" she said, but the older woman was already pushing herself to her feet and moving to the small window above the kitchen sink. It was covered in a patchwork curtain peppered with roses and lilacs softly illuminated against the sunshine outside. She pulled it open and the wagon lit up with warm dappled light. When she turned back to us, there was a wide smile on her face.

Sofi was running her fingers down the page, touching the book almost reverently, her eyes filled with wonder. No one else said anything, but I could feel the thrill in the air around us. We had done it. We had done *magic*.

I'd forgotten that I'd been furious with Aggie on the way over here, completely at my wit's end with her mysterious misdirection and perpetual avoidance of any actual truths. I nodded at the page they'd been reading from, then looked back at her. "Can you understand any of it?"

"Here," she said, lowering her hand next to Mirtel's and pointing at a word on the page. At the same moment, Sofi ran her finger down the length of the spell, right through Aggie's delicate, bird-like wrist. Aggie flinched away, and I gave Sofi a look, nodding infinitesimally toward her hand and then away. She seemed to get the hint, pulling her hand against her chest and looking mildly embarrassed.

"Do you know the word?" Mirtel asked, and Aggie nodded.

"I remember it from one of our prayers. We used to say it at the end, when we took a piece from the loaf of bread we all ate from. 'It is done,'" she said.

I pointed to the word and repeated the translation for Sofi.

Mirtel gave her a nod, and she seemed to steel her shoulders before saying firmly, "*Valmis.*"

Nothing happened.

"Oo-kay," I said. "Good try. But if that ends the spell, why are the lights still out?"

No one said anything for a long moment, then Sofi looked up at me, her eyes gleaming with an idea.

"The lights only went out when Mirtel and Aggie both spoke the words together."

Mirtel began to smile. "Of course. The bond must be

what makes it work. Why don't you two try it." She gave Sofi an encouraging smile.

With a deep breath, Sofi glanced over to me again, nervous and uncertain. I wasn't quite as supportive as Mirtel; I shrugged, not really believing any of this was actually going to work. But I still muttered, "*valmis*" in her direction, so she'd know how Aggie had pronounced it.

She nodded and gave me a thankful smile, then repeated the word in a whisper-thin voice, "*Valmis.*"

Immediately, the lights in the wagon flared, blazing brightly before settling to their usual soft glow.

"Holy shit," I said quietly. Sofi was gaping at the book, leaning away from it as if it might bite her. Mirtel's face was stoic, but there was a triumphant gleam in her eyes. Aggie watched us all with her usual skeptical glare.

"Did we..." Sofi began, a tentative smile tugging at the corners of her mouth. "Did we just... cast a spell?"

Mirtel was grinning widely, looking decades younger. There was something wild in her eyes, and I could see why everyone in town had thought her crazy.

"That," she said, touching the pages in front of her almost reverently, "was most certainly something magic."

The two of them laughed softly, not seeming to know how to process this. I exchanged an unsettled glance with Aggie, who seemed as troubled as I suddenly felt. I couldn't put my finger on it, but something didn't sit right with me. Maybe it was because the only reason the magic seemed to work was because half of us were dead.

Still, it made sense. The whole purpose of the bonding was to tap into some sort of power source that neither living nor dead could access on their own. It was strange, but as unsettled as I felt, I also felt as if something—something maybe I was meant for—had been fulfilled.

"Darja?" Sofi asked suddenly, her smile fading. "Are you okay?"

"Sure," I said, but I wasn't sure I meant it. This felt...big. And I didn't really know if we should celebrate just yet. But Sofi was looking like a kid who'd just discovered a pile of presents under the Christmas tree, and I couldn't take that away from her. Not yet.

"I mean, hey," I said, trying to sound nonchalant, "I'm a ghost *and* a witch. I'm like a whole horror movie, all in one."

Sofi laughed, but Aggie harrumphed. "I don't like this," she said, and neither did I, but we had the book, and we could sound out some of the words, so...what could it hurt?

Feeling reckless, I plopped myself down next to Sofi and leaned over the pages. "So, what else have you got?"

Sofi's eyes lit up. She looked over at Mirtel and gestured toward the book. "Should we...?"

Mirtel seemed enchanted by the whole thing. "Well, I'm not sure how much we can accomplish, and of course, we must be cautious...but yes. Why not?"

"Why *not*?" Aggie hissed. "Mirtel, what are you thinking? We don't understand this magic. It could be *dangerous*."

"Turning the lights on and off is far from dangerous, Aggie. We might just...test this out. After fifty years, I'd like to think something good might come of this."

Aggie clenched her jaw. Mirtel didn't seem to notice, but I could feel a crackle of angry energy pierce the air.

"You think this is nothing more than parlor tricks?" she said. "You think *this* is what I died for? What Darja died for? All those other girls? Is that what we are? Nothing more than magicians' assistants?"

"Aggie, please," Mirtel said. Sofi was looking back and forth between Mirtel and the empty space next to her. I was sure even though she couldn't see Aggie, she could sense the electric hum that was growing more and more resonant.

"There's no reason to be upset," Mirtel continued. "If we could all just remain calm—"

"CALM?" Aggie screeched. The gray aura around her suddenly flared brilliantly, blindingly white, and a sound like a sonic boom shook the wagon. There was a flash and everything around us trembled like an aftershock. When it stopped, Aggie was gone.

"Oh, dear," Mirtel muttered. Sofi's mouth was open and her eyes darted around the wagon.

"Could you see that?" I asked.

"I felt it," she said. "What happened?"

"She's pissed," I said.

At the same time, Mirtel said, "I've upset her. It isn't the first time, and I doubt it will be the last. She'll come around though. She always does."

"Should we leave?" Sofi asked.

"No, dear. Let's give her some time to cool off. In the meantime," Mirtel leaned over to retrieve the book, which had fallen from their laps during Aggie's explosion, "let's see what else is in here."

———

Twenty minutes later, we had tried two more spells, with zero success. The problem was clearly on my end. I didn't know any of the words, and couldn't even hope to sound them out. I was beginning to get weary and frustrated, but both Mirtel and Sofi seemed somehow energized.

Sofi flipped a page and pointed. "What about this?" It was a brief spell—just two short paragraphs spread across two pages. Beneath the words there was an illustration of a woman. Her eyes were closed, but in the center of her forehead there was a third eye, wide open.

"There," Mirtel said, pointing to a word at the top of the

page. "That means 'two,' I think. Or 'twice.' And this here, it's something to do with seeing. 'Vision,' maybe?"

Sofi looked lost in thought. "Twice," she said softly, running a fingertip over the drawing of the three-eyed woman. "Twice seeing? Two visions?"

"Second sight," Mirtel exclaimed, shaking her head as if she couldn't believe she hadn't realized it sooner. "It makes sense, doesn't it? With the illustration?"

The look Sofi shot me over Mirtel's shoulder told me it didn't make any more sense to her than it did to me.

"The *second sight*," Mirtel said again, as if we were missing something obvious. "Clairvoyance. The ability to see the dead."

"Well, you two already checked that off the bucket list," I said, but Sofi leaned forward and studied the page, clearly intrigued.

"Do you think that means...could we see each other's bonded? Or other...dead people?"

Mirtel shook her head. "I'm not sure. But the spell seems simple enough."

"Speak for yourself," I snapped, even though of course she couldn't hear me. The paragraph on my side of the book appeared to be complete and total gibberish. Short, yes, but I was sure I couldn't begin to pronounce half the words.

"Let's try," Sofi said, shooting me an appealing look. "What have we got to lose?"

I was irritated, but I knew the two of them weren't likely to let my protests stop them, so I waved her on.

"Go ahead," she said to Mirtel. "Let's see what happens."

Mirtel sounded out the words on her page in a jerky, staccato sort of rhythm that sounded unlike any actual language I'd ever heard before. When she reached the end, she turned her eyes expectantly in my general direction.

I gritted my teeth, not wanting to continue, but Sofi was

watching me intently, and so I began sounding out the words, certain I was butchering them. I got to the last line, stumbled over the final phrase and halted, feeling stupid for even attempting it.

It took a moment for me to notice that Mirtel was staring. Not in my vicinity, but *at* me. And Sofi was staring at her.

"Dear God," Mirtel said breathlessly. I met her eyes, a thrill of excitement tinged with terror blazing through me. It all felt suddenly very real, and though I knew we had done magic, I wasn't certain what the implications of that would be—what it would mean if the living could see the dead. "Oh, my dear," Mirtel continued, her eyes going soft and a little wet at the corners. "Aren't you lovely?"

"*Was* lovely," I corrected, but there was no sting in my voice.

Mirtel nodded. "Yes, of course. You were. I'm so very sorry."

My shoulders slumped and I felt some of the tension seep out of me. "Thank you," I said quietly, and I meant it.

"Well then," she said briskly, picking up the book and closing it firmly. "That will certainly make conversing a bit easier. But I think that's quite enough magic for one day."

"Do you think..." Sofi said softly, looking both afraid and intrigued. "Will I be able to see Aggie?"

"Well," said a voice from the back of the wagon, "can you?"

We all turned to see Aggie walking toward us and I heard Sofi gasp.

"I suppose that's a yes," Aggie said tightly, but she nodded at Sofi, a sort of half-smile flitting across her lips. "Hi," she said quietly, and Sofi beamed back at her.

"Aggie," Mirtel said, relief evident in her voice. "I'm glad you've come back. Oh, isn't it thrilling?"

"Is it?" Aggie said, but there was no more fight in her voice. She sighed, her shoulders sagging. "I hope you know what you're doing."

"As much as any of us do, dear," Mirtel said.

The four of us looked at each other for a long, silent moment, the unspoken, *Now what?* hanging in the air between us.

"I think we need to find Stephen," I finally blurted out.

Sofi glanced up sharply. "What? Why?"

"*Why*? So he can tell us what the spells are before we go setting a forest fire or blowing up town hall. We can't mess around with this, Sofi. We don't understand this magic, and we don't know where it comes from. He's the only one who knows the magic, but isn't Vaikesti."

"Darja, this is ridiculous—"

"He's the only one who can help us," I said with finality. Sofi frowned, but she didn't protest again.

I just hoped I was right.

CHAPTER 15

SOFI

I let it go the first time Darja suggested taking the book to Stephen, sure that the others would protest too. But the second time she brought it up, I couldn't stay silent.

"How can you even consider trusting him with a book of *spells?*" I exclaimed hotly, laying my hand protectively over the pages. Darja opened her mouth to respond, but I cut her off. "I know he can't use them. It doesn't matter. He's creepy. He's been stalking us, taking pictures, and he's not from around here."

Darja scoffed. "He's not from Vaikesti, so he must be eeeevil." She drew the word out mockingly, waving her hands like an actor in a cheesy horror movie, and I scowled. I couldn't understand why she wouldn't take this seriously.

She must have seen my expression, because she dropped the act. "Okay, fine, what do *you* think we should do with the book?"

I looked to Mirtel and Aggie for help. It was still strange that I could see the pale ghost girl in her high-necked, old-fashioned white gown, a scowl seemingly permanently affixed to her face. She didn't appear to be paying attention, but Mirtel glanced between Darja and I, waiting to see how I would respond.

I huffed out a breath. "I don't know. Maybe take it to the Town Council? They might know how to translate it."

"The *Council?!*" Darja exclaimed. "You mean the ones who have been overseeing hundreds of years of Vaikesti-sanctioned murders? *That* Council?"

"I..." I cast around for an answer. Of course, she was right. But it was still hard to shake that feeling, ingrained since birth, that the community elders were where you took your problems. They were supposed to be our protectors, and even though I knew the truth, I wasn't sure how to rewire my brain with this new knowledge of reality.

"What about my dad?" I suggested. "He'll know what to do with it."

Darja's incredulous expression didn't change. "Your dad? The one who drugged Mirtel and kept her strapped to the bed last night?"

"But he was trying to help her. He didn't know..." I was floundering, and I knew it. "Besides, he *knows* me. He would listen..." I trailed off under the weight of all three gazes.

Mirtel finally broke in, lifting the heavy book off my lap and closing it gently before setting it on the tiny kitchen table. "All right, we don't have to decide right now. We'll keep it here until we can all agree on what's best."

Neither of us argued, but I could still see the stubborn light in Darja's eyes. The problem wouldn't go away. We needed to have the book translated, and there were really only two options: the Vaikesti elders, or Stephen. Neither option seemed safe.

Leaving the book on the table, Mirtel came back over to us, and I watched the way her gaze lingered on Darja as she resettled herself in the rocking chair. I wondered what it must be like for her, to be able to see another bonded dead. To know she wasn't alone after over fifty years. I couldn't imagine how I would feel if we hadn't found Mirtel and Aggie. If Darja and I were the only bonded pair, and we couldn't tell anyone or figure out what had happened. I shuddered at the thought, feeling the prick of tears in the back of my eyes as I looked at Mirtel.

My train of thought was abruptly derailed by a loud knock on the door. Mirtel startled as well, but recovered quickly, heaving herself to her feet once again and going to answer the door. On her way by the kitchen she paused to push the book into the shadows under the cabinets.

I didn't imagine that Mirtel had many visitors at her wagon, and it was a shock to see the dark form that stood in the doorway. His features were obscured by the bright sunlight that backlit him against the sky, but he was still instantly recognizable.

"Hello, can I help you?"

"Jared?" My voice rose over Mirtel's as I realized she might not know who he was.

"Sofi?" He squinted into the interior of the wagon, then chuckled as Mirtel stepped aside to let him in. "If I didn't know better, I'd think you were following me," he said with a wink.

"More like, he's following *you,*" Darja said.

Aggie looked over. "Who is that?" Suspicion was clear in her voice.

"That's the infamous Jared," Darja informed her.

Mirtel looked at them and raised an eyebrow. "Girls," she said with mild reproof, and I groaned inwardly as Jared's eyes darted around the small room.

"Are you here to see me?" I cut in before anyone could make the situation worse.

Jared abruptly seemed to remember why he was here,

and his demeanor changed, his spine straightening as he turned to Mirtel.

"No, I'm actually here to see Ms. Parn. I'm Officer Braden." He reached out to shake Mirtel's hand. "I wonder if I could speak to you for a few minutes. Privately," he added, casting an apologetic glance my way.

"Oh. Of course, I..." I looked around. I didn't want to leave yet, not if Jared was here about his investigation into Darja. And I didn't want to leave the matter of the book unsettled.

Mirtel seemed to catch my hesitation. "Why don't you go feed the chickens, dear?"

I nodded gratefully, sending a smile her way before letting myself out the door.

I could hear Jared's voice behind me, "I didn't realize you two knew each other." The sound was muffled as the door swung closed on Mirtel's response.

Darja had used whatever dead-person magic she had access to, and was already standing in front of me as I made my way down the steps and out onto the lawn. Aggie must have remained inside.

I knew Mirtel had already fed the chickens that morning, so instead I followed Darja down the path that led to the riverbank, ducking through the trees before settling next to her on a log and staring out over the swiftly moving water. It was beautiful here, and I could understand why Mirtel had chosen this spot to park her wagon.

Darja broke the silence first. "Do you think he's here about me?" Our argument about the book may not be forgotten, but it was at least put aside for the moment.

"I don't know. I mean...probably. He said he was going to follow up with anyone who knew you."

I paused before glancing over at her. I really didn't want to start another argument. "It...it could be a good thing," I said carefully. "Him looking for you, I mean. It's what you wanted, right? For the truth to come out? For people to be held responsible?"

Instead of attacking me like I'd feared, she gave a small sigh. I knew she didn't need sleep any longer, but still, she looked tired. She looked how I felt.

"I don't know," she said softly. "I mean, yes. That's what I want. I want this whole charade to be stopped. I want someone held responsible. But I don't know...what do you really think he'll find if he looks for me? No one is going to tell him the truth."

I sat quietly. She was right. Vaikesti's secrets were buried deep. What chance was there that someone would tell the police what had happened? Jared wasn't even Vaikesti. And yet...

"Someone did report you missing," I reminded her. "That must mean something."

She shrugged. "I mean, it could have been one of the younger girls at the *koolis*. They wouldn't know what had happened. It's happened before, and if that's the case, it'll get shut down real quick."

I hadn't thought of that. Of course, to anyone under eighteen, it *would* seem like she'd just disappeared. And the *tajas* surely already had a way of dealing with that.

"What do you *want* to happen?" I asked.

Darja fiddled idly with one of the sleeves of her dress. "See, that's the thing. I don't really know. I mean, do I want someone to be arrested? Yes. Do I want the Ceremonies to stop? *Yes.* But..." She paused, staring up at the canopy of branches overhead. "I guess what I really want is for them to *understand*. I want them to see how it was wrong. I grew up with those girls, you know? The *tajas*. The girls at school once a week." She gestured at me. "All the adults in the community. I *knew* them. They knew me. My whole life. And they just *stood* there."

She pulled her knees up to her chest and her shoulders heaved, and I knew she would be crying if she'd been able. I slid closer on the log. I couldn't wrap my arm around her shoulder. Couldn't hold her hand or offer her any physical comfort at all, so I just sat there by her side.

"And you," she went on, her voice muffled by her dress. "You're the only one who sees how wrong this is, and it's just because you're part of it."

Guilt flowed through me like a wave, hot and liquid. I wanted to think more of myself. I wanted to believe that I would have felt the same at seeing a ritualistic murder even if the bond hadn't happened. But how could that be true? When not a single other person in town had reacted any differently?

Because the truth was, even if I *had* been horrified, or thought it was wrong, I would have let the elders explain it away. I would have let them convince me that it was what Darja had wanted, and that everything was okay. Because it was easier to believe a lie than to change your whole worldview.

But as I sat on the log, close to Darja but not touching, I hoped we both were wrong. I hoped it wasn't some confused girl at the *koolis* who had reported her missing to the police, but maybe someone else out there who was feeling guilt. Someone else who saw how wrong this was, and was maybe a little braver than we were.

———

It seemed like forever before Mirtel joined us down by the river. Aggie wasn't with her—or at least, I assumed she wasn't. I didn't know if the spell would fade over time and maybe she had already disappeared from my sight.

Mirtel's eyes were tight as she sat next to us on the wide log. Darja didn't wait for her to speak.

"What did he want?"

It took her a moment to answer. "He was asking about you." She confirmed our suspicions, and I saw the spell must still be active.

"He really must be asking everyone in town," Darja said, raising her head from her knees. "I didn't even *know* you."

Mirtel's lips were compressed into a line, and I realized there was something she wasn't telling us.

"What is it?" I asked.

She hesitated. "I think I might be the main suspect."

"*What?!*" Darja and I spoke in unison. "Why?"

"Apparently I've been seen 'hanging around the *koolis*,'" she responded.

"What, delivering eggs? But I never spoke to you. And the *tajas* in the kitchen knew why you were there."

Mirtel sighed. "Yes, I told him that. It didn't seem to sway his opinion of me."

"They just want a scapegoat," Darja spat. "It's easy to blame things on the town crazy lady."

"Jared wouldn't do that," I protested.

Darja's expression suggested that she didn't agree, but she just said, "They can't arrest you or anything, can they?"

Mirtel shook her head. "He still has other people to interview. It seems like the department is taking this seriously. But he implied that he'd be back."

Her words were encouraging. If the police were taking Darja's disappearance seriously, that must mean that it wasn't one of the *koolis* girls that had reported her missing. But if *Mirtel* was a suspect...that wasn't what we wanted at all. I couldn't believe that Jared would use her as a scapegoat. He was better than that, I knew it. But the rest of the department...I didn't know. His father was the Sheriff, and Jared had been so excited to be assigned his first case. And even if they had no direct evidence, Mirtel was already an outcast in the community.

I didn't know what to think.

"Is there any other reason they might look at you?" Darja asked. "I mean, if all they have is that you've been seen at the *koolis,* which you have a perfectly good explanation for, then they *can't* suspect you, right?"

The older woman's mouth turned down in a frown, and I met Darja's glance briefly before biting my lip and looking back to Mirtel.

"What is it?" Darja asked.

Mirtel seemed reluctant to answer, but after a long pause the words came out quietly. "There was an investigation when Aggie disappeared. I was a suspect then, too."

I sucked in a breath and Darja went still by my side.

That wasn't good.

Darja opened her mouth to respond, but Mirtel cut her off. "I think you girls should go for now." Her voice was quiet. "I need to collect the eggs."

Her excuse was flimsy, but it was clear she wanted to be alone. I rose immediately and glanced at Darja, who was hesitating.

"I'd like to stay and talk to Aggie, if that's all right."

I wasn't sure who she was asking permission from, but I nodded as Mirtel said, "I think she's back by the wagon."

We were all subdued as I said my goodbyes and made my way to my car alone.

I didn't know what to do—I didn't think there was anything I *could* do, and the thought was frustrating. I felt like I had no control over anything. My thoughts were a tangle in my head as I pulled my dented Honda out onto the road toward town.

I didn't know how to help Mirtel, and I didn't know what to do about the book. We needed answers, not more questions, and at the moment, that damn book seemed like the only lead we had. But I didn't want to take it to Stephen. I just didn't trust him. There had to be some way to...

Suddenly, an inkling of a plan took root in my mind. What if...what if there was some way to remove suspicion from Mirtel...by giving the police someone else to focus on. And if that also happened to work in my favor with the book...

I tried not to focus on my motivations as I pulled into the driveway and jumped out of the car, leaving the engine running. Was this the right thing to do? No. Probably not. But it was for Mirtel, I told myself, ignoring the guilt that clawed at me. I let myself into the quiet house and grabbed the camera from where it sat on my bedside table.

It was for Mirtel.

CHAPTER 16

DARJA

I found Aggie sitting around the back of the wagon, watching the chickens pecking enthusiastically at the scraggly grass that surrounded their coop. Her arms were wrapped around her knees and her chin was perched on top of her hand, just like I'd found her in Mirtel's exam room at the doctor's office. Her dark hair was piled on top of her head as usual, but it looked somehow looser, if that were possible—wisps of deep chocolate brown framing her face and curling at the back of her neck.

"Hey," I said, lowering myself down beside her. She glanced at me out of the corner of her eyes, but otherwise didn't acknowledge me.

"So...that was some messed up shit, huh?" I said lamely.

She shrugged, the barest movement of her shoulders, but at least it was a response.

"I know you're worried about Mirtel—" I began.

"Mirtel can handle herself."

"Sure," I agreed. "Of course. But it must make you feel...helpless."

She barked out a laugh. It seemed to startle her as much as it did me. "Like that's anything new. I've been feeling that way for fifty-two years."

There was nothing I could say to argue that, or offer any comfort, so I said nothing, hoping my silence at least provided some sense of solidarity. I might have just been imagining the way she leaned in toward me, the feeling that maybe some of those walls she'd built up over the years were finally ready to come down. I wanted to tell her if they did, I'd be there to catch her. And if I couldn't, I'd help her dig out of the rubble.

I wanted to tell her, but I didn't. As the quiet stretched out, I began wondering how much time had passed. Was it different, for the dead? Was it an eternity, or just an instant? Before I could dwell too long on it, she spoke.

"I can't help thinking there's some kind of connection. Some...*reason*...that the bonding worked for us, but not for anyone else. And if we figure that out..."

I'd thought the same thing. "Then what?" I asked, though it didn't seem like a question with a ready answer.

"Then maybe..." She shook her head, staring off at the river, rushing fast and high after the spring rains. "Maybe we could be free."

I cocked my head, not really sure what she was saying. "You mean...like, reverse the bond?"

"Or break it."

"But what does that mean? For Mirtel and Sofi? For—" I'd been about to say, *for you and I,* but caught myself just before the words could escape my lips.

She looked at me then, her eyes glinting like flint on steel. "They'd be free, too. No longer haunted by ghosts from their past. And we..."

"We'd what?"

Her lips went thin, and I could see the frustration on her

face. "I don't *know*," she said, something both yearning and plaintive in her voice. "But don't you think there's more than *this*? This can't just be it, can it? This pointlessness?"

I didn't know, and if I was honest, I was afraid to think too hard about it.

"What do you think happened to the spirits of the other girls?" I asked, though I wasn't sure I wanted an answer. "Where did they end up?"

"Where does anybody's spirit end up?" she said, and I could hear a waver in her voice. "If we never break the bond, we won't ever know."

Aggie looked like she wanted to cry. And even though we couldn't, I reached out a hand, as if brushing away an imaginary tear before I realized I would only be touching thin air.

Except...

Warm.

Soft.

Real.

My hand made contact with her cheek, and the whole world exploded.

In that split-second, her eyes made contact with mine, wild with surprise and fright, and then I was plummeting, rushing through space in a free-fall that shoved my heart into my throat.

What is this, I thought as I spun through a vast nothingness. *Is it the spell? The second sight... and something more?*

It was reckless, to work the spells before we knew what they could do...what the consequences could be. Reckless and foolish and—

The fall stopped abruptly then, and I had the sudden, sickening feeling of *existing* again. My body felt too heavy and the sun shining around me was too bright. I closed my eyes against the queasy feeling in my stomach, willing the dizzying waves of nausea to end. I took a deep breath, and then gasped.

I took a breath.

A shriek sounded somewhere off to my right, and I opened my eyes, squinting against the sun that blazed hot on my skin.

I was standing at the end of a dirt road dotted with small, shabby houses. A broken down pickup truck perched on cinder blocks in the field across the way, where waist-high grass waved gently in the breeze.

Two small girls were sprinting down the road in my direction, laughing shrilly. No more than five or six, they were both wearing patched-up dresses that had seen better days. One of them was carrying a rag doll, one black button eye dangling by a thread, and it seemed this was the object of the other's pursuit.

I had no idea what had happened, but I stood rooted to the ground, unable to move. As they approached, I heard the creak of a tattered screen door opening from the house across the street. A woman stepped out onto the porch, wiping her hands on a towel tucked into the apron string around her waist.

"Aggie! Mirtel!" she called, and the two girls slowed to a walk, still playing keepaway with the raggedy doll as they neared the rickety wooden steps.

The one who'd been doing the chasing, smaller than the other, with a wild mess of dark hair falling down her back, swiped the doll and immediately hid it behind her back.

"Hey," the other girl protested, but the smaller girl just giggled, dancing up the steps and ducking behind the woman's skirt.

"Mirtel," the woman said, wiping her brow and leaving a trail of flour across her forehead, "your mother wants you home for dinner."

The girl looked disappointed, but she nodded and said, "Thanks, Aunt Henny," then stuck her tongue out at the other girl before dashing away down the road.

I staggered backward a step, completely off-kilter. Aunt Henny? Did that mean that Aggie and Mirtel were... cousins? I couldn't begin to wrap my head around how I was here, seeing this—memory?—and feeling like I was actually inhabiting my body again. The mother and daughter on the porch paid me no mind, so I didn't think they could see me, but I could feel everything—the heat, the hard-packed earth beneath my feet, the tall grass that brushed my fingertips. It was overwhelming. Intoxicating. And terrifying.

Up on the porch, Aggie's mother was scolding her for taking the doll, and Aggie, face smudged with dirt and knees skinned and red, was doing her best to look contrite. They turned to walk into the house, and I found myself following without a thought.

I had barely made it across the road when the earth tilted suddenly, and I was spinning again.

This time, I landed with a thump against something hard and unforgiving, a painful jolt radiating through my hip. I looked around and saw I was in the Vaikesti cemetery, at the far edge up on the ridge, where the graves were overgrown and mostly untended. I had fallen against a headstone, craggy and crumbling, unmarked except for two dates carved into the base. A small group of mourners huddled around an open plot at the highest point on the ridge, pulling their coats around them against the cold wind that howled through the bare trees. I caught sight of Aggie, wearing a dull gray coat, her hair in a long braid down her back. She wasn't much older than before, maybe only seven or so, and her eyes were swollen and red.

As I watched, a small figure darted over the crest of the ridge. She had no coat, and her cheeks were bright pink from the cold. "Mama!" she screamed, shoving her way through the gathered adults. "*Mama!*"

Aggie's mom ran toward her and caught her around the waist before she made it to the gravesite, catching her up in her arms and shushing her softly. Mirtel continued to scream, thrashing against her aunt's grip and reaching out toward the open hole in the frozen ground.

Aggie looked on, stricken, and I watched, unable to tear my eyes away from the heart-breaking scene. Mirtel had said her aunt had taken her in after her parents died. She and Aggie must have grown up together, as sisters. At least, until Aggie was sent away to the *koolis*. I was desperate to know what had happened, but with a growing suspicion I was going to find out, I felt suddenly unsure I wanted to see it.

I huddled against the gravestone behind me, shivering in the chill air, until Mirtel's cries began to sound further and further away, and the whole scene in front of me went blurry before tilting sharply sideways. I was expecting the falling sensation this time, but it was no less jarring when I landed butt-first in the grass.

Disoriented, it took me a few minutes to realize I was back at Aggie's rundown little house. This time, I had ended up in the backyard, wedged between a ramshackle old garden shed and a fence that might have once been white, but had darkened to a dingy gray. It was twilight, summer, and I could see fireflies winking through the honeysuckle that grew wild over the back hedge. The air was scented with its perfume, sweet and flowery, as the barest breeze stirred through its reaching branches.

Aggie was sitting on the concrete stairs that led up to the back door. She was older, a teenager, her dark hair brushed straight and parted down the middle. Her t-shirt was black, with a logo for a band I'd only ever seen worn by one of the outsider kids at the county school. Her jeans were snug, flaring out sharply around her ankles. And she wasn't alone. Another girl, one I was certain was not Mirtel, sat next to her, hip-to-hip on the narrow steps.

She was all light to Aggie's dark, hair so fair it appeared to glow nearly white in the fading dusk. I couldn't see the color of her eyes from my vantage point behind the shed, but they were luminous. She stared off into the distance, a serious expression on her face. She was perhaps older than Aggie by a couple of years, maybe old enough to have been through her own Spring Day Ceremony.

I felt like the worst kind of intruder, waltzing in on a quiet moment between friends uninvited. But I couldn't look away. Every new scene so far had shown me something previously undiscovered about Aggie's history, and I was entranced by it.

As I watched, Aggie lowered her hand to rest atop the other girl's. They kept their eyes cast steadfastly away from one another for a long moment, until finally, the older girl pulled her hand away.

"Aggie," she said softly, "you know we can't."

Aggie looked more defiant than disappointed, a challenge evident in the hard set of her jaw.

"Aren't you tired," she said, "of always being told what we can't do?"

"Don't..."

"I am. I'm tired of this town, and all its secrets."

The other girl's expression was wounded. She pulled her hand away and held it to her chest.

"You know I can't tell you what happened."

"I didn't ask you to," Aggie said stubbornly. "I haven't asked you for anything."

The older girl laughed, but it was tinged with bitterness. "Haven't you?"

Aggie moved swiftly and suddenly, pulling the girl's face toward her and pressing their lips together. I sucked in a breath as I watched, feeling my cheeks flame. I saw the girl's shoulders go rigid, then slowly relax into the kiss. After a long moment, during which I felt certain my heart had stopped beating for the second time, she reached out to caress Aggie's cheek.

Pulling away, she gave Aggie a soft, sad smile. "I'm sorry," she said, pushing herself off the stairs and dashing through the back gate. Aggie sat unmoving, as if cut from marble. I wanted to go to her, to tell her the girl was a bitch and she could do better, but I was rooted to the spot.

I couldn't bear to look at Aggie's carefully composed face, so I took in the rest of the dilapidated house. An empty carport sat to one side, its roof leaning precariously, a jumbled collection of rusted bicycles in a heap beneath it. Along the edge of the house, orange daylilies stretched up toward the window ledges. There, in one of those windows, I caught sight of another face. Mirtel. I wondered how much she had seen. I wondered what she thought about it.

I watched until Mirtel vanished from the window. There were footsteps from inside, and then the creak of the back door opening. But it wasn't Mirtel; it was Aggie's mom, looking much older and surprisingly frail. She eased herself down onto the steps beside her daughter, smoothing Aggie's long hair and tucking it behind her shoulder.

"Dr. Ilves is here, Aggie."

Dr. *Ilves*? Sofi's dad? But that was impossible. He wouldn't even have been born yet. Then I remembered a photo I'd seen tucked around the vanity mirror in Sofi's room. It was her family, gathered in front of the municipal building for the ribbon cutting when the new doctor's office had opened. Her father had been smiling broadly, holding a pair of oversized scissors, and next to him, an older man with the same blue eyes as Sofi. Her grandfather, then. He must have been the town doctor before his son took over.

I was drawn back to what was happening by Aggie's sharp intake of breath.

"Why?" she asked, her eyes going wide with sudden terror.

Her mother looked down, still playing with a lock of her hair, winding it around a finger and then releasing it.

"You're getting older, Aggie," her mother said softly. "And there's been...talk. Around town."

"Who cares about talk?"

"A lot of people, sweetheart. They just...they want to make sure you're prepared to assume your role as a woman of Vaikesti."

"You mean they want to make sure I'm going to get married and pop out a bunch of babies," Aggie said venomously.

"It's just an exam," her mother said soothingly. "Every Vaikesti girl goes through it. It's over before you know it."

Aggie pushed her mother's hand away from her hair. "I won't," she said.

"Aggie, you must. If not...between this and the rumors... Aggie, they could send you to the *koolis*." Her mother looked desperate, weak and frightened, and I felt for her.

But I felt for Aggie more.

"I. Won't." she repeated. "He's not touching me. Send me wherever you want to. But tell him he's not needed tonight."

"Aggie, he's the doctor. He runs this town—"

"I said 'NO'," Aggie shouted, shoving herself up from the stairs and turning to face her mother. "Send me away, then. At least you'll have Mirtel for company."

Her mother looked as if she'd been slapped. "Aggie—"

"This is on you," Aggie said in a dangerously quiet voice. "Whatever happens now, you did nothing to stop it."

Her mother began to cry, but Aggie seemed unmoved. She pushed past her and charged up the stairs, letting the back door slam behind her.

I sat against the shed, stunned by everything I'd seen. I wasn't sure what to do, but before I could even think about it, the world was once again spinning and lurching.

This time, there was no landing. I was back on the river bank, out of my body and hovering next to Aggie, who was watching me with wide, horrified eyes.

"Oh, Aggie," I whispered, reaching a hand out to her again.

Her energy crackled and she flickered in and out like static. "Go," she said quietly, and then, when I made no move to leave, "GO!"

She blinked out then, leaving nothing more than a buzz of electricity in the air and a smell like ozone after a storm.

I didn't know what to do. I didn't know how to process everything I'd seen. I didn't know if our spell had triggered something that allowed us to touch, to share the deepest, hidden parts within us.

One thing I did know—I needed to talk to Sofi.

CHAPTER 17

SOFI

The second Darja barreled into my room later that afternoon, it was obvious something was wrong.

"What is it? What happened?"

I'd been sitting on my bed, trying not to think about Stephen's camera. I wouldn't say I was feeling guilty, exactly, but I was definitely starting to question my motives. Those thoughts were all pushed aside, however, with Darja's next words.

"I saw Aggie's *memories.*" She collapsed onto the armchair by my window. It was still a strange effect, like she was sitting on it but the fabric didn't fold or crease under her weight.

"What? What do you mean, 'saw her memories'?"

"I don't know. I touched her arm—like actually physically touched her—and then I just...*saw* things. It was like I was there, actually watching her, as a kid, then later, and—"

"Whoa, slow down." I held up my hands. I'd never seen her like this, so flustered. "Tell me what you saw."

She did, or at least she tried, describing watching as an

invisible outsider during some of the more intense moments of Aggie's childhood.

"What do you mean, they're related?" I broke in.

"Mirtel and Aggie are cousins. They grew up together, until Aggie went to the *koolis*."

The implication of this hit me. "You mean they sacrificed her *cousin* at Mirtel's bonding ceremony?" I tried to imagine it. What if the sacrifice at my ceremony had been someone I'd known my whole life, someone I'd grown up with? My own *cousin*. I shuddered.

"Why did they send her to the *koolis*, then?" I asked. If she had grown up as a regular member of Vaikesti, she must have done something to be sent there.

Darja paused for a second, her fingers worrying at a thread in her sleeve. "She...she was arguing with her mother. She refused to see the doctor when he came, and...I don't know. I only saw flashes."

I got the feeling there was more she wasn't telling me, but I didn't push it. "The doctor? My dad? Wait, no..." I did the math. "You mean my grandfather?"

Darja nodded. "She started screaming. She didn't want to take the exam."

I could almost understand that. Each girl in Vaikesti underwent a physical examination at puberty. They claimed it was only a routine physical check, but everyone knew it was really a check for reproductive health. Vaikesti was a small community, and the Council always wanted to ensure the health of anyone coming into child-bearing years. To be sure the magic would pass on through the generations, they said. Typically, the town doctor performed the exam, though I'd been checked by a nurse since the doctor was my dad. And the *koolis* kids didn't get checked, since they weren't considered full members of Vaikesti.

I remembered my own exam. It certainly hadn't been

fun; it was a little invasive, and there were lots of personal questions and a blood draw, but it wasn't something I'd risk being sent to the *koolis* to avoid. Clearly there was something else going on.

"What do you think she was so afraid of?" I asked, but Darja was chewing on her lip and I didn't think she heard me.

After a minute she glanced up at me. "Is it possible we're cousins, too? You and I, I mean?"

"What? No. How could we be?" I laughed. "My mom has a sister and a brother, and my dad has two brothers and a sister. I mean, I have a lot of cousins, but I think I know who they all are."

Darja looked pensive, and went back to chewing on her lip.

"What about you?" I asked. "What's your family like?" It occurred to me that I still knew so little about her.

She shrugged. "I don't know."

In a sudden flash I remembered what the *taja* had said when I'd been to the *koolis* that day. Darja had been at the *koolis* since she was a child. Her mother had been young and her father hadn't been identified. I remembered the expression on her face when Ms. Kross had revealed that Darja's mother had been a sacrifice as well.

I sat up straight on the bed. "I'm so sorry, I didn't mean—"

"No," Darja said softly, picking at the edge of the chair cushion. "It's okay. I was young. It's not like I remember them. My mom...I mean, if she was a sacrifice—"

I winced at the words, but Darja didn't, "—then she had to be younger than eighteen when she had me. And I don't know who my father was. He could have been anyone. We really could be cousins."

She looked up at me, and I felt my cheeks heat. "You're

suggesting that one of my uncles cheated on his wife, fathered an illegitimate child, and then turned them both over to the *koolis*."

Darja shrugged, not bothered by my tone or my words. "Someone did it," she pointed out.

"It wasn't my uncles," I said firmly. I knew it sometimes happened; Vaikesti wasn't immune to scandal, but I couldn't imagine any of my three uncles, men I had known since birth, doing something so terrible. And even if they had, they were all honorable men. They would have dealt with the consequences, not just swept it under the rug. It wasn't possible.

Darja didn't push it.

"I guess we could be, like, second or third cousins or something," I said after a moment. "I mean, most of Vaikesti is probably related in some way. Or maybe you're related to Mirtel or Aggie somehow." I shrugged. "Maybe the magic is tied to them."

"That doesn't explain how it worked for *you*, though," she pointed out.

I leaned against the wall and let my head fall back. "So we have another mystery, then. We need to find out who your parents were."

There was a long stretch of silence, but my thoughts felt like lead, sitting heavy and dull in my brain. I couldn't deal with any more mysteries. Instead of finding answers, we were just piling up more questions.

I felt more so than heard Darja shift in her chair. She dropped her feet to the floor and sat up straight, looking at me.

"You know, there's a place where we could maybe find the answer to that question."

"What? Where? I—"

But suddenly I knew what she was going to say before she said it. "No. We are *not* going back to my dad's office."

She looked at me earnestly. "Sofi, we have to. He has files on everyone in town."

"He would never share other people's files with us. That's illegal. What would we even tell him?"

She just stared at me, and when the pieces clicked into place, I felt like an idiot. Of course she wasn't suggesting we *ask*.

"Darja, *no.*" I glanced around, even though we were obviously alone. "We would get in so much trouble. And it's *wrong.*"

"How is it wrong for me to know who my parents are?" she demanded. "And you know Mirtel and Aggie would show us their files if we asked them."

I raised an eyebrow.

"Well, Mirtel would," she amended. "But it's not wrong. We *need* that information."

"We can't," I said weakly.

"We have to." Her voice was firm. "We'll go tonight, when it's dark."

I shook my head, but I already knew I was going to lose the argument. It was inevitable.

At least I wouldn't lose the fight about the book. I looked at my empty nightstand, feeling somewhat less guilty. Turning in the camera wasn't nearly as bad as breaking into my dad's office, and with Stephen out of the way, that would be one less thing to worry about. Then at least—

"Sofi."

I looked up at the tone of Darja's voice, and realized she had followed my gaze, and was staring at the empty spot on my nightstand where the camera had sat. My eyes were wide when they met hers.

"What happened to the camera?" she asked.

A million thoughts raced through my head in that moment: how to respond, what lie to tell, how to change the subject. But I knew she'd seen the answer on my face the second I'd met her eyes.

My voice came out as a whisper. "I took it to Jared."

"You *what?*" She stared at me. "How could you?"

No, that wasn't fair. She couldn't calmly suggest we break into my father's office and go through his medical files, and then in the next second look at me like *I'd* betrayed *her.*

"I did it for *us.*" I snapped. "If they think Stephen had something to do with your disappearance, then they won't be looking at Mirtel."

Darja rolled her eyes. "Oh, and I'm sure it had *nothing* to do with the fact that you don't want Stephen to translate the book."

I didn't back down. "That too," I retorted. "I don't trust him."

Her form began to crackle around the edges like I'd seen Aggie's do. "Everyone is hiding something. You don't trust Stephen, and I don't trust Jared. Aggie has secrets, and my parents, and your dad, and the Town Council, and…and…"

"Darja—"

"Well, who the hell *can* we trust?" And with that, she sparked out like a burst of static, there and then gone in a flash as her anger got the better of her.

I fell back on my bed, tears pricking hot behind my eyelids. My voice was a whisper. "I trust you."

―――

Darja was gone for hours. I forced myself to come downstairs for dinner and did my best to act normal, though I could barely pay attention as the conversation flowed around me. Afterwards I retreated to my room, where I laid on my bed again, brooding, until I fell asleep.

I didn't know if it was simply Darja's suddenly returning presence that woke me or if I would have woken regardless, but the blinking light on my alarm clock read 2:24am when I came suddenly awake to find her there, pale and translucent in the moonlight streaming through my window.

"Where have you been?" I asked groggily, sitting up and rubbing sleep from my eyes.

"With Aggie." She didn't elaborate, and through mutual silent agreement neither of us broached the subject of Stephen again.

"Are you ready?" she asked, perching on the corner of my bed, and I realized I didn't have the strength to try to argue again. It was illegal, and wrong on so many levels. But at the same time, Darja was right. Didn't she have the right to know who her parents were?

I didn't answer, just pushed back the covers and hastily threw on some clothes, barely stopping to glance at what I grabbed. I wrapped my cardigan around my shoulders.

"Let's go."

We didn't pass a single other car on the road on our way to the municipal building, which was good because I might have turned around if we had. We parked at the far edge of the lot under the trees, like it would make any difference, and snuck around the back of the building. Darja rolled her eyes when I made her go on ahead to scout the way, but she went anyway, her white dress shining like a beacon in the night that guided only me.

The municipal building itself was locked, but my dad's office had two entrances, one from inside the building and another from the outside. There were no security cameras; crime was fairly rare in Vaikesti. Well, discounting murder, anyway.

My heart was hammering in my chest as I crept up to the back door and fished my dad's key from my pocket. It'd been almost too easy to slip it off his keyring where it hung by the door as I'd left the house, and the key felt slippery in my fingers as I fumbled it into the lock and turned it. The door swung open on silent hinges and I slid inside quickly, then closed and locked it behind me.

I expected to feel relief once we were safely inside the office, but if anything I was more tense, my nerves ratcheting tight.

"Wait here; I'll go make sure there aren't any patients staying overnight," Darja said in a low voice, and I nearly jumped.

How had I forgotten that? If there were patients here, there would be nurses as well. I was a terrible criminal. I wavered as Darja slipped silently off, unsure if I should stay here or wait outside. Where was the biggest danger? But she was back before I could make a decision, shaking her head.

"No one's here. Come on. Where does he keep the files?"

I led the way down the hallway toward the reception area. I had to unlock a second door before we could slide behind the glass-windowed front desk, where a series of tall filing cabinets lined the back wall. It occurred to me that Darja could have just passed through the walls; she had no need of keys.

"Jeez, this is archaic," she commented as she moved around the copier toward the file cabinets. "Don't they use computers here?"

"They do, for newer patients, but they don't have the manpower to input all the old stuff," I explained. "The files we're looking for are probably still on paper. Which is good, because I don't have the computer passwords."

Darja looked like she hadn't thought of that. Maybe my

partner in crime wasn't exactly a criminal mastermind, either.

When I reached the file cabinets though, I was at a loss. "You don't even know your parents' names, do you? And would you even have a file if you lived your whole life at the *koolis?*"

Darja shot me a look. "I have a file. We weren't completely segregated, you know. We had nurses at the *koolis,* but if we needed any more serious medical attention, they brought us here."

I felt a rush of embarrassment, *again,* at how little I knew of the *koolis,* but I shoved it aside.

K, Kallas. I opened the labeled drawer, and flipped through the neatly organized row of files, the guilt gnawing at me. I tried not to look at the names as I flipped through.

Halfway through I found it. Kallas, Darja. I pulled it out and quickly closed the drawer. The file was thin, but it was there.

I crouched down to sit on the floor and placed the file before me, Darja by my side. I glanced quickly at her face, but her expression was unreadable. I opened the file.

Kallas, Darja

I scanned down beneath her birthdate.

Mother: Kallas, Mari

Father: Unknown

I released the breath I hadn't realized I'd been holding. It hadn't occurred to me that she'd been given her mother's last name. And still no information on her father. Whoever it was, he hadn't even admitted it to the doctor. I wondered if the only person who knew might be Darja's mother, the secret lost entirely with her gone.

I glanced again to Darja, who was sitting perfectly still, her face pale. I flipped through the rest of the file, but there was nothing of interest in there. Chicken pox as a pre-teen, wisdom teeth removed two years ago.

"Get her file."

I didn't have to ask who *her* was. I rose and put Darja's file back, sliding it into place before pulling out the file directly after hers and sinking back down to the floor.

This file was much thicker than Darja's had been. A normal Vaikesti kid, then. I opened it to the first page.

Kallas, Mari

Mother: Liina Rebane

Father: Sander Kallas

I checked her birthdate and did the math. Her mother was only sixteen when she'd had Darja. Maybe fifteen when she'd gotten pregnant. Was her father some other teenager who'd made a mistake? If so, he had likely gone on to have a normal adult life, his secret safely covered up, I thought bitterly. No such luck for the obviously pregnant Mari.

I turned the page and began to flip through Darja's mother's file. I was right: a normal Vaikesti kid, albeit an accident prone one, with a standard array of doctor's visits: broken bones, colds, the flu, etc.

By my side, Darja's eyes seemed to swallow the information hungrily, and I realized this was more information about her family, about *herself*, than she'd ever been given. I wished we'd been able to find the name of her father, another link for Darja to build a mental picture of what her life was, or could have been.

Finally I reached the last page and turned it slowly.

A death certificate. May first. The day of her Spring Day ceremony.

Darja reached a trembling hand out, her fingers hovering over the gold embossed letters of her mother's name. My eyes pricked with tears, and I blinked fast to keep them from falling. It was so unfair. A whole life, thrown away in the blink of an eye.

We sat in silence for a minute, and I let Darja take the time she needed. Eventually she seemed to pull herself together and sat up, gesturing at me to close the file.

"You can put it back," she said softly.

I rose and did so, and as my back was to her she said quietly, "Thank you. For doing this. I know you think it's wrong, but...it helps. Just to know."

I nodded, not sure if she saw or not. We were no closer to knowing anything. For all we knew, she could still be related to Mirtel or Aggie, or me, or anyone else in town. But it didn't feel like a waste, coming here, if it gave her any connection with her mother.

"Should I pull Mirtel's file? Or Aggie's?" I asked.

She cleared her throat, and when she spoke again her voice was back to normal. "Yes, definitely. Both."

Parn, Mirtel

Saar, Agnes

Both files were normal, and the family ties were easy to see. Mirtel and Aggie's mothers had been sisters, and a quick check showed that Mirtel's parents had died in a house fire when she was seven years old. The two girls were barely six months apart in age, and their files were similar, up until a note signified the abrupt end of Aggie's file with "*moved to* koolis," written in a bold hand. I checked the date. She'd been sixteen. I wondered what those two years had been like when Aggie had been at the *koolis* and Mirtel had not.

In Mirtel's file, the results of her reproductive exam were listed as 'normal,' a note that was conspicuously absent from Aggie's file, but there was nothing else of interest in there, no answers to our questions beyond what we could have gotten simply by talking to Mirtel and Aggie ourselves.

And yet, as we replaced the files and triple-checked that everything was in its place, turning off the lights and locking the doors behind us, I still didn't think the trip had been a waste. Just the look on Darja's face as she'd knelt on the floor, silently running her fingertips over the embossed name of her mother, had been worth it. That had meant something.

I slept late the next morning, tired from all the recent sleepless nights. Darja was gone again when I rose, and while I still felt a strange tugging loss inside when she wasn't nearby, I was sure she needed space to process what she'd seen, both from Aggie and from my dad's office.

I wasn't sure where dead people went when they needed time alone, or if she even was alone, but I would wait until afternoon at least before I tried to hunt her down.

Feeling a little lost and unsure of myself, I decided to head to the police station to check in with Jared. Maybe he'd been able to deal with Stephen, and I could go to Mirtel's wagon that afternoon so we could figure out what to do about the book. One thing was for sure—we needed it translated one way or another.

The police station was quiet when I got there, but the lady at the reception desk pointed me back to Jared's dad's office, where I found Jared sitting at the desk, a laptop open in front of him and one hand running idly through his hair.

"Sofi." He looked tired, but his smile was genuine when he saw me. "Hey, grab a seat." He gestured across the desk at the two worn chairs and I sank into one gratefully.

"Thanks." I glanced around. "Does your dad ever actually use this office?"

He gave a short laugh. "Not really. He works mostly out

of other stations around the county. There isn't a lot of crime in Vaikesti, so this office is here for whoever needs to use it." He paused, looking at me closely. "How are you? I'm sorry if I startled you yesterday, out at the old lady's house. I didn't expect her to have company."

"Oh, that's okay." I fiddled briefly with the hem of my t-shirt. He hadn't been at the station the day before when I'd brought the camera over, and I wasn't quite sure how to broach the topic. I decided to dive right in.

"I brought that camera in yesterday, from the guy at the festival? Stephen? I left it at the desk, and I wanted to make sure they gave it to you. It seemed like something you should have."

Jared smile faded and his brow creased. "Yes, I got it. Thanks for bringing it in. I really appreciate that."

I paused, wanting to ask what he'd done about it, but unsure how appropriate that might be.

He rescued me from my indecision by leaning across the desk toward me. "Sofi, are you okay? I'm a little worried about you."

"About me?"

"Yes. I assume you looked at the pictures before you brought it in?"

I nodded, still confused.

"You were in some of the pictures," he clarified, and I realized he must be concerned about Stephen taking pictures of me.

"Did it give you what you needed? Were you able to arrest him?"

"Who, Stephen?" Jared scowled. "No. I mean, don't get me wrong, he's definitely a nuisance, and I don't like him hanging around here, but he's not doing anything illegal. Not yet, anyway."

I tipped my head to the side. "What are you worried about me for then?"

"Because he has pictures of you with that crazy old lady. Mirtel."

Oh no.

"I'm worried that she might be dangerous," he went on, "and I'm not sure you should be hanging around with her."

I groaned internally. I'd given Jared the camera to take the focus *off* of Mirtel, not make him look at her even harder.

"Honestly, I think she's just lonely," I said, trying to figure out how to steer the conversation back to Stephen and failing.

"I'm sure she is," he said, looking at me warmly. His eyes were a soft brown, his face open and earnest, as if he honestly cared about my well-being. Not for the first time, I desperately wished I could just tell him everything.

"But there's something strange going on with her, too," he continued. "I just think it would be safer for you to keep your distance. At least for now."

I sighed, but gave him the nod he obviously wanted to see. Things never got simpler, only more and more complicated, every step of the way.

CHAPTER 18

DARJA

Aggie's anger was still there when I returned, hovering around her like a storm cloud, heavy and rumbling. But she didn't protest when I sat with her at the edge of the river, careful not to hint at any of the things I'd seen in her memories. And after a few moments of silence, I could feel some of the tension begin to ease. I couldn't explain it, but something about her presence, fierce though it was, had a calming effect on me. I hoped I could do the same for her.

I talked aimlessly for a while—meaningless chit chat that normally would have gotten an eye roll and an exasperated sigh. Eventually though, she joined in, and the conversation turned to heavier topics, though the words flowed easier. We talked about what it had been like to die (no surprise, we both thought it sucked), and how we still felt we were meant for something more in the afterlife. Some sort of finality, maybe—a resolution to all the horror we'd been through.

Once our words were spent, we sat in silence, watching the late morning sunlight reflecting off the rushing water. I could see tree limbs waving lazily as they arched over the banks, but could feel no breeze. It left an aching longing within me, and it startled me to realize how deeply and profoundly I missed being alive.

I wanted to touch Aggie again, not to get sucked into her memories, but just to have that brief flash of contact, of something normal and remembered and familiar. Something solid. Everything in this world of the dead felt so fleeting and ephemeral, as if it all might slip away at any moment, leaving me in void and darkness.

Of course, I didn't dare reach out to her again. I had tempted fate a few times in my life, but I wasn't stupid. And getting on Aggie's bad side wasn't on my post-bucket list. If I'd ever been on her good side...I wanted to stay there.

After a few more moments, she spoke again.

"What you saw," she began haltingly, "with Rina..."

I didn't have to ask who Rina was. There was only one person she could have been.

"I get it," I said quickly, so she wouldn't feel she had to explain.

"How could you?" she said, twisting her hands in the ivory lace that pooled in her lap.

"*I get it,*" I repeated firmly. "I'm...not so different...from you and Rina."

She looked at me then, dark eyes wide and surprised. I nodded and gave her a small smile.

"Turns out we're batting for the same team," I said, and she frowned, confused. I didn't bother to explain, but after a moment, her expression cleared, and her eyes got impossibly wider.

"You...?"

"Yep. Me."

"Is that why you were sent to the *koolis*?"

I shook my head. "I was born there." I filled her in on

what Sofi and I had discovered at the doctor's office, including my theory that the two of us might be distantly related.

She nodded. "It makes sense, doesn't it? The strongest magic always uses blood."

"Does it?"

She smiled slightly, and her gaze went hazy and faraway, as if she were remembering something from long ago. She opened her mouth and started singing in the old language. Her voice was low, lilting and sweet.

I recognized it at once. It was a song we always sang to close out our daily reflection at the *koolis*. "What does it mean?" I asked. I'd never bothered to learn the translation.

"*Bless us, oh, mother. Let us be bound in spirit, as we are bound in blood. Let it bathe us in the magic of the earth, and connect us to your power.*"

I felt more certain than ever that Sofi and I had a tie that went even deeper than our bond. But what if this was just another of Vaikesti's secrets? Could we ever find an answer, and if we did, what else would it unravel?

"We have to get Stephen to translate that book," I said, and Aggie nodded.

"Maybe there are other books," she said. "Histories or genealogies that would show your relation."

I nodded. "I have to go," I said.

"Where?"

"To find Sofi. And then to find Stephen."

Sofi was back in her room when I flickered in right on top of the cat, who gave me an irritated yowl and then immediately curled into his chair cushion and went back to sleep.

She was sitting on her bed, a pile of old photos scattered

in front of her. She looked up, unsurprised, when I appeared, but I could see the relief on her face.

"Whatcha doing?" I said, trying to sound casual.

She gestured at the photos, some of which were yellowed and crinkling around the edges. "I got to thinking," she said, tugging at a few brittle corners and pulling out some black and white photos of families dressed in stiff clothing, wearing dour expressions. "I know we aren't first cousins. But what if we're related further back in our families?"

"You mean, like, second cousins?"

She nodded. "Or third. Or twice removed. Or whatever it is."

"I think you're onto something. But listen, Sofi, we need to talk about Stephen."

Her face screwed up in an unpleasant frown, but she sighed, resigned. "I know." She filled me in on her talk with Jared that morning, and how he was still persistently, doggedly pursuing Mirtel as a person of interest.

"So I threw Stephen under the bus," she said, a deep red flush coloring her cheeks, "and it was all for nothing."

I had to literally bite my tongue to keep the *I told you so* from slipping out. I could see she was feeling terrible about it, and there was no sense making her beat herself up more than she already was.

"So," I said, "how are we going to find him?"

"I have no idea," she said. "Jared made it pretty clear that he needed to get the hell out of Dodge."

A sudden thought occurred to me. "He was booked into the jail, right? After the festival? They'd have to have his address on file."

Sofi's eyes widened and she shook her head violently. "No," she said. "You've talked me into trespassing more than enough for one lifetime. We're *not* breaking and entering into the sheriff's office."

"Maybe we won't have to," I said, formulating an idea. "You're a part of this investigation now. If you tell them you have more information on Stephen, they'll probably pull up his file. I'll just *poof* behind the desk and take a peek at the computer when they do."

Sofi looked uncertain, but after a minute, she nodded. "Fine. But we're not committing any more crimes."

I made an *X* shape over my chest and grinned. "Cross my heart."

"Okay. But come with me—I need to find something before we go."

———

What Sofi had been looking for was a family copy of our spiritual text. Written in the old language, no one ever really read it anymore, but every Vaikesti home had a copy or two, usually passed down from generation to generation, and usually containing an extensive listing of the family's genealogy.

We found it in a sideboard in the dining room, hidden by stacks of chipped china and mismatched fluted glasses. Sofi carefully pulled it out and began scanning names, frowning as she ran her finger down the list of untidy scrawl. My attention, on the other hand, had drifted to the other contents of the sideboard, including a set of gold-plated flatware in an open wooden case.

The utensils were badly tarnished, but the finely detailed filigree curling along the handles was strangely familiar. I peered closer, and found a delicate monogram etched into each piece. It was the letter *I*. I gasped, a memory rushing back with the force of a wave, strong enough to knock me off my feet.

Nobody at the *koolis* had much in the way of personal effects, least of all me, but I had always kept a small box hidden in the bottom drawer of my dresser, tucked safely under my school uniforms. It contained a few trinkets from some of the girls I'd gotten close to over the years, and the only remaining artifacts I had that connected me to my mother. A threadbare blanket Ms. Luts said I'd been wrapped in as a baby, and a small golden teaspoon. Ms. Kross had given it to me when I'd turned sixteen. She'd never revealed how it came to be in her possession, only that it had been one of the few belongings my mother had left behind.

I had taken the teaspoon out every night, tracing over the ornate swirls, the metal cool against my fingertips. Every night, I'd wondered how my mother, poor, alone and bearing the shame of an unwanted pregnancy, had acquired such a piece of finery.

I'd also wondered what the letter *I* stood for.

I realized Sofi was staring at me.

"What's the matter?" she asked, slipping the book back into its nook and looking down at the flatware set.

"I... I've seen this before."

She raised an eyebrow. "You've seen our old silverware set?"

I nodded, still reeling. I didn't know what it meant, but I knew for sure that this was the link to my connection with Sofi.

"I'll fill you in after we visit the sheriff's office," I said, trying to keep my voice steady. "And then we need to go to the *koolis*."

———

As it turned out, our ploy to find Stephen's address was unnecessary. He was there, in the municipal building, pacing in front of the door to the sheriff's office, ranting about his camera and how it was illegal confiscation of property.

When Sofi entered the building, he stopped dead. "*You*," he said, pointing a finger at her. "Do you know where it is?"

Sofi took a step back. "Uh...where what is?"

Stephen huffed. "My camera. They took it, right? After the festival?"

"I...I don't—" Sofi looked over to me desperately, her eyes pleading. I tipped my head back toward Stephen and tried to look encouraging.

"They've got your camera," she confirmed, and Stephen's shoulders sagged. I couldn't tell if he was relieved or defeated, or maybe a little bit of both. "I think," Sofi continued, "that I can help you get it back."

His eyes snapped up to hers. "You can?"

She nodded. "Yes. But I need some help from you in return."

"What do you mean?" he asked, his eyes narrowing behind his glasses.

Sofi nodded toward the entrance to the library, at the back of the municipal building lobby. "It's about the book."

CHAPTER 19

SOFI

I still didn't trust Stephen. I felt bad for what I'd done, using his camera to try to set him up as a suspect in Darja's disappearance, and I understood that he was our best option—maybe our *only* option—to get the book translated, but I still didn't trust him. None of that explained why he'd been skulking around, taking pictures of us in the first place, and even if his motives were harmless, I couldn't understand his fascination with the Vaikesti.

To my relief, getting the camera back wasn't too difficult. Jared had made copies of the images and added them to Stephen's file, and with another warning to stay away from Vaikesti he released the camera back to its owner, who had the good sense to keep his mouth shut this time.

Stephen eyed me warily as he followed me out the front door of the municipal building and across the parking lot to my car. Darja kept shooting meaningful glances my way, but I didn't know what to say, how to explain, so I simply said, "I'll show you when we get there," and gave what I hoped came across as a sincere and apologetic smile as I gestured him into the car. Surprisingly, he didn't balk or ask any questions, but I could feel his suspicious gaze on me as I pulled out onto the road.

Darja had passed through the closed door and settled into the backseat, but as soon as we hit the road she flickered and phased out of sight. I wondered how much control she had over the transition. I wouldn't put it past her to have deliberately gone on ahead just to avoid the intensity of the awkwardness that permeated the interior of the car like a dense fog.

By my side, Stephen took in our surroundings with a wary gaze. I heard his soft, indrawn breath when I turned off the road and onto the dirt path that led toward Mirtel's wagon. He clearly knew where we were, and I could feel the unasked questions building in the silence between us.

I jerked the car to a stop and flung the door open, eager to escape the stifling interior, and Stephen followed suit, sparing a glance at the cluster of chickens before following me up the path to the door.

I'd been right; Darja had gone on ahead to alert the others, and the three of them were gathered around the wagon steps, watching us approach. I sagged with relief at the familiar faces and joined them, putting distance between myself and the outsider. The spell from the day before was still active—we were all able to see each other—and I wondered how long it would last and if it would fade naturally or had to be deactivated. There was so much we didn't know.

"You must be Stephen." Mirtel's voice was warm and welcoming and I frowned; clearly I was the only one here who had a problem with the guy.

"And you're Mirtel." Stephen's tone was polite and his eyes were wide, and I realized he wasn't suspicious, he was *fascinated*. He may be wary, but his expression was also intensely curious, and I realized this might be the most interaction he'd ever had with the Vaikesti that didn't involve being shunned or arrested. I tried to suppress a snort, and Darja raised her eyebrow at me.

"I am indeed. Welcome to my home; we've all been expecting you."

I saw Stephen's eyes dart to the side, clearly checking to see if he'd missed a person before he gave Mirtel a cautious smile. Across the steps Darja's mouth had stretched into a grin. She was actually *enjoying* this.

"Well, come on in everyone," Mirtel said, ushering us up the stairs and into the tiny space. "We have a lot to talk about. Does anyone want tea?" She didn't wait for us to answer before bustling to the kitchen and setting about the familiar routine.

The small space was cramped with the five of us, but oblivious, Stephen gingerly took a seat on the worn loveseat, his eyes huge behind his glasses as he looked around, drinking in his surroundings. He had clearly never been inside a Vaikesti home before. I took a seat in the armchair in the corner, putting as much space between us as possible, and watched as he took in the worn quilts, the piles of books, the shabby decor.

"Look at him." Darja was watching Stephen too. "What do you think he expected to find in here? Pentagrams and chalices full of blood?"

I snorted, my face flaming with the effort to keep in my laugh, and Stephen's eyes flew to me.

"Okay, girls," Mirtel said mildly from the kitchen where she had laid out three teacups and was waiting for the water to boil. "You know he can't hear you, so let's give the poor boy a minute to adjust."

At her words, Stephen grew very still. He opened his mouth, then closed it. His eyes landed on me again, and despite myself I actually felt a small stab of pity. I knew firsthand what it was like to have your whole world turned upside down, to find out that everything you thought you knew was wrong. I wouldn't wish that feeling on anyone. I forced myself to give Stephen a small reassuring smile. I knew there was no way to ask for his help on the book without revealing everything we knew—Darja, Aggie, the bond, everything. I prayed I was wrong about him. I prayed he would be worthy of the huge amount of trust we were about to place in him.

The piercing whistle of the kettle broke the silence, and Mirtel quickly poured the tea and joined us in the cramped living room, distributing steaming cups before settling into the rickety rocking chair.

"Stephen, we find ourselves in a difficult situation," she began, leaning forward and meeting his eyes, "and you appear to be one of the only people who can help us."

"Me?" His voice came out in a squeak and he pushed his glasses further up his nose.

Mirtel nodded. "I realize this is all very sudden, but we hope you'll be willing to help." She glanced my way. "Sofi, would you get the book?"

I rose and hefted the book from where it sat on the kitchen counter, then deposited it onto the coffee table in front of Stephen with a *thump*.

"This is the book I was looking at in the library," he said, glancing up at me as he carefully opened the cover. "With the blank pages. The one you ran off with."

I nodded, reclaiming my seat in the corner. "We need you to translate it."

His mouth fell open and I watched as a hundred questions seemed to pass through his mind. Finally he settled on, "You can't translate it? It's *your* language."

Affronted, I opened my mouth to reply, but Mirtel cut

me off. "I'm afraid most of us don't speak the old tongue any more. It's primarily ceremonial, and most of us only know a few words here and there." She took a sip of her tea. "Sofi led me to believe you have been studying the language. Do you think you could translate it accurately?"

"The whole book?" Stephen flipped through the pages, his auburn hair falling over his forehead, obscuring his expression. "I mean...yes, probably." He looked up. "But...why?"

I grimaced. "I don't suppose you'd be willing to just do it and not ask any questions?"

Darja snickered from her spot on the floor by the table, and Mirtel glanced my way, a soft reprimand in her eyes.

Stephen looked at me, his expression uncertain as if he wasn't sure if I was joking. "Um...no."

I sighed and slouched down in my chair. "You'll regret it," I muttered under my breath.

"What?" he asked.

"Nothing." Best to jump right in. I slid out of my chair and joined Darja on the floor in front of the coffee table, reaching out to flip through the pages until a familiar spell was facing up.

"You said this was a spell book, right?"

He nodded, staring hard at me.

"Well, you were right. And we figured out how to use it. The page with the words," I indicated the page on the left, "is meant to be read by the living." I gestured to Mirtel, who obligingly read the familiar words there—the first spell we had ever tried.

"And this page, the blank page," I moved my hand across the book, "isn't actually blank. It's filled with words, you and I just can't see them. This page is meant to be read by the dead." I nodded to Aggie, who, with a long-suffering look, spoke the words and finished the spell.

I caught sight of Stephen's expression, his eyes huge and round, for only a second before the lights went out.

It seemed as though all sound had been sucked out of the wagon along with the light, and the silence was absolute for a moment before Darja began to chuckle. "Damn, Sofi. I didn't realize you were so theatrical."

I ignored her, and after a moment Mirtel's soft voice broke in. "*Valmis,*" she said, and Aggie repeated the word. The lights immediately flickered back on, and the four of us all turned toward Stephen.

He looked thunderstruck.

"It...you...it's real."

He leaned forward, his fingers hovering above the blank page of the book as if afraid to touch it, then he suddenly sat up straight, staring around wildly as the significance of my words penetrated.

"The dead. How—who?" He fixed his gaze on me, and I found myself unable to interpret his expression. "I'll help you," he said. "Anything you need. But you have to tell me everything."

A lump formed in my throat. How to explain? How to *begin*? I looked helplessly at Mirtel, and she met my gaze silently. If we did this, we were betraying secrets the Vaikesti didn't talk about even amongst each other. To share them with a stranger, an *outsider,* I didn't think any of us had really considered what that would mean. What a real betrayal that was. Mirtel gave me a slight nod, pain mixed with the encouragement on her face, and I turned to Darja. Her face was stony, her expression hard as her eyes bored into mine, and I knew without a doubt that she had no reservations. She had already been betrayed; nothing was holding her back, and if Stephen could hear her, she would have been talking already. I took a deep breath and gave her a firm nod. My loyalty was to her, and I would not let her down. If she believed so strongly this was the right thing to do, I would trust her, even if I didn't trust Stephen.

I twisted to face the boy on the couch, his shocked expression at odds with the intensity of his eyes, his need to know, to *understand*. I took a deep breath and began to talk.

It was hard.

It was hard to spill the secrets the Vaikesti had protected through generations.

It was hard to relive the Ceremony yet again. The fire. The screams only I could hear. The magic that became real. I told him about meeting Mirtel at the *koolis*. I tried to backtrack and explain what the *koolis* was, but he already knew. He knew so much about us already. I introduced him to Darja, who he couldn't see. Mirtel introduced him to Aggie, who sat stonily in the corner. I told him about the book, about finding him with it in the library, realizing Darja could see the text where I couldn't, all of us gathered here, sounding out words together in this same spot just the day before. The spells we had tried. The spells that had *worked*.

So much we knew.

So much we didn't understand.

Through it all, Stephen sat motionless, questions brimming in his eyes but he held them back, letting me get it all out.

Finally my words began to dwindle, and I slumped back, resting my weight on my hands. Despite my exhaustion, strangely I also felt lighter.

Stephen sat back against the mismatched cushions, and I could see from his unfocused gaze that his mind was racing, trying to process everything he'd learned.

"So, you'll help us?" Mirtel asked, leaning forward. "The book is too dangerous to use without understanding what it says. But with it, with your help…maybe we can understand what has happened to us."

Stephen seemed to pull himself together with an effort, and he nodded. "Yes, of course I'll help. I'll translate the book, but..." He glanced down, skimming his fingers again over the blank page. "I can't see the words. I'll need..."

He trailed off, but Mirtel nodded. "Aggie can read them to me, and I'll write them down for you. We need to know what both sides say."

"Of course. Also, I'll need to take the book with me."

I started, sitting up. "What? Why can't you do it here?"

He gave me an apologetic shrug. "I told you, I'm not fluent. I have texts at school that I'll need to help me translate it. I assume you need it to be pretty accurate."

I grumbled, and he looked at me, his eyes softening.

"Sofi." He waited until I looked up, meeting his gaze. "Don't think I don't know what it means that you shared all this with me. I understand the risk you've taken, and I don't hold it lightly. I'll take good care of the book. I promise. Here," he added, jotting something on a scrap of paper from his backpack and handing it to me. "Here's my number. You can check in with me any time."

I nodded, accepting the paper from his outstretched hand. I would trust him, because I had to. But as I watched him lift the heavy book and slide it carefully into his backpack, I prayed we hadn't all just made a huge mistake.

CHAPTER 20

DARJA

The mood in Mirtel's wagon was somber after Stephen left. I was glad he'd been so willing to help us, but I wasn't sure he understood what was at stake. Still though, it felt like a relief to bring someone inside our little circle... even if that someone was an outsider and outright 'enemy' of Vaikesti.

Mirtel busied herself clearing away the teacups and saucers, bustling and *hmph*ing like it was a major chore, when in reality I thought she probably just needed something to do with her hands while she processed what we'd just done.

What we'd just done. That sounded pretty melodramatic, especially when our scale went from, 'clueing in helpful stranger,' to, '*being burned alive.*' Still, Mirtel and Sofi remained quietly introspective, and I could see from their worried and somewhat guilty expressions how hard it was for the two of them to grapple with such an enormous break with tradition, no matter how flawed—how deadly—that tradition was.

Aggie, on the other hand, appeared to be slightly more optimistic. She'd seemed to relax somewhat since our talk, and I wondered if maybe a few of those walls were starting to tumble. And when I caught her gaze and gave her a cheeky and exaggerated wink, I swore I could almost see the corner of her mouth tug upward. She composed herself quickly, however, rolling her eyes and crossing her arms in front of her chest. Well. They couldn't all be victories.

I waited a few more minutes while Sofi brooded and Mirtel put away her charmingly chipped china with a little more force than was strictly necessary. Finally, I slid over to Sofi's elbow, quiet, easy, like approaching a horse I was pretty sure would spook.

"Hey," I said, noticing as I did that she was picking absent-mindedly at a few loose threads fraying from one of the patchwork pillows on the small sofa.

"Hey," she replied, her tone muted and distant.

"I think we're doing the right thing," I offered, feeling a bit worried at the uncharacteristic indifference I could sense in her. I couldn't see it, but it was pervasive, like an aura hovering all around her. Not something I would have put any stock in...*before.* But I supposed any witch doctor hoo-doo bullshit was possible at this point.

"I hope you're right." She turned to look at me, and her eyes were tired. Blue as ever, but crinkled at the edges, with dark smudges beneath. I doubted she'd been sleeping enough since the Ceremony, and I made a silent promise to let her rest.

I put my pledge to the test later that night, staying in her room as she drifted off to a restless sleep. I felt like a creeper, but I wanted to make sure she could recharge. We had a long road ahead of us, and we weren't going to get anywhere if she was dead on her feet. Besides, that role was already taken.

It wasn't hard to convince Sofi to come to the *koolis* with me the next morning, and that worried me more than anything. I knew she was feeling overwhelmed, like we all were, but she was taking it the hardest. Of course, with Aggie and I already dead, and Mirtel having lived a very long life, Sofi was the one with the most to lose. In just a few days, her entire world had been shaken to its core, literally everything and every person she'd believed in suddenly called into question.

I decided to ride with her in the car, instead of flickering my way to the other side of town. My attempts at small talk, however, were met with resigned, clipped answers or pointed silence. Eventually, I dropped the conversation and stared out the window, marveling at how everything looked so familiar...but so different at the same time. More and more, I could feel that this was no longer my world, no longer the place I was meant for. I'd never felt any particular sense of belonging before, when I'd been alive, but at this point, the absence of it was palpable, like a wound throbbing with each beat of my heart...except I no longer had one of those, either.

Finally, we turned down the road that led through a tall grove of trees to the *koolis* beyond, looking, as usual, industrial and antiseptic. The surrounding woods were dappled green, heavy with unfurling spring buds. Even the field that lay to the east of the school looked idyllic, ankle-high corn stalks bathed in golden morning sunlight.

But the *koolis*, set down haphazardly in the middle of this Midwest paint-by-numbers beauty, looked even more intrusive, like the uninvited guest at a party. If I'd been alive, I would have shivered. Not all my memories in this place were bad ones, but enough of them were tinged with loss, longing and loneliness that I couldn't muster any sort of fondness at seeing its flat gray roofline cutting a dark trench across the azure sky.

"You remember what we need to do?" I asked finally, breaking the lingering silence between Sofi and me.

She sighed. "Yes, but I still don't understand—"

"I'll explain everything once we get in there," I promised, giving her what I hoped was an encouraging smile. She didn't return it.

Sofi parked in the lot designated for *tajas* and got out of the car. She didn't look back to see if I was following, but I stuck close behind her, hovering near enough that I could almost smell her shampoo. Classes were just beginning, but there would likely be a few stragglers finishing up breakfast in the cafeteria, and *tajas* on the prowl, watching for anyone daring to break any of the many rules *koolis* students were expected to uphold at all times.

I felt a flutter of nerves as Sofi strode through the front doors. I had to admit, there was something courageous, almost reckless about her actions, and though I was worried for her, I also admired her strength. I wondered what it would have been like to have been friends in life. The concept had never occurred to me before, but I thought that I would have liked it. Would have liked her.

She made a beeline for the front office, turning on a blazing smile just as she rounded the corner and stepped up to the reception window, all traces of the emotions she'd been holding in for the last few days suddenly evaporated.

"Hi there," she chirped, putting her hands on the counter and leaning toward the plexiglass window, peering in at the sour-faced *taja* sitting at the desk on the other side. "I was wondering if Ms. Kross is in?"

"Where else would she be?" the woman behind the glass barked, but Sofi's smile never wavered.

"Ha, of course. Right. Well...would it be possible to see her?"

The woman's frown deepened. I'd seen her around, but students didn't interact much with the administrative staff. And thank goodness, because the look of her would have sent most of us cowering in our beds.

"What do you need with Ms. Kross?" she asked. Her hair was steel gray and wiry, much of it attempting to escape her mercilessly tight bun—not that I could blame it for wanting to be as far away as possible.

"Oh," Sofi said with a tinkling laugh, "I've visited her here before, and she said I could come back anytime." She leaned in closer, looking around conspiratorially, then whispered, "It's about Darja Kallas."

If this had any effect on the old crone, she didn't show it. But she did slide a guest badge beneath the glass, pushing it forcefully toward Sofi's splayed hands.

"She'll be on breakfast duty," the woman said in a near growl, nodding her head toward the cafeteria that sat at the opposite end of the hall.

Sofi took the badge and dropped the lanyard quickly around her neck. "Thanks so much," she said, then turned and dashed down the corridor before the receptionist could change her mind.

Feeling like a proud (if delinquent) mama, I trailed behind, taking in the familiar gloom and quiet of the *koolis'* interior. In any normal school, I imagined it would be noisy during meal time, bursting with pent-up adolescent energy, but instead the cafeteria sat like a tomb, the only sounds the scrape of cutlery and the occasional thump of the vending machine in the corner. High, narrow windows let in a slant of diluted sunlight, but it faltered and then died before reaching anyone at ground level.

In the shadow of the farthest corner, I saw Ms. Kross,

sitting at a table thumbing absently through an old textbook with one hand while mindlessly stirring her tea with the other. She wasn't looking at either, instead gazing off into the distance, a blank expression on her face. She seemed older, I noticed. Tired. I tried to feel bad for her, but I couldn't muster any sympathy.

Sofi approached slowly, the manufactured smile slipping from her face as she got closer. She had one hand on the chair opposite before Ms. Kross glanced up, startled, the spoon clattering sideways out of the cup, spattering the table with dark droplets of tea.

"Sorry!" Sofi said, swiftly pulling out the chair and sitting down before looking around to see how much attention they'd attracted, but no one even spared us a glance.

Ms. Kross was immediately on-guard, carefully closing her book and straightening her red top smartly. "What's this about?" she said, none of the warmth she'd shown on Sofi's last visit apparent in this cold, gray mausoleum. Could it be guilt? Or was she really as emotionless as I now suspected? Not a murderer, exactly. But an accomplice, to be sure.

"I'm Sofi Ilves," Sofi said, keeping her voice quiet and even. "I was here last week about...about Darja Kallas."

"I remember," Ms. Kross said. "I meant, 'why did you come back'?"

Sofi shifted in her chair. "Well, I remembered you said I could, if I ever wanted to talk more about...about Darja."

Ms. Kross's eyes lowered quickly to the table, but her expression remained stony.

"And..." Sofi continued, her voice beginning to falter. "I just thought...I thought you might be able to help me learn more about her—about her life here."

Ms. Kross barked out a sharp and unexpected laugh. "There's not much more to it than this," she said, waving a hand dismissively around the room. "Lessons, chapel, meals. Punishment," she added, almost as an afterthought. "So, now you know." She opened her textbook again and began reading.

"Yes, well…umm…" Sofi cleared her throat and, for the first time, looked over to me, meeting my eyes pleadingly. I gave her a nod, then tilted my head at Ms. Kross.

"Right," Sofi said, "I'm sorry to interrupt you. It's just… Darja and I knew each other from school. From the days she was there. We were…friends. Well, before she…died. My other friends, they're mostly younger than I am. They haven't had their Spring Day Ceremony. I don't have anyone to talk to and I—"

"I understand," Ms. Kross said with a deep sigh. She gave Sofi a searching look. "It's so hard," she said. "On you girls. We ask so much of you. Keep our secrets, don't ask too many questions. It's an unfair burden."

I could see, in her downcast eyes and the creases around her mouth, she wasn't completely unaffected by what had happened. In some ways, she was just as much a victim of Vaikesti as the rest of us.

But only in some ways.

"It's just," Sofi began, apparently sensing the same weakening in Ms. Kross' walls, "Darja mentioned something—a box. She said you gave it to her, a long time ago, to keep some of her things in. She thought you might still have it, and I wondered if maybe…I could see it?"

Ms. Kross's eyes sharpened. "Why would she think I would have it?"

"Oh, uh, I meant *I* thought you might have it," Sofi said quickly, covering her misstep. "That you might have kept it…afterwards."

Ms. Kross looked around, then back to the envelope. Her face gave away nothing, but her eyes were fierce.

"Come with me."

The box was in storage, and though the less-than-accommodating admin seemed reluctant to allow us into the records room, with a firm nudge from Ms. Kross, she finally relented.

Half an hour later, we were back in Sofi's car, idling in the parking lot while Sofi gently lifted the lid. I tried not to dwell on what Ms. Kross was thinking, back in her room, rehashing her conversation with Sofi. Was she guilty? Did she regret leading me to my death?

Annoyed with myself, I forced the thoughts away and focused on the box, thin and shoddily constructed. It had once been a jewelry box, though a very cheaply-made one. The remnants of a pasted-on forest scene were barely visible on the lid, disintegrating everywhere the glue didn't hold.

Sofi hadn't said much since we'd got back to the car, but I could tell by the way she was eyeing the box that she must be curious. She held the lid open and placed it gently on the car's center console. Inside, I could see what was left of my old baby blanket, barely more than a handkerchief's worth of fabric. Sofi looked up at me and I nodded at her, trying not to let her see how nervous I was. Delicately, she lifted the blanket and shifted it to the other side of the box. Beneath it, gleaming a brassy sort of golden-silver was the teaspoon, the handle curling intricately around the engraved *I*.

Sofi was shaking her head, reaching out a finger to trace along the curve of the spoon. "But how..." she said. "And *why*?"

I shook my head, too. "I don't know, but I know this spoon was my mother's most treasured possession. It's the only thing she kept from her life before."

Sofi's brow furrowed. "Could she have been a cleaning lady for my family? A babysitter for my sisters?"

"Stealing a fake gold-plated spoon? For what? It couldn't be worth anything. And obviously it wasn't all that precious, if no one's ever noticed it missing in all these years."

Sofi frowned. She lifted out the spoon and scrutinized it, as if she thought it might be an imposter. Then, she held up the box, peering inside. "That's it," she said, sounding frustrated. "We went through all that for this? What does it even prove?"

"It proves we're connected," I said, wishing she could feel the same current of excitement that was rushing through me. Our families were somehow linked, and the spoon was evidence of that. It might bring up more questions, but it got us one step closer to unraveling this mystery.

"It proves your mom was in my house at some point," she said stubbornly. "That's all." She was still holding the box, fiddling mindlessly with it. She flipped it upside down and gave it a little shake, like that was going to do anything. However, when she turned it back over, she did a double take, leaning over in her car seat to get a better look.

"What is it?" I asked, straining to see. And there it was. Inside the box, where the bottom should have been, one corner of thin plywood had popped up. Sofi lifted it up and looked beneath, but the bottom of the box, from the outside, was still intact.

"What the hell?" she breathed. She reached a finger gently inside and began to pry up the loosened corner. It came away with little resistance, one corner splintering as Sofi continued to lift, revealing a very thin compartment beneath.

"Holy shit," I said quietly. All those years, I'd never thought to look—never would have imagined the plain box held any secrets within its flimsy walls.

Sofi reached underneath the wood and pulled out a thin stack of letters, all of them sealed. There were six in total, and each one had a *return to sender* stamp across the front.

The sender was listed as M. Kallas. My mother. I reached out a hand, wishing I could trace my fingers over the ink, wishing I could feel her spirit in the curving, swirling letters beneath.

I glanced up at Sofi, hoping she could see how grateful I was to her for finding this—for bringing me this piece of my mother—but her face was stricken, and she wasn't looking at me. She was staring at the envelopes, all addressed to the same person.

Dr. Robert Ilves.

CHAPTER 21

SOFI

The wave of foreboding that swept over me when I saw my father's name on the envelopes was dense and real, like I had stepped into a thundercloud.

We drove home in silence, Darja in the back and the box with its letters sitting like a live viper on the passenger seat by my side. I could barely keep my eyes on the road as I drove, my gaze jumping to the box every few seconds.

A large part of me wanted to throw the letters away, or tuck them back inside their hidden compartment and pretend they never existed. Because whatever we were about to read, whatever might be found in a stack of letters written by a sixteen-year-old pregnant girl to the upstanding, married town doctor—my *father*—it probably wasn't going to be good.

The second we arrived, I ducked into the house and made a beeline for my bedroom, ignoring my mother's greeting from the kitchen and slamming the door behind me. I immediately pulled the letters from the box.

Darja's eyes were intently focused as I pulled the first

letter from the bottom of the stack and flipped it over. The envelope was still sealed, and I felt a bit like I was committing a crime as I slid my thumb under the edge of the flap and ripped it open with a jerky motion.

The letter inside was written on thin, cheap paper with the *koolis* letterhead stamped across the top, and I felt Darja lean close, drawing in a sharp breath at the looping scrawl of the words. She had probably never seen her mother's handwriting before. I took a deep, painful breath, and began to read.

Dear Dr. Ilves,

I know you told me not to tell anyone about what happened, but I had to tell my mother. I was scared, and I didn't know what to do, and you told me I shouldn't come see you. I'm so sorry. I didn't say anything about you, I swear. She thinks it was a boy from school.

But I think there's been some sort of mistake. They came last night and took me to the koolis. Do you know what's going on? I'm scared.

Mari

I felt like I was in a haze, like time had ground to a halt. Automatically, my hands found the next letter and ripped it open.

Dr. Ilves,

I've been here for two weeks now. I know you know I'm still at the koolis. How could my own mother do this to me? Can you help me? I won't tell anyone, I swear. You know I've never said anything before. But I can't stay here. I feel sick all the time, and the tajas are awful. I can't stay here another seven months. Please help me. I miss you.

Mari

I felt queasy. Darja was motionless by my side. The third letter was more of the same. The tone changed to pleading, then anger. Mari's mother came to visit on a rare family day, and while she swore she hadn't been the one to send her daughter to the *koolis*, she still told Mari it was better this way. At least until the baby came.

But then the baby came. And Mari stayed at the *koolis*. My hands shook as I opened the final letter.

Robert,

I was going to write that your daughter is three weeks old now, but despite your role in this, she is not your daughter, she is mine. *No one will ever love her the way I do. I named her Darja. Isn't that beautiful? She is named after a Saint, and martyr, which is perfect because she does not deserve any of this. She does not deserve to be raised here, in this hell, paying for your sins. But at least she has me, and I will keep her safe.*

I don't know why I'm bothering with this; it's not like you'll ever read it. I won't write you again, and I hope you live to regret what you've done.

Mari

The last letter fell from my hands in a flutter of paper as my legs gave way and I sank to the carpet. It was only when I heard the choked gasp coming from my own throat did I realize I was crying. Thick, wrenching sobs boiled out of me, and I couldn't seem to catch my breath.

What had just happened? I didn't know how to process all the emotions roiling in my gut. How was this even possible? My own father, who had been there my whole life, who wasn't perfect, sure, but had always been a perfectly decent dad; a little absent maybe, a little preoccupied with work and a little overly concerned with his public image as the benevolent town doctor, but he was always good to his family. How had I judged him so incredibly wrong? Was I *blind?*

Did my mother know? The thought stole my breath. Surely not, because how could she possibly live with a secret like that? And yet, I had first-hand knowledge of how deep secrets were buried in Vaikesti. I didn't know what to believe anymore.

"I think you need a Kleenex."

Darja's voice jerked me out of my spiraling thoughts, and I realized she was right. I was probably quite a picture, with snot running down my face and my eyes swollen half shut. But as I grabbed a tissue from the nightstand and blew my nose, it suddenly occurred to me how selfish I was being. This news affected Darja as much, if not more, than it did me, but when I paused long enough to look at her face, the expression I saw held no trace of my own feelings.

There was no pain there, no betrayal, and why would there be? She'd already known her mother had been betrayed by someone, just not *who*. Instead, her face held a kind of tentative hopefulness, a bit of light shining in her eyes, but held in check as if she knew she needed to let me process my emotions at this revelation.

Wiping the tissue across my face again, I met her eyes and raised a questioning eyebrow.

She gave a half shrug and couldn't quite contain the smile that pulled at the corner of her mouth, before giving voice to the thought that might have been the first thing I should have realized.

"I guess I have a sister."

CHAPTER 22

DARJA

I have a sister.

The words echoed in my mind, tumbling over each other in a sort of frantic ecstasy as I tried, unsuccessfully, to tamp them down.

A sister. And not just any sister. Sofi.

Sofi is my sister.

I had decided to give her space to deal with the avalanche of emotion our discovery had triggered. For me, the revelation was like a cloud opening up, raining down on the parched earth below. To Sofi, it must have been like a dam breaking, roaring and rushing, ripping a path through everything she held dear, leaving destruction in its wake.

I was angry, of course. Angry that the respected town doctor, twice my mother's age, had taken advantage of her and then abandoned her, pregnant and frightened, at the mercy of the *koolis* and the *tajas* who ran it. But Sofi...I couldn't imagine the betrayal she must be feeling.

Still, there was no helping the rush of...*joy*...I felt in discovering the truth. I had a family. A dysfunctional one, but a family nonetheless. I had siblings. Aunts and uncles, nieces and nephews. And I had Sofi.

And it turned out Aggie had been right—it *was* blood that created the bond, blood that bound us together in life and in death. It was good to know, but still...I wasn't sure the knowledge of why the bond worked would actually help us.

I had left her in her room, hoping she'd be able to get some rest once I stopped hovering over her. She didn't ask where I was going, but then again, I didn't have many options. I had told her goodbye and then flickered out, reappearing at Mirtel's wagon.

I hovered near the front steps for a moment, unsure what to do. I couldn't knock at the door, but it seemed wrong to just appear inside, completely unannounced. I waited, indecisive, watching the chickens scratch the dusty ground in search of a late supper. I was a bit lost in my reverie until I heard a voice.

"Darja?"

It was Aggie. She had appeared around the side of the wagon, her long dress fluttering around her ankles as the chickens, seemingly unaware, bobbed right through her. I guessed they weren't as perceptive as cats.

"Hey," I said, and I could hear the quiver in my voice. Aggie could apparently hear it, too, and she gave me a searching look. "Sorry to come by so late."

It wasn't really all that late yet, but it was getting there. Dusk was settling over the river beyond the wagon, heavy with the violet haze of twilight. A fine mist hung low over the ground, blanketing the world in a fuzzy, otherworldly sort of glow—a perfect evening for two ghost girls to have a chat.

"Where's Sofi?" Aggie asked, a note of worry in her voice.

"Sleeping, I hope. Mind if we talk for a bit?"

Aggie shook her head. I moved past her, closer to the water's edge, and we took up the same spots we'd been in the other day. I had thought about how to ease into the subject of my parentage—play it cool, indifferent, state the facts and nothing more.

Instead, I blurted out, "Sofi and I are sisters."

I waited for a shocked response, but Aggie said nothing. I searched her profile in the dimming light, but there was nothing in her expression to give away her reaction.

"So it was the blood after all," she said after a long moment. "How did you find out?"

I told her about seeing the flatware at Sofi's house, and the memory it triggered of the teaspoon, and everything that happened after. The words poured out of me in a flood that I couldn't have stopped even if I'd tried. When I was finally all tapped out, Aggie stayed silent. I thought her dark eyes were a little wider than before, but it was hard to tell in the late evening light.

Finally, she turned to me, her face calmly schooled in a neutral expression. "How did Sofi take it?"

"Okay," I said. "I think. She's upset, finding this out about her father—"

"*Your* father," Aggie interjected, and I nodded, though the thought felt foreign and distant.

"Our father," I amended. It felt strange on my tongue, like a religious epithet I didn't really mean.

"And you?"

I paused then, uncertain. I was overcome with happiness, to learn the truth and know that Sofi and I were inextricably, irrevocably entwined. And yet...

"I never had a real Christmas at the *koolis*," I said slowly, "but I think it feels like that. Like I woke up and found the biggest present under the tree with my name on it." I shook my head. "But then...somebody takes it away before I can open it."

It was, I realized then, a strange sort of grief. Just as I had begun rejoicing at the news that Sofi and I were sisters, I was also instantly in mourning—mourning for the relationship we never got to have... for all the things I never got to have. The sense of loss was enough to send me reeling. My shoulders heaved, and I sobbed, tearlessly, wishing for all the world I could just cry out all the pain. I shook with the overwhelming wave of emotion, unable to speak, unable to do anything but choke over the thick, bitter ache that gripped me like a vice.

Eventually I realized that Aggie was whispering my name, over and over, hushed and solemn, her own voice heavy with feeling.

I looked over to her then, just in time to see her reach out a hand, tentatively, somewhat warily, and place it over mine. I braced myself for the shock to come...but nothing happened.

That wasn't exactly true, though. It wasn't the jarring feeling of being pulled into someone's memories this time. Instead, I felt warmth. The warmth of a touch that was almost human...almost alive. The spell we'd done seemed to work in increasingly mysterious ways. I didn't want to intrude on Aggie's memories again, and I didn't think I wanted her stumbling around through mine. But this...this I could get on-board with.

I looked down at our hands, not quite solid, not quite corporeal, but joined together all the same, and then I looked up at Aggie.

I could see my surprise reflected in her face. Her eyes were round, and for once, there was no sign of her trademark frown. She seemed younger, somehow. Full of wonder and impossibly beautiful.

"Aggie," I said quietly, terrified of upsetting the delicate balance of this moment. But when she met my gaze, I saw the barest hint of a smile tug at the corners of her mouth. I lifted my hand slowly, not sure what I was even hoping for, and ran my fingertips over her cheek. Like our joined hands, it wasn't quite the same as touching a living person, but it was the closest I'd come since this all had happened, and it was more than I could have imagined. Aggie's eyes drifted closed as she leaned into the touch, turning her face and pressing her lips against my palm.

The sudden snap of a twig echoed through the moment like a gunshot. We jumped apart, and I looked wildly around for the source of the sound. If I'd had a heart, it would have been racing, and not because of the loud intrusion.

"There," Aggie hissed, keeping her voice to a whisper, even though Mirtel was the only living soul around that could have heard us.

I swiveled around and looked back toward the wagon, its faded jewel box colors even duller, like an unpolished emerald, in the full dark.

Everything was in shadow, especially here at the backside of the wagon. The light that hung over the front door spilled a golden glow that didn't reach more than a few feet in any direction. Back here, it was pitch black. I squinted through the darkness as another branch cracked beneath the feet of someone—definitely a person—with a not-insignificant amount of bulk.

"Is that..." I whispered, creeping closer, feeling Aggie at my heels. "Is that Jared?"

"The cop?" Aggie said, and I nodded.

"What the hell is he doing?" I wondered, sneaking toward him. There was no reason for either Aggie or I to sneak around, but we both kept our voices hushed as we inched toward him.

He was bent over something at the edge of the wagon, and it looked like he was exerting some force on it. I peered closer, and saw that it was Mirtel's root cellar, not much more than a shallow hole in the ground with two ply board doors on top, secured with a padlock. I'd seen the one at the *koolis*, much larger than Mirtel's but nearly as primitive—just a cool place to store canned food during the winter months—and I wondered what on earth Jared could expect to find inside.

"Should I tell Mirtel?" Aggie whispered behind me, and I jumped.

"Yeah. She should definitely know about this."

Without a word, Aggie flickered out. A few moments later, I heard the low creak of the front door. Jared, apparently, did not, as he went on wrestling with the lock.

Aggie flickered back in behind me just as I saw Mirtel round the corner, wearing a velvet dressing gown that matched the exterior of the wagon to a T.

"You won't find much in there this time of year but sweet potato slips," she said, and Jared froze, dropping whatever he'd been using to try to prise the doors open.

He straightened up and turned, a broad smile already stretching across his face. "Ms. Parn, good evening. I apologize for sneaking up on you like this."

"Well, dear," Mirtel said, a slight edge beneath her kind old-lady voice, "it seems *I'm* the one who's snuck up on *you*."

Jared laughed. "No, you're right. And again, I'm sorry. I didn't want to wake you if you'd already gone to bed."

"So you thought it'd be better if I died of a heart attack after hearing an intruder outside?"

Jared kept smiling, but it was growing strained. "Of course not," he said. "I just..." He sighed then, running a hand over his close-cropped hair. "I was hoping to make some progress in the investigation. This missing girl...it's just...it's got the whole town on edge."

Mirtel nodded. "Of course. I assume you have a search warrant?"

This seemed to catch Jared off-guard. Even in the darkness, I could see that his face had gone pale.

"Well, er...I mean...not...exactly," he finished lamely.

"Ah," Mirtel said, raising an eyebrow. "Well then, I suppose I'd better invite you in."

Jared's shoulders relaxed. "If it's okay," he said, "I'd like to talk to you for a few minutes."

"Of course."

"I could come back," he said quickly, apparently thrown by Mirtel's cooperation. "Tomorrow, maybe?"

Mirtel sighed. "No, of course not. Come around to the front. I'll make some tea."

The two of them disappeared around the side of the wagon, and I looked back at Aggie.

"Should we follow?"

She rolled her eyes. "What do you think?"

A few moments later, Mirtel and Jared were sitting across from one another in the tight space, sipping from their steaming cups. Aggie and I were bunched together near the curtain that separated the front of the wagon from the sleeping space. Any other time, I might have been distracted by the tingle I felt at her nearness, and the memory of what had happened on the bank of the river, but I forced myself to focus on the conversation at hand.

"So you were looking for...what, exactly? In my root cellar?" Mirtel said, peering at Jared over the rim of her teacup.

"I have no idea," he said, looking defeated. "I just...I'm

worried about Sofi. I know she doesn't want you being involved in all this, but after last time—"

"Last time?" Mirtel interjected, There was a sudden sharpness in her voice, a far cry from the little old lady offering the young officer tea.

Jared may not have been the brightest bulb, but he wasn't the dimmest, either. He schooled his face into a neutral expression.

"We have to investigate all relevant leads," he said carefully.

"You mean me?" Mirtel said. "I'm the lead? Because of... because of Aggie."

Jared nodded. "Your cousin, right? Look, I'd be lying if I said we had piles of evidence connecting you to either case, but it feels like more than a coincidence, doesn't it?"

Mirtel eyed him coolly over her tea cup. "You're the detective; you tell me."

"You were investigated before."

She nodded shortly. "I was."

"A *koolis* girl goes missing right after her 18th birthday and—"

"Right after Spring Day," Mirtel said, an edge in her voice.

If Jared was supposed to get the hint, it seemed to have missed its mark. "I can't just drop it," he said, sounding almost apologetic. "If you're not involved, I'll find out, and you'll be in the clear."

"How kind," Mirtel said.

Jared's frustration was clear in his tight voice. "Look, I don't think you're some small-town serial killer going around murdering young girls. But I haven't proven you're not yet. Right now, I just want to get the case wrapped up, so Sofi can..."

"Move on?" Mirtel said, and Jared nodded.

"This has all really gotten to her. She said she didn't know the missing girl all that well, but I can tell it's bothering her. I remember her from school, and she was always so cheerful and upbeat. Now…it's like…like someone's died."

I felt a shiver run through me at that, and Aggie and I exchanged a look.

"And what if someone has?" Mirtel said.

"We don't know that."

"Mmm," Mirtel said.

"No, it's more likely she's run away. It's happened before, a time or two. My dad's told me some stories about the *koolis* girls."

"Your dad, the sheriff?"

"That's right. He's found a couple, actually. Brought them back safe and sound. I'm guessing this Darja is another one. Probably hiding out somewhere nearby."

"And you think she might be hiding out here?" Mirtel asked, and I snorted. Jared wasn't going to win any *detective of the year* awards, but even a broken clock is right twice a day.

"Look, I don't really think you have anything to do with this," Jared said, gazing intently down into his tea. "But I just want Sofi to know I'm taking this seriously. I want to find whatever I need to clear you, so she can stop worrying."

That surprised me. I'd always thought he was a player in school. Popular, athletic, and always with a cheerleader hanging on his arm, and his every word. I doubted he'd ever even known I'd existed. But he genuinely seemed to care about Sofi. Maybe I hadn't been giving him enough credit.

"And Stephen?" Mirtel was saying. "How does he play into all this?"

Jared frowned. "I wish I knew. That little…rat…knows something, and I'm going to find out what."

Mirtel shifted, taking a long drag of her tea. "And how will you do that?"

"I've got eyes on him," he said. "He's not going to get too far without us knowing what he's up to. We'll find out, and if he's involved, I'll make sure the whole town knows it."

I looked at Aggie, and could see my worry reflected in her eyes. If Jared really did have Stephen under surveillance, he'd find out about the book for sure. We needed to let Sofi know, so she could get word to Stephen. But how could she do it without being found out?

As we waited there, not voicing our fears, Jared finished his tea and placed his empty cup on the table beside him.

"Sorry to have kept you up so late, Ma'am," he said, running his hands over his pant legs and getting to his feet. "And I'm sorry for, you know..."

"Trying to break into my root cellar?"

Jared's face flushed. "Yes, Ma'am. I apologize."

"It's no problem," Mirtel said, standing up. He held out a hand, and she shook it.

"If you do hear anything," Jared said, pausing at the door, "give me a call at the station."

"I will, dear," Mirtel said, then nodded a goodnight and closed the door firmly behind him.

"Well," she said, turning and looking at Aggie and I, "we've got some work to do, girls."

CHAPTER 23

SOFI

Sleep that night was slow in coming, and restless when it finally did. I must have risen from my bed what seemed like dozens of times, rereading the letters in the dim glow of the bedside lamp before I finally shoved them all back in the box and buried it in my drawer under a pile of sweaters. Even then, I could still see the words on the back of my eyelids.

She thinks it was a boy from school.
Your daughter is three weeks old now.
Your daughter...

I clenched my hands into fists to keep them from trembling.

The sun was barely peeking over the horizon, sending wavering rays of light out to reach tentative fingers over the manicured lawns of my neighborhood, when the resentment and anger that was lodged in my chest finally drove me out of bed. I threw on my clothes in a blind rush and was out the door on silent feet and into my car before the thought had formed fully in my head. I didn't know where to go; I just needed to get away. Away from the ridiculous tangle my world had become—secrets and betrayal woven together into a tapestry I could no longer recognize as my own life.

The problem was my whole world was Vaikesti. I could count the number of times I'd been beyond our city limits on one hand. Where could I possibly go?

My phone had GPS though, and I loaded up the map as I drove, turning out onto the main thoroughfare that ran through town, driving too fast on the deserted roads. I turned right, then right again, and took the ramp onto the interstate, a move I'd never done outside of driver's ed. I let the roiling thoughts in my brain drown out the little voice that questioned what the hell I was doing, and sped up, merging into traffic with a wobbly jerk of the steering wheel, and then I was out of Vaikesti, heading south and away.

It was only when I took the exit a little over an hour later and found myself driving through the narrow, tree-lined streets of Springfield University that the little voice in my head pushed through to the forefront. What the hell was I *doing*?

I wasn't sure what had possessed me to seek out Stephen of all people, except that while we had dragged him into this mess, he wasn't really *part* of it. Not the way I was. He was the only non-Vaikesti person I'd ever really known, and while I still wasn't sure I trusted the guy any further than I could throw him, maybe an outside perspective was exactly what I needed.

The problem was I had no idea where he lived.

I pulled into a large empty parking lot and turned off the car. The lot was surrounded by enormous buildings with large placards outside of their arched front entryways. I skimmed the signs.

Bellmont School of Engineering.
College of Liberal Arts.
Springfield Memorial Student Union.

The buildings were all constructed of red brick—larger certainly, but not otherwise unlike the buildings at home—and yet I still felt like I had entered a foreign world. The sun had barely risen over the treetops, but I could see a few people about, likely students heading to class. For a moment I imagined a different reality, where I was one of those students, heading to a science lecture without a care in the world. What would it be like?

I blew out a breath, then pulled myself together and retrieved my phone from the passenger seat, where it had been acting as navigator. I opened my contact list and let my thumb hover over the newest entry, added just a couple of days ago after our revelation at Mirtel's wagon.

Stephen Jennings.

Would he even be awake yet? Maybe he was in class. I shouldn't even be here. Would he think I was crazy? Well, more crazy than he probably already thought?

In the end, I couldn't bring myself to call, so I settled on a text message.

It's Sofi Ilves. I'm here, on campus. Can we talk?

To my immense relief, he answered immediately.

Sofi! I'm in the grad apartments at 242 Littleton Street. Apt 4. Come on over.

GPS got me there with no issues, but my hands were shaking as I climbed out of my car in front of a depressing-looking series of low, brown buildings with identical small windows and metal stairs. By the time I found myself standing outside of apartment 4, so identified by a tiny tarnished plaque on the door, my palms were damp and I could feel my heartbeat thudding in my ears. This was a mistake.

I'd barely knocked before the door swung open.

Stephen didn't look much better than I felt. His eyes were wide and slightly manic behind glasses that sat crookedly on the bridge of his nose, and his hair was a wild mess. When he saw me though, he smiled a bit self-consciously and straightened his glasses, pushing them further up on his nose.

"Sofi. Come in. Sorry it's...I wasn't expecting you."

He stepped aside to give me room to enter, and I moved into the brightly lit space.

I hadn't really stopped to think what his apartment might look like, but if I had, I imagine this would be exactly what I would have pictured. The place was small, with an open kitchen and living room, and a short hallway that presumably led to the bedroom and bathroom. It wasn't dirty, exactly—no piles of clothes, no dishes in the sink—just unkempt, with overflowing bookshelves and papers littering nearly every surface. He clearly lived alone. A shiver chased up my spine. I'd never been in a boy's apartment before.

Stephen entered behind me and shut the door, but I stayed by the relative safety of the wall.

"Are you...is there...?" He glanced around cautiously, and I understood what he was asking.

"No, Darja's not here. It's just me."

He paused, then nodded. "Did you want to see the translation?" And just like that, I felt more at ease. No questioning why I was there, no comment about how it was barely seven in the morning or how it was strange that I would be here at all.

"Yes," I said, trying to keep the relief from my voice. He beckoned me further into the room and I followed, my eyes landing on the couch that dominated the space. It was thick and plush and comfy looking, strewn with blankets and papers. The large coffee table had been pulled up close, and was stacked high with books and other documents, sheaves of paper covered with pencil scratches and other notations. Our Vaikesti book was laid open in the center, next to a laptop, and I could barely see the top of the table through the mess. It looked like months of work had taken place here, and he'd only had the book for what—two days? Suddenly his red eyes and messy hair made sense. I glanced between him and the table.

"Have you even slept?"

He gave a short laugh and sat at the edge of the couch, reaching over the coffee table to move books out of the way and pull papers toward him as if the whole mess made sense to him, before shooting a quick glance my way.

"I, uh…I really wanted to get to work on it. Here's what I've got so far."

I sat down on the edge of the couch and he pushed a heavy binder in front of me. Carefully, I flipped it open, revealing page after page of translated text. Many pages had lines scribbled out, or post-it notes affixed to the edges, and comments filled the margins. But the amount of work that had been done was staggering.

"Holy shit. Did you already translate the whole book?"

He laughed again. "No. I mean, well, I only have a few pages of the, uh…the…dead portions of the text. I got them from Mirtel yesterday. She and…Aggie…are working on writing down the rest. So I've just been working on the parts I can see. I'm probably two thirds of the way through it."

I was stunned. I leaned over the book, reading a few lines to myself. His handwriting was small and cramped, but easy enough to read. I flipped through the pages, seeing where he'd left spaces for the missing sections to be filled in.

"That's...that's really amazing. Thank you for helping us with this, Stephen."

"No, thank *you,* Sofi, for trusting me with this. It means more than you can imagine."

I wondered again what he was getting out of this. I mean, he'd said he was doing research on the Vaikesti, but...why?

The silence stretched between us, and finally I gave voice to my thoughts. "Why are you so interested in us? Why have you been taking pictures, and why are you doing this for us?"

He didn't answer right away, and I glanced up at him. He wasn't looking at me. His eyes were focused on the mess of papers, but it didn't seem like he was really seeing them. After a moment he turned and cautiously met my eyes.

"I told you I was a graduate student here."

It wasn't a question, but I nodded anyway.

"I'm doing my thesis on..." He trailed off.

"On the Vaikesti?" I asked.

He gave a half shrug and I could see a faint flush crawling up out of the collar of his shirt. "On religious cults."

"*What?*" I sat up straight. "We're not a *cult.* We don't predict the end of the world and poison people with kool-aid."

"Doomsday cults are only one category," he said, pushing his glasses up his nose, and his voice took on a slightly lecturing tone. "A cult is really just a social group that has...unusual religious or spiritual beliefs. There are other common characteristics, but—"

"Our spiritual beliefs aren't *unusual,*" I countered hotly, and even I could hear the false note in my voice. "It's not like we b-brainwash people or...or murder..." And just like that I was crying again. I ducked my head, turning away, as the pain in my chest from the previous night's revelation—hell, from the previous *week's* revelations—mingled with the supreme embarrassment of being unable to control my emotions in front of Stephen.

Stephen. Who had been skulking around, taking photos, and writing papers about us like we were bugs under a microscope—because *of course* Vaikesti was a cult—and who I didn't even *like*, and yet who hesitantly slid closer and put a tentative but surprisingly comforting arm around my shoulder.

"I'm sorry," I managed a minute later, wiping my nose on my sleeve before Stephen rose and offered me a tissue. I studied him as he came back to the couch, and he watched me in return as if he wasn't quite sure what I was going to do next.

"Why us?" I asked. "Why the Vaikesti?"

One corner of his mouth rose in a smile. "Well, you're really close by, for one thing. So that's convenient. And for another... you're really secretive. No one really knows anything about the Vaikesti. Except for me," he added quietly.

"You know you can't tell anyone about all this," I said, narrowing my eyes. "You can't write about it in your thesis. You can't show anyone this translation."

He nodded. "I know."

"Then why help us?"

He shrugged, and didn't quite meet my eyes. "I've been interested in this stuff for a long time. Besides," he added, looking at me again, his expression intense," if everything you told me is true, this is bigger than a grade, or a thesis. This is...life-changing."

I nodded. I couldn't argue with that. We fell silent again, and I twisted my hands in my lap as he continued to watch me. Finally he said softly, "Why did you really come here?"

"What?"

"You didn't come to see the translation. There's nothing to see until it's done, and this was a long drive for you to make, alone, when the sun is barely up. Did something happen?"

That was all it took for the story to come pouring out. I stared down at my lap as I talked, twisting the hem of my shirt in my hands, and I told him about the letters, and my dad, and Darja's mom, and what it could mean for the bonded pairs, and what it meant to *me*.

Stephen was nothing if not a good listener. He didn't interrupt as I recounted the anger and betrayal.

"And I just had to leave, you know? I've barely been outside of Vaikesti my whole life, and it's suffocating, all the secrets and lies. And you're the only person I know who isn't part of all that." I glanced down at the open binder on the table. "Though I guess you are now, aren't you?"

He didn't get a chance to answer before I felt the change in the air and spun around to see Darja standing by the window that looked out over the parking lot. She seemed so out of place with her flowing white dress, slightly transparent flowers still threaded through her carefully styled hair, against the backdrop of a modern student's apartment. And yet, her presence still calmed me.

I glanced back to Stephen, who had not missed my odd reaction. "Darja's here," I told him, and his eyes widened a fraction.

But Darja didn't move from her spot by the window, just turned to peer out and gestured with a hand. "Someone's watching the apartment."

CHAPTER 24

DARJA

"So what did Jared say, exactly?"
"He said, 'I've got eyes on him.'"
"Whatever that means," Sofi muttered.
"*That's* what it means," I said, gesturing toward the window. The car was a block down the street. Nondescript. A beige Corolla, or something equally invisible on a college campus. But the man inside—he was out of place. Dark sunglasses, even in the hazy light of early morning, collar pressed and crisp—too crisp for a hungover student coming home after a night of partying. I'd watched him for at least half an hour. Aside from occasionally sipping from a styrofoam cup and consulting a clipboard propped against the steering wheel, he hadn't moved.

Sofi was sitting on Stephen's couch, half-hidden behind a mountain of papers. Her feet were tucked beneath her and her hair was a wild tangle down her back. Her eyes were red, and I wondered if she'd been crying. Stephen had sprung up when I'd flickered in, looking a little at sea until he'd finally settled uneasily into the armchair facing the window. He looked surreptitiously around the room now and then, presumably seeking signs of the ghost that was suddenly haunting his ratty little apartment.

Sofi chewed on her thumbnail, her expression troubled. "Should I just...call Jared? Tell him Stephen's not a threat and to leave him alone?"

"Sure," I said, moving closer to Stephen and waving a hand in front of his face. He didn't react. "And while you're at it, you can also let him know that you're part of an ancient magical cult that performs ritual murders on innocent girls."

Sofi flinched at the word *cult*, but said nothing. I snapped my fingers an inch from Stephen's ear. Nothing.

"Stop that," Sofi said, but her attention was on the pages in front of her. "If they find out about this..."

"What? They'll think we're all lunatics? Or witches? Maybe burn us at the stake?" I snorted. "That ship has sailed, don't you think?"

Sofi frowned at me, but said nothing. Stephen was perched on the edge of his chair, fingers splayed over the armrests, digging into the worn corduroy fabric.

"Look," he said finally, glancing at Sofi then casting his gaze around the room, still managing to look everywhere but at me, "this is all really...fascinating. Weird as hell, but fascinating. But shouldn't we maybe try to think up a plan that doesn't involve me as the secret society-obsessed murderer?"

"Of course," Sofi said. "But maybe he's watching you the same way he's keeping tabs on Mirtel. So he can prove you didn't do it."

Stephen and I gave her equally skeptical looks.

"For now, though," she continued, "I think we need to get the book and the translations out of here."

"You mean without Miami Vice down the street noticing?" I asked.

Sofi nodded. "Maybe we should just wait him out?"

"The problem is," Stephen said, "that your car is parked right outside. It'll get back to Jared, if it hasn't already, and he'll know you were here."

Sofi looked thoughtful. "I can tell him I came here to confront you. To demand that you delete the pictures you took at the festival, and leave us alone."

"You think he'll buy that?" I asked, and Sofi shrugged.

"Do you have anything better?"

Stephen ran a hand through his already messy hair and huffed out an irritated breath.

I nodded toward him. "What's got his panties in a bunch?"

"This is insane," Stephen muttered.

Sofi and I exchanged a glance.

"Which part?" she said.

"Oh, I don't know. Maybe being suspect number one in the disappearance of a teenage girl. Or translating a book of magical spells that actually work. Or maybe having a *dead girl in my apartment*."

"He's not wrong," I said. "That is all actually bat shit crazy."

"You're not helping."

Stephen let out a frustrated groan. "And *this*," he said, gesturing vaguely around the room. "Hearing one half of the conversation. It's...maddening."

Sofi's eyes went wide. "What if you could hear both sides?" she said, and began rummaging through the papers in front of her.

"What do you mean?" Stephen asked warily.

"What if there's a spell?" she said. "Like the one we tried

that let the four of us see each other. What if there's one that would let an outsider see the dead?"

"You mean someone who isn't bonded?" I asked. I didn't know why, but the idea of it felt wrong somehow. I trusted Stephen to help us, but bringing him so deep into our circle —into our secrets—it gave me a chill I couldn't quite shake.

"Exactly," Sofi said. Then, to Stephen, "Have you come across anything like that?"

Stephen shook his head, looking a little dazed at the prospect. "I'm not sure. There were a couple of spells that mentioned second sight. So, it's possible. But...what the hell are we going to do? About the book, I mean. And Jared. And getting you out of here without rent-a-cop getting suspicious?"

"Well, you're right about my car," Sofi said. "Of course, it'll get reported to Jared, and he'll know I was here. But we need to get the book hidden, and finish the translation. I'll take it to my house. We can meet up at Mirtel's tomorrow and get to work."

"And Jared? Do you really think your story will fool him?"

"I'll take care of Jared," Sofi said, sounding confident, though I could see the worry in her eyes.

"Okay then," Stephen said with a sigh. He pulled the armchair closer to the coffee table and began rifling through pages. A few moments later, he pulled a loose sheet out of the stack, running his fingers down the words and mouthing along with them.

"I think...I think this could be it," he said, handing the page to Sofi.

"Gifting the Sight," she read aloud. "Where's the rest?"

"I don't have the other half yet. If Darja could..." He looked expectantly across the room, missing me by a good six feet.

217

"Happy to help," I said flatly. I moved toward Stephen and peered over his shoulder. He was paging through the original manuscript, searching for the spell. He found Sofi's side and flipped the page, revealing three paragraphs of small, tidy scrawl.

It took almost an hour to dictate the page, sounding out unfamiliar words until finally I went letter-by-letter, with Sofi reciting each one for Stephen, who copied it down meticulously on another sheet of paper. He went through each word of both halves of the spell with us, coaching us on pronunciation and translating as he went.

Finally, we were ready to give it a try. I felt a nervous flutter low in my stomach, and wondered if Sofi felt the same. If she did, she gave nothing away. She held onto her page with a firm grip, not so much as a ripple evident in the thin paper.

She recited the words carefully, her voice steady and low. I followed along, and when she finished, I picked up seamlessly with my half of the spell. Unlike Sofi, I could hear the waver in my voice.

When I uttered the last word, we both stared expectantly at Stephen.

"Is it...is it done?" he asked, glancing around the room.

Sofi's face fell. "It didn't work then."

"Maybe we're missing something," he said.

"Like what?" Sofi asked.

"I have no idea." Stephen glanced back at the book. He turned the page to my half of the spell, and I gasped.

Below the writing was a rudimentary drawing I hadn't paid attention to before. Three small dots were positioned as the three points of a triangle. Between them were three straight lines, with an X in the middle of each.

"Sofi," I said, "take Stephen's hand."

She looked at me askance, then sighed. "Darja wants me...wants us to...hold hands."

Stephen's expression was surprised, and I thought his cheeks might have gone ever so slightly red, but he reached over and took Sofi's hand.

"Now, tell him to hold out his other hand."

"Hold out the other one," she said. He dutifully stretched it out, palm up, though I could see by the tight set of his jaw that he was apprehensive. I placed my hand over his, my fingers dissolving like mist where they encountered his skin. I reached out my other hand toward Sofi and she met me halfway, shivering when her fingers passed through mine.

I nodded at her, and she began reciting the spell again. I said my half, more confidently this time, and when I finished, I could feel a warm tingle spreading down my arms and through my fingers. I watched Stephen, whose eyes had gone wide behind his glasses. He looked at his hand, where it was joined with mine, then up to my face, directly into my eyes.

"Holy shit," he breathed.

None of us said anything for a long moment after that. Finally, Sofi huffed out a soft laugh.

"Stephen," she said, "I'd like you to meet Darja. My sister."

CHAPTER 25

SOFI

The sun was just beginning to set as I made my way through the atrium of the municipal building and into the police station.

It had been nearly a week since Darja and I had left Stephen's apartment, sneaking the book past the lookout in a borrowed backpack and hoping I looked more casual than I felt.

We'd gotten the book back to Mirtel's and filled her and Aggie in on everything that had happened. Stephen had showed up the next day, wearing a hooded sweatshirt and sunglasses that I'd pointed out made him even more visible to anyone watching, but he'd informed me proudly that while the beige car had followed him when he'd left his apartment, he'd "lost the guy" on the way. I'd wondered if Stephen even realized that this wasn't some thriller action movie, and how much was really at stake here, for all of us.

He and Mirtel had quickly gotten down to business, and with help from Aggie and Darja, slowly but surely, the translation progressed.

In the meantime, my mother had mentioned in passing that she hadn't seen me much lately, and asked what I'd been up to this summer, and I found myself spending more time hanging around the house so my parents wouldn't get suspicious. Darja split her time between me and the others, and the discomfort I felt while seated at the dining room table, trying to make conversation over dinner with Darja's still form hovering in the corner or pacing behind my chair, was almost more than I could handle. And it wasn't just her; I barely knew how to be in the same room as my father anymore. Every time I saw his face, all I could think of was Darja's mother. Had she looked like Darja? Did my mother know? What on earth would my father think if he knew what was really going on? What kind of a person was he really? Did I even know him at all?

It was enough to tie my stomach in knots.

After nearly a week of this, I figured I had played the role of dutiful daughter enough, and fled the house. Jared had sent me a text earlier that day asking me to drop by the station, and it'd seemed like the perfect opportunity to get away, both from my parents and from the mass of bodies packed into Mirtel's tiny wagon. Plus I needed to speak to him anyway, to figure out a way to draw attention away from Stephen. The translation was too important to risk falling into the wrong hands.

Jared was waiting for me in his dad's office, files stacked on the desk and the computer open in front of him.

"Sofi, hey," he greeted me, gesturing to the open chair. His smile was genuine, and it put me at ease. I knew we had to be careful around Jared, especially with the ongoing investigation, but I genuinely *liked* the guy, and it was nice to spend a few minutes with someone who wasn't really part of this whole mess my life had become. Being with Jared was easy, and he seemed to be one of the only people I knew who wasn't harboring any deep, life-changing secrets.

I smiled wryly to myself as I took a seat across the desk. Ah, how I missed that life.

"What's got you smiling today?" he asked, his eyes warm.

"Oh, nothing, things are just a bit crazy at home and it's nice to get out of the house for a bit. It's really good to see you."

He nodded. "It's been a few days. Look, Sofi, I asked you to come because I wanted to talk to you about something."

I knew what was coming, but I let him ask anyway.

"We're still following all the leads we can on this case, you know, the missing girl?"

I nodded. "Darja, right? Do you have any suspects yet?"

He looked down at the desk. "No real suspects, but some leads. I'm still looking into them. Anyway, I wanted to ask you about Stephen."

There it was. I kept waiting.

He paused, then finally met my eyes. "I know you went to see him. You've been at Mirtel's, and now at Stephen's too. I'm worried about you."

I wondered if he really *was* simply worried about me, or if he suspected something. But judging by his open, earnest face, I was pretty sure it was the former. I found the thought strangely flattering.

I felt the faint beginnings of a blush, but I forced myself back on task.

I nodded. "Yes, I went there. I'm sorry. I know I should stay out of it, but I was worried. And I thought maybe... maybe I could help you."

His brows shot up.

"I thought maybe he would tell me something," I went on. "Something he might not be willing to tell you."

"And?" Jared leaned in.

I shook my head. "He says he's studying the Vaikesti for a school project." Well, at least that much was true. "He'd never even heard of the missing girl, and despite the pictures, he really doesn't seem to know very much about us."

Jared's expression was concerned. "Sofi, you really shouldn't have gone out there. What if he really had been part of it? He could have hurt you."

"I know. I'm sorry," I said in a quiet voice. "I just hate all this...mystery and secrecy. And I'm worried about that girl. If she's hurt, and I could have helped..."

I hated lying to him, but it seemed a necessary evil these days.

Jared's face softened. "Sofi, that's what the police are here for. You can't take it on yourself. Leave it to me, and I promise, we'll find out what happened to her."

I wondered what he would say if I told him the missing girl in question was in fact dead, but was also hanging out back at Mirtel's house with his two main suspects and another dead girl. I couldn't imagine it would go over well.

I sighed. "I know. I'm sorry. I'll stay out of it."

He reached across the desk and took my hand, and my pulse leaped at the contact. "Trust me. We'll figure it all out. Just keep yourself safe, okay?"

I nodded, and he released my hand. I felt a little rush of disappointment.

"Sofi," Jared said, and I glanced up, catching a different note in his voice.

"When all this is over, would you...maybe want to go out sometime?"

The disappointment vanished as my heartbeat sped up, a warm flush spreading across my face. "Out?"

He nodded. "Yeah. I like you, Sofi. I'd like to spend some more time with you."

I hesitated. We had grown up together, and I knew his parents as he knew mine, but he wasn't actually part of Vaikesti. My parents would flip at that, and though their opinions were growing less and less important to me day by day, I didn't know if I was ready for yet another break in tradition. And tradition aside, when this was all over, whatever *this* even was, I would still be bonded to an invisible dead girl, and know more about life and death and murder and betrayal than any girl my age should ever have to deal with.

But Jared looked at me with clear eyes and a hopeful expression, and I forced myself to forget about everything that had happened since the first of May, pretend that I was still that naive girl I'd been. And damn it, didn't I still deserve a little happiness? A bit of normalcy? A date with a cute guy, was that so freaking much to ask for?

So I smiled back at him, and said, "Yes, I'd really like that." And when he reached across the desk and took my hand again, I squeezed his and smiled like a lunatic and felt *normal* for the first time in what seemed like forever.

Until with the barest change in air pressure that only I noticed, Darja flickered into existence at my side and said, "Sofi, we need you. The translation is finished."

CHAPTER 26

DARJA

It was stifling in Mirtel's wagon. Granted, in my current body-less state, I couldn't really feel heat or cold, but I could certainly feel the stuffy, tense, too-close-for-comfort claustrophobia that permeated the tiny space.

We were all there, the living and the...not-so-alive...and after a week spent poring over unfamiliar words, mystifying and primitive illustrations, and maddening pronunciations, we were all on-edge. Sofi had been absent for much of the drudgery, a fact I both resented and envied. I knew she was struggling to balance it all without arousing her family's suspicions, or leading Jared straight to us, but she also had the option to turn off all the noise, to sleep in a warm, comfy bed, to get in her car and drive away, to shut her door and tune out the world.

I didn't have that, not anymore. I felt as worn out as I ever had in my entire life, but apparently, in the afterlife, the sweet relief of unconsciousness no longer existed. And even though I could flicker out when I felt like it, I still wasn't sure I actually *went* anywhere—it was more like the sudden absence of existing, and it left me feeling unsettled every time. Besides, though I could flit and flutter between Mirtel's and Sofi's, if I got much further away from my erstwhile sister, the bond would begin to tug at me, pulling me toward her whether I liked it or not. I was tethered to her, and while I had grown to care for her more than any other person I'd known in life, I still couldn't reconcile myself to the idea of spending eternity bound to another soul, especially when neither of us had had a say in the matter.

"Trying to escape out the back?"

I jumped at the sound of the voice, low and lightly teasing, and then tried to cover it with a smile. I had hidden away in Mirtel's bedroom, which was really more of an exceptionally well-padded closet, leaving the others to argue over the pronunciation of the word *ülestõusenud*, or something equally incomprehensible. I'd been so lost in my thoughts that I hadn't noticed Stephen pop his head in, his glasses perpetually askew, his hair standing on end. He looked like a mad scientist who hadn't slept in a week—an assessment I thought wasn't too far off the mark. A mad linguist, perhaps.

"Hey," I said, nodding for him to sit down on the bed. "How's it coming?"

Stephen shrugged, then tried to stifle a yawn. "Mirtel and Aggie are arguing over which spells are safe to try out, and Sofi's trying to keep the peace. And failing," he added, with a crooked smile. He was really quite charming, I thought, in a nerdy sort of way. And he seemed to genuinely want to help us. I couldn't really see why Sofi was still so wary of him.

"It seemed like a fight was brewing," I said in agreement. "That's why I decided to retreat."

Stephen laughed. "Smart move."

We sat in comfortable silence for a few moments, then I

noticed he was looking at me with a shrewd sort of intensity.

"What is it?" I asked.

"I just keep wondering," he said, narrowing his eyes and scrutinizing me until I wanted to squirm away from his gaze. "What's it like?"

"What's *what* like?"

"Being dead." His words were blunt, but his voice was gentle.

I shook my head. "It's not like anything, really. Or maybe it's like nothing. Does that make sense?" I didn't wait for an answer. "Like, I don't eat or sleep. I don't walk or run. I don't get sleepy, but I feel worn out. I feel sad, but I don't cry. At least, not like a *real* person—"

"You *are* a real person," Stephen said emphatically, and I smiled.

"Am I?"

"You are. Just a...recently deceased one."

I laughed. "Okay, I'll take that."

Stephen was watching me keenly once again. "Are there..." He faltered. "Are there...others?"

"Other dead people?"

He nodded. "Yeah. I mean, like, do you see other ghosts?"

"Just Aggie."

"Why just her?"

I shrugged. "I have no idea. I can feel, sometimes, that there's something...else...out there. Something...more."

"You mean, more in the afterlife?"

"Maybe? I don't know. Just, sometimes, I can feel this...sensation. Like there's something all around me. And I can hear...voices. Not words, just muffled voices."

Stephen grimaced. "Sounds like a horror movie."

"Well, it's weird, but it's not scary," I said. "More than

anything, it just makes me feel...sad, I guess. Like I'm not where I'm supposed to be."

"Like you're stuck." It wasn't a question, but I nodded anyway.

"Exactly."

"Does Aggie feel stuck, too?"

"Why do you think she's always so pissed off?"

Stephen laughed, then grew serious again. "Is that why you want this translation? Do you think you'll find something that will help you cross over?"

I couldn't help but scoff. "Cross over? Like, go into the light?"

"Okay, maybe not exactly like that. But, yeah. Release your spirit, or whatever. Yours and Aggie's."

I felt a little pang at that. I didn't know what it would mean, to move on to whatever came after this. I knew it wasn't supposed to be like this—this in-between, uncertain monotony—this nothingness. And yet, this weird sort of fugue state had brought me my sister. It had brought me Aggie. Could I give them up—to be free?

"Sorry," Stephen said suddenly, apparently reading my stricken face. "Didn't mean to cause an existential crisis."

I laughed shortly. "No, that would be the fault of the assholes who murdered me."

I had said it lightly, but Stephen looked pained. "I'm really sorry," he said. "About what happened to you."

I nodded my thanks. "That's what I want," I said. "Justice. I want these creeps exposed, and this stupid ritual stopped for good. I don't want any other girls to die, and I'm so tired of all the secrets. Secret ceremonies. Secret spells. Secret magic. All for what?"

"And this... secret magic?" he said. "I mean, it's real. So what does that mean? The ritual worked, but..."

"But that doesn't mean it's worth someone's life," I said,

and Stephen nodded. "I want us to learn everything we can about it. That's why we're here. Why *you're* here. I want to know what it is, where it comes from, and why it requires human sacrifice. And then I want to shut it down."

"How?"

"Who the hell knows? But I'm not going 'into the light' until I do."

He laughed. We sat in companionable silence for another moment, and then I noticed a shadow cross the doorway. I looked up and saw Sofi standing in the doorframe, an uncertain expression on her face.

"Hey," she said, and I wondered how much she'd overheard. It wasn't anything she didn't already know, but still, her stricken face made me think she'd seen a boogieman. Or, more accurately, a ghost.

"Umm, Mirtel and Aggie are ready to try a few spells," she said, forcing a smile. "They're outside."

"Well, we probably shouldn't leave them alone with a book of magic spells for too long," Stephen said, standing up and squeezing past Sofi. She shrank back as he moved around her, careful not to let him touch her. I felt an eye roll coming on, but tried to control the impulse.

"You coming?" she said, eyeing me cautiously.

"Wouldn't miss it," I said, and she smiled, but it didn't reach her eyes.

———

Mirtel and Aggie were setting up around the backside of the wagon. Near the river's edge, there was an ornate cast iron bench that apparently had a colorful history...literally. Layers of paint had been chipped and worn away, revealing many past lives—turquoise, chartreuse, bubblegum pink— and though it had obviously been intended to be mostly white, it took on a bit of a tie-dyed effect. Mirtel sat on the bench, her mismatched, jewel tone clothing adding to the craziness, making it hard to look directly at her.

In front of the bench were upturned produce crates. I'd seen them before, back when I'd only known Mirtel as the Egg Lady—she'd always had them stacked with cartons of eggs whenever she came by the *koolis*.

Stephen had taken up a seat on one of the crates, and was busy shuffling through a stack of yellow pages torn from the numerous legal pads we had been using for the translation. Aggie hovered nearby, looking miffed, and I assumed that meant whatever she'd been arguing against, she'd gotten overruled. The diffused sunlight of late afternoon filtered over and through her, casting her in warm gold. God, she was stunning.

Our eyes met, and she scowled. I grinned back, lifting my eyebrows suggestively. She turned her back to me, but not before I saw a half-smile tilt the corner of her mouth.

I wanted to say, *You're so into me,* but even if we'd been alone, I wouldn't have dared. Truth was, I was pretty into her, too, and I didn't know what that meant—two dead girls falling for each other—but it sent my stomach swirling and my palms itching and my heart pounding (metaphorically), and honestly, I didn't hate it. I hadn't felt that way since— well, I couldn't remember ever feeling that way.

I continued staring unabashedly at her until she gave me a *look* over her shoulder, then nodded toward the others. I didn't care, but maybe she did, being from a different time and all. In any case, I turned my attention toward the crate that sat in front of Mirtel. There was a piece of green velvet fabric, frayed at the edges, draped over the top, and on it, a small pile of dirt. I cast a questioning glance over at Sofi, but she made an inscrutable face and went to stand next to Mirtel.

"Ah, Sofi," Mirtel said, a soft smile stretching her wrinkled cheeks. "You have it, then?"

Sofi nodded. "I do. I'm not sure it's right, but—"

Mirtel waved a hand dismissively. "We'll soon know either way, dear. Now, everyone come a bit closer."

I had no idea what was about to happen, but I did as Mirtel asked, moving to Stephen's other side. Aggie was next to Mirtel, and Sofi between us, so we formed a sort of circle around the crate.

Stephen cleared his throat. "Right. So, here's what we've got. Mirtel and Aggie have been practicing the pronunciation on this one, so we'll let them try the spell." He handed a sheet of paper to Mirtel, who held it out so Aggie could see.

Mirtel gave Sofi a nod, and I saw her dig into her pocket and pull out something small and gray. She cradled it gently in her palm, then stepped toward the crate and lowered herself to her knees. Carefully, she placed the small object on top of the pile of soil. I leaned in to get a closer look. It was a seedling, shriveled and wilted, its scraggly roots pitifully twisted. It was a sad little thing, misshapen and pathetic, and I felt something inside me clench, knowing it would never grow—never put down roots, never unfurl new leaves, never drink deep after a spring rain or bloom under the summer sun.

I swallowed hard, unprepared for the surge of emotion this little plant had caused. While I pulled myself together, Mirtel started reading, her words stilted and unsure. Aggie took over when it was her turn, her voice like a poem.

When she said the last word, she looked at Mirtel, then down at the plant. We all followed her gaze, waiting for something to happen.

Nothing did. We sat in expectant silence, none of us wanting to be the first to speak—the first to call it a failure. Mirtel's face was crestfallen, and it hurt me to see it. Sofi was clenching her jaw so hard I could see a vein pulsing at her temple. Maybe magic wasn't so real, after all.

Disappointed, I turned back toward the wagon. That was when I heard the gasp. I wasn't sure if it was Sofi or Aggie, but I whirled around when I heard it, my eyes immediately going to the shriveled up little seedling.

Except it wasn't so shriveled anymore. Before my eyes, the seedling started to change. Slowly, the gray, ashy color faded, replaced by a light wash of green that crept up the length of the stem. The roots stretched and curled, turning white and plump, questing like a child's fingers against the dirt below. We stood, frozen in place, as the sprout began to uncurl, stretching upward and spreading out two perfect, jewel green leaves.

None of us were breathing—living or dead. Nobody said a word. Tears shimmered in Sofi's eyes, and even Aggie looked moved, her lower lip trembling as she stared at the tiny, tenacious little plant.

Nobody seemed to want to break the spell—not the one we had cast on the sprout, but the one that had fallen over all of us. Sofi and Stephen sat back down on the overturned crates, and Aggie moved closer to Mirtel. We watched the newly sprouted leaves wave gently in the breeze, and as it seemed to stretch even closer to the sky, I felt something opening up inside—bursting forth to seek out the light.

It felt a lot like hope.

CHAPTER 27

SOFI

In the week that followed, the mood inside Mirtel's wagon shifted from a sort of heavy anticipatory tension to what one could almost call optimism. It was the most I'd felt like myself since before my Spring Day Ceremony.

No one seemed more excited than Mirtel, however. With the magical regrowth of the dying seedling—and none of us seemed to want to spend too much time considering the implications of *that*—she seemed almost invigorated, flipping excitedly through the book in search of other spells for us to try.

And to all of our collective amazement, they *worked.* They all worked.

We coaxed seedlings to grow; we levitated small household objects; we caused a flurry of snowflakes to fall from the late spring sky over the brightly painted roof of Mirtel's wagon.

It was amazing, unlike anything I'd ever even imagined might be possible, and I threw myself into the spells with a feeling of mingled awe and relief, like we finally might have found the answer to all of our problems, even if we didn't quite know what that answer might be, or even exactly what problem we were trying to solve.

Surprisingly, only Mirtel seemed as completely smitten with our newfound power as I was. Aggie was her usual skeptical self, and I could hear her arguing with Mirtel through the wagon's thin walls as I stepped outside to feed the chickens. I wondered idly if she even had the capacity for happiness after so many years stuck in limbo, and the thought sobered me.

Darja seemed cautious, overly so in my opinion. I understood her hesitation; I could see as well as the others that we were dealing with things we didn't fully understand, things that were bigger than us and likely had ramifications we didn't fully grasp. I understood that magic was *dangerous,* as she kept unhelpfully pointing out. But as much as I tried to reason with her, it was like the awe she had felt in the beginning had shifted to trepidation. We could conjure snow out of thin air, for crying out loud. I found it hard to focus on the negatives when faced with something so wondrous.

It was Stephen, however, that surprised me the most. As the days passed and we got further through the book of spells, he grew progressively quieter and more withdrawn. It was like the boy who had been so excited to work on the translation, to be a part of whatever this was, had ceased to exist, leaving behind someone who was clearly fighting some internal battle I didn't understand. But instead of making me suspicious of him, as I had been before, I found myself worried. He wasn't cautionary like Darja, or skeptical like Aggie, he was just...troubled. Like the magic was personal to him somehow.

I'd been feeling somewhat closer to him after the

morning spent at his apartment, but I still didn't really know him at all.

Thanks to either the presence of our bond, or perhaps her own powers of observation, I wasn't the only one who had noticed something was bothering Stephen.

"Take him with you," Darja said to me in a low voice.

It was late afternoon on a Tuesday, and my parents had once again begun to comment on how little time I'd been spending at the house recently. Coupled with the fact that it was my niece, Mia's sixth birthday, and I didn't have an excuse to miss the party.

"I can't take him with me to a family birthday party," I stage-whispered back to her. "He's not supposed to be in Vaikesti. Remember the arrest? Besides, he's still a suspect."

"He's not supposed to be taking pictures at festivals," she countered. "It's not illegal for you to invite him to a birthday party. Besides, you can just leave him in the car; you're not going to stay long anyway." She cast a meaningful glance at me. "And you need to talk to him. Find out what's going on."

I sighed, but didn't argue. She was right, anyway. After my visit to his apartment, Stephen and I seemed to have called an unspoken truce. I wasn't sure what his problem was, but I at least had to admit he probably wasn't up to anything nefarious after all.

To my surprise, he agreed to come with me without much convincing. He was quiet in the car though, no sign of the slew of personal questions about my family that I'd expected, and finally I glanced over to where he was staring listlessly out the passenger's window.

I jumped right in.

"So, what's going on with you?"

He blinked over at me, seeming a little surprised to be pulled out of his thoughts. "What do you mean?"

I sighed impatiently. "Clearly there's something wrong.

Ever since we started trying out the spells, you've been..." I waved my hand vaguely in the air. "...weird."

I'd expected him to blow me off, to roll his eyes and look back out the window, but he surprised me by tipping his head against the headrest and blowing out a breath.

"I know. I guess...it's just a lot, you know? To take in."

I couldn't argue with him there. With all this magic dumped in his lap, I imagined he must be feeling similar to the way I had after my Spring Day Ceremony.

He went on. "I just never expected it to be...*real.*"

We were both silent for a moment, then he tilted his head toward me.

"Do you ever wonder...how your life might be different if you'd known from the beginning?"

I raised an eyebrow. "What do you mean?"

He glanced away. "If magic had always been part of your life...would you have done things differently? Would you..."

I wasn't sure what he was getting at.

"Well, I sure wouldn't have participated in the Ceremony," I joked, trying to lighten the mood, but he didn't answer. "Honestly though," I went on, "how could you know what choices you'd make under different circumstances? If magic had always been a normal, everyday part of my life, we probably wouldn't all be in the situation we're in now, right?"

His voice was quiet as he stared through the windshield. "But would that be better or worse? If power like that was normalized, would we use it responsibly, because we knew the cost? Or would we all be doing terrible things because we'd been raised that way?"

I wasn't sure he was even still talking to me, and not himself.

He turned to me again, and the expression on his face

surprised me. It was almost pleading, his tortured eyes wide as they connected briefly with mine.

"What am I missing?" I asked. I'd been on autopilot through the drive, and I realized we'd turned onto my street. I pulled into the driveway and cut the engine, turning in my seat to face him fully.

"Is it worth it?" he asked.

"Is what worth it?"

"You said you wouldn't have participated in the Ceremony if you'd known. Is that true? If you'd known what was going to happen, if everyone had known the bond was going to work, would you have done it?"

I felt cold. When I'd said that, I'd assumed if the community knew the magic was real, they never would be sacrificing girls, but I suddenly realized how ridiculous that was. They were sacrificing girls based on the mere *chance* the magic might work. If they knew it really did, they would...well. Who knew what they might be capable of?

I didn't answer Stephen's question, but I didn't need to. It was clear he could see the answer in my face.

"What are people willing to do for power like that?" he asked me, and I knew he wasn't looking for a response. His voice dropped even lower, so quiet I could barely hear it. "What would *I* have done?"

I felt it again, that certainty that I was missing something, and I opened my mouth to ask again, but just then the front door opened and my mother poked her head out of the house. She smiled when she saw me and called out with a wave.

"I thought I heard a car. What are you waiting for, *kallike,* come in."

I waved back and gestured that I'd be right in, but when I turned to Stephen once again the tortured expression was gone, replaced by his normal calm.

That wasn't the end of it though. I needed to know what was bothering him, what his cryptic comments meant. I made a mental note to bring it up again later, and if I didn't get anywhere, maybe Darja could try.

I unbuckled my seatbelt and reached for the door handle, then hesitated. "Do you want to come in?" I asked.

It was probably a bad idea. After all, the last time my family had seen Stephen, it was at the Spring Day festival, camera in hand, where he'd caused a scene and managed to get himself arrested. Not to mention he was still a suspect in Darja's disappearance. But Darja was right. It wasn't illegal to invite him to my house. Besides, he hadn't actually done anything illegal in the first place.

"Don't you want me to wait in the car?" he asked, seeming to read the hesitation on my face. "I don't want to cause trouble with your dad..."

My lip curled at the mention of my father. "I don't care what *he* says. You're *my* friend, and you can come if *I* say you can."

"Okay," he started to reply, but I was already climbing out of the car and stomping toward the house. Just let my dad *try* to say something.

Inside the house, Stephen's wide eyes scanned the foyer, taking in family pictures, the hand-lettered sign above the door that read, "Õnnista seda kodu," the dried bouquet of blue cornflowers that sat on the small table by the entry. I could practically see him mentally cataloguing everything and filing it away, and I felt a surprising sense of relief that he seemed to be acting like himself again.

Laughter and voices were coming from the kitchen, and I made my way there, beckoning for him to follow. Rounding the corner, I was immediately surrounded by the noise and bustle of family, but for the first time I felt removed, like I didn't fully belong there anymore, and a swell of sadness filled my chest. I missed Darja. This was her family just as much as it was mine.

My sisters Hanna and Arina were gathered around the kitchen island with my mom, voices raised in good-natured argument. On the floor, Hanna's son, two-year-old Marten, scooted by, in hot pursuit of my poor cat, Sprat, who darted around the corner and out of sight. One of my aunts was carrying a platter piled high with food out toward the dining room, and I could hear the shrill voice of another aunt coming from the living room, where the deep baritones of my uncles and brothers rumbled in laughter.

I stood awkwardly in the doorway until my sisters glanced up.

"Sofi. Finally. I haven't seen you in weeks," Hanna chastised, coming around the island to grip me in a hug. "Where have you—who's this?" she asked, catching sight of Stephen. Her voice wasn't judgmental, merely curious, but I caught Arina exchanging a glance with my mother.

It wasn't like I couldn't bring a friend to a family gathering—I'd brought friends over plenty of times before, as had my sisters, and there was never any shortage of food, not in a Vaikesti house. But there was no way they didn't all remember him from the Spring Day festival. I'd known it would be awkward, but I'd assumed they wouldn't make a scene. Had I misjudged them?

I held my breath, but to my immense relief, my mom simply wiped her hands on her apron and crossed the room to shake his hand. "Yelena Ilves," she said, smiling pleasantly as Stephen introduced himself, then simply asked, "Will you be staying for dinner?"

I blew out my breath and sent Stephen an encouraging smile, relieved that there wouldn't be any trouble after all.

I was wrong, of course.

The trouble came about half an hour later, when we

were all filing into the dining room, where all the extra leaves had been added to the table, chairs wedged in at every angle to accommodate my unwieldy family. Up until then, I'd spent the time catching up with my sisters, then showed Stephen my room, which he'd taken in with shy curiosity, and we'd managed to avoid my father, who'd stayed cloistered in the living room with my uncles and brothers.

I should have known the trouble would come from him.

He entered the room last, and the second he caught sight of us he went completely still. "What are *you* doing here?" His voice echoed through the room, suddenly quiet save for the giggles of the oblivious children.

I stiffened, anger flushing my cheeks at my father's tone.

Stephen, to his credit, mustered a smile, and held out his hand. "I'm Stephen Jennings, a friend of your daughter," he introduced himself.

My dad made no move to cross the room to take his hand. "Like hell you are," he snapped, his gaze flying to me. My jaw set. How dare he speak to my friend like that, after all he'd done? If he knew what I knew—

"What were you *thinking,* Sofia," my father demanded, "bringing an outsider into my house?"

His house? It was *my* house too, as much as it may no longer feel that way. I opened my mouth to retort, but he cut me off, turning his attention back to Stephen.

"You are not welcome here." His voice cracked like a whip. "In fact, you are not welcome in this community, and you are *certainly* not welcome with my daughter. You may leave now."

With that, he pulled out his chair and sat, clearly considering the discussion to be over. I opened my mouth again, ready to let the vitriol inside me fly out, when suddenly I heard my mother give a muffled cough, and the words died on my lips.

I glanced over at her, to where she was staring down at her lap, red staining her cheeks, clearly uncomfortable with my father's outburst. My eyes jumped involuntarily to my sister Hanna, sitting on my mother's right, the person I would have considered my biggest ally. She, too, was looking away, not meeting my eyes. My gaze did a circuit of the table, taking in all the faces: my aunts, uncles, brothers, nieces and nephews, even my grandmother, her tiny body wedged in between my aunts. Not one of them spoke up, not one of them would even meet my eye, and suddenly shame and embarrassment flooded through me, hot and bitter. I never should have brought him here. I knew better, and all I was doing was ruining Mia's birthday party.

My father glanced up at me again, and his face was even and smooth. "Sofi, *kallike*, are you staying or going?"

It was the endearment that did it. Proof of his absolute certainty that his word was law, and I would never disobey him. That I was a good daughter, who had simply made a poor choice, and of course I would show Stephen out, and never see him again, and it was my choice if I wanted to return to the table or not. My heart thudded down into my feet as I realized he was right. I would obey.

Besides, it was better this way. Better not to make a scene, not to upset the children.

"I'm sorry, father. I'll go." I crossed the room and bent to kiss my mother on the cheek. "I'll see you soon, Mama."

I turned, and felt the eyes of the whole room on my back as I headed to the door, Stephen hot on my heels.

I could feel him behind me, vibrating with tension, but he waited until we were safely in the car and pulling out onto the street before he rounded on me.

"What the hell was *that*?"

The uncharacteristic anger in his voice startled me and I glanced over, surprised.

"What?"

"'I don't care what *he* says. You're *my* friend, and you can come if *I* say you can,'" he quoted my own words back at me. "How could you let him talk to you like that?"

"It was better that way; I didn't want to make a scene," I argued, feeling somewhat taken aback, but he scoffed.

"So it's better to do what he says? Let him believe he's right?"

The heat rose in my cheeks. "What was I supposed to do?" I demanded, glancing over at him. "Who cares if he thinks he's right?"

He looked away, but the frustration was still clear in his tight voice. "I just didn't expect you to act like that."

"Like what?" I said, my own frustration rising. Just when I thought he was getting back to normal, here he was again, acting weird.

"Like you're still..."

"Still what?"

He threw up his hands. "Still part of a cult." He turned to face me, his auburn hair falling into his eyes. "I thought you had changed, that you weren't part of this any more. I thought..." His voice dropped, the anger falling away. "... maybe you'd understand."

We'd come full circle, I realized, and this was part of the same conversation we'd started in the car on the way over.

"Stephen," I said, trying to keep my voice even as I turned out of the neighborhood and headed back toward Mirtel's. "Understand what? What aren't you telling me?"

He looked at me, emotion brimming in his eyes, but he didn't speak for a long moment. I gave him space, trying to pay attention to the road in front of me, and waited. I had trusted him with my biggest secrets, sought him out when I needed to tell someone about my dad. I wasn't sure when our dynamic had shifted, when I'd stopped viewing him with suspicion and he'd stopped thinking of me as something to study, but I hoped he knew that if he needed someone to talk to, he could trust me.

Finally he spoke, his voice coming out in a whisper. "I've...done things in my life that I'm not proud of. I found out what happens when someone thinks they're acting for the greater good, and chooses how they want to define what is right and wrong. I..." he paused, looking frustrated. "I don't know how to explain."

"Start at the beginning?" I suggested.

His glasses slipped down his nose, and he pushed them up impatiently. "Sofi, you're not the only one who has experience with cults."

My eyes grew round. "You were in a cult?" I still didn't like the word, didn't like it applied to myself and my friends and family, but I had to admit, I could see his point.

"Not exactly. But I know what it's like to have people tell you you're doing the right thing, and for you to believe it, when you're not doing the right thing at all. I know what it's like to hurt people, because you think you're supposed to. And I don't want to see you fall back into that world."

I pulled into the dirt yard behind Mirtel's wagon and shut the car off, turning again to face him.

"Please, Stephen. Stop being cryptic. Talk to me; tell me what happened."

He opened his mouth, but then both of us jerked in surprise when Darja flickered into existence, her body forming in the passenger's seat, right on top of where Stephen was leaning toward me. Her transparent arm disappeared inside of his solid one, and he flinched, even though he couldn't have felt anything.

"Shit," she exclaimed, "I forgot you'd be sitting there."

But before she had a chance to move he'd leapt back, flinging open the door and bolting out of the car.

"Wait," I called after him, but he only paused long enough to shoot me a look I couldn't interpret. Then he was climbing into his own car, parked just a little ways up the path, and backing out toward the street.

Darja and I both turned in our seats, watching him go.

CHAPTER 28

DARJA

The pale purple crocus hung in midair, its petals drooping heavy and pendulous, bending its thin stem nearly in half. I watched as it floated, spinning lazily in the breeze as it bobbed closer to the river's edge. It hovered for a moment, suspended in all its springtime glory, before hurtling into the water, swiftly carried away by the current.

"What did that poor flower ever do to you?" I asked, casting a sidelong glance at Aggie. She ignored me, reaching out her hand and pantomiming the motions of picking a flower. Another crocus, this one pure snowy white, lifted out of the earth near the river bank, bits of soil scattering beneath it. Aggie moved her fingers gracefully, and I watched as the flower bent and spun and whirled at her whim. She ushered it slowly toward the water, twirling it with one finger, tumbling it over and over itself before twisting her wrist violently, splaying her fingers and casting it beneath the river's surface. She'd been playing with this spell in particular since we'd cast it earlier in the morning, and I could see a wistful sort of expression on her face when she cupped her hand to lift a teacup, or stretched it out to smooth a rumpled blanket. And I understood; it was the nearest she could get to touching something. That was why she didn't end the spell, but kept the magic flowing through her, like a fountain—like that stream of energy made her feel a little bit more alive.

I cleared my throat. "Anything you need to talk about?"

She shot me a look, and I gathered the answer was no.

It had been like this for a week—experimenting with spells, testing the boundaries of our newfound powers, and learning about all the magic we'd never noticed in the world. It seemed to vibrate in the very air around us, humming with an energy that felt both thrilling and unsettling. I wasn't sure if it was the whole *being dead* thing, but Aggie and I were noticeably standoffish when it came to testing out new spells. Sure, it didn't take too much coercion to get us to participate, but we did so almost grudgingly. I figured that was just Aggie's personality, but as for my own hesitance…I didn't really understand it. I was fascinated by the magic, and I felt a flutter low in my belly every time a new spell worked. And yet…

"Mirtel has taken to the magic," Aggie said suddenly, and I looked over at her, surprised. She'd left the poor crocuses in peace, but I could see her fingers still moving minutely at her side, almost as if she were caressing the tips of the petals.

"Sofi, too," I said quietly. "It must be exciting for them. To know that it really exists."

"It exists because we died," she said sharply, and I winced.

"I don't think our deaths brought the magic into being," I said carefully.

"No, but we wouldn't be able to use it otherwise," she said.

I couldn't argue that.

"Are you worried about it?"

"Of course I'm worried about it," she snapped. "Anything that requires a sacrifice—anything that calls for blood—cannot be totally benign. And yet, here we are, squealing and giggling over these spells like little girls."

"But nothing bad has happened," I said, though I wondered who I was trying to convince.

"Yet."

I nodded. "Yet."

"I'm worried that Mirtel is...too caught up in it. Too deep into the magic. She's forgetting about why we're here—why we're doing any of this."

I laughed, but there wasn't much humor in it. "Why *are* we doing this?" I wondered. "Levitating flowers and changing the weather? It just seems so..."

"Pointless?" Aggie suggested.

"In a way. I just wanted to know *why*. Why kill these girls, year after year? Why go so far to get nothing in return? And why *us*?"

Aggie said nothing, but I could see the years of pain etched into her face, clouding her eyes.

"What else is out there?" I went on, gathering steam. "This isn't living, but it isn't dying, either. This isn't what being dead is supposed to be."

Aggie looked at me then, and for a moment, it felt that time, as I knew it, had come to a stop.

"Isn't it?" she asked quietly.

"No," I said, then again, firmly, "*No.*"

She smiled then, just a little, and that same clenching feeling released a bit. She opened her mouth to speak, but then I heard the bang of the wagon door, and footsteps thudding gently down the front steps.

"Hey, you two," Sofi said as she popped around the backside of the wagon. "What's going on out here?"

I shook my head. "Just...practicing," I said vaguely, waving my arm toward the vandalized bed of crocuses.

Sofi smiled, and even though I was worried, it was good to see her sunny expression. She'd been acting a little off this week, and I couldn't quite pinpoint why. When I'd asked, she'd said she was just tired.

"We've got another one," she said, grinning like a kid in a candy store.

I looked over to Aggie, whose expression was carefully schooled and calm.

"Another what?" I asked.

"Another spell. It's from further back in the book, so we think that might mean it's more advanced." She looked around, as if we might be overheard, then ducked her head and whispered conspiratorially, "It's a good one."

I returned her smile, though it didn't feel genuine, and started to follow her back to the wagon. Before we'd gotten around the house, Stephen's car rumbled up the dirt drive. Sofi froze, and I could see the muscles in her back tense.

We waited there while he put the car in park, shut it off and got out, waving congenially.

"Hey, everyone," he said. He smiled at me and Aggie, but when he got to Sofi, it faltered.

"Hi," I said, glancing back and forth between the two of them. Sofi wasn't making eye contact, and Stephen just looked worried. Sofi had filled me in on what had happened at her house, and it seemed the awkwardness of the failed dinner was still hanging like a cloud over both of them. I gave Stephen a smile, and I could see a little bit of the strain ease from his expression. "Uh...how's it going?"

"Good, good," Stephen said, shutting his door and leaning against the car. "Just thought I'd stop by and see how you've all been." His eyes lingered a little too long on Sofi as he said this, and I was pretty sure he wasn't that concerned with *all* of us.

He hadn't been around much this last week, come to think of it, and when he had, Sofi had conveniently had very pressing errands to run, or appearances to make with her family.

"Well, you're just in time," I said with false cheerfulness. "Sofi has a new spell for us to try, and—"

A sharp glance from Sofi shut me up quickly. I snapped my mouth shut and tried to keep the smile plastered across my face. Sofi rolled her eyes, then finally looked over to Stephen.

"Mirtel's inside," she said shortly. "If you want to—"

She was cut off by the shrill ring of a cell phone, sharp and too-loud in the still spring air.

"Sorry," Stephen muttered, going a little red in the cheeks. He dug his phone out of his pocket and glanced at the caller ID, frowning. "Sorry," he said again, "I just need to..." He gestured with the phone and then swiped to answer it.

"Hey," he said, turning away from us, but still leaning against the car. He was trying to appear casual, but I could see that he was trying too hard.

"Yeah," he went on, "yeah, thanks for—what? When? Are you sure?"

Sofi, Aggie and I all exchanged a skeptical look. I could see Stephen's shoulders stiffen, and the way the backs of his ears went suddenly red. Something was up.

"Where the hell *were* you?" he hissed into the phone. "You said—yeah, I know. But...did they take anything?"

We all waited for the answer, not really understanding the question.

"*Shit,*" Stephen yelled, and we all jumped. "No, forget it,

249

just...just...forget it." He hung up the phone and slammed his other hand hard against the side of his car.

He turned around slowly, not meeting any of our eyes, his jaw clenched and his face white as...well, *me*.

"What's going on?" Sofi finally asked, looking like she was torn between wanting to comfort him and wanting to run from him.

Stephen shook his head, breath coming hard and fast, flaring his nostrils.

"I just...it was so...so *stupid* of me," he said. "I just wanted to have something...some *evidence*...and I didn't think..."

"Okay," I said, not liking the sound of where this was going, "let's start with a softball. Who the hell was on the phone?"

Stephen took a breath, then finally met my eyes.

"Another TA," he said. "From my department. I asked him to stay at my place while I left to keep an eye on things."

"Keep an eye on *what?*" Aggie said.

"My apartment. My stuff. I knew they were watching me, so I wanted to keep it safe, but he went out for a soda...for a freaking *soda*—"

"What *stuff* was he keeping an eye on?" Sofi asked, her eyes narrowing.

Stephen opened his mouth, but nothing came out. He sucked in a breath, then glanced around at each of us, something pleading in his eyes.

"I made a copy of the book," he said finally, his voice tight.

None of us said a word, too stunned to even formulate a question.

"I wanted to have a copy. In case I needed it...in case I needed to prove..." He shook his head, puffing out a ragged, angry breath. "It was dumb. I know that."

"So, you made a copy?" I asked. "Of the original?"

Stephen shook his head morosely. "Of the translation."

Sofi's face was pale. "Both sides?"

Stephen nodded, and I could see tears building around his lashes.

"And now it's gone?" Aggie asked.

Stephen's voice was choked and hoarse. "Yeah. Jared's guys. They came by as soon as I left. I'm so sorry, Sofi—"

"Shut. Up." Sofi's voice was barely a whisper. "Shut up, you...you...*traitor*."

Stephen put up his hands as if warding off a physical attack. "Sofi, I didn't mean—"

"You didn't *mean*," she shouted. "You didn't *mean* to betray us? You didn't *mean* to expose every secret this town has? You didn't *mean* to jeopardize the progress we're making? What exactly did you *mean* to do?"

Stephen shrunk back like an animal, wounded and cornered. He shrugged helplessly. "I don't know, I just...I just wanted to prove that you believe in something that's real."

Sofi pressed her mouth into a thin line. "I don't need you to tell me what I believe," she said coldly. "Or what's real."

Stephen blinked then, something about her words seeming to spark something inside him.

"Really?" he said, pushing himself away from the car and stepping toward her. "You've needed someone to tell you what you believe all these years, haven't you? Aren't I just one more?"

"Shut up," she said, backing away from him. He was tall, I realized for maybe the first time. And also, for the first time since I'd known him, he was mad.

"No," he said, leaning forward, putting his face close to hers. "You came to *me*. You pulled me into all this crazy shit. You dragged me to your dad's house like you aren't the freaking Manson family—"

"Shut *up*," Sofi said again. "You don't know me *or* my family and we aren't—"

"You *are*," Stephen said, pointing his finger at her. I felt something flare up within me, some sort of sisterly compulsion to protect her.

"You," Stephen went on, inching closer, "are a sycophant. You're a follower. And if you'd stood up to them, if you'd said something at your Ceremony, *she'd* still be alive." He pointed at me then, and I felt something boil over inside me.

The spell. The spell that Aggie had been using on the crocuses. I called it up then, the magic. Felt it move through me, gathering in the tips of my fingers, tingling and sparking like electricity.

"*Back. Off*," I said, hoping he could hear the warning in my voice.

He looked baffled.

"You're *dead*," he said, shaking his head. "This...this *cult* is responsible for your death. And hers," he said, gesturing to Aggie. He'd stepped several feet away from the car, and the three of us had moved closer together.

"You need to leave," I said, balling my hands into fists at my sides.

He cocked his head, his expression disbelieving. "Are you all *insane*? All I've tried to do is help you. I'm risking everything...for what?"

Behind us, the wagon door banged open. "What on earth is all this racket out here?" Mirtel said, pulling her velvet amethyst robe closer around her.

Stephen looked around wildly. "I just wanted to *help*. But now I see...I see how blind you are." He took a step toward Sofi and she shrank back. "You're in too far," he said, and Sofi shook her head. I could see tears streaming down her cheeks. "You are," he said again. "You won't stand up to him. You won't stand up for *her*—"

I'd had enough. I raised my fists and flung open my hands, pushing a wall of energy toward Stephen. I didn't have much control of the magic yet, but he'd been taken off guard, and it was enough to send him sprawling onto his back. The air whooshed out of him and he lay still, staring up at the blue sky stretching peacefully above.

Sofi was staring at me, eyes wide, but no longer crying.

"Let's go," I said, heading toward her car, parked just down the drive.

"Uh...where?"

"To see Jared. We have to get to him...before anyone else does."

Sofi nodded and followed behind me. Stephen was slowly getting to his feet, and Aggie and Mirtel retreated to the wagon. We got into the car and Sofi started the engine. Without a backward glance, we were off, magic crackling around us like static electricity.

It didn't feel half bad.

CHAPTER 29

SOFI

It was times like this that I wished Darja was still alive, if only so she could take over and drive the car. Because I could barely focus on the road. My hands were sweaty on the steering wheel, my mind racing a mile a minute. How could Stephen have been so *stupid*? How had I let myself trust him? What were we going to do?

I must have voiced this last question aloud, because Darja ceased her angry muttering from the passenger's seat and answered me.

"We're going to talk to Jared. We're going to get the book back before it falls into the wrong hands and people start asking questions." Her voice lowered to a growl. "And then we're going to kill Stephen."

I knew she was joking, but I didn't laugh. I'd been such an idiot. I'd been so blinded by the excitement of the spell book, so carried away by the illusion of power and control that it had given me, something I'd never before felt in all my life, that I'd completely missed the bigger picture. I'd avoided Aggie's warnings and Darja's hesitance, and willfully ignored how *dangerous* all of this was. Instead of finding answers and solutions, our secrets just kept growing and compounding, and I was going to drown in them.

The dead girl in the seat next to me was crackling with magical energy, a real, physical presence that she could use to interact with the world around her, and I didn't know how to wrap my head around that. And Stephen had *lost* the translated book. And something was happening between Darja and Aggie—I didn't know what, and I was afraid to ask, afraid of everything around me moving so fast, afraid to lose her, the one person closer to me than anyone had been my whole life. And she was *dead*.

Hysterical laughter bubbled up inside of me and I choked on it, forcing it back even as we pulled into the parking lot at the municipal building and I realized I barely remembered a second of the drive over.

I killed the engine and turned to face Darja.

"Sofi," she said, and the ferocity in her eyes grounded me slightly. "Pull your shit together. We have to get this book back."

I nodded and took a deep breath, trying hard to get some semblance of control over my roiling emotions. Then I wiped my sweaty palms on my jeans and swung myself out of the car, hurrying toward the police station with Darja at my back.

Jared was there, talking with the receptionist, and at the sight of him my palms started to sweat, hysteria building once again. He must have seen something in my eyes because he quickly ended his conversation and ushered me to his dad's office.

I shut the door behind me.

"Sofi, what—?"

"Did you take something from Stephen's apartment? A book? A binder full of papers?"

His expression turned wary, and Darja stormed around the desk to stand next to Jared where I could see her. "A little finesse, maybe?" she said, and I forced myself not to look at her.

I sighed and dropped into a chair.

"I'm sorry. Stephen said something is missing from his apartment. It's the translation of an old book. And I just thought, since you'd been watching him..."

Jared's eyes were cautious. "You know I can't go in there without a warrant. I was just...keeping an eye on him."

Crap. It hadn't occurred to me that I was accusing him of breaking the law. Even though that was obviously what he'd done. I needed to slow down and think.

"I'm sorry," I said, working to erase any trace of impatience or accusation from my voice. "I didn't mean to imply...it's just that he came to me and said he's missing a binder, and I know you were having him watched...I thought maybe you'd know where it went."

The caution in his eyes melted into worry. "Sofi, why are you still hanging around with him? You promised me you wouldn't go back there."

"I haven't been back to his apartment, I swear."

It was technically true, but Jared's expression made it clear he knew it wasn't the whole truth.

"You promised you'd stay out of the investigation," he said. "But I know he's been to your house, and you've been spending time with him. I don't want you to get hurt."

A thread of guilt twisted in my gut. I had ulterior motives here, but that didn't mean everyone did. Jared didn't know what was really going on, and his words had a ring of truth. He really was worried about me. He was trying to protect me, and he didn't understand why I kept getting involved.

I sighed, and my voice was small when I answered. "I'm sorry. I...I'm trying to keep out of it, I really am. It's just, well, Stephen...and Mirtel, they're my friends. I don't think they've done anything wrong, and I want to help."

My blood heated with anger at the thought of sitting here, defending Stephen, when it was his fault we were here in the first place, but I tamped it down, and relaxed when Jared looked at me and smiled softly.

"Sofi, always rooting for the underdog. Darja was an underdog too, it seems. Is that why you want to help so much?"

Darja stiffened and shot a glare at Jared, but he just continued to look at me, oblivious, and I found myself smiling back at him.

After a long pause, he leaned closer. "Sofi, listen, I..." He glanced around, then lowered his voice. "I did take the binder from Stephen's apartment."

"Duh," Darja put in, but I kept my gaze on Jared and my expression smooth, tamping down the thrill of excitement that he'd admitted it, and maybe we were one step closer to getting it back.

"I know I shouldn't have gone in there," he went on, "but it seemed like it might be important. I know you want to be friends with the guy, and you're right, he probably isn't involved with the missing girl, but you have to admit he's too interested in the Vaikesti, and I thought maybe he'd stolen those papers."

"What were they?" I asked.

"What did he say they were?" Jared asked.

Darja shot me a warning glance, but I just shrugged. "He said they were for a school project, and he was freaking out because he only had one copy."

"Hm." Jared leaned back. "That makes sense, I guess. I couldn't tell what they were. It looked like a bunch of spells or something—"My heart flew into my throat, terror spiking through me, but he continued on,"—you know, like some New Age witchy bullshit. Maybe he's going to try to raise the dead." Jared laughed, and I chuckled weakly.

"Anyway, I was wrong; it wasn't anything important. I was just going to put it back."

Darja raised a meaningful eyebrow at me and I took a shaky breath. "I could take it, if you want. I could put it back, and then you wouldn't get in trouble for...anything."

Jared gave me a warm smile, like he really thought I was just looking out for him, and I felt that sense of guilt again. He really was a good guy. If I ever got out from under this mountain of lies and deception, maybe we really could go out to dinner together, like two normal people.

"That's sweet, Sofi, but you don't have to, I can—"

"I really don't mind," I said, in a tone I hoped was earnest and not impatient. "I don't want you to get in trouble," I repeated.

He hesitated again.

"Oh, come *on*," Darja muttered angrily, and though he couldn't hear her, his response seemed directed at her.

"All right. Let me go get it."

He rose and crossed the room, and I breathed a sigh of relief when the door closed behind him.

"I didn't think he was going to admit it," Darja commented, and I nodded at her with wide eyes.

"I can't believe he's going to give it to me," I said in a low voice. "We'll have to destroy it, and make sure Stephen doesn't have any other copies lying around."

"I'm just glad it was this easy to get it back," Darja said, moving around to my side of the desk. "I was half afraid—"

The words died on her lips as Jared came back through the door, and when I saw his expression, my pulse spiked.

"What's wrong?" I asked.

"It's not there." He kept his voice low and shut the door behind him.

"What?!" At another swift glance from Darja I moderated my tone. "It's not where?"

"I hid it in the copy room, but it's not where I left it. Someone must have found it."

"Why would you have put it there? Wouldn't you keep it in evidence or something?" I raised my eyebrows, trying to keep my heart from beating out of my chest. This was *so* bad.

Jared stared at me like I was slow. "I didn't have a warrant. I wasn't supposed to be in there, let alone take anything; of course I had to hide it."

Darja turned and slipped through the door, no doubt to poke around on her own.

"Well, did anyone else know it was here? You have to find it." Without Darja's calming presence, my control on my emotions was slipping, and I could hear the edge of panic in my voice.

"No one else knew it was there." He tilted his head and eyed me oddly. "It's not that big a deal, Sofi. I told you it wasn't anything important. Why do you care so much?"

"I just...he said it was his only copy," I said lamely. "He was really upset."

"I'm sure it'll turn up, and when it does I'll put it back, okay? He'll think he misplaced it or something."

Jared kept talking, but I tuned him out, my brain frantically turning over the options. Someone else must have known. Had someone seen him take it? Did someone else know what it was? Had someone stolen it from Jared?

"Okay?" Jared was watching me expectantly.

"What?"

"I said I'll see you again soon, okay? Don't worry, I'll find it, all right? Just take care of yourself, Sofi."

I rose, still a little shell-shocked, and let him usher me out the door. Darja was waiting for me in the car.

"It's not there," she told me without preamble. "I looked everywhere I could; I don't think he's lying."

"Of course he's not lying," I snapped. "Someone else must have taken it. But who? And why? Do you think someone knows what it is?"

She shook her head. "I don't know. It must be someone who works there, right?"

I didn't want to face Mirtel until we knew something, so I headed to my house instead. We turned the puzzle over, talking it through and getting nowhere, and by the time I reached the house we were on the verge of snapping at each other, nerves taut and fraying.

The house was silent as I stormed upstairs to my room, my skin buzzing with anger and frustration. Darja followed behind me on silent feet, but I half expected she would disappear at any second, off to seek out Aggie and do whatever it was they did together. It made my mood darken even further, and as I stalked down the hall I didn't even hear the voices coming from inside my parents' bedroom until Darja's urgent, "*Sofi,*" stopped me in my tracks.

I turned to snap a question at her, but her expression pulled me up short, and only then did the hushed voices behind the door filter into my awareness.

"Dozens of them, maybe hundreds, spells for everything you could imagine." It was my father's voice, excitement clear in his words.

No.

I felt the blood drain from my face.

"But the Town Council *has* spell books," said my mother, her voice muffled through the door, and I stepped closer, holding my breath. "The magic doesn't work, you know that. How is this any different?"

I met Darja's eyes, and I knew the shock there mirrored my own. How had this happened?

But my father continued on, oblivious to our silent presence outside the door. "It *is* different," he insisted, and my gut churned with acid. "These spells *work.*"

CHAPTER 30

DARJA

I was pacing the floor. As much as a ghost could pace, anyway. Occasionally, I cast a worried glance over at Sofi, who was curled up on the soft yellow duvet on her bed, staring blankly toward the window. Every so often, I would walk through Sprat, sleeping in a sunny patch on the floor, causing him to awaken and hiss at me half-heartedly, before immediately falling into another doze.

Sofi hadn't said more than a handful of words since we'd gotten to her room, but we both knew this was bad. Really bad. I thought she should confront her parents immediately, come up with some excuse or ploy to get the book away from them, but the look she gave me when I said as much shut me up pretty quickly.

So instead, I paced, muttering to myself about this stupid cult and this stupid town and the stupid people in it, and Sofi sat, silent, unmoving, sightlessly staring.

I wasn't sure how much time had passed, but the patch of sunshine had moved away from Sprat, turning his blazing orange fur to dull rust. I could see Sofi's head nodding every so often, and eventually, she let it droop back against her fabric-covered headboard.

As much as I longed to *do* something, I couldn't begrudge her the rest. She hadn't been sleeping much lately, and it was showing—in the shadows that tinged the delicate skin beneath her eyes, and in the subtle shift in her demeanor. The cheerful, naive teen I'd seen in school was gone, replaced by a young woman who was searching for something. A woman who had *seen* things.

I'm not sure how long Sofi slept, but when she finally blinked her eyes open and stretched her neck, wincing painfully, I could see something different in her. Some sort of resolve that hadn't been there before. She took a breath and got out of bed, tugging down her shirt and *shooing* Sprat off of the pink flip-flops she'd discarded next to her chair.

She looked at me then, her jaw set firmly, her brow pulled down low. "Come on," she said. "Let's go."

I knew better than to ask questions as she stormed out into the hallway, swiveling her head to look from room to room as we walked by. We passed two more bedrooms, then what appeared to be an office, and finally a closed door right before the hall spilled out into the open kitchen. Everything was cloaked in shadows as the light dwindled outside, but I could see a glowing strip of yellow between the door and the threshold.

Sofi barged past me—or, rather, through me—and pounded her fist against the door.

"Mom?" she called. "*Dad*. I need to talk to you."

No answer.

She stopped pounding, and I waited for something to happen—a sister or niece or nephew to come flying up the basement stairs, or a great-aunt to shuffle in disapprovingly. The house remained silent. Sofi's gaze flicked down at the light spilling onto the hall carpet, then back up at me. She tilted her head in a meaningful way.

I sighed. "Fine," I said, and pushed myself through the door.

It was a jarring feeling, definitely not a pleasant one, but it'd be a neat trick at parties. If the dead had parties.

I gave my surroundings a cursory glance before deciding to take another route out of the room.

Sofi jumped when I flickered in right at her shoulder, shooting me a vicious glare.

"What the *hell*, Darja?" she hissed.

I shrugged an apology. "There's no one there," I said, and before she could ask, "and no sign of the binder."

Sofi scrubbed her hands over her face and briefly over her flyaway hair, which frankly, had seen better days. I was about to gently suggest she might want to squeeze in a quick shower when her phone pinged loudly, and both of us jumped. She dug around in her pocket and pulled it out, barely looking as she swiped away the lock screen.

She cocked her head and her brows furrowed together. "It's a text," she said. "From my sister."

"What's it say? 'Our father's a creep and this whole town is built on lies'?"

Sofi waved away my sarcastic remark and continued staring at the screen. "There's a meeting," she said, "at the old bonfire grounds."

I shuddered. It wasn't a place I wanted to return to. But from the look on Sofi's face, and the firm set of her jaw, I had a feeling that was exactly what was about to go down.

"The Council is meeting," she continued, "and some of their family members who are of-age. She thought I should come."

"But we don't really need to—"

"We absolutely need to," she said, and I knew there'd be

no arguing with her. "This is about the book, Darja. You know it is. They have it. They *have* it, and somehow they know it works, and we've got to—"

"Got to what?"

"We've got to get it back."

———

Sofi drove us to the outskirts of town, and I tried desperately not to look out the window. I hadn't been coherent enough to pay attention to the scenery the last time I'd made this drive, but just knowing where we were headed was enough to set off waves of dread inside me. I didn't realize we were there until Sofi shut off the engine and unbuckled her seat belt.

I forced myself to look out at the field, and saw...a whole lot of nothing, really. It was like any other field. Green, mostly flat, with patches of newly-turned earth rising in mounds like ripples in the sea. At the far end of the expanse, a line of trees stood thick and watchful, like sentinels. And beyond the trees, through the thickest vegetation, down a ravine and past a trickling stream...

The clearing where I'd died.

Correction. Where I'd been *murdered*.

Sofi's hands were white on the steering wheel. I could see her chest rise and fall rapidly in time with her quickening breath. Mine would be doing the same, I assumed, if I could still breathe. A sudden memory flashed in my mind—the backseat of Ms. Kross's car, the vinyl of the headrest against my cheek, the feeling of simultaneously flying and falling...

I wasn't sure I could go back there. I half-expected Sofi to say something along those lines, but when I looked at her again, her gaze was focused intently out the windshield, on something I couldn't or didn't want to see. She unbuckled her seatbelt and opened the door decisively.

I could see then that there were other cars here, too, lining the gravel road that edged the field. As Sofi got out and shut the door behind her, I flickered reluctantly to her side. The ground was soft enough to show lines of footprints, leading back to the woods. Sofi's flip-flops sank into the earth as she stepped over a sagging wire fence.

We knew where to go. I imagined the path there was etched permanently into both of our memories. Even then, when I'd been in a haze of drugs and confusion, the details had been in sharp focus—the smell of the damp earth, of the far-off smoke, the distant sound of women laughing…

Sofi and I walked in silence, too lost in our own minds to speak. At the treeline, I could hear the voices of men and women chattering excitedly. I wanted to cry. I wanted to scream. I wanted to do anything but cross through that line of trees. But through the bond, I felt something. Something calming. Something like comfort. Sofi reached out then, and I let my hand float next to hers, a silly pantomime that eased some of the worry that flared in my chest.

We moved together through the woods—Sofi pushing branches out of her way, muttering curses when one occasionally caught her in the face. By the time we reached the clearing, she'd gathered scratches on both cheeks, twigs in her hair, and her eyes had gone completely wild.

She looked fierce, this sister of mine. Not to be messed with. It would seem we shared the same blood, after all.

We hadn't talked about what we'd do when we confronted the Council about the book. And we hadn't worked out a plan for what to do if things went sideways.

So, when we burst out of the trees and into the meadow, I braced myself for…anything. What happened was…nothing.

Well, not nothing. As expected, the entire Council and some of their adult family members had gathered in the clearing. They were seated in a semicircle, facing away from us, staring raptly at the dais in front—in front of the remains of my funeral pyre.

We stayed near the shadows, still taking in the scene before us. On the dais, Sofi's dad, leader of the Council, stood behind something that looked like a lectern or a pulpit. In a chair to his side sat Sofi's mom. She was wearing a soft floral dress and her hair was wound up on top of her head. She sat primly in her seat, but she was beaming at her husband, something electric in her eyes.

The doctor was by turns pacing the length of the small dais, then pausing to stand behind the lectern, clutching it as if it were the only thing tethering him to the earth. He waved one hand in the air, and I realized with a jolt that in it he was holding the copy of our book.

His voice was raised, though I hadn't registered his words. As he went on, the Council members nodded along, some of them exclaiming and waving their arms. I saw then that, below the dais, at the front of the crowd, two Council members stood apart, a man and a woman I'd seen once or twice at the school. Parents of Vaikesti kids, maybe, or school employees. They each held a sheet of paper in their hands—both were trembling.

Sofi's dad was working himself into a frenzy, his booming voice seeming to shake the very trees around us. "Now," he shouted, waving at the two people standing below him, "now we will see the true power of the old ways. Now we will know the path that has been laid before us—the chosen people."

A cry went up from the Council, but then the doctor held up a hand and a hush fell over them.

I stole a glance over at Sofi and whispered, "Should we

—?" but she shook her head and watched, transfixed. Her father—*our* father—gestured to the two people below him—Henri and Marleen Luts, I suddenly remembered—and they lifted their sheets and began to read. I hadn't noticed the small mound of dirt at their feet—it was small, inconspicuous, but as I watched, I could see the dirt begin to shiver. The mound trembled and the assembled Council members leaned forward, breath held, waiting.

For a long moment, nothing else happened. The words they'd spoken had been familiar, the same spell the four of us had used to bring the seedling back from the brink of death. As I watched, the two readers glanced at one another with uncertainty. I recognized the look. Then, more dirt began to spill down the sides of the mound, and a seedling, vibrant green and heavy with leaves, burst upward, uncurling and stretching toward the sun.

The roar from the Council members thundered in my ears. Henri and Marleen stared at one another, dumbfounded. I felt the same. Could they really do magic, without one of them being dead? How could they access the kind of energy that had demanded my blood, and Aggie's? Had just the words been enough all along?

I watched them as the plant continued to grow, straightening out and climbing higher and higher. Then, I saw something that stopped me cold.

I thought it was just me at first. I was seeing double. An afterimage, like when you stare at a silhouette against the sun. Henri and Marleen were...flickering. Like I did, I supposed, when I flickered in and out. Their bodies remained, but there was something else—something like a reflection—superimposed on top. The reflections looked exactly like them, but they were gray, wavering, not at all solid. As I watched, the reflections began to change—their faces crumpled, and they writhed as if in pain.

"Sofi," I hissed, trying to catch her attention. She was too busy watching the plant— obviously a stalk of corn—begin to flower and then fruit.

Henri and Marleen looked ecstatic, but their reflections —twisting in agony—were slowly pulling away from their bodies. The Council members' cries had reached a crescendo, some of them praising our ancestors, some thanking the doctor for bestowing this blessing on the town.

I looked frantically from face to face, seeing the same blind rapture in each expression. No one else could see the reflections, flickering frenetically as they tried to stay tethered to their bodies.

And it hit me. They weren't reflections. They were *souls*. The magic, meant to be read and performed only by a bonded pair, wasn't intended to be performed by two living, unbonded people. It wasn't the words. It was the blood. And I was seeing the consequences when the rules of the magic were not obeyed.

"Something's wrong," I said, too quietly. Sofi kept watching.

"Something's *wrong*," I said again.

Finally, she tore her attention away from the spectacle. "What?"

"The magic. It's not supposed to work like this."

"But it *does* work," Sofi said, nodding toward the corn stalk.

I shook my head. "It doesn't. It's killing them."

She looked at me then, her eyes narrowing. "What do you mean, 'killing them'?"

"Their souls. It's...damaging them. Sucking them out...or something. This isn't how it's supposed to be."

"You can see that?" she asked. "Their souls?"

I nodded, swallowing past the hot tears that had begun

to burn my throat. "We have to stop this."

Marleen and Henri appeared outwardly normal, but I could see that some of the shine had gone from their eyes. They looked dazed, blank. No one on the Council seemed to notice or care. The reflections—the souls—were floating off, flickering in and out, mouths open in soundless screams.

"Sofi, please," I said, my voice barely above a whisper. "You have to do something."

"But what do I—?"

"*Stop* them."

"What can I—?"

"Now, Sofi!" I was shrieking, unable to contain my horror. The souls were flickering faster. "Please."

Sofi threw herself out of the shadows and into the crowd. "Stop!" she screamed. "STOP."

No one heard. They couldn't, over the chaotic celebration of the small crowd. The flickering stopped. The souls were gone.

The magic had destroyed them.

CHAPTER 31

SOFI

I couldn't make sense of anything. The Council was in chaos, their reaction to proof of the reality of magic not, disturbingly, unlike my own had been. But the blind fervor, that was different. The cheering, the shouting, it all swirled in my head, a cacophony of sound. Next to me, Darja was frantic as well, gesturing wildly and pleading nonsensically —something about souls, I couldn't quite understand—and up at the front of the crowd stood my father, a triumphant light shining in his eyes. In the midst of all the pandemonium a stalk of corn waved in the gentle breeze, tassel shining and leaves unfurled to the sun as if it had been growing there for months rather than minutes.

My breath caught at the sight, no different than the magic we had been performing for weeks, but my former sense of triumph and excitement shriveled in the face of the blind elation of the Council members.

They don't understand.

For a moment I believed the thought was my own, until

Darja repeated it, her hands raised as if to grip my shoulders before sliding ineffectually through my skin.

"They don't understand," she repeated. "*You* don't understand," and her face was so distraught it snapped me back to awareness. Gathering my wits, I pushed through to the front of the crowd.

"Sofi, you came." My mother's face lit at the sight of me. "Did you see?" She gestured at the corn, but the joy in her expression faltered as she took in my face. I ignored her though, pushing toward my father.

He hadn't seen me yet, but my steps halted as Eliise Tam stepped up beside him at the pulpit. She was quickly joined by the rest of the Council, who clustered around them, some shaking hands with Henri and Marleen, others hesitantly reaching out to touch the stalk of corn.

Eliise spoke quietly to my father for a moment, before turning to the gathered group and raising her voice.

"As you all know, Vaikesti's sesquicentennial celebration falls on Midsummer Day this year. Our committees have been working hard all year on the plans for the festival, which has promised to be the biggest event in Vaikesti history. It is nothing less than a miracle," she said, her clear voice at odds with her stooped form, "that our magic has returned to us now, on the threshold of such an important and historic celebration. I am thinking that we should not waste this opportunity that has been laid before us."

My gut twisted uneasily.

"I agree," said another woman, a Council member I knew by sight if not by name. "It's the perfect opportunity to demonstrate what we've found to the entire town. Perhaps we could do something large scale? A demonstration of some sort?"

"Yes," my mother chimed in, looking excited. "What about the blessings? The blessings over the fields have always been a traditional Midsummer ritual. What if we add spells in this year? Make a spectacle of it?"

The others were nodding, and I began to feel sick.

"Perfect," my father said with a smile of approval, running his hands over the thick binder of pages. "This year, our blessings will be more than prayer and hope. This year, we leave nothing to chance."

"Everyone can be involved," another man put in, his fingers caressing the silky leaves of the corn stalk. "Imagine what we could do to the crop fields if everyone participated."

"Sofi," Darja gasped, and my blood turned to ice in my veins at the mental image of the entire town out in the fields, using broken magic to curse our crops. What would it do to the townspeople? To my family? My friends?

I heard Darja's words in my head again. *Their souls. It's... damaging them. It's killing them.* My horror rose, choking me. I couldn't even tell if the feeling was all my own or if Darja's emotions were leaking through our bond. Beside me she flickered, as if she was too distraught to be able to control herself.

"No!" Heads turned to face me before I realized I'd spoken, and my feet carried me up to the dais. I focused my beseeching gaze on my father and the other Council members.

"You can't do this, you have to stop. You don't understand what you're doing—"

"Sofi? What are you saying?" My mother's face pinched with worry.

I ignored her.

"That book. It's not meant to be used that way; it's—" but I stumbled, unsure of what to say. I had to stop this, but I had no idea how to start.

"What would you know about any of this?" my father cut

in. His voice was calm and cool, and my face flushed with anger.

"More than you do," I snapped. "Those words aren't meant to be read by the living." I pointed to Henri and Marleen, who still stood to the side, faces strangely blank. How long would they even live like that? "You're *hurting* people. You can't let this get out of hand."

Though things had gotten out of hand a long time ago, I knew.

Eliise stepped closer, eyebrows raised questioningly, but my father waved her back, indicating he would just be a moment. Beside me, Darja still flickered, her mouth forming words I could only half hear.

"I don't know what ideas that boy, that...*vōōras*...has been putting in your head," my father said coldly, "but this is none of your concern. If you've decided to turn your back on your people, you can't expect—"

"Sofi," my mother cut in anxiously, placing a soothing hand on my arm, "why don't we talk about this later. We can all go home after—"

I pushed her hand away, trying to block out Darja's distracting form as she struggled to stabilize herself, phasing in and out first to my left, then behind my father, then by my side again, her voice crackling in agitation as if through a faulty telephone connection. "You have to...don't let them...I can't..."

Around me, the other Council members were whispering, a concerned undercurrent of low voices distracting me further.

I ground my teeth and tried to focus on my father, my blood pressure rising until I could feel my heart beating in my ears. "I *haven't* turned my back on my people," I ground out, "but you have to *listen* to me. Magic doesn't work the way you think it does. You—"

"Honey," my mother tried again. "You don't have to worry, we have a plan. I know this is new and scary, but we're all going to work through it together at the celebration."

My father was speaking over her, "—completely inappropriate. You don't know the first thing about the sacrifice that we—"

"Have to go—" Darja snarled by my shoulder, then phased out again.

"Dammit!" I yelled, my voice echoing through the clearing, and in the silence that followed I turned and grabbed the stalk of corn, ripping it from the ground with a harsh yank. Clumps of dirt showered from the healthy rootball as I spun, brandishing it first at my father, then at the open-mouthed Council members who stared aghast as if I had just defaced a sacred monument.

"Is this worth your *lives?*" I yelled, my skin tingling as anger and stress bubbled up through me and overflowed, tears of frustration stinging my eyes. "Would you *kill* for this?" I shook the plant harder, and my mother stepped back. "Because you already have." I whirled again, toward my father, and my face twisted into a snarl. "And you think I don't know about *sacrifice.*"

At that moment, Darja phased in by his side, whatever she'd been saying coming in half-formed words I couldn't understand, and I turned on her before I could stop myself.

"Darja, *stop.*"

She phased out again, leaving behind the empty air I knew was all anyone else had seen all along, and I realized my mistake.

My mother went deathly pale, and the angry expression on my father's face faded in an instant, leaving behind a strange blankness that set alarm bells ringing in my head.

An instant later Darja was back, her voice low but clear.

"Let's go."

I dropped the broken stalk of corn at my father's feet, turned, and ran.

CHAPTER 32

DARJA

"Oh, dear. This is quite a pickle, isn't it?"

Mirtel's words were light, but I couldn't deny the heavy truth in them. We were back at the wagon, which seemed even smaller and more constricted than usual. Sofi was pacing in a tight circle between the table and the kitchen sink, her eyes bright and wild with worry. Aggie was in the corner, her presence crackling with furious energy. I couldn't tell if she was mad at us, at the townspeople, or the whole situation.

I wasn't sure how I was feeling. The look on our father's face when Sofi had spoken to me had sent a jolt of electricity coursing through my body. Between that and all the flickering in and out while I'd tried to warn Sofi about what was happening, I felt raw and charged and ready to ignite. The wagon seemed even smaller than usual—claustrophobic and suffocating.

"I can't believe I did that," Sofi hissed, continuing her rounds, and I could feel the anxiety coming off of her in waves. In contrast, Mirtel was sitting in calm repose—so calm it was maddening.

I could feel myself beginning to go static, and I knew I was about to start the same uncontrollable flickering as before.

"I need a break," I gasped, barely registering it when everyone turned and stared at me. "Sorry," I said, though it came out as more of a growl. And before anyone could say anything, I flickered out.

I ended up just on the other side of the wall, behind the wagon, where the grass turned to dust as it met the river. It was almost as if my energy had been sapped so profoundly that I couldn't manage to take myself any farther. Still, it felt better—freer—out in the open air, and I found myself mimicking the motions of breathing, lifting my chest and letting it fall in a slow rhythm, trying to remember the way it felt.

I wanted to scream. I could feel it bubbling up in my throat. Or it may have been a hysterical laugh. Or a tearless sob. It was as if a dam had been opened up inside of me, and all the emotions, all the fear and the anger of this last month was rushing out, threatening to swallow me up.

When I felt a pair of arms come around me, I froze. It wasn't a sensation I had much experience with, even in life, and it stunned me into silence.

"Mirtel and I renewed the spell," Aggie whispered against my ear. Her lips brushed my neck and I shivered in her embrace. I leaned into her, surprised at how warm she felt. How...*alive*.

I whirled around before I could think about what I was doing and caught her lips with mine. It was desperate and messy and so real my body ached with wanting. I thought I might shake apart. I thought I might lose my mind. Lose myself. But if I was losing myself in her, I suddenly didn't care.

The heat between us crackled and sparked, and I worried I might flicker out if I didn't get it under control. Reluctantly, I pulled back, keeping my hands wrapped around her arms, but allowing a little distance between us. Her dark eyes burned like coals, and there was a ferocity in her gaze that terrified me and thrilled me at the same time. I reached a hand up, trailing a finger over her bottom lip, then up her cheekbone before pushing my fingers into her hair. It felt like silk, and I wanted nothing more than to release it from its pins, but that seemed to be outside the rules of the spell.

Instead, I contented myself with drinking her in—the way she looked, the way she felt. I didn't know what was coming, and though I felt adrift in the uncertainty of it all, she was my anchor.

"I can't believe," I whispered, pressing my forehead against hers, "that I had to die to find you."

She laughed hoarsely. "Maybe all these years, I've just been waiting."

Her words sent a shiver through me. "Hope I was worth it," I said, half-joking, though I could hear the tinge of uncertainty in my voice. You'd think facing death would give a girl some courage, but apparently not.

She leaned in and kissed me, softer than a moth's wings. "So worth it," she murmured against my lips.

The sound of Sofi politely clearing her throat felt more like the crack of a whip. We sprang apart, and though I was pretty sure it wasn't possible for me to blush, I could feel the heat in my cheeks.

"Uh, hi," Sofi said, looking anywhere but at us. "I mean, sorry. Sorry to...anyway. Mirtel has a...thing...she needs to talk to us about." Sofi's cheeks were decidedly pink, and I felt a rush of affection for my sister.

Something inside me loosened, and I felt for the first time in a while that things might work out.

I took Aggie's hand in mine, and with Sofi in the lead, we went back into the wagon.

"But how did you get this?" Sofi said, shuffling through the stack of papers in her lap.

Mirtel looked sheepish. "I remembered seeing this book in the archives at the library. It's a history of our people, but it's in the old tongue."

"And this?" I said, gesturing to the loose sheets of printer paper scattered over her small table.

Chagrined, Mirtel opened her hands in a placating gesture. "I asked Stephen to translate."

"You *what*?" Sofi said, looking up sharply.

"It was before…well, before recent events," she said sheepishly.

"Why didn't you mention this before?" Aggie said, and I could see she was surprised that Mirtel hadn't even told her.

"I thought it might be nothing," Mirtel said, taking a sip of her tea. "Just a jumble of meaningless places and dates. I wasn't expecting to…*find* anything."

We all stared at her, and finally, Aggie spoke. "And what you found was…?"

Mirtel took a deep breath. "What Darja saw was right, I'm afraid. The book describes the bond between souls, and how the magic is meant to be used. But it also warns about what happens should the magic fall into the wrong hands."

"And?" Sofi prompted. She was scanning the pages in

front of her ceaselessly, but her eyes were glazed and I wasn't sure she was actually taking anything in.

"And it's as we feared," Mirtel said. "Spells require energy—a great deal of it, actually. Two living people can't access that amount of energy, not without serious consequences. That's why the bond exists. The living partner and the..."

"The dead," I said flatly.

Mirtel looked uncertain. "Well, technically, yes. But not just dead. Or not completely dead. You and Aggie exist somewhere outside the realm of the dead, at least according to this."

Even though I'd known this wasn't the way the afterlife was supposed to be, this still felt like news to me. "So we aren't actually dead?"

"You are. At least, physically. But you haven't crossed into the spirit world, the..." Mirtel shook her head, searching for the right words, "...'great beyond,' as it were. You're in some type of in-between. But in that place—the space between life and afterlife—that's where the magic lies."

"What does this mean?" Aggie said. I could hear something in her voice, a slight hint of hope mingled with her usual skepticism. "Can we...cross over? Or cross back?"

"I don't know, dear. I'm still trying to understand it myself, though I imagine it's beyond what any of us could comprehend. What I do know is that to use the magic, without harm, the bond must be present. But when the spell is performed by an unbonded pair, all of that energy comes from within them."

"From their souls," I said, and Mirtel nodded.

"What happens to them?" Aggie asked.

Mirtel took a breath and placed her teacup gently on the side table. "Eventually, it will kill them," she said, and I could hear Sofi make a soft, pained sound. "Their bodies will live on, for a time, but their souls will be...depleted. Destroyed."

"And where do their souls go?" Sofi asked. She looked like she might be sick.

Mirtel shook her head. "No one knows. The mythology of our people says they're stuck in *porguwaaris*."

Nobody said anything. Finally, I broke the silence. "Which is—?"

"According to Stephen's translation, limbo."

"And what does that mean?" I asked. "What happens to them?"

"They're just...stuck," Mirtel said, gesturing helplessly.

"Like us," Aggie said.

"No," Mirtel said quickly. "You're not in limbo, you're in—"

"The in-between. Well, that's a relief."

Mirtel sighed. "Aggie, it's not the same. They're being punished for misusing magic. You and Darja and other bonded girls—"

"Are what?" Aggie said, the pitch of her voice rising dangerously. "Rewarded for our good deeds? Allowed to exist in the world as long as we never experience it? Moving through eternity with no end in sight?"

I reached out and touched her hand, but she yanked it away from me. I moved back quickly, trying not to look hurt.

"For now," Mirtel said, "we need to focus on stopping the festival, before the entire town loses their souls."

CHAPTER 33

SOFI

The stress of the past few weeks was nothing on what I felt in the aftermath of the revelations at the Council meeting. The bond that had been forged between the four of us—five if you considered Stephen as part of our ragtag group of magical misfits, which I assuredly did not—began to show the strain.

Our new understanding of what exactly had happened to those two poor Council members who had performed the spell on the ear of corn caused bile to rise in my throat every time I thought about it. The ramifications of what would happen if the entire village gathered to cast magic on the crops at Midsummer were terrifying to consider. The souls of all the Vaikesti—destroyed. My parents. My friends. My family. Inevitable death for everyone I'd ever known or cared about.

The excitement and camaraderie of working together on trying new spells and solving shared problems devolved into bickering and pointless stress-fueled squabbles. Mirtel, Darja, and I, at least, agreed that our priority had to be stopping the community-wide disaster that loomed only a few short weeks away, though figuring out how to do that was an exercise in futility.

We lost days in squabbling, nerves ratcheting higher with every moment that passed.

Mirtel was convinced our answer would be found in the spell book, and spent all her time scouring the entries for anything that might help us. She insisted we needed Stephen's help since he was more familiar with the material than the rest of us, which Darja and I both adamantly refused.

For my part, I was convinced Jared was our best bet, and we should ask him for help in talking sense into the Town Council. If we told him everything, he'd help us, right? He'd have to. Darja and Mirtel both shot this down.

Darja was convinced I needed to talk to my father, because he had the power to put a stop to this, but I refused. I was avoiding my father at all costs—she hadn't seen his eyes when I'd slipped up and said her name at the town meeting.

When our voices rose over each others for the thousandth time, each of us arguing the same points to the same unyielding audience, Aggie finally spoke for the first time, commenting in a toneless, offhand voice that maybe we should just let it happen, maybe the world would be better off if the Vaikesti were left to destroy themselves. I heard Mirtel's breath hitch in the shocked silence that followed, looked up into Aggie's cold, unfeeling face and over to Darja's unreadable expression, and suddenly I'd had enough. I paused only long enough to grab my keys from the tiny kitchen table before storming out of the wagon.

No one followed me.

―――

"I don't need them."

I growled the words, a mantra to...convince myself? Reassure myself?

Whatever. It didn't matter. They could do whatever they wanted. Mirtel could bury herself in translated spells to her heart's content, searching for something that didn't exist. I wouldn't stop her. Darja could stay with Aggie and rejoice over the deaths of everyone I knew, for all I cared. *I* was going to do something. I was going to figure out how to stop this.

I did the only thing I could think of, I went to see Jared. If I told him everything—*everything*—would he believe me? The thought of spilling all of our secrets to an outsider, even one who had grown up with the Vaikesti, made my stomach twist. We'd tried that with Stephen, and look how that had turned out. But what other options did I have? I needed help.

When I pushed through the door to the police station, Jared was at the front desk, talking with the receptionist. Both their eyes went wide when they saw me, and Jared straightened, his eyebrows climbing as he took me in.

"Sofi? Oh my God, are you all right?"

I paused for the first time to consider how I might look. I hadn't been home since the meeting just over a week ago. I'd been camping out on the cramped sofa in Mirtel's wagon, wearing the same clothes. I hadn't seen a hairbrush in days. My appearance was probably pretty rough, and I didn't want to think about how I might smell.

"I'm fine," I said quickly, not at all sure my voice matched my words. "Can we talk? In private?"

"Of course," he said quickly, and his arm came around me, hand resting supportively at my lower back. I nearly sagged at the contact, the strength of his arm holding me up.

The idea of pouring out all my troubles and letting someone else be strong for a change was so enticing.

We'd only just turned and he'd begun to usher me toward his father's office when a voice rang out behind us, cold and filled with steel, and I froze in place.

"Sofia."

The warmth of Jared's hand fell away as I turned to face my father. His face was the same, familiar face I'd known my whole lifetime, dark blond hair over a wide brow. Pointed nose, smooth-shaven square jaw. But his eyes were enigmatic, his expression unreadable, and the contrast between the familiar man and the unfamiliar twist of fear I felt in his presence was unsettling.

"We haven't seen you at home recently," he said. "Your mother is worried. Could you come talk with me for a few minutes in my office?"

"I need to talk with Jared," I said weakly, glancing toward my would-be savior, but whatever message I was trying to convey telepathically was lost on him.

"I'll be here all afternoon," Jared informed me with a smile. "Just come back when you're done with your dad."

Before I had a chance to protest, my father's hand locked around my upper arm like a manacle, and he started to move away, leaving me no choice but to stumble after.

His strides were long, and I had to hurry to keep up as he marched us across the atrium and into his office, the door banging shut behind us. Despite the hour, the office was empty, and my heart sank. No patients or nurses present to provide a buffer.

Only when he had led me into his office and shut the door did he release my arm, and I sank into one of the thick leather chairs by his desk.

Rather than round the desk, he took the matching leather chair beside me, then turned to face me and leaned in close. I tried not to shrink back. He was my *father*, I reminded myself.

He wasted no time.

"Is she here right now?"

I did lean back then, pushing my spine into the cool leather of the chair.

"Who?" My voice came out in an unconvincing whisper.

When he slammed his fist down on the desk it took me completely by surprise, and I flinched, my throat tightening with shock.

"Don't play dumb with me, Sofi, this is too important." He leaned forward even more, and his eyes burned into mine. His next words came out a little breathless. "It worked, didn't it? The bond? How did you make it work? Why didn't you *tell* us?"

At that, my tongue finally loosened. "*Tell you*?" The words came out in a bit more of a shriek than I'd intended. "Tell you what? That your inhumane murder ritual worked? That you've ruined my life?"

"Ruined your life," my father scoffed, sitting back in his seat. "Sofi, you're so young, and I know it's hard for you to see this, but it really isn't about you. This is for the greater good of our entire community. If you had told us earlier, we could have—"

"Could have what?" I demanded. "Made it worse? You already have no idea what you're doing with the spells in that book. This isn't for the greater good. *I'm* the one who's trying to *stop* you from destroying the community."

"Ah yes, the book." He turned his bright eyes on me again. "That was you, too, wasn't it? Wherever did you find it? Really, Sofi, we should be thanking you. You have no idea the service you've done in having it translated."

"No, you don't understand." I blew out a breath.

Darja had been the one insisting I should talk to my

father. Well, here he was. She wouldn't be able to say I hadn't tried.

"Listen to me," I said, scooting forward in my chair. "We saw the spell from the town meeting. Darja was there too. We *both* saw it."

His eyes widened and he drew in a breath, as if he'd known it was true, but hadn't been quite able to believe it without my confirmation.

"The magic doesn't work the way you think," I continued on in a rush, stumbling over myself in an effort to get the words out. "The spells have to be read by bonded pairs. The magic draws through the dead half of the pair, from the earth, from, from—" Dammit, how could I explain something I barely understood? I pushed on regardless. "When you have two living people recite a spell, there's no link for the magic to come through. It comes from the person's soul. It *kills* them!"

"Both Henri and Marleen are fine. It didn't kill anyone," my father said, raising an eyebrow.

"Not yet, but it *will*," I insisted. "And their *souls*—"

"Sofi," he broke in, his voice suddenly gentle, "I know you don't want to share this magic. I understand that. It's hard to be the youngest child, isn't it? Never anything new of your own, always in your sibling's shadows."

"*What?* No—"

"And then something amazing happens, just to you. I know you want to hold on to that. Keep it for yourself. But this is bigger than you. It's bigger than *me*. You saw what it did for that single stalk of corn. Imagine what it could do for a field. For the whole community."

I spluttered, barely able to form words.

"You aren't doing this for the *community*," I spat. "If you cared about them at all, you'd listen to me. This is purely selfish." My voice dropped low as anger seethed through me. "We know, by the way. What you did. To Darja's mother."

He froze.

"I know who you are," I snarled, unable to stop myself. "Does Mom know?"

I'd crossed a line, I knew it, but it was too late to take back the words. His eyes went black and his expression shuttered like a wall falling into place.

"That's enough."

He rose, and I shrank back into my chair for a brief second as he loomed over me, my heart pounding as if I'd just run a marathon. He stalked around to the inside of the desk and yanked open one of the drawers, then bent over it as he reached deep inside.

"You don't even know the gift you've been given," he said in an icy voice. "And one way or another, you *will* use it to help us."

He straightened, and the brown eyes that bored into mine were cold and unfamiliar. Onto the top of the desk he laid a tray, neatly arranged with a pair of gloves, alcohol swabs, and a series of small vials. Next to them gleamed a syringe.

All the air left my lungs in a rush, and I scrambled to my feet, but he was faster. He was around the desk and between me and the door in a flash.

I opened my mouth to yell, not that there was anyone to hear me. A heartbeat later, Darja flickered into existence.

"Sofi, you need to come quick. Mirtel's found something, a spell, and—what the hell is going on here?" Her transparent eyes took in the tray on the desk, the wild eyes and posture of my dad blocking the doorway, and whatever was on my own face.

"Darja," I squeaked, and my father's eyes swung to my

face, then followed my gaze, triumph passing over his features.

"She's here," he breathed.

With his attention momentarily diverted, I grabbed the tray from the desk and swung it at my father. It hit him square across the face, supplies scattering, and a dull clang echoed from the metal.

"Go," Darja gasped, and I did, shoving past my father and wrenching open the door even as his hand came up to grasp at my arm.

The fabric of my shirt slipped through his fingers as I scrambled out into the hallway, Darja on my heels.

Choking on the panic that coursed through my bloodstream, I ran.

CHAPTER 34

DARJA

"I can't believe that...that...*asshole*!"

Sofi said nothing, just stared ahead, her fingers white where they were wrapped around the steering wheel. She hadn't said a word since we'd gotten in the car, but the growl of the engine as she pressed harder and harder on the gas seemed to echo what she was feeling.

I was nearly vibrating with rage. What would have happened if I hadn't shown up when I did? If I hadn't surprised Sofi and snagged his attention away from whatever he was planning to do with the instruments on that tray? I didn't want to think about it.

"Some *father*." I spat the word out as if it tasted bad in my mouth. Which it did. I wouldn't trade having Sofi as a sister for anything in this world or the otherworld...but I resented the fact that we both had to share DNA with Dr. Evil.

Sofi was still silent, and when I looked closely, I could see that her lower lip was trembling. I couldn't imagine how hard she was working to keep it together, when all I wanted to do was fall apart.

"I should have blasted him," I muttered, more to myself than anything, so I was surprised when Sofi responded.

"With what?"

"With *magic*," I said. "I should have sent him straight into the next county."

I saw a grim half-smile quirk the corner of Sofi's mouth. "You could have done it, too," she said softly.

"Well, I didn't need to, because apparently my sister is a badass."

She laughed at this, but I could hear the edge of desperation in it.

"What are we going to do, Darja?"

"We're going to go back to the wagon and get Mirtel and Aggie. The Council's going to be after us now for sure. It isn't safe for us to stay here. We need to leave."

"And go where?"

I sighed in frustration. "I don't know. Somewhere... away from this stupid town and this stupid cult."

Sofi glanced at me out of the corner of her eye. "So, you want to just run away?"

I shook my head. "No. I'd like to light a match and watch the place burn first. But since I'm probably going to get vetoed on that, I think we should go somewhere safe until we can figure out how to stop the festival."

"But where?"

"No idea. For now, just drive."

Sofi tightened her grip on the steering wheel and I heard the engine rev. "That I can do."

Aggie was outside when we pulled into the drive, wearing her trademark frown. She looked stunning. Grouchy, but stunning.

"Hey," I greeted her as I flickered over to her side. I raised a hand to brush it against her cheek, and her eyelids fluttered shut. But my fingers met only mist, dissolving into nothingness. She must have ended the spell. But there was no time for hurt feelings just now.

Sofi got out of the car, looking even more wild and unkempt, and Aggie tilted her head, her eyebrows furrowed.

"What happened?" she asked Sofi. "Are you okay?"

Sofi shook her head. "No. None of us are. Is Mirtel inside?"

Aggie nodded. "Yes, but—"

The door swung open then, and Mirtel stepped out onto the wooden stairs, smiling with relief when she saw Sofi.

"Oh, I'm so glad you're back, dear," she said, knotting a scarf around her hair. "It's time for us to be going."

I was just about to ask her if she could read minds when she bent down to retrieve an ancient-looking carpet bag from inside the doorway, and I caught a glimpse of a figure behind her, lanky and hunched awkwardly, as if trying to make himself less conspicuous.

"Stephen?" Sofi said, and her voice was a mix of betrayal and relief.

"I called him," Mirtel said, her tone placating. "Sofi, we need him. He can help us. I've got something to show you, once we're somewhere safe. But just now, I don't think it's wise for us to stay here."

"You're not the only one," I muttered.

Sofi's jaw was clenched, but I could see her shoulders had gone slack. I didn't think she had any more fight in her at that moment.

"You're right," she said with a sigh. "We were just coming here to tell you the same thing. So, where are we going?"

Stephen straightened up and ducked around Mirtel, taking her bag and carrying it down the front steps.

"My parents' house," he said, giving Sofi a sheepish smile.

"And exactly how are you going to explain your entourage of ghost girls and an old lady?" I asked.

Stephen laughed, but I was mostly serious. "They aren't there," he said, opening the trunk of his car and putting Mirtel's bag inside. "It's their summer house, but they won't be there for at least a month."

Sofi and I exchanged a glance. I barely knew Stephen *had* parents, let alone that they owned a summer house. I shrugged at Sofi—I had to admit, I was curious.

Sofi shook her head, somewhat ruefully. "Okay," she said. "Let's go."

———

The sun was just beginning to sink into the horizon as we pulled into the long, curving drive. As it turned out, Stephen had been wrong—it wasn't a summer house...it was a summer *mansion*. It rose up from behind a dense cover of evergreens, sprawling just beyond an ornate iron gate. Through the trees, I could see a silver shimmer, and I realized the house must be situated right on the edge of a lake.

We'd driven more than an hour outside Vaikesti, and with each mile, I'd felt a little of the tension of the last few days begin to release. Stephen and Sofi had made polite, if slightly strained, conversation in the front, while Mirtel hummed contentedly to herself in the back. Aggie and I had squeezed in too, since we didn't know where the house was or how to transport ourselves.

But I wouldn't have wanted to miss experiencing it like this, pulling through the gate and driving slowly through the trees until the full majesty of the house was revealed. I didn't know what the style would be called, though it made me think of an old English manor, all ivy-covered brick, boxy hedges and climbing roses. I hadn't ever seen anything like it, which wasn't surprising, since I hadn't ever really been outside of Vaikesti.

"Oh, my..." Mirtel breathed as we pulled into a four-car garage, and I concurred. It was overwhelming in every way —a bizarre mix of very old and very modern, designed to blend as seamlessly as possible.

There were no cars in the garage, just what looked to be a workshop set up in the far corner, complete with massive power tools whose names and purposes I didn't know, and wall-to-wall toolboxes in blindingly shiny chrome.

Stephen parked his car and got out, fumbling with a light switch that looked like something out of a sci-fi movie. The lights came up slowly, creating a soft glow that seemed to emanate from all around us, though I couldn't see any light fixtures anywhere.

At the door, Stephen punched in a lengthy series of numbers on a keypad that lit up beneath his fingers. He seemed to be holding his breath while it beeped at him for a long moment, and then we heard a distinctive "click" from the door as it unlatched.

"Come on in," Stephen said over his shoulder. He pushed open the door and paused for a split second, seeming to steel himself before stepping inside.

The lights came on automatically as we filed through the doorway, illuminating our way through an entry hall and into a massive, gleaming white kitchen.

"Air on," Stephen said into the empty room.

"Turning on air conditioning," said a female voice, and we heard a whoosh as the system kicked on. Sofi and I looked at each other with raised eyebrows. We weren't total bumpkins. We understood the technology. Just like most other teens, Vaikesti kids (or at least, those not in the *koolis*) had smartphones and video games. But most of the homes were simpler. More old-fashioned. I'd never seen anything like *this* before.

Stephen shook his head. "It's so over-the-top, I know. My parents had it all installed last summer. Apparently, all the neighbors have smart houses, so that means they should, too."

None of us said anything, until finally Mirtel murmured, "Goodness."

Stephen seemed embarrassed, but I couldn't imagine why. His parents had to be filthy rich to afford this kind of place. My only question was why in the hell would he drive a Honda if he was that loaded?

I didn't get a chance to ask, because my attention was stolen as Stephen said, "Open blinds," and the woman confirmed, "Blinds opening." We heard a mechanical whir, and then a flood of light spilled in as the blinds in the adjacent living room began to lift.

The entire wall seemed to be floor-to-ceiling windows, and as the view was slowly revealed, I went completely speechless. The lake extended out almost endlessly from the back of the house, glimmering orange and red in the fiery glow of the setting sun. I could just make out the opposite shore, a solid wall of green without another house in sight. I couldn't believe Stephen had never told us about this place. It was heavenly.

"We can sit outside," he said finally, gesturing toward a set of French doors that led out onto a massive, three level deck. Just outside the doors was a kitchen outfitted with stainless steel grills and a full-size fridge. An enormous table stretched most of the length of the deck, and on the other side was a large covered hot tub.

Stephen led us down a set of stairs to the middle deck, which was covered in cushioned chairs and chaise lounges.

Below us was the bottom deck, which led out to a small beach and a boat dock.

Sofi took it all in, then turned to Stephen. "Wow. This is..."

Stephen's face went beet red. "It's obnoxious. Practically obscene."

"I think it's gorgeous," Sofi said softly, but Stephen only went redder, if that was even possible.

He pulled over a small table and started arranging Adirondack chairs around it.

"Mirtel, do you have it?" he asked.

"Oh yes," Mirtel said, settling herself into a chair and pulling the binder out of her bag. She placed it on the table and opened it up. "This," she said, "is the answer to our little problem."

"Little?" Aggie asked incredulously, and Mirtel gave her a sly grin.

I wasn't sure if I was annoyed with Mirtel's sunny attitude, or comforted by it. Sofi didn't seem to be sure, either. She eyed the pages warily.

"What is all this?"

"A spell," Mirtel said. "Or, an anti-spell, if you will. These are the instructions to counteract the magic the town is planning to cast at the festival."

Aggie shook her head. "What does that mean, exactly? What will we have to do?"

"Essentially, we'll cast the same spell at the same time. If the power of our spell is balanced with theirs, the spells will cancel one another out."

"Wait," I said, looking around at the others, who all looked as skeptical as I felt. "Our magic has to be as strong as the magic of the *entire* town?"

Mirtel's smile slipped, but it didn't fade. "Well, that is the rub. But I believe if we work now to hone our skills and harness as much of the magic as possible, we can match their power."

"And, uh, how long is it until your...uh...festival?" Stephen asked, pushing his glasses up his nose.

Sofi's face was grim. "Two weeks," she said.

"So...two weeks for the four of you to become as strong as...hundreds of other people?"

I sighed, watching the sun sink down into the water. "I guess we've got some work to do."

CHAPTER 35

SOFI

As I stood under the rainfall showerhead in Stephen's parents' lake house bathroom, in a shower large enough for four grown adults, I let the hot water wash days' worth of grime down the drain and thought to myself that there were worse places to hide out.

Never mind that our plan had so many holes it was practically a sieve. Never mind that the five of us could still barely speak without arguing. Never mind that part of me was still afraid my father would find me here and drag me back home to...what? Perform medical tests? Force me to do magic? I didn't know what he'd had in mind, but I sure didn't want to find out.

I let the thoughts spiral down the drain with the water, before shutting off the tap and stepping out of the glass enclosure. The towel I wrapped around myself was softer than a cloud, and I ran the plush fabric through my fingers as I dried off. We'd left in such a hurry, I'd had no time or thought to stop at home and pack a bag as Mirtel had. Stephen had assured me that the house was well stocked though, and he'd found a pair of his own dark sweats for me to change into, only slightly too large after I rolled the waist and cuffs. I'd gaped at him in disbelief when he'd handed them over. "You have an entire spare wardrobe here? At your parents' *summer* house?"

He'd flushed in clear embarrassment, so I'd accepted the proffered clothes and disappeared into the bathroom. How much money did Stephen's family *have?* And why was he living in a dingy student apartment? I was only beginning to understand that I really didn't know anything about him at all.

Except my own assumptions. Well, those and the fact that he'd listened to our outlandish story, accepted it, and gone on to help us with a difficult and time-consuming translation out of the goodness of his own heart. Of course, then he'd made a copy of the translation that had gotten stolen and landed us in this new mess. But here he was again, hiding us away at his parents' house, helping us for seemingly no reason, at no benefit to himself. I really didn't know what to make of him.

I pushed those thoughts aside as well and marched back out to the enormous dining room, where the group was gathered around the table. Stephen sat by himself at the far end of the heavy carved-wood table, flipping through pages and muttering to himself. I gave him a wide berth and slid in next to Darja instead.

"How's it going?"

She nodded down the table at Stephen. "He's going through the book again, searching for anything else that might help us. I don't think he's going to find anything though."

"And you guys?"

She gave a weary sigh. "More of the same. We were waiting for you to keep going."

Before I'd left to clean up, we'd split into two groups, Mirtel and Aggie, Darja and I. We took turns with one group casting a spell, while the other group cast the counterspell, cancelling out the first group's magic. We'd repeated the process what seemed like a hundred times, until all four of us knew the complicated words by heart and the magic never failed. When the time came, the plan was that all four of us would cast the counterspell together, in the hopes that our magic would be enough to stop the magic of the entire community.

But there was so much we didn't know, so many assumptions we had to make. We didn't even really know what the Town Council had planned. Were they going to split the townspeople into groups of two, and have each of them perform the spell? Would they all be in the same place? Would our counterspell even work if they were spread out, around different fields in the community? Were they going to try other spells too? Not to mention, we didn't know what was happening in town while we were hiding out here by the lake. How many spells had they tried? How many people had already unknowingly given their souls for this magic?

The other faces around the table looked resigned, their thoughts clearly running along the same lines as mine. We'd argued enough at this point, and none of us had the energy to point out the obvious yet again. That this plan was doomed to fail. That the four of us would never be strong enough to stop the combined magic of all the Vaikesti. That even in the slim chance that we did succeed, it likely wouldn't matter. The Town Council had the book—they would just try something else. If anything, our plan was a stopgap, a temporary solution to a much larger problem.

To solve the real problem, we either had to get the book back—and who knew how many copies were floating around at this point—or we had to make everyone understand. And if I couldn't even get my father to listen to me—one single person—how could I possibly get the whole village to listen?

It was hopeless, and I could see my expression mirrored on Mirtel's face across the table. The sadness in her eyes was a stark contrast to her usual cheery demeanor, and it made my heart sink even further. If Mirtel didn't think we had a chance, we were *really* screwed.

To my side, Darja glanced up from the silent conversation she seemed to be having with Aggie, shaking her head slightly, and I looked away at the rawness of Aggie's expression. I wondered again at the relationship that was clearly forming between the two dead girls, but I was determined to stay out of it. Their relationship might be as doomed as our plan, but I wouldn't take from Darja the only happiness she was likely to know, no matter how temporary it might be.

Darja was the first to break the silence.

"Look, we all know the plan sucks. But unless anyone has a better idea, we need to pull it together and keep practicing. It's the only way to get stronger, and we have to make sure we all know the spell by heart."

Mirtel glanced over, the weariness on her lined face making her appear even older than she was. "Should we try something new? Work on range, maybe?"

We'd tried so many variations at this point. We'd learned that the magic didn't only work with a bonded pair. Mirtel and Darja were just as capable of casting a spell as Mirtel and Aggie. We'd learned that the counterspell didn't have to be said at the *exact* same time as the spell it was canceling, as long as some of the words overlapped. But if the first spell was finished, the second one wouldn't affect it.

We hadn't yet considered the distance between the two spell casters, though, and that would be a big variable. If the Vaikesti were all scattered throughout the fields, and we couldn't get to them all, it might be over before we even started.

I nodded. "That's a good idea. Darja, should we go outside? And you two can stay in here?"

"We'll do a spell," Mirtel said, "and you two do the counterspell. Go where you can see us from the window," she instructed, "so we can be sure to do it at the same time."

Which just added another problem to the mix—what if the Vaikesti were all spread out and we couldn't see when the spells were taking place? But I didn't say anything, just headed outside with Darja on my heels.

The floor-to-ceiling windows in the dining room looked out over the thick green forest, and we headed deep into the woods, as far from the house as we could be while still able to see the figures through the window.

I saw Stephen's head come up, watching us, and muttered to Darja, "Ready?"

She nodded. We hadn't taken the papers with us; after all this practice, we knew the words by heart.

I waited until I saw Mirtel's hands lift in a signal, and I started reciting the spell. I didn't stumble over any of the unfamiliar pronunciations anymore; the words were easy and smooth as they fell from my lips. The second I finished, Darja started in on her part. When she was halfway through, I saw the lights in the house flicker out, casting the figures inside into shadow, and I knew their spell had worked. I held my breath as Darja finished her lines, muscles tense, but as I'd hoped, the counterspell worked, and a second later the lights came back on. Even through the distance I could see the relief on the faces in the house.

I blew out my breath.

"Should we try further?" Mirtel asked when we were together again in the dining room.

"But if we can't see you, how will we know when you're casting the spell?" I protested.

"We could pick a time," Darja suggested. "Maybe take the car and drive away a distance, then we both do our spells at two o'clock, and see what happens? Find out what the end range is on this thing?"

Mirtel nodded. "That's a good idea. Once we know how far we can go, we can keep practicing and see if the range increases as we get stronger."

So we did. And once we had the answers there, we tried something else, and then something else, until the days were flying past and we'd tried every combination and tested every variable we could think of, until our exhaustion overpowered our worry.

There were some things we couldn't try. We desperately wanted to know if the counterspell could wipe out more than one spell at once, or if it was just a simple one-to-one ratio. But there were only four of us, so there was no way to test the theory.

The list of what we *did* know was growing too, though. After days of experimentation, we knew that our range did indeed grow with our powers, and by the time we felt satisfied with that experiment, we could counter spells that were being cast over three miles away, even though the timing was still a problem. We also discovered that while the spells worked with any living and dead pair, it turned out they were much stronger when performed with a bonded pair.

As the days wore on, only Stephen left the property, running out to buy food while the rest of us stayed hidden, until finally Aggie, of all people, reminded us that she and Darja couldn't be seen by anyone else—a fact I'd somehow almost forgotten. She suggested the two of them go back to Vaikesti to do some reconnaissance and see if they could find out anything more about what was happening in town, or what the plans were for the Midsummer festival.

It seemed like such an obvious oversight that I mentally kicked myself for not thinking of it first, then went on to wonder what else we might be missing.

The two of them left right away, and returned hours later, overflowing with information about the plans the town had made for the approaching festival.

There was something else there too, I noticed. The two transparent, white-clad figures stood close together, and an expression I'd never seen graced Aggie's face when she looked at Darja. It was almost...soft. But by the time we'd all gathered inside, clustered around the dining room table again, the two were all business.

"It's not everyone," Darja said in a rush. "They want to turn it into a big event at the festival, so they're targeting just the fields around the fairgrounds. They've asked for a hundred volunteers to split into pairs and cast the spells, and everyone will be in sight of the grandstand at the fairgrounds, so they can make a big spectacle of it. Then, if everything works, they'll go out and magic up the rest of the fields later once Midsummer is over."

"Then they'll all be within our range," Mirtel said, breathing out a sigh of relief, but I wasn't so sure. Fifty spells to cancel. That was still a lot, when we didn't even know if we could cancel more than one at a time.

Aggie directed a frown my way. "It's good that we're here. Your father is searching for you, and he's furious. They have the police looking for you as well."

My heart skipped a beat. "Do you think they'll—?"

"No," Darja cut in. "They won't look here. They've searched Stephen's apartment, but they're still looking in town. Your car is parked at Mirtel's, so they're focusing on that connection right now." She glanced at Mirtel, then lowered her voice. "But I'm pretty sure he suspects that you're bonded too."

Mirtel just nodded, like it was to be expected, but my breath was still stuck in my throat. No matter what happened at the festival, there was no going back after this. No way to return things to the way they had been. I suddenly felt very cold, and very alone, even surrounded by these people I cared so much for. What would my life look like once this was over? Where would I go, and who would I be?

I glanced up to see Stephen watching me from across the table. His eyes were sad, and it was almost like he could read my thoughts. Almost like he understood how I felt. I looked away, then shook my head. It didn't matter.

It felt like we were gearing up for war, and there was no time to expend thought or energy on anything other than the upcoming battle. Because it was true. We had battle plans to make, logistics to figure out. Lives to save. And barely any time to do it.

Because Midsummer was only two days away.

CHAPTER 36

DARJA

I didn't know how much more Sofi could take—how much more *any* of us could take. She was curled up in an Adirondack chair on the middle deck, gazing into the flames Stephen had coaxed to life in the brick firepit. Mirtel had gone in to rest, and Aggie had disappeared not long after. Stephen had retreated back into the living room, so it was just the two of us left overlooking the edge of the lake, watching as the sun sank beneath the still surface of the water to the west.

"I'm really sorry," I said. Sofi didn't look at me; she just blinked, though whether it was reflex or recognition, I wasn't sure.

"About your—*our*—dad," I went on. "And just...everything that's happened."

Sofi said nothing, and after a moment, I heard a tinny *pling* from her cell phone. She swiped it open, typed something quickly, then put it back in her pocket. When she was done, she looked back at the fire, her cheeks bathed in flickering shadows, her eyes hooded.

I decided to keep trying. "It must feel like your entire life is upside down," I said, edging closer to her. "I didn't know him—any of them—before. But I wish—"

"You wish *what*?" she said, snapping her head around to cast the full weight of her stare on me. I was startled and shrank back, flickering a little as I did.

"You wish you'd gotten to know him?" she said, sitting up and swinging her legs over the edge of the chair. "You wish you'd had the chance to be one of daddy's little girls? That he'd loved you, or said he did? You wish you'd spent your whole life believing your family was perfect, only to find out you were wrong?"

What the hell? The sudden outburst was so out of character for Sofi, and though I understood the pain she was going through, I couldn't help feel a flicker of anger in response.

"I'm sorry," I said, "but *what*?"

"Oh, you're sorry?" Sofi said. "Sorry about *what*, Darja? That my dad is some kind of cult leader? A religious fanatic? A scumbag who messes around with underage girls? That he's complicit in the murder of how many girls? *Of his own daughter?*"

"Well," I said, starting to warm up to the brewing fight, "as the daughter he helped murder, I think I have a little more right to be pissed off than you do."

I could feel that we were teetering on a precipice, and it wasn't one I was sure we could climb back from. We were all at our breaking point, and every day, I felt Sofi retreat further into herself, pulling away from me, away from our bond. I resented him for that, and just then, I resented her, too.

"You aren't the only one he's betrayed."

Sofi laughed, a harsh, unpleasant sound, twisting her

usually soft and delicate features into something sharp and jagged, like stone. She stood up, stepping towards me.

"And you didn't spend eighteen years holding him up as some kind of hero."

I could feel the anger smoldering inside me, catching and spreading through my chest and into my throat.

"So what you're saying," I said, and I could hear the venom in my tone, "is that because my *entire life* has been shit, I can't understand how hard it is for poor, perfect Sofi right now?"

She recoiled as if I'd hit her. "You have no idea," she snarled.

I laughed. "You're right about that. I have no idea what it's like to grow up in a home with parents and brothers and sisters and aunts and grandparents. I have no *clue* what it must be like to celebrate holidays surrounded by people who love me. To have someone give me a birthday present. To never be hungry. Or lonely. Or scared. So excuse me, *sister*, if I can't muster up much sympathy for your idyllic little life."

When she slapped me, it didn't connect, of course, but I felt it just the same. I went instantly hot and cold where her hand passed through me, and I felt for a moment that I would dissolve into particles—of energy, or dust—and fly away.

We stood, staring at one another, for a long, drawn out moment. I thought she might be holding her breath, and I thought that if I could still breathe, I'd be doing the same. The pause stretched out, and then her phone *pinged* again, sending her fumbling in her pocket.

I couldn't see the screen as she swiped it open, but even if I'd tried, she only glanced at it momentarily before snapping it off and spinning on her heel, stalking toward the door to the living room.

"Where are you going?" I shouted after her, not quite ready to give up on the fight.

"To bed," she shouted, and slammed the door so hard the glass panes inside it rattled.

"Fine!" I yelled after her, but she was already gone.

I stayed out on the deck for a while, losing track of time, which seemed to get easier and easier the further I got from my mortal coil. When I saw the moon hanging low and heavy across the opposite shore, I went inside, glancing at the lump on the couch that appeared to be Stephen, hidden under a pile of heavy quilts and surrounded by open books and loose pages.

Further down the hall, I passed Sofi's room, but didn't dare intrude. The next door down was Mirtel's, and I thought I might try to talk to her, to see if she had any wisdom to impart.

As I approached, I could hear the raised voices from the hallway.

At first I backed away, thinking it was none of my business and I'd just shove off and pretend I'd never heard anything. But then I heard my name. *Darja*. Said with such longing and pain that I found myself suddenly rooted to the spot.

"In all these years..." It was Aggie talking, and I could hear the rage and the tears mingled in her voice. "...she is the only thing that's ever been *mine*."

"Then I can't understand why you're talking like this," Mirtel said, in a voice clipped by the strain of trying to keep it under control. "It's just...nonsense. Crazy talk. I won't hear anymore of it."

"You don't get a choice. Mirtel, if there's some way...some way we can escape this...*together*—"

"Together without me? Without Sofi? And what becomes of us? Of your bonded?" There was a quaver then, in Mirtel's voice, and I could hear that whatever grip she had on the conversation was about to slip away.

"You *live*," Aggie said forcefully. "Alone. As it was always intended. It isn't the natural order of things, to remain here, *after*..."

"Trapped, you mean?"

I could hear a sigh, though I wasn't sure who it came from.

"Yes," Aggie said finally. "Bonded. Trapped. It's all the same."

"And yet," Mirtel began, the pain in her voice like a lance in my side, "if we hadn't been bonded, you and Darja would never have crossed paths...on either side of the veil."

"How dare you?" Aggie said, but I could hear that most of the fight had drained out of her. "How dare you throw Darja in my face? As if I'm not allowed some happiness?"

I faded back then, into the shadows, embarrassed to have been listening in on such a deeply personal conversation. My cheeks felt hot, a memory of what it was to blush, and I suddenly wanted to cry, to sleep, to curl up somewhere soft and warm and escape into unconsciousness.

Instead, I went back to the deck, and stared out at the water until the moon drooped low, like a pregnant belly, and then dipped slowly beneath the surface. I waited until the sun was fully above the horizon to go back inside, where Stephen was stirring on the sofa, fumbling, eyes shut, for the glasses he'd left at the other end of the coffee table. Taking pity on him, I waved my hand and levitated them into the air, floating them over to the opposite side of the table and plinking them down next to his questing hand.

He blinked, suddenly awake, and when he caught sight of me hovering nearby, must have realized what I had done.

"Thanks," he mumbled, sitting up and stifling a yawn. He was all gangly limbs and messy hair, and I could imagine exactly what he'd looked like as a little boy—awkward, bumbling, and sweetly strange.

I smiled and turned to go.

"Wait up," he said, gathering some of the papers from the floor and shuffling through them. "I wanted to talk to you about something."

"Okay, shoot," I said, molding myself into a position that suggested I was sitting in the overstuffed chair next to the couch.

"I had an idea, for the festival," he said. "I was thinking, once we get to the edge of town, we cast a spell—on the whole village—so they can see you and Aggie."

"On every person in town? Won't that take up a lot of the energy we need to perform the counterspell? And besides, why?"

Stephen frowned. "I think if they could see the sacrifice they're making for this...this *magic*...they'll understand it's not worth it. They'll see that you two had to die for it. That *they're* dying for it. You can tell them you weren't a willing sacrifice—that none of the chosen girls have been. But it won't be real to them if you're just invisible boogeymen."

I nodded, but I wasn't totally convinced. "How could we manage it though? Isn't it too risky? And don't we need to hold hands? Besides, we're exhausted after a few hours of casting spells on each other, let alone an entire town."

"It can be done," he insisted. "The hand-holding was your interpretation of the symbols in the book, but it's not necessary. You've worked plenty of spells together without anyone making physical contact. And you're right that it'll take a lot of energy, but here's what I'm thinking: if we make you and Aggie visible, we might be able to convince them not to try the spell. Once they see you and they know the magic is real—and really dangerous—they might give up."

"So, we wouldn't need our energy for the counterspell?"

"Exactly." Stephen pushed his glasses up and peered at me nervously over the frames, as if worried about getting my approval.

I shrugged. I didn't think there was a chance in hell it would work, but he looked like he needed a win. "I mean... sure. I guess. We should probably get the others on-board, though."

Stephen's expression was relieved. "Yes, absolutely. I can talk to Mirtel and Aggie, if you'll talk to Sofi."

I tried not to roll my eyes at this. "She won't bite, you know. Besides, I doubt she's still pissed at you."

Stephen raised a skeptical brow. "Really?"

"Maybe a little. But she'll get over it. She likes you."

Stephen's eyes snapped up to meet mine. "She does?"

I smiled. "She does. She may not admit it, even to herself, but I think you've grown on her."

"Like a fungus. Great."

I laughed. "Like a friend. Like someone she can rely on. She doesn't have too many of those these days."

"You're right," Stephen said, and his hunched shoulders went a little straighter. "She needs people on her side. And... I like her, too."

"I know you do."

I started to say more, when I spied a movement over his shoulder, through the window. It was Mirtel. She'd somehow managed to sneak out onto the deck, quiet as a cat. And, like a cat, she was curled up on one of the lounge chairs, her book of Vaikesti history open in her lap. She wasn't reading it though; she was staring out over the water, her face troubled. The lines around her eyes and mouth had deepened overnight.

I nodded at her and Stephen turned to look out the window, then gathered up his papers. "Wish me luck," he said.

I didn't respond, but secretly wished luck for both of us. I went back down the hallway where I'd eavesdropped on their conversation. When I got to Sofi's closed door, I lingered for a moment, wondering how to politely request entrance when I couldn't knock. I cleared my throat, waited a minute, then leaned closer, putting my mouth close to the door jamb.

"Sofi?" I called. "Can I...can I come in? Please?"

There was no answer. I thought about making my case, presenting my apology, pleading with her to let me in, but I settled for whispering a half-hearted, "Sorry," and flickered myself into her room.

Sofi was nowhere to be found. But just as I began to panic, I saw a sheet of paper on top of the still-made bed. My name was scrawled across the top in Sofi's looping handwriting.

Darja, it said, *I'm sorry about our fight. I wasn't being fair to you. I feel like this is my mess to clean up, and I hate dragging all of you into it. That's why I have to leave. Jared knows what's going on, and I think he can help. He can stop this. He can shut down the festival. I had to tell him...I'm sorry. I'm sorry for everything. Love, Sofi.*

Lifting my hand, I levitated the note into midair, bringing it closer and reading it again, then once more. I stood there, unmoving, for a long moment, then slowly, I closed my fist. The note crumpled, then dropped to the floor.

I could hear the static crackle around me, could feel myself begin to flicker. I closed my eyes and searched, reaching out with my mind, my spirit...whatever it was that was connected to her.

And I felt it. The tug. The one that had grown fainter the longer we were bonded. Or maybe I'd just gotten used to it. But the one that was still there, binding us together. The festival was just a day away, and if we had any hope of stopping the Council, we had to act. So I would follow the bond. I would find her. And I would bring her back.

CHAPTER 37

SOFI

I hated the way talking to Jared made me feel like I was betraying my friends. But I didn't know what else to do. We'd been cooped up at Stephen's parents' house for nearly two weeks, testing our abilities and trying to prepare for something entirely out of our league, and it felt like we were just running in circles. We weren't going to be able to stop this on our own. There were too many what ifs. What if the counterspell only stopped one spell at a time? What if we weren't strong enough? What if our information about the festival was wrong?

No.

We needed help, and Jared was the only person I could think of who I could trust. He could get his dad to help. The Town Council might not listen to me, but surely they would listen to the sheriff. He was an actual authority. He could stop this.

I took Stephen's little red Honda, feeling bad as I swiped the keys from the kitchen hook. It was the only car we had, and we would need it to get everyone to town in the morning, but I would be back by then. And if I could get Jared to cancel the festival, or at least to stop the magical display, maybe we wouldn't need to come into town at all.

I checked the clock on the dashboard display. Eleven forty-five. Then I glanced at my phone, resting on the passenger's seat. No new messages. I thumbed it on to make sure, checking the last couple of messages.

Jared: Can you meet me outside the back door to the police station?

Sofi: I can be there by midnight.

God, I hoped he would listen. I'd started to try to explain everything by text, and quickly realized this was too much to deal with and we'd have to do it in person.

He was there when I pulled up, silhouetted under the streetlight that lit the back parking lot, and when I ran up to join him he grabbed me and pulled me into a hug. His arms were tight around me and I melted into the embrace, my fears of betraying the others eclipsed by the relief I felt in his arms. He would fix this, he *had* to.

"Sofi, where have you *been?*" he asked, his voice muffled against my hair. "Nobody has seen you in weeks. I've been so worried."

"I'm sorry," I said into his chest, then pulled back. "I'll explain everything. There's so much to tell you, and practically no time. But I need your help."

He took my hand in his and pulled me out of the pool of light and around the back of the municipal complex to where the sidewalk wove through town. The moon was barely visible, a waning crescent high in the starry sky.

"Sofi," he said, pulling my attention back to him. "Are you okay? Your texts...they didn't make sense. All about magic and the festival and the missing girl? What's going on?"

It's now or never. I took a deep breath, clutched his hand tight in mine, and tried to figure out where to start.

"The missing girl you've been looking for? Darja Kallas? She's...dead."

Jared's steps slowed and he pulled me around to face him. His voice was cautious. "What are you talking about?"

"Look, I barely know how to explain. There's so much..." I blew out a breath. I didn't have much time; I just had to spit it all out. "Okay. I don't know how much you know about Vaikesti customs, but when Vaikesti teenagers turn eighteen, there's a ceremony..."

I went on to—for the second time in my life—divulge all of the community's most closely held secrets to an outsider, and though Jared was certainly less of one than Stephen had been—he had at least grown up here with us—it certainly didn't feel any less wrong or strange. I described Darja's sacrifice. I described the magical bond that the ceremony was intended to create, and I explained how it had worked, tying us together.

Jared's eyes were huge and round, but he didn't interrupt, pulling me instead to sit on a park bench off the sidewalk not far from the fairgrounds, and let me pour it all out.

I let my gaze wander as I spoke, afraid to look at him and see whatever expression was on his face—horror? Disbelief? Disgust? Instead, I stared out into the dark night, my eyes drifting over all the shadowed shapes in the distance by the fairgrounds that would be the preparations for the festival. There would be tents waiting to be filled with food, kids' activities like face painting and treasure hunts, booths filled with farm-related games, spaces cleared for dancing. There would be livestock judging and baking competitions and traditional artwork. Everything would be decorated with flowers and brightly colored ribbons.

But at the moment it was all just a series of shadowed

lumps in the distance, dark and vaguely sinister against the nearly moonless night sky.

My hands clenched around the edge of the bench as I described the events of the last couple of months. I told him about Mirtel and Aggie. About the spell book and Stephen's translation. About casting spells—*real* magical spells.

At that, I heard a sharp indrawn breath, and I turned to face Jared again. His gaze was fixed on me, his expression intense and unreadable. God, I hoped he believed me.

I kept going, telling him about how the book had turned up in the hands of my father, and everything we'd learned about my father and Darja's parentage. Part of me felt guilty spilling those secrets, but a larger part of me felt vindicated. *You owe him nothing,* I reminded myself viciously. And his precious secret was finally out. I wondered what the fallout of that revelation might be. Would Jared arrest my father? Could he, after all this time? Did I care? I wasn't sure.

I ended with the most important part of all—what we'd learned by watching the villagers cast a spell, and what the village had planned for the following morning. "It's going to kill them," I told him, my voice wavering. "It's not the way the magic is meant to be used, but they don't know any better. It's our fault, for making the translation, and copying down those blank pages, and we have to stop it." I gazed at him imploringly. "That's why I need your help. We don't know what to do. *I* don't know what to do. And it's almost too late. I need you to help me stop this. Stop the festival, stop the magic, or it'll destroy the town. It'll kill everyone."

My voice broke on the last word, and I turned my face up to his, afraid of what I might find there. He'd been so quiet during my tale.

The expression I found was not at all what I'd been expecting. I'd figured he would be shocked, or maybe disbelieving and I would have to work harder to convince him of the truth. What I did not expect was a broad smile and shining eyes.

"Sofi," he breathed. "That's *amazing*." He took my shaking hands, clutching them tight in his own. "*You're* amazing. It's true? The bonding worked? You can do magic?"

"What?" My stomach twisted in confusion. "Yes, I—"

"I always knew you were special, Sofi. This just proves it. Tell me more. Tell me about the magic."

The nervous adrenaline that had been running through me the whole time I'd been talking shifted, turning sharp and metallic.

"You knew. How could you—what did you know?"

"Some of it," he admitted, his smile not fading. "Not all of it. I didn't know the bonding *worked*."

"*What?* But you're not Vaikesti. How could you—?"

His smile finally faded, his expression turning soft. "Oh, come on Sofi. Don't be naive. My dad's the sheriff, and teenagers have been going 'missing' for years. Of course we know what's going on."

I couldn't seem to take a full breath. "But you—you've been investigating her disappearance for weeks."

He raised an eyebrow. "Well, sure. We have to keep up appearances, right? It'd look pretty strange if we didn't even *try* to find her. But Sofi, this is amazing. Everything makes so much sense now."

He jerked on my hand, pulling me in for a hug. I didn't even have the wherewithal to pull away, my mind was racing too fast, trying hard to process everything that was happening.

"I was so worried about you," he said against my hair. "I couldn't figure out why you kept hanging around with that Stephen guy, and the crazy lady—she's bonded too?—it explains so much. But it's okay, Sofi, everything is going to be okay now. I'll take care of you."

He leaned back, holding my shoulders in both hands, and I felt like a ragdoll, my head stuffed full of cotton.

The realization, when it hit, was cold and painful and horrifyingly obvious.

"It was you. Of course it was." My voice was a whisper. "You lied to me when you said the book had gone missing. You're the one who gave it to my dad."

"Well, actually, I gave it to *my* dad," he corrected. "I didn't even know what it was, not really, it just looked like something that might be important. He took it to the Council." He turned his beaming smile on me again. "I can't believe it was *you* that found it, though. You're going to be a hero, Sofi. Don't you realize that? You're the one who brought magic back to Vaikesti. They'll say you saved your people."

I jerked out of his hold. "Didn't you hear anything I said? The magic is going to destroy them."

He shook his head. "Sofi, c'mon, that can't be true. They've already been using it, trying out spells, and no one's *dying*. You've got it wrong. Look, you've done your part; you found the book. Now you can leave it to the Council. They know what to do with it."

He took my hand again, and I jerked it back as if his touch had burned me. "I was wrong to come here. Darja warned me, but I didn't listen. I thought you could help, but no one can help us now." I pushed unsteadily to my feet.

"Wait." Jared rose as well, stepping close, and I took a stumbling step back. "Sofi, calm down. Everything is okay. The hard part is over. I can *help* you."

"Help me? How?" I demanded. "By stopping the festival? Because that's the only help I need."

"No, listen to me." He made a frustrated gesture. "Don't

you see? Sofi, I'm going to be the sheriff someday. And you—you're the one who brought magic back to Vaikesti. Don't you see the influence we could have, if we're careful, and use it correctly? You can't just throw away that kind of power. The two of us together, we could—"

"We?" I choked on a laugh. "There's no *we*. You betrayed me from the start, and I was too stupid to see it. I have to go." I turned and started to hurry back down the path.

"Sofi, wait—"

I didn't wait to hear what he had to say. I needed to get back to the others. I needed to tell them what had happened. We needed to move forward with our plan.

"Sofi!"

But my stupidity never seemed to cease. Had I actually thought he would just let me go? Would I ever learn?

I'd barely made it to the end of the block before I heard his footsteps behind me, pounding on the pavement. With a gasp, I lurched into a run.

"Damn it, Sofi, don't make this harder than it needs to be."

But I never stood a chance. He wasn't even winded when he caught up, and Stephen's dented Honda was in sight behind the municipal building when Jared tackled me to the ground. The air blew out of my lungs with the force of my landing, and I didn't even have time to react before the feel of cold steel clamped around my wrists.

———

No one could say I didn't fight. I screamed, and swore, and spat, but no one came to help me. I kicked at the door of the car that had been parked around the corner as he forced me into the back. I tried reasoning with him as he pulled away from the curb and drove into the night. I tried begging and sobbing. Pleading.

Nothing worked.

I needed Darja. I wasn't even sure what she could do, but I needed her. If nothing else, she could tell the others, and they could come help me.

"When this is over, you'll thank me, Sofi," Jared told me, glancing in the rearview mirror. "I'm only trying to keep you safe, I really am. Your dad has been frantic since you've been missing. He calls me every day. I promised him."

I renewed my struggles.

It didn't take me long to realize he was driving toward my house, but after a tense phone call with my dad, he swung the car around and we ended up back where we'd started. I didn't make it easy for him to get me out of the car and into the municipal building, but rather than take me to the police station as I expected, we ended up in my dad's office.

By the time my father arrived I was drained of energy, my wrists bruised and sore, and sweat from my efforts plastered my shirt to my back. I couldn't muster anything beyond a glare.

Darja, where the hell are you?

They took me into one of the patient rooms, the same one Darja and I had rescued Mirtel from what seemed like a lifetime ago. My father barely spared me a glance as he entered, turning to Jared instead.

"Help me with this."

I used what little strength I had left to fight them as they released my handcuffs and transferred me to the hospital bed, but it was no use, and they locked down my wrists and ankles in the restraints there instead.

"Thanks, son. I've got it from here," my dad said with a dismissive nod to Jared.

Jared, who to my satisfaction looked just as tired from my struggles as I felt, glanced my way in concern. "Are you sure? I can—"

"I've got it," my father repeated, and his voice made it clear he would not be listening to any arguments, even from a police officer.

With only another quick glance my way, Jared left.

My father turned his attention to me.

"Where have you been? No," he cut himself off. "It doesn't matter; I don't have time for this. You'll stay here until the festival is over, and I'll deal with you then."

Part of me felt that I should try again, try to explain, try to make him listen. *Someone* had to listen, to understand. But the greater part of me was too tired. Too overwhelmed. Too traumatized. I heaved a sigh and turned my face to the wall, unable to even look at him.

I heard his footsteps head toward the door.

Good. Just leave me alone. Go away so I can wait for Darja in peace.

But rather than leave, he called down the hall. "Mrs. Rebane, I'm ready for you now."

I jerked my head around, just as my dad's nurse entered the room. Sandra Rebane was a plump, older woman with gray hair and a ready smile, always sneaking lollipops and stickers to kids as they left the office. But right then her smile had been replaced by a solemn expression and a furrowed brow, and she gripped a piece of paper tight in her hands. She glanced between my father and the paper, conspicuously refusing to meet my eyes.

My heartbeat leaped again. *What—?*

"Go ahead, Sandra."

"Et varjata elu ja surma sidet..."

As soon as I heard the words pass her lips, the spell given life by her shaky voice, I began to scream.

"NO! Stop. Don't do this."

She ignored me, focusing her attention on the page in front of her, and my father ignored me as well, his foot tapping against the tile floor as he waited for his nurse to stumble through the words.

When she finished, she let out a shaky breath, and my father jerked the paper from her grip, starting his own recitation.

"Dad, no. Oh my God, you don't know what you're doing. *Stop.*"

It didn't matter what he'd done, how many times he'd betrayed me; even if he deserved it, I couldn't bear to watch my father lose his *soul*.

Tears filled my eyes, but he didn't stop, and when the last word crossed his lips he turned his attention to me again, peering close, and the look of utter shock and horror that I knew had crossed my face must have been clear proof that the spell had worked.

Because I hadn't even realized my bond with Darja was something I could sense, a tangible feeling inside me, until it was suddenly gone. A vast, gaping emptiness yawned inside me.

A scream wrenched from my throat.

"*DARJA!*"

With a satisfied nod, my father turned and left, ushering Mrs. Rebane ahead of him. Distantly I heard the click of a lock as he shut the door behind him, but I barely noticed. All my attention, everything within me, was focused on the absence, on the bond that was no longer there.

CHAPTER 38

DARJA

I was on my way back down the hall to find the others when Aggie materialized in front of me. I swallowed a scream and tried to smile, but I could feel the tremble in my lower lip. The smile on her face dissolved, replaced by a look of concern that softened her eyes and made me want to melt into her.

But I couldn't melt. Not yet. Not until we got Sofi back.

"What is it?" Aggie said, looking more worried the longer I said nothing.

"It's Sofi," I managed to say over the lump in my throat. "She's gone."

Aggie's eyebrows shot up. "What do you mean, 'gone'?"

I shook my head, still not fully understanding it myself. "She left a note," I said. "She's gone to see Jared. She thinks...I don't know, she thinks he can help."

Aggie looked horrified. I'd expected she'd be angry at Sofi for spilling the secrets of the Vaikesti to an outsider, but the naked fear in her eyes surprised me.

"I think she...I think she kinda likes him?" I said, feeling a bit defensive of Sofi's choice, even though I thought it was a stupid one.

Aggie shook her head. "That's not it. Don't you see, Darja? Sofi's in *danger*. This is not something the *Vaikesti* take lightly." Her eyes clouded. "They never have. Why do you think, in all these generations, not a single Vaikesti girl knew about the ceremony before the very day? Why do you think decades of missing girls have never made the nightly news? Why isn't our town crawling with police, detectives, FBI?"

I shook my head. A creeping sense of dread was brewing deep within me, and I could feel tendrils of fear snaking up my spine.

"Because," Aggie said, "no one who knows more than they should has been around long enough to tell anyone. We didn't come here just to practice our little spells. We came here to protect Sofi."

"But they wouldn't...they wouldn't *hurt* her," I said, my voice thin and uncertain. Even to my ears, it sounded absurdly naive.

Aggie looked torn between irritation and compassion. I was pretty sure I knew which would win out in the end, but instead of prickling, Aggie drifted closer, her eyes pitying, brows furrowed with worry. The magic crackled between us, enveloping us in some kind of force field. It was us against the world. I wished more than anything that I could sink into it, that I could sink into her and forget about life and death and anything else that would disturb this delicate thread between us.

Aggie raised her hand, sweeping a lock of hair behind my ear. "Sofi is a threat to the Vaikesti," she said softly, and I nodded, though my mind was more focused on the electricity that arced along the path her finger traced down my jaw. "That's why she needs you," she went on, moving her other hand up to my waist. "We protect our Bonded."

And we did. I knew she'd done the same for Mirtel, and some faraway corner of my still-functioning brain wondered how many times they'd argued over the years, Aggie talking Mirtel down, taking the metaphorical matches when the older woman had been close to lighting a blaze.

Aggie leaned in closer, pulling me toward her. There was no breath to feel, but there was warmth against my lips. A tingling that raced through my body, and it was suddenly so much more—so much better—than anything I'd ever felt while I'd been alive. Her nose brushed against mine, and I felt my eyelids flutter closed.

"There'll be time for this later," she murmured against my mouth. "Once she's safe."

It was like I'd unexpectedly stepped into an ice cold shower. The emptiness, the lack of warmth, when Aggie pulled away shocked me into opening my eyes, bringing me back to the present. The cocoon of magic we'd been wrapped in was still there, but I could see beyond it. I had a job to do, and Aggie was right—there would be time for the rest of it later. An eternity for the rest of it.

"Right," I said, pretending I couldn't hear the quaver in my voice. "We've got to go after her."

Aggie nodded, looking decidedly disheveled.

"Where is she?" she asked. "We need to know what we're marching into."

I closed my eyes and felt for the tug, ready to follow it to wherever Sofi was.

There was nothing.

I opened my eyes and looked at Aggie, who was watching me curiously. Maybe I'd just been distracted, caught up in the moment with her. I shook my head, gathering my concentration, and closed my eyes again. I could feel the familiar sensation around my waist, behind my navel, like a rope that ran around and through me. I followed it outward, knowing it would lead me to Sofi. I inched my way along the imaginary rope, willing Sofi's energy—her magical presence—to make itself known.

But Sofi wasn't there.

When I opened my eyes again, I could see Aggie's worry, plain on her face.

"What is it?" she asked, though I could hear from the dread in her voice that she already had an idea. That same dread was creeping through me as well, a tightness that started in my chest and unfurled insidiously through my entire being.

I shook my head, not wanting to give voice to horrifying reality. Finally, I forced myself to answer. "She's not there."

"What do you mean she's not there?" There was panic in Aggie's voice, and I knew that it was because she alone understood the implication of that—of not being able to feel your Bonded.

"There's just...nothing. When I came down the hall, I could feel her, like always, and now... it's gone." I looked up into Aggie's eyes, the horror of the situation dawning on both of us. "Our bond is gone."

Aggie's jaw clenched, and I could see that, like me, she was fighting back an onslaught of emotions. "I'm going to get the others," she said finally, and I nodded, feeling numb. She flickered out, and for the first time since I'd taken my last breath, I knew what it was to feel well and truly alone.

"What can this mean?" Mirtel said, wringing her hands together. Stephen was pacing the kitchen floor, frantically alternating between adjusting his glasses and tugging at his hair. Aggie hovered between Mirtel and me, as if she wasn't sure which of us needed her more.

The truth was, we all needed each other, more than ever. And above all, I needed Sofi. I needed her safe. I needed her near. I needed to know that the other half of my soul—my sister—was not in danger.

"Is there magic that can do this?" Aggie asked, and Stephen stopped suddenly in his rounds. Without a word, he ran to the coffee table in the living room and began manically rifling through the heaps of papers piled there.

"If it's a spell," Mirtel said, looking at Aggie and me hopefully, "that's good, right? It just means someone has worked magic on her. It doesn't mean..."

It doesn't mean she's dead.

Because though none of us had said it, we all knew there were only two logical reasons our bond would be severed. Magic. Or...the alternative.

"Here!" Stephen shouted from the living room. We all shuffled in as he waved a sheet of paper triumphantly over his head. "I think I've got something." He held the spell out toward us as we all craned in to read it. It was untranslated except for the title: *Smothering Spell*.

I shook my head as the rest of the spell, all the words in the old language, seemed to wriggle and squirm on the page in an incomprehensible jumble. "What does it mean?"

"I can't find our full translation," Stephen said, frowning down at the page as if he could guilt it into giving up its secrets. "I did this one a while ago, before we really understood the magic. But I think it's a spell to dampen it somehow. It can't destroy the magic, but it can muffle it, like throwing a blanket over it."

"But I can't feel *anything*," I said, the shrillness growing in my voice.

"That's because of the distance," Stephen said, pushing

up his glasses. "We know she left to go back to town, so she's out of range. Normally, I think you'd be able to feel *something*, but the distance combined with the spell makes it almost impossible to sense the bond."

"What do we do?" Aggie asked. "Can we end the spell if we didn't cast it?"

Stephen shook his head, looking dismayed. "I don't know. But even if we could, probably not from this far away. We've got to get back into town."

"And what about the festival?" Mirtel said, quietly. We all turned to look at her. The festival was the last thing on my mind.

"For all I'm concerned," I said, feeling my frustration swell up within me, "the festival and everyone near it can burn."

Mirtel looked pained, but stubborn as ever. "There are many lives at stake," she said.

"Sofi's life is at stake," I shouted, hearing the crackle in the air and feeling the charge of my anger.

Even though it wasn't directed at him, I saw Stephen back up a step. He put his hands up in a placating gesture.

"No matter what," he said, his voice quiet and low, "we have to get back to Vaikesti." He glanced at Mirtel. "Without two bonded pairs, we won't have the strength to stop the townspeople."

Mirtel's face crumpled, and I thought she might cry. I knew she didn't want any harm to come to Sofi, but I also knew she'd been fighting her whole life—labeled the town crazy lady, shunned and ostracized—to save the town from itself. I felt pity well up inside me, but it wasn't enough to squelch my anger.

"We can't do this without Sofi," I said through gritted teeth. "If she isn't safe, none of us are."

"If we go now," Aggie said, "we'll have time before the

festival. We already know she was going to see Jared, so if we find him, she'll be there." She sounded far more confident than I felt, and I was grateful for it.

Stephen nodded. "You're right," he said, "we need to leave right now. If she went to see Jared"—he spat out the name as if it tasted bitter on his tongue—"she might be at the jail. We need to give ourselves time to work on an escape plan. Mirtel, I'll pull the car around, if you want to grab your stuff."

Mirtel nodded, still looking morose, and disappeared down the hall to her room. Aggie and I waited in silence. I wondered if she'd be upset with me for taking a harsh tone with Mirtel. If she was, I knew I'd hear about it. I took her quietness as a good sign.

Mirtel emerged from the hallway a few moments later, threadbare bag and spell binder in hand, and we moved toward the front door. Before we reached the entryway though, Stephen bounded back in from the garage.

"I'm an idiot," he declared, picking up random objects he'd scattered over the kitchen island, obviously searching for something.

"What is it?" I asked.

"Sofi took the car," he said with a brittle sort of laugh. "I don't know if I was thinking she just teleported herself back to Vaikesti or what."

"So what do we do?" I asked. "Can we even get a cab this far from civilization?"

Stephen huffed another mostly humorless laugh. "We can barely get an ambulance out here," he said. "A discovery I made right around the same time I learned I'm highly allergic to bees."

"So what are we supposed to do?" Aggie said.

Stephen sighed. "I don't know. Maybe the two of you could phase back to Vaikesti and—"

"And what?" Aggie said. "We can't make ourselves visible without a bonded, we can't drive a car—we can't even talk to anyone."

"Great plan," I said darkly. "Besides, if Aggie and I use up our energy getting back to Vaikesti, we'll be worthless later. With both of us out of commission, we won't stand a chance."

"I know that," Stephen said, yanking open drawers and pawing through the contents. "Just...give me a minute, okay?"

We waited impatiently while Stephen tore apart the kitchen, finally resorting to upturning drawers and dumping everything from utensils to potholders on the floor. Finally, we heard a clattering sound, and Stephen scrambled under the island to fish out whatever had skidded beneath it.

"There we go," he said, holding up a set of car keys. He got to his feet and looked at the rest of us expectantly. "Come on," he said, "and cross your fingers."

I hadn't realized that in addition to the massive garage attached to the side of the house, there was also a sprawling outbuilding on the property. "It's the guest house," Stephen mumbled, obviously embarrassed, as he led us around to the back of the building. There was only a single garage here, and instead of a fancy voice-controlled opener, Stephen crouched down and inserted a key into a rusted latch. With some effort, he hoisted up the door, and we all peered into the darkness.

A few dusty slats of light from a high window illuminated the...car? Beast? Hulking heap of metal that crouched menacingly in the depths of the garage.

"What. Is. *That*?" Aggie said.

It might have been cool, at one point. But, fifty years past its prime, it was more rust than paint, and the gaping engine compartment looked like a better home for an evil goblin than a motor. Pinning our fate on this scrap metal hellspawn seemed like a risk.

"It's my dad's project," Stephen said with a wry grin. "He loves this thing more than he loves me."

"God, what did you ever do to him?" I said. Stephen's cheeks went red.

"Well, it's certainly some...jalopy," Mirtel said, tossing her bag in through an open window. She turned back to Stephen. "How many horses does she get?"

Stephen and I stared at each other, while Aggie rolled her eyes.

"I, uh," Stephen stammered, "I have no idea."

Mirtel held out her hand and looked expectantly at Stephen. "Keys, please," she said after a long moment. "I'm driving."

CHAPTER 39

SOFI

I felt like a husk, a hollow shell of a person that had been drained of all energy, all emotion, all thought, everything that had made me human. I was exhausted and numb, and the only emotion I could muster was a faint trace of annoyance that my weary body wouldn't just let me sleep.

But every time I came close, I would jerk awake, a subtle feeling of wrongness, of something missing, pulling me back and reminding me of everything that had happened.

I must have fallen asleep eventually though, because the next time I jerked awake, the bright glow of sunlight was visible through the window. The same window through which, just moments later, a heavy rock came flying. The sound of breaking glass was loud in the small room, and I let out an involuntary shriek, my hands pulling ineffectually at their restraints as my nerves jumped, adrenaline flooding my system and forcing me fully awake.

"Who's there?"

I watched as a cloth-wrapped hand came up, carefully breaking out the remaining shards of glass before reaching through and forcing open the latch. Another hand joined the first, pulling up the frame, and then a voice I couldn't quite place hissed through the opening. "Are you alone?"

"What? Who—"

"Are you *alone?*" the voice repeated.

"Yes, but—"

I broke off when a face appeared in the empty window, followed by the rest of the body. The woman heaved herself up onto the sill, swinging her legs awkwardly through the narrow space to drop to the floor on the inside.

The face belonged to the last person I would ever have expected to see.

"*Ms. Kross?*"

Darja's old *taja* from the *koolis* didn't stop to acknowledge me, instead crossing the room to poke her head out of the door and peer down the hallway. Only then did she turn back to glance at me. "Keys?"

"What?"

"*Keys.*" She gestured at my restraints.

Oh. My mind was slow, bogged down with confusion.

"I'm sure my dad took them. There should be a second set in the nurse's office, but it'll be—"

I didn't get the word 'locked' out before she fumbled with the door and disappeared down the hallway, but she must have found a way into the office because she was back only a few minutes later, a ring of keys on a lanyard clutched in her hand.

She crossed straight to the bed and began working on the shackles that bound my ankles.

"Ms. Kross, what the hell—wait." I bolted upright, staring out the window. "What time is it?"

She seemed to know what I meant, because without stopping she said, "Nine-forty. Everyone is gathered at the fairgrounds."

"What?!" My heart leaped into my throat. The ceremony was set to start at ten. Had the others made it back to town? Were they at the fairgrounds or were they out looking for me? "Hurry," I shouted, as the lock around my ankles finally sprang free and she moved up, grasping the restraint around my left wrist.

"Don't worry," she said roughly. "I'll get you there."

What was even happening?

"Ms. Kross, what are you doing here? What's going on?"

She only spared a quick glance my way, but I could see the agonized look in her eyes.

"I followed you and that officer. Last night. I know everything."

Wait—*what?*

"Why?" I demanded. "What were you—?"

She dropped the restraint abruptly, raising her head to meet my eyes, and I flinched at the emotion there.

"Look, I'm the one who reported Darja's disappearance to the police."

"Why would you do that? You know what happened to her. You were there." I felt like my head was spinning, and fury burned in my blood. "*You're* the one who drugged her and threw her into the fire!"

Her eyes dropped to the bed. "I know," she choked out. "I didn't think it would affect me like it did. I've been attending Spring Day ceremonies ever since my own, and at the *koolis*...well, let's just say Darja's not the first girl I've lost to the flames."

"'Lost to the flames,'" I spat. "Like it was an accident. Like it wasn't something *you did*." It occurred to me after the words were out that maybe I shouldn't antagonize the woman before she'd finished unlocking my bindings, but I couldn't hold back my contempt. It didn't matter though— the contempt didn't seem to be one-sided.

"I *know*," she said again, tears filling her eyes. "I see Darja's face every night when I close my eyes. If I could take it back, don't you think I would?" She dashed her hand against her face, wiping away tears. "I don't know what I was thinking; I knew it wouldn't make any difference, but I thought maybe if the police started looking...maybe if people knew, then..."

I sighed tiredly, my chest loosening as the anger drained away. "Well, you're too late, they already knew."

Her head shot up again, fire lighting her own eyes. "I heard. I can't believe..." Then her eyes widened. "I also heard...is it true? Your binding *worked*?"

I nodded. I hoped it was still working, even if I couldn't feel it.

"Is she..." She cleared her throat. "How is she?"

I didn't even begin to know how to answer that. "She's dead," I said flatly, then jerked my remaining bound wrist. "And the rest of the town will be too if you don't hurry up and let me out of here."

Ms. Kross hurried around to the other side of the bed and made quick work of the last restraint.

"*Can* you stop it?" she asked as I sat up, rubbing my wrists. "The festival?"

I shook my head. "I don't know. Probably not. But I need to get there, *now*."

"Come on, my car is outside."

I was sure everyone would be at the fairgrounds by this point, and I doubted anyone would be left guarding the office, but we went out through the window just in case.

Ms. Kross hesitated by the side of the car. "Will you...will you tell Darja I'm sorry?"

"Come with me and you can tell her yourself." I opened the passenger's door and slid into the seat, before giving her a hard look. "She won't forgive you. But you should tell her anyway."

We'd agreed that the five of us would come to the fairgrounds early, before the crowds started to arrive, so we could find a good place to hide where we would still be able to see everything that was going on and cast our spells. That, of course, was before I'd decided to take matters into my own hands and screwed everything up. I had no idea where they would be hiding, if they were even here at all, and not off trying to find me. God, I was such an idiot.

The parking lot at the fairgrounds was filled to overflowing, and Ms. Kross pulled her car into a spot in the grass. The second the engine was off I ducked out of the car and into the crowd, keeping my head down and trying hard to avoid notice. Everyone knew everyone else in this town, and I had to get through the crowd before someone saw me who knew I wasn't supposed to be there. I didn't wait for Ms. Kross. She could keep up if she wanted to.

I had desperately hoped that whatever spell my father had cast on my bond with Darja would fade with proximity, and I'd be able to feel her again once I got close enough, but nothing changed as I carefully maneuvered around the clusters of people. I prayed that didn't mean they weren't here. And what if my father's spell had done more to our bond than make me unable to feel it? What if it meant we couldn't do magic together? I shivered despite the hot June morning, and rubbed my palms against my arms.

Unsure of where to go, I headed in the general direction of the main stage. I stayed near the furthest edge of the crowd, where I was practically hidden by the orchard trees, trying my best to avoid the families on picnic blankets, the kids running wild with ribbons streaming from their hair. I could remember countless other Midsummer and Spring Day festivals, when it had been me running across the lawn, chased by my brothers and sisters. I felt a pang, but I ruthlessly tamped it down. It was too late—I could never go back to that naive innocence. I wouldn't want to.

It had to be after ten o'clock by then, and I could see the cluster of Council members gathered on the stage, but nothing seemed to be getting started just yet. The barest wave of relief flooded through my tightly-ratcheted nerves. At least I wasn't too late.

I was jerked out of my musings at the sight of a pair of familiar faces, and ducked my head, letting my hair fall to curtain my face as my pulse sped. Anna Saar and Liz Koppel sat together on checked blankets, surrounded by their families, laughing together over some private joke. I immediately changed direction.

"Where are we going?" a voice hissed beside me, and I startled. I'd forgotten Ms. Kross was even here.

"I don't know," I whispered back. "If they're here, they'll be hiding somewhere nearby, but we didn't have a chance to—"

The words choked off in my throat as I caught sight of another pair of faces. My alarm this time though wasn't at the fear of being recognized, but instead at the horror of the vision in front of me. The two faces belonged to Henri and Marleen Luts, the pair that had performed the first spell together at the town meeting less than a month before. The couple looked...awful—as if they'd aged decades in a single month. Both were hunched in their lawn chairs, grey-tinged skin hanging loose on gaunt frames, dark bags beneath dull eyes, hair lank and pale. Bile rose in my throat. Darja had been right—not that I'd ever doubted her—but faced with the two withered bodies of people who not four weeks earlier had been vital, healthy-looking people, it was obvious that something in that spell had gone terribly wrong. How did no one else *see* this? Or maybe they did, but they just didn't care.

"I think I know where they are." Ms. Kross's whisper broke into my trance and I wrenched my attention away.

"What?"

"Look."

Edging close to my side, she indicated toward the front of the crowd. "Watch the flap under the stage."

It didn't take long to see what she meant. The stage was raised on a platform maybe four or five feet off the ground, and dark plastic sheeting ran around the edge like a skirt. Near the front center, the flap had been pulled back slightly, a small window into the darkness beneath the stage, but as I stared, I thought I detected a flash of movement.

"There it is again," Ms. Kross said in a low voice.

"I saw it. Let's go."

Keeping my head down and my hair swinging in my face, I hurried toward the edge of the crowd and together, we circled the raised platform until we were out of sight of everyone on the lawn.

I sucked in a breath and ducked through the plastic, Ms. Kross close on my heels.

It was dark beneath the stage, dank and cool, the ground soft under my shoes. I tried not to picture all the spiders down here with us as I carefully maneuvered around the thick wooden support beams, hunching over awkwardly as I hurried toward the front of the stage.

The whispered voices might not carry beyond the barrier of the skirt, but they were loud enough to my ears in the near-darkness, and a palpable rush of relief flooded my veins as I recognized Mirtel's voice.

I couldn't help myself.

"*Darja.*" It came out in a whisper-shout, and the answering call of "Oh God, *Sofi,*" was like music to my ears. Squelching footsteps came closer, and then they were there, all of them, hunched over in the cramped space beneath the stage, and I nearly sagged with relief as my dead bonded half-sister threw her arms around me. I couldn't feel a thing except a lingering sensation of cold, but it was still the best hug I'd ever received.

CHAPTER 40

DARJA

She's alive. Sofi's *alive*.

I repeated it to myself like a mantra, like thinking it over and over would make it true, and not a dream I'd soon wake from. I wished I could feel her hug so damn much it hurt, but this misty, incorporeal embrace was all we had... and I was happy to cling to it. We'd searched high and low, and the desperation that had taken hold when we'd finally given up and headed for the festival had been crushing. But our relief and joy and our *sisterhood* filled up the emptiness where our magical bond used to be. There was a new bond to replace it, a different one, and we didn't need magic—or bodies—for that.

Still, though I'd fought it so hard at first, I missed the bond—missed the feeling of not being so alone. So when Mirtel handed the binder to Sofi and I saw her flip to the smothering spell, I smiled. We read the words that would end the spell with wavering voices, and when the magic surged between us, I felt almost whole again.

I didn't have long to enjoy the sensation though, as I

noticed in the half-darkness over Sofi's shoulder, another figure skulking just out of sight. I squinted and leaned forward, and then felt everything in me go suddenly rigid.

"What the hell is *she* doing here?" I hissed, backing away from Sofi. She bit her lip and cast her eyes toward the ground.

"She sort of...rescued me," she said, gesturing vaguely toward Ms. Kross, who had her arms wrapped tightly around her *koolis* polo shirt, which was the same deep crimson as fresh blood in the creeping shadows.

"She *what*?" I said, forcing myself not to look at the woman's face. I knew I couldn't control myself if I did. I knew I couldn't hold back the anger...the betrayal.

"We have another spell to do," Sofi said gently, flipping through the pages until she found the visibility spell.

"No," I said firmly.

Sofi smiled softly and nodded. "Yes. She helped me today. And I think this... I think this would help her."

I shook my head, but I could already feel myself giving in. "Do you really think she deserves to be helped?" I asked.

"If we waited for everyone to deserve help, we'd be in a world of trouble."

I couldn't argue with that. I nodded my assent, and we motioned for Ms. Kross to come closer so we could perform the spell.

I heard her intake of breath, and knew that it had worked. When she spoke, I clenched my jaw and stared resolutely at the ground.

"Darja, I—" her voice wavered and then faltered. I could hear sharp, short intakes of breath, and I realized she was crying.

I swallowed down whatever nameless emotion was rising up in my throat, and moved my gaze carefully back up to Sofi's worried face.

"She found you?" I said, hearing—and despising—the hoarseness in my voice.

Sofi nodded. "I was tied up," she said, rubbing unconsciously at her wrist. "My dad, he—" At this, Sofi's face crumbled, and the tears she'd been holding back started to flow.

"Sofi," I said, reaching a hand out toward her, though I knew I couldn't comfort her like I wanted. Sniffling, she shook her head and wiped her tears, lifting her chin almost defiantly.

"Anyway," she said, "Ms. Kross was following me, and after my dad left, she snuck in and got the keys—"

"He had you *locked up*?" I said, feeling a burst of anger flare inside me. Sofi gave a short nod.

"That son of a bitch." I balled my hands into fists at my side.

A grim smile touched Sofi's lips. "Yeah," she said softly. "Yeah. He also cast the smothering spell on our bond."

I suddenly understood the phrase, 'seeing red.' I was livid with our father, and I was aghast that he could show such cruelty to his own daughter. In reality though, I was mostly mad at myself. How could I not have thought to check his office? It seemed completely idiotic in hindsight. A sudden thought occurred to me.

If our dad had cast the spell without a bonded...

"But that means..."

"I know," she said quietly. "I know what it means."

We stood there in silence for a long moment, before Ms. Kross leaned into the dim light. Her dark brown curls were loose around her face, and she looked older than I remembered.

"Darja," she said again. "Darja, I'm so sorr—"

"Don't," I said, still refusing to meet her gaze. "You don't get to do that."

Her expression was stricken, but she nodded and stayed silent.

I could feel the others behind me, uncertain what to do, probably wondering if I was going to go all *Carrie* on them.

"And...thank you," I said finally. "For saving her."

Ms. Kross's chin trembled. She must have thought better than to try to respond, but she swallowed hard and gave me a terse nod before looking away.

"We have to get moving," I said, my own voice sounding a little less steady than I would have liked. "Sofi, are you still up for this?"

Sofi nodded, her mouth set in a grim line. "Absolutely."

"Stephen," I said, nodding to where he was awkwardly crouched behind Mirtel and Aggie. Behind his glasses, I could see that his eyes were shining, and I thought that maybe he was just as relieved as I was to see that Sofi was safe. "Are you ready?"

Pushing his glasses up on his nose and straightening his shoulders as best he could in the tight space, Stephen nodded. He moved past Sofi to retrieve his camera bag, and as he did, I saw his fingertips brush the back of her hand. She looked after him, something like relief on her face. Stephen grabbed the bag, hefted it by the strap then slung it over his shoulder. "Okay," he said. "Ready."

Mirtel smiled at Stephen, then looked at each of us in turn. "It's been an honor," she said, "being a part of this with all of you. Well," she added, looking at Ms. Kross, "not you. But the rest of you, truly an honor. Thank you for making an old woman feel a little less crazy."

I smiled, feeling hopeful for the first time in a long while. "Let's do this," I said. Together, we crept toward the back of the platform, where a seam in the vinyl covering was slightly open and waving gently in the breeze. The light glimmered around the edges, creating a honey gold halo that looked almost welcoming. If I hadn't been pretty sure we were walking to our doom.

Ms. Kross sidled up to me, still keeping her head down, though I wasn't sure if it was because of the cramped space or the weight of her guilt. I hoped it was the latter.

"What can I do?" she said in a whisper.

"Don't you think you've done enough?" I shot back, but there was no real rancor in my voice.

"Darja, I can never make this right, I know that. I made a mistake. The worst mistake of my life."

I scoffed. "And yet, here you are. The one who still *has* a life."

I saw her wince out of the corner of my eye. Guilt it was, then. Good.

Still, I could feel some of the tension ease out of my shoulders. "You can keep an eye out," I said finally. "Did Sofi explain what's going on? What we're trying to stop?"

Ms. Kross nodded.

"Good. Stephen is going to be recording the whole thing, and we'll be focused on the spell, so if you can act as lookout, that'll help."

"Why is he recording it?" she said, even as she was nodding her agreement.

"Leverage," I said. "In case something goes wrong, we want proof of what's been happening in Vaikesti. We want to know that there may be some kind of justice for the girls... the girls...."

"Girls like you," she whispered, and I nodded because I couldn't speak.

Slowly, as if approaching a feral animal, she reached out a hand and placed it on, or at least near, my arm. It was familiar, almost soothing, and I remembered that, of all the teachers and students in the koolis, even as 'Kross the Boss,' she had been the friendliest face through most of my teenage years.

"Let's go," I said, moving to catch up with the others. There would be time to analyze those feelings…later.

We had just huddled around the opening at the back of the stage, ready to step outside, when we heard footsteps above us, heavy and loud. The entire platform creaked and shivered, and I wondered if it would come down around our ears before we could even get started.

There was a squeal of feedback as someone turned on the PA system, and then an echoing *tap tap tap* on the microphone.

"Welcome, citizens of Vaikesti, to our annual Midsummer Festival. It's always a wonderful occasion, but it's even more special this year, as we mark 150 years of community, caring and culture."

The voice was female, and older, but I didn't recognize it. I looked to Sofi, and her face was carefully schooled in a blank expression. I couldn't tell if she knew the mystery speaker or not.

"Now, I know this has been quite a year for our little village, and there have been many exciting developments. I know you're all anxious to get underway, but to commemorate this very special occasion, I'd first like to lead you in a prayer of prosperity. Please, everyone, join me."

The woman's voice was reverent as she began speaking in the old language, its lilting phrases washing over me in a way that felt both comforting and agonizing. I'd repeated this prayer countless times while I was growing up, heard it recited by the teachers and townspeople before every harvest, but I hadn't known then. I hadn't realized the magic it was channeling, the power it invoked. And it horrified me.

The rest of the townspeople joined in, their voices lifting in chorus, the prayer becoming rhythmic and staccato, like a chant. They didn't know, none of them knew, what they were praying for. None of them knew what the answer to that prayer would be—what the blood magic would bring down on them. I felt sick to my stomach.

"And now," the voice resumed in a normal tone, "I'd like to welcome to the stage the Council leader of our beautiful town, who also happens to be my husband." I went still as ice shot through me and the voice above chuckled. "Robert, would you like to join us?"

Sofi's father. Which meant the voice belonged to Sofi's mother. I didn't know if she was aware of what was going on, of what her husband had done, but if she was...if she could come out and speak like that, and lead the town in prayer, knowing how her husband had treated their daughter...

I couldn't think about it right then. I was sure Sofi was thinking of it, though. And imagining the pain she was feeling tore a hole in me. But we'd talk about it later. I'd comfort her later. There would be time for that...later.

There were different, heavier footsteps moving across the stage, and some whispers that weren't quite caught by the microphone. Moments later, the voice of Sofi's dad—our dad—came booming out, seeming to fill up the space around us like thunder.

"Glad Midsummer," he said cheerfully, and the townspeople responded in kind. "Thank you all for being here today. As you know, this festival marks a momentous day for the people of Vaikesti, our heritage and our way of life. It is my pleasure to lead the town in one of the most meaningful rituals of our ancestors. And this year," he said, his voice slightly teasing, "it's actually going to work."

There was scattered laughter from the gathered crowd. I could almost hear a buzz of excitement ripple through them, and the pit in my stomach grew heavier. I looked over

349

to Sofi, whose face was still blank, and she gave me a nod. That was our cue, then.

As our father continued with his speech, we crept out from under the platform. Or at least, the living among us did. Aggie and I simply phased through the vinyl covering and into the sunshine.

It was spectacularly bright, and I could see the others blinking blindly as they got their bearings.

"Stay low," Sofi hissed, crouching down onto the grass, and the rest of us followed her direction. She nodded at Ms. Kross and pointed to the back corner of the stage. There was a large speaker set up there, and she could stay hidden while keeping an eye out for approaching danger. There was also a set of stairs leading up to the stage directly behind the speaker, so she could climb up there unnoticed. Ms. Kross nodded her understanding and moved silently away from us. Stephen took Sofi's hand, and ignoring her look of wide-eyed surprise, tipped up her chin and planted a soft kiss on her lips. Then, wordlessly, he followed Ms. Kross, pulling out his camera as he went.

Well. Stephen had grown a pair. How about that?

I exchanged a look with Aggie, and I could see a smile tugging at the corner of her lips. I wanted to kiss her, too, but there would be time for that...later.

Above us, on the stage, our father was calling up the first five pairs to work the spell. They would perform it as a trial, he explained, and when it was successful, which it would be, the rest of the hundred volunteers would pair up to work it again. I'd gotten a look at the stage as we ran for cover, and had seen the boxes lined up in the center. About four feet across and two feet wide, and at least a foot deep. All were filled with dirt. This was the setup, I realized. It was to be a performance, showing off the magic in front of the entire town. This time though, the utter arrogance of it all worked in our favor. If they were going to put on a show first, it meant we could work the counterspell in phases, so we wouldn't need as much power to stop them.

This was going to work. It was actually going to work.

There were more footsteps across the stage, as the ten townspeople—guinea pigs—took their places. The crowd clapped their encouragement, and I heard some nervous laughter from the stage. After a moment, a hush fell over the crowd, and I wondered if our father was gesturing for them to be silent. He must love having that kind of control.

The voices began tentatively, in unison, and I could feel a tremble of magic beneath my feet. Was this where it came from, I wondered? From the earth itself? I wondered if the townspeople could feel it, too. But there was no time to dwell on it, we had to act...fast.

The four of us took our positions, Sofi and I standing across from each other, and Mirtel and Aggie next to us, in the same stance. We began chanting in hushed whispers, and I could feel an arc of electricity along the bond we shared. I wanted to close my eyes, wanted to let the magic envelop me, consume me, but I kept my gaze focused on Sofi, drawing power from her presence.

The four of us continued, a soft rhythm of words that once had no meaning, and had come to hold the future of our world, our people. I could barely hear the chanting from the stage, drowned out by the magic that was twining around us like a living thing. It was warm and cool at the same time, creeping in tendrils up and down my back, licking at my ankles and shivering around my fingers. We simultaneously raised our hands, as we had practiced, almost as if cupping water for a cool drink. Then we lifted our arms and opened our hands, releasing our counterspell.

With a *whoosh*, I felt the magic move through me and

out of me, leaving me feeling suddenly achingly hollow. I looked at the others, and knew they felt it, too.

The voices above us went quiet.

The silence seemed to stretch for an eternity. Had it worked? Had we stopped them?

I could feel my tight expression breaking into a hopeful grin. But then, the cheering started. It was a wave of ecstatic laughter and hoots that sounded more like hyenas than humans. I looked at the others and saw my own dazed and uncertain expression mirrored back at me.

"Well," our father's voice boomed out, with a hint of a chuckle. "We haven't worked out all the kinks yet, I suppose. But three out of five isn't bad."

I looked at Sofi, and saw my panic reflected in her eyes. Since neither Sofi or Mirtel could see for themselves, I phased up to the stage, and gasped at what I saw. Three of the five boxes were overflowing with vibrant green vines and heavy, ripe fruit that shone like jewels. The last two were barren. The four townspeople standing nearby looked disappointed, even ashamed, but they looked healthy.

The others...

The others were shells of themselves, gray and worn, looking like they'd been through a war. They'd aged a decade in mere moments. With horror, I realized the counterspell had worked...but not enough. All that power, all that magic, and we'd only stopped two pairs.

I phased back down to the others and shook my head. Sofi buckled to her knees, and Aggie looked stricken. Mirtel's face was unreadable, but she walked over and placed her hands on Sofi's shoulders, shushing her softly.

It had worked. Just not enough.

We had failed.

CHAPTER 41

SOFI

It was over. The odds had been against us every step of the way, and we'd failed. Our magic wasn't enough, and six more people had just been condemned to death. An empty, hopeless feeling twisted in the pit of my stomach.

"The magic of Vaikesti is *real*." My father's voice boomed through the microphone as he shouted to be heard over the roar of the crowd.

"Our town has been blessed by the earth; the magic of our ancestors returned to us, and it is up to us, to all of us, to use the gift we've been given to pave the way for our children, our children's children. Will you join me?"

The crowd cheered, the clamor so great I couldn't pick out any individual voices. The pit in my stomach grew, threatening to overwhelm me.

"Join me in a spell," he called, his voice full of promise. "A spell to bless our fields. If we all join together, we can use the gift we've been given to ensure the greatest harvest of our time."

More cheers. My skin was cold, my hands clammy.

"Everyone who has agreed to participate should already have their spell pages. You can start pairing up."

His words faded into a drone in the background of my spiraling thoughts. This was it. I couldn't see the crowd, but my mind's eye filled in the blanks. A hundred volunteers. And when it worked, the rest of the community would join in. My sisters would pair up with their husbands, their children watching as their parents' souls withered and died. My grandmother. My aunts, my cousins. Marta Kask and Liz Koppel and Anna Saar. My whole community, everyone I'd known my whole life long could be lost in the blink of an eye, all because I hadn't been able to stop it.

"Get up, Sofi. Come on, child." Mirtel's voice was coaxing, her hand soft on my arm, and only then did I realize I'd fallen to my knees.

I stumbled up with her help, my cheeks wet with tears I hadn't known I'd been crying.

"It's not too late," she told me, her hands against my cheeks, drying my tears. Her eyes were soft, but I couldn't quite read her expression.

"You've done your best, Sofi," she told me. "You should be proud." Her wrinkled hands cupped my face as her eyes searched mine. "But there's still a chance left; we can still stop this, but I need you to trust me. Can you do that?"

My head bobbed in a jerky nod. I trusted Mirtel to the ends of the earth, but what did she mean? We'd tried and failed. What else could we possibly do?

"Aggie?"

The girl was already there, standing by Mirtel's side, her face set in grim lines.

"It's time," Mirtel said.

Aggie gave a quick nod, and threaded her arm through Mirtel's. The older woman couldn't have felt anything, but she squeezed Aggie's arm nonetheless, and the pair turned, stepping a little distance away from me before facing each other. Though I knew they couldn't touch, it almost looked like they had linked hands, Mirtel's skin paper-thin and pale, Aggie's bone-white with a luminescent transparency.

Darja had appeared by my side. "What are they doing?"

I shook my head. "I don't know. Mirtel said—"

"Is everybody ready to make history?"

I jumped at the sound of my father's voice through the loudspeaker, the raucous response from the crowd drowning out my words.

Mirtel and Aggie had started to speak, eyes locked together as they chanted in unison. Finally the crowd quieted and I could hear their hushed voices.

"Õnnistus maa peal, esivanemate võludest..."

Their voices overlapped, twining together, and my breath caught. What was this spell? What were they doing?

A movement out of the corner of my eye caught my attention, and I turned to see Stephen. A flush rose quickly to my cheeks as I remembered the feel of his mouth pressed to mine, the intensity in that brief kiss and my surprise at how much I had liked the sensation, but the expression on his face pulled me up short. He still had his camera on his shoulder, but his face was devoid of all color, mouth open as he stared in horror toward Mirtel and Aggie.

I took a step toward him. "What—"

Once again, my words were cut off by the noise of the crowd. But this time, rather than cheers, their voices were raised in unison, a wave of sound as hundreds of voices chanted together in the old tongue.

No.

I took a step toward the crowd, wanting to see, feeling like I was being pulled in too many directions at once.

"Sofi." I only heard Darja's voice because it was right in my ear, and I turned again, following her gaze back to Mirtel and Aggie. I could *feel* it, the power they were drawing, feel it thrumming through the air like a plucked wire.

A seed of hope took root inside me. What was this spell? Could it really work? Did we still have a chance?

Their mouths closed, their spell finished, and a second later the magic released, a blast of power that dwarfed anything we'd ever used before. It shot out in a great burst, with Aggie and Mirtel at the epicenter, and flooded the crowd, an enormous wave of magic. I turned in awe, following the invisible wave of power as it swept outward, crackling like electricity. My feet carried me forward a step as if I might run alongside, keeping pace with the magic as it swept through the entire town. I'd never felt *anything* like that before.

The voices of the crowd wavered, finishing their spell and then dissolving into a hushed murmur of confusion and speculation.

"Well now, folks, let's everyone keep calm." It was my father again. "Obviously the spell didn't work, but I'll have to confer with the Council to figure out what happened. Don't lose heart, everyone."

The seed of hope in my chest bloomed, suffusing my limbs with joy.

It had worked? It had *worked*. They had stopped the ceremony.

I spun to face Darja, my breath coming out in a gasp. "Oh God, Darja, we—"

My words shriveled and died at the sight that greeted me.

CHAPTER 42

DARJA

"Aggie?"

Her name was a whisper on my lips, hushed like a prayer. But there was no soul inside me left to pray, and nothing to pray *to*. There never would be again.

It was all wrong. I didn't know what was going on, but I knew that much. The spell Aggie and Mirtel had cast seemed to break something loose inside me. My bond with Sofi was still there, but I felt suddenly unmoored, like a ship tossed around on a roiling sea.

There was magic sizzling around us, crackling through the air. Though my eyes were fixed only on Aggie, I caught Stephen out of my peripheral vision, sprinting toward us with horror etched across his face. When he got close, he pulled up short, and I could see his hair standing on end.

My fingertips hummed with electricity. This was *magic,* deep and wild and unfathomable.

And it had done something to Aggie.

I went to her in what felt like slow motion, my whole being moving as if through molasses. After what felt like an eternity, she turned her head and looked at me. She was smiling, but there was pain—pain so strong it threatened to consume me—in her eyes.

"It worked," she said, and her voice was both relieved and disbelieving. "It actually worked."

I shook my head. "What worked? Aggie, what are you—" She slumped then, and I caught her in my arms, her spirit light as a feather.

"Oh, Aggie," I said, as I lowered us gently over the grass. "Aggie, what did you *do*?"

She smiled again, but it was weaker. In my arms, what once had felt warm and soft and almost alive felt more like porcelain—cool, unyielding, and so, so fragile.

Behind me, I heard raised voices, hysterical and frantic. It was Sofi, screaming at Stephen to tell her what had happened. What *was* happening.

I turned my head in time to see Stephen shake his head, his face stricken. "The spell," he said, running a hand through his hair, the static around us making it cling to his fingers. "The spell..."

"*What spell?*" Sofi demanded. "What did they *do*?"

"I thought it was too dangerous," Stephen said, almost as if talking to himself. "That's why I took it out of the book. I don't know how she—"

"*What. Spell,*" Sofi ground out.

Stephen looked at her, his eyes brimming with tears. "The *Spell of Sacrifice*. It was in the old text. I translated it, but I never showed it to anyone. I didn't think anyone should be able to...to do that."

Sacrifice.

The words sent ice through my veins, and I let out a sound that was more animal than human.

"No," I said, "Aggie, *no*."

"It's too late, Darja," she said, raising a hand to my cheek. "We had to. There was no choice."

I wanted to cry. I wanted to pour out an ocean of tears and drown in it, with Aggie by my side. The bitterness I felt at not even being able to grieve threatened to consume me. But it couldn't, not yet. Not while I still had Aggie here with me. Not while I could still cradle her in my arms.

"You knew?" I whispered. "You knew this would happen?"

Slowly, almost painfully, Aggie nodded. "Mirtel explained it all. It was our last resort. I don't—I don't want to leave you, but—"

"So don't," I said, my voice almost a growl. "I just found you. I didn't even know...I didn't think it could *be* like this—"

My words were cut off by Sofi's scream. "Mirtel!"

I had been so focused on Aggie I hadn't even spared a glance for the older woman. I looked at her then, and swallowed down a scream of my own.

Mirtel's face was gray, ashen and nearly lifeless. She was swaying on her feet, the velvet of her skirt rustling softly against the ground. I didn't know what Sofi saw, but what I could see...

I couldn't bear it. I couldn't understand it. And I couldn't stop it.

As the life literally drained from Mirtel's body, I could see something soft and wispy, like an exhale of smoke, twisting its way out of her chest. It clung to her at first, like a mist, then, as it grew larger, it whirled around her like a shroud.

My eyes darted back to Sofi, who was frozen in terror. Just as Mirtel's body began to collapse, Stephen jumped behind her and caught her, moving her carefully to the ground.

The white mist stayed where it was, hovering above the body it had once been chained to. As I watched, Aggie gripped my hand tighter, and the mist slowly took form—arms, legs, a pile of wild, flyaway hair, and finally a face, recognizable, but unlined and carefree in a way I'd never seen.

"Mirtel," I said softly. "Oh, Mirtel..."

Sofi ran to Mirtel's body and dropped to her side, apparently not seeing the apparition of Mirtel's spirit. I couldn't find the words to tell her there was no one left in there anymore; it was just a shell.

The spirit smiled gently at me. It was tremulous, sad... but also relieved. "I'm so sorry, Darja. I wouldn't have done this if there'd been another choice."

I shook my head fiercely, refusing to comprehend what she was saying. "No. No..."

"Aggie," she said then, looking lovingly at the spirit growing ever colder in my arms. "Aggie, my darling girl, you're free now."

"NO!" I roared, clutching Aggie to my chest. "Not like this. It wasn't supposed to be like this."

Aggie put a single finger to my lips. "Shh," she whispered. "It's okay. I didn't want to leave you. I *don't* want to leave you..."

"So *don't*," I choked out over my tears.

Aggie smiled, a genuine smile that seemed to light her eyes from within. "I have to, Darja. Whatever is supposed to come after life...this wasn't it. It was never meant to be this way. Now I can move on, knowing that it wasn't in vain. Knowing that it brought me to you."

"Aggie, *please*."

"It's going to be okay," she said. Her eyes flickered, then suddenly grew lighter, a pale shade of gray, like the sky just before a breaking dawn.

"No," I said, though I knew it was too late for that. The

spell couldn't be undone. Her spirit grew lighter, until I could see the green grass through her tremulous form.

"I'll wait for you," she said, her voice thin and faraway. "Wherever I go, I'll wait for you there."

"I love you," I said frantically, pleadingly, desperately wanting her to hear it, to *know* it.

"I know," she said, echoing my thoughts. "I know you do. I love you, too."

I leaned down and placed a kiss on her lips. I could barely feel them beneath mine, but I stayed like that for a long moment, feeling her against me, memorizing every line, every curve, every inch of her.

When I opened my eyes, she was gone.

I looked up to see Mirtel's spirit, still hovering above us, but she was fading, too.

"Goodbye, my friend," she said. "Take care of the others. They will need you."

Through my pain, I choked out a raspy, "Goodbye." As Mirtel's spirit seemed to dissolve into nothing, I looked over to Sofi and Stephen, still crouched around her body.

Sofi's eyes met mine, and a surge of magic arced through the air. I could feel it building inside me, charging up through the earth and into me, buzzing all through me.

Vaikesti had done this. All of this. Every person in this town was culpable. My father chief among them.

I could hear the whine and hum of the magic as I slowly stood up, splaying my hands and feeling the power dart between my fingers.

They'd killed me. They'd killed Aggie. Twice. They'd brought her to me, and then they'd taken her away.

They were all going to pay. Every last one of them.

CHAPTER 43

SOFI

I couldn't seem to catch my breath. Mirtel's body was limp and my searching fingers couldn't find a pulse. The apparition that had been Aggie was nowhere to be seen, and Darja was muttering to herself, nonsensical words I couldn't quite make out. My heartbeat was loud in my ears, a too-fast thrum that made my head pulse with each beat.

I turned my wide gaze on Stephen.

"How do we stop this?"

"What?" His gaze was fixed on Mirtel's crumpled form. I shifted, putting myself directly in his line of sight.

"You said 'sacrifice.' You know what they did. Can we reverse it? What can we do?" My voice broke on the last word, shaky and tremulous.

He shook his head, whether in answer to my question or in disbelief, I didn't know. "It's too late. They sacrificed themselves. A bonded pair, no longer tied to life, can pull so much more magic than they ever could otherwise." His voice was hoarse, just as broken as mine. "For just a moment, they were strong enough to stop the ceremony. But...with the link gone, it's over. They're gone."

Much as I tried to deny it, it was obvious, from Mirtel's lifeless form if not from his words. Darja's choked gasps were loud behind me. I wanted to go to her, comfort her, but I had no comfort to give.

"Mirtel knew," Stephen said, laying a hand on my arm. "She chose this—*they* chose this. I'm so sorry."

"I—"

"Is this your doing?" The voice was a harsh rasp, and I spun at the sound.

My father stalked around the side of the stage. He looked ill, and the sight tore a gasp from my mouth. The magic he'd cast in his office had taken a toll on him, same as the rest. His pallor was grayish, his features sunken and wan. How could no one *see* this? How long could he possibly survive in this state?

"What have you done?" he demanded, moving closer. "You just couldn't leave it alone, could you?"

"Sofi?" Another figure stepped out from behind him. I hadn't even realized he wasn't alone.

My mother's voice was confused. "*Kallike,* what's going on? What is this?" Her eyes lighted on Mirtel's still body and her hand flew to cover her mouth.

Two more Council members crowded close behind, grim faces taking in the scene behind the stage.

"Who is responsible for this? What's happened to her?" Eliise Tam demanded, her voice strong despite her stooped form.

"*She* stopped you from destroying the town," I snapped, my pain morphing to anger. Darja appeared suddenly by my side, static crackling between us.

"*She* stopped you from murdering your friends and relatives," I spit out.

"That's enough," my father said. "We've heard plenty of—"

"*She* just gave her *life* for you," I screamed, not caring who heard me.

The buzz of conversation from the crowd on the other side of the stage fell silent.

"She gave her life for all of you," I choked out, tears streaming down my cheeks, "and if I could take it back, I would. You're not worth it!" My voice broke as I shouted, the words clawing their way out and tearing my throat to shreds in the process. "She was worth more than you ever were. Every single one of you."

"That's *enough*," my father thundered, and then he was coming forward, reaching for me with outstretched hands.

"Take her," he instructed, and Jared was there too—had he been there the whole time?—handcuffs clenched in his hands, though his eyes were wide. There was a flurry of movement then, too fast for me to follow.

A heavy sound of impact, a grunt of pain, and then my father landed on the ground with a groan and lay still. My mother let out a shrill scream. Stephen was shaking out his hand, his knuckles already red and swelling.

"Don't you dare touch her," he snarled, stepping between Jared and me.

"What is wrong with you, girl?" Eliise Tam demanded, her hand clenched tight on her cane. "Why are you trying to sabotage this? Betraying your people, your own family? After all this town has done for you?"

"I—how—*Look* at him," I exclaimed, pointing at my father's prone form. "He's *dying*. If you cast that spell on the crops, you'll all die too. It's not—you won't—"

There was a rasping sound next to me, cutting into my thoughts, and it took me a moment to realize it was Darja.

She was laughing—or crying, I couldn't tell—and she wrapped her fingers around my upper arm. Cold sliced through me, and though I couldn't feel her touch I immediately covered her hand with mine.

"Enough," she grated out. "Let's go."

CHAPTER 44

DARJA

These *idiots*.

These narcissistic, arrogant, ignorant fools. Every last one of them so focused on wishing some fairy tale into existence they couldn't see the devastation in front of their faces.

They *would* see it though. Soon.

"On stage," I growled to Sofi. "*Now*."

Sofi nodded and pushed past her mother and Eliise Tam, who stood there stupidly, not even trying to stop her. Behind us, I could hear Stephen and Jared arguing, but I couldn't be bothered to care. Let them figure it out.

Sofi climbed the steps that led onto the stage as her mother and Eliise finally moved to where our father lay crumpled on the ground. I couldn't care about him, either. It was less than he deserved.

I phased up to the stage and took my place next to Sofi. Her hair fell in wild tangles over her shoulders and tear tracks streaked down her face, but her jaw was set and her shoulders were straight and strong. She strode toward the mic and flicked it on, ignoring the squeal of feedback that cut through the milling crowd.

They turned questioning gazes up toward the stage, and I wondered if they were surprised not to see their fearless leader coming to console them.

"You've been tricked," Sofi said, without any introduction. "Your beliefs and your superstitions are real. But they will kill you. If you don't stop this—stop the magic—you'll be dead before you ever see a harvest."

There was a rumble of outrage from the townspeople, mingled with outright laughter from a few.

"My father is not who you think he is. The magic is not some gift to you from our ancestors, to do with as you please. Until now, you thought it was a myth." Sofi's voice cracked, but she carried on. "But you went on with the rituals anyway. You murdered innocent girls, even when you thought the magic was a made-up story. You *killed*...for what?"

A cry of protest went up from the crowd, but Sofi shook her head. "You have blood on your hands. All of you."

"They were willing," came a woman's voice from the back of the gathered townspeople. "They chose this."

Sofi scoffed. "Did they? Are you certain?"

Several women in the crowd nodded. A few looked frightened, but most were just bewildered or angry.

"Why don't we ask one of them?"

Sofi looked to me and I nodded at her. A hush fell over the townspeople. In spite of their outrage, they couldn't help themselves. They wanted to see more magic.

Disgusted, I reached my hand out to Sofi as we spoke the visibility spell in unison. The magic, angry and raw, had ebbed after Mirtel and Aggie's spell, but I could feel it again, jittering up through my feet and humming across the bond Sofi and I shared. I could also feel the remnants of the magic the two of them had called up when working their spell. I grasped at it, too, pulling it into me and adding to the energy Sofi and I were drawing up. We'd never cast the spell on more than one person, and I knew it was going to take some effort. Together, we opened our arms wide, as if bringing the crowd into an embrace.

We raised our voices together to finish the spell, and a gasp went up from the crowd. It had worked, then.

"See," Sofi said into the mic, gesturing at me. "See what your rituals have done. This is Darja...my sister."

The crowd erupted in chaos.

"Yes," Sofi snarled, "it's her. The girl you *murdered* in the name of your religion. And she wasn't the first. Not by a long shot. Darja," she said, looking over to me. "Were you a willing sacrifice?"

I laughed mirthlessly. "Not even close," I said, and my voice elicited more gasps and shouts from the crowd. "I was drugged. I was taken from the *koolis* and brought to the ceremony against my will. They put me on the pyre, and they let me burn."

I looked out into the crowd, meeting as many eyes as I could. Most of them quickly shifted their gaze. "*You* let me burn."

I could hear more dissent coming from the townspeople, excuses and explanations, all of them meaningless. Just as I was about to speak again, I saw a figure approaching from the side of the stage.

"It's all true." Ms. Kross shouted her words as she dashed to my side. "I gave her the drugs. I put her in the car, and I marched her into the fire. I let this happen." She paused for a moment, gasping over sudden sobs that shook her shoulders. "I *made* this happen," she finally said, her voice hoarse and thick with tears.

"Amazing." We all whirled around at the voice, soft and

calm, even reverent. Eliise had made her way back onto the stage, Sofi's mom hovering right behind her.

"Darja," she said, stepping closer and raising her arms toward me, "what a gift you have given this town. Your sacrifice brought our magic back to us."

I shook my head, too dumbfounded to speak, but Eliise continued on, turning first to the crowd. "I'd like to ask the younger members of our town to defer their questions for now. I'm sure this is a very confusing time. Your families will be able to explain once we've got this resolved. There is nothing to fear." She turned back to me then. "And that's because of you, Darja. You gave us back our birth-right. And we know now, why it worked this time."

The crowd waited with baited breath. They apparently did not know why it had worked.

"It must have worked because you weren't given a choice. The blood sacrifice must be made out of pain, out of betrayal. All the others—they gave their lives willingly to our cause, but we didn't know then that their gift of life could not raise the magic. I am sorry, my child, that you had to go through this horror, but your death has brought new life to all of Vaikesti."

The crowd began to cheer. I watched, disgusted, as several women fell to their knees, their arms raised in reverence. Some were weeping. Others began to pray in the old tongue.

"*Bullshit,*" I shouted, and I could feel the air pulse around me. "None of them were willing. None."

"Now, Darja," Eliise began. There was a smile on her face, but her eyes were sharp and piercing. "You weren't there when the others made their sacrifice. How could you know? The Ceremony has been one of Vaikesti's dearest, most protected secrets for decades. I can see how you might think that—"

"I don't *think* anything," I bit out. "You're murderers! All of you. And the last time it worked, she wasn't willing either. She wasn't—"

"The last time?" Eliise cut in sharply. "You mean it's worked before?"

I couldn't control the feeling that surged up inside me. And I couldn't begin to explain to her what Aggie and Mirtel had done—what they had given up—to save these ungrateful sycophants.

Sofi was looking between us worriedly. I knew she could sense the magic that was building in me, knew she understood that I was on the precipice of doing something we couldn't take back. I also knew she wanted it, too.

"They have to learn," I said to her between gritted teeth.

"Are you sure?" she asked me in a hushed voice. I nodded.

"They have to understand what they've done."

I raised my hand and the binder rushed toward me in a *whoosh*. I caught it deftly and then pushed it out between us, hovering in the air, pages flapping until it landed on the one I wanted. The one I'd seen at the lake house, but hadn't pointed out because it seemed too extreme. Too punishing.

"This one," I muttered to Sofi, and she nodded.

In front of us, the crowd was coming out of its stupor. Most were watching the scene play out before them eagerly, too stupid to understand what was about to happen. They stood there like cattle to the slaughter. Electricity crackled in the air around me. I lowered my hands, palms down toward the ground, and drew in as much magic as I could. The sky darkened as heavy clouds gathered. The sunny day turned to twilight, cloaked in shadow.

"Girls," Eliise said warningly. Her voice was light, but I could hear the strain beneath it. "I don't think we need to—"

"Oh, we need to," I said, drawing up more magic than I'd

ever held before. Lightning shot through the sky, and a rumble of thunder silenced the murmurs of the crowd.

I thought of Mirtel, of what she had been through, forced to exist as an outsider among her own people, a victim of their selfishness and recklessness. Branded the town crazy lady, shunned and cast aside, when all the time, the magic lived in her. It lived in her because Aggie had died.

Aggie had...

The clouds burst then, a downpour of rain beating against the people of Vaikesti, who did nothing but watch on, wide-eyed and awed. Frightened, maybe, but not enough. Not nearly enough.

I would give them something to fear.

"Darja," Sofi said, and I nodded at her.

"Now," I said, bringing the book closer.

"Now," she echoed, and we began to chant.

There was power inside me, flowing between us, building like a storm as we recited the spell, building to a crescendo as I looked out over the townspeople—the people who had taken my life, and the lives of two of the people I most cared about—and I screamed the final word in a whirlwind of fury and rage.

Lightning split the sky and the rain fell like a curtain of iron as the magic erupted from us in a roar that shook the very earth. Eliise stumbled to her knees, and to my right, Ms. Kross held on tightly to the PA speaker. I couldn't make out much in the crowd, but I could hear the screams of hysteria and confusion.

The magic flowed out of us for another moment, and then it was gone, leaving me completely hollow. No more anger. No more vengeance. There was nothing inside but emptiness.

Sofi wavered as the magic ebbed, holding onto the mic

stand to keep her footing. The clouds still lingered, but the rain stopped. There was no more electricity in the air. Just a smell of ozone and ash.

The crowd was in chaos. I glanced at the wooden boxes and saw the plants they had grown had all withered to brown husks, the boxes themselves singed black along the edges. And in front of us—the field was charred and gray, not a blade of grass or a wildflower spared, as far as the eye could see.

We had done it. The land that Vaikesti was built on—the land that built Vaikesti—was dead. The blight had spread farther than I could have imagined, turning the rolling hills of farmland in all directions a sickly shade of gray, as the newly emerged crops wilted, shrunken and stunted.

The land was destroyed. The town was in devastation. They would not recover.

I smiled.

CHAPTER 45

SOFI

The crowd before us looked bedraggled and stunned, their clothes clinging wetly to their skin as their glazed eyes stared around, taking in the devastation of the land all around them. I wasn't much better.

It was like all the color had been sucked out of the world, leaving it pallid and gray, and I certainly felt like all the energy had been sucked out of *me,* leaving me as wilted as the crumbling grass beneath the feet of the crowd.

Is this really what it had taken? Had we saved the town or destroyed it? I wasn't sure if the distinction even mattered to me anymore.

"C'mon girls, let's go."

I felt a hand under my elbow and turned to see Sheriff Braden. *When had he gotten here?* I stiffened, but Jared's dad only nudged us out of the way and took the microphone from its stand.

"Festival's over, folks. If everyone could please return to your homes, we'll get this all sorted out."

Sorted out. Like it was some kind of misunderstanding. Like we hadn't just cursed the very earth we stood upon.

The crowd was starting to wake up, muttering amongst themselves as they began to shuffle around, gathering their belongings. Darja's hand was nothing but a shock of ice on my arm.

"We have to get out of here," she said in a low voice.

"Wait—Stephen," I muttered, turning and hurrying down to where we'd left the group clustered behind the stage.

Little had changed. Eliise Tam and the other Council members were still there, looking stunned and horrified, still frozen in place as they took in the devastation all around them. My mother was crouched by my father's side. He seemed to have regained consciousness, but was groggy and disoriented, and I didn't bother to see if he was all right. Jared had a grip on Stephen, but it was as if both of them had forgotten what they were doing, their eyes lifting to us as we joined them on the crumbling gray soil.

Sheriff Braden was right behind us, and his gaze landed on Mirtel. His expression turned stony and business-like, and he turned to his son.

"Jared, call the coroner to come pick up the body."

Jared nodded, his eyes wide and dazed.

"All of you," the sheriff turned, taking in the rest of us with a hard look, "are coming with me to the station. We'll need statements from each of you before we figure out how to proceed."

My mother paled, her hand tight on my father's arm. "What about Robert? He needs medical treatment."

Eliise Tam spoke over her. "Those girls are the ones who—"

"*Those* girls just saved the town," Ms. Kross snapped.

Eliise spun on her. "I'm supposed to believe—"

Ms. Kross didn't back down. "I don't care *what* you—"

"*Enough,*" Sheriff Braden roared. "*Everyone* is coming with me to the station, and we will sort this out there."

A hand slipped into mine, solid and warm.

"Let's go," Stephen said quietly.

"What about Mirtel?" I protested.

"There's nothing we can do," Darja said, already turning away as Stephen pulled me after her.

"Wait—" Sheriff Braden's voice rose over the commotion, yelling after us. "You three have to come to the station, too."

The group was still in chaos, arguing and hurling insults, and when I glanced back the sheriff had already turned his attention back to Mirtel's body, apparently expecting us to obey his command without question.

Stephen wrapped his arm around my shoulders, and we quickly ducked around the edge of the stage, making our way out into the field and out of sight.

When we were well out of earshot, Darja turned to glare back, biting words out under her breath. "I'm dead. I don't have to go anywhere, and I'd like to see you try to make me."

"This is a *car?*"

It was some kind of scrap metal behemoth, but Stephen had pulled out a set of keys and seemed to be suggesting we all climb inside, like I hadn't risked my life enough already.

The corner of his mouth pulled up in a hint of a smile, but the sadness in his eyes didn't waver. I climbed in.

"I'll see you back at the house," Darja said. She was gone before I could respond, her body vanishing like mist.

The engine roared to life as I stared at the space where

she'd been standing, taking a little comfort in the fact that I could at least feel our bond again.

"Is she going to be okay?" Stephen's voice was quiet.

"I...I don't know," I said, turning to look at him. Would she? Would any of us?

But he seemed to accept my answer. His worried eyes scanned my face, his attention only half on the road as we made our way out of town.

"I'm sorry," he said, pushing his glasses up the bridge of his nose. "I'm so sorry, I...I knew about that spell. I didn't include it in my translation—I thought it was too dangerous. But Mirtel must have found it anyway; I didn't know, I'm so—"

"It's not your fault," I said, laying my hand over his where it rested on the center console. His gaze dropped to stare at my hand for a second, and then he turned his palm up, threading our fingers together.

"I still wish none of this had ever happened," he whispered.

"Me too," I said, staring unseeing out the window. "Me too."

We were silent most of the way to Stephen's parents' lake house. Whether it was due to exhaustion or an inability to find the right words, I didn't know, but he didn't let go of my hand and I didn't pull away either, finding comfort in the connection.

True to her word, Darja was waiting for us inside. The place had been huge even when all five of us had been there, but with Mirtel and Aggie gone, it was enormous. Their absence was glaring, like a wound that wouldn't heal, making my chest constrict until I could barely pull in a breath.

We gathered in the dining room, the space that had become our makeshift headquarters over the past few weeks, and I tried to ignore the papers still strewn across the heavy wood table, the teacup Mirtel had left sitting in one corner, the warm peppermint-and-mothballs smell of her that still permeated the air. I tried to ignore the feeling that they might at any second walk around the corner. I tried to ignore my certainty that no matter how much I might be hurting, Darja was certainly hurting more.

Stephen sat slumped in a chair, his eyes downcast, while Darja stared vacantly out the window toward the woods. Both of them looked as lost as I felt.

"So, what do we do now?" I asked, glancing between the two of them.

"We have to go back to Vaikesti," Darja said, at the same moment Stephen said, "We can't go back to Vaikesti."

I glanced between them in confusion.

"We have to go back to Mirtel's wagon," Darja said. "We need to go through her things."

Stephen was shaking his head. "We can't; it's too dangerous. They'll be looking for you again—for all of us."

"But—but where will we *go?*" My voice broke on the last word. I didn't just mean right then, either. I'd lived my whole life in Vaikesti. What was I—*who* was I—without it?

They both seemed to understand my real question, but neither seemed to know how to respond.

"We have to go back to Mirtel's," Darja repeated. "We can't let them go through her wagon. She'd want us to take her things with us."

Stephen shook his head again, and I knew he had a point, but Darja was right. Mirtel had no relatives, and I couldn't imagine letting the police or the Town Council paw through her things.

"What if...we went in at night?" I suggested. "We could be quick...it's not very big."

He sighed, and I could tell he wasn't going to fight us on it. "As long as we hurry."

We waited until the moon was high in the sky. It wasn't like any of us were sleeping anyway. Even after the events of the day, I knew I should be exhausted, but my mind was still spinning, and I couldn't imagine trying to relax right then. So instead we all climbed into the car and made the drive to Vaikesti one last time.

It was obvious even before we crossed the town limits. Even the air felt different—hot and stale, odorless, and an odd silence blanketed the town. There was no buzzing of insects, none of the quiet night sounds I hadn't realized were there until they were missing.

"What have we done?" I muttered under my breath, but it was obvious what we'd done. We may have saved the lives of the citizens, but we'd sucked the life out of Vaikesti as surely as if we'd burned the town to dust.

It was quiet as we drove through the streets, not another car in sight, until we reached the gravel turn-off that led down to the banks of the river where Mirtel's wagon sat in its lonely clearing.

It was a shock to see. I hadn't been sure our magic would have reached this far, but it had. The little wagon, once cute and charmingly weathered-looking with its dull, chipped patina, only looked sad. It fit in perfectly with the barren earth of the surrounding clearing, once-lush grass crumbled to dust underfoot. The trees on the river bank were still living, but their branches hung limp and heavy over the sluggishly-moving water, and my breathing was ragged as I tried to hold back my tears at the sight of what had become of the once-picturesque scene.

"Come on," Darja said quietly, and I felt a brief pulse of cold as her fingers hovered above my arm before she moved toward the wagon. I ducked, stroking the feathers of a lone chicken pecking idly in the dirt as I tried to compose myself before following her up the path.

"*Sofi.*" Stephen's call was strangled, and all my muscles tensed as I spun, searching for him in the dim moonlight. Had we been caught? Was someone waiting for us here after all?

Darja's sharp indrawn breath came from the same direction as his voice, and I found them standing over what had once been Mirtel's tiny vegetable garden, tucked under the trees to the side of the wagon.

"Oh God," I gasped, one hand flying up to cover my mouth as I took in the sight. It was Mirtel, her body laid out peacefully in the center of the patch.

With her eyes closed, I could almost pretend she was sleeping, and in her folded hands she clutched a profusion of blooming flowers—lilies and salvia and even a cluster of bright blue cornflowers spilled over the faded patchwork vest she'd been wearing. The flowers were bright and colorful and unaffected by the destruction of our magic—they clearly hadn't been picked from the earth.

My eyes filled and overflowed, tears tracking down my cheeks as I dropped to my knees next to her body. "How...?"

"Jared," Darja said quietly.

"Why would he do this?" Stephen asked, his brows pulled down and his lip twisted. "Is it supposed to be some kind of warning? A threat?"

"It's an apology, I think," I said through my tears. "A peace offering."

"The Vaikesti burn their dead," Darja said, the glint in her eye showing the irony of the statement was not lost on her. "He's giving her back to us. To honor in our way."

We did.

We honored her the best way we knew how, with a small pyre by the riverside. We laid Mirtel's body to rest wrapped in her favorite patchwork quilt, the blooming flowers spread out on top, and we held hands and sang as the bright flames lit the night, lazy spirals of smoke licking up toward the sky. We sang in the old tongue, unable to escape our roots even in the tragic aftermath of all that had happened because of those roots.

I let my tears fall into the dust and prayed that whatever the future held, it would be better, and brighter, and would somehow ease the pain that clenched around my heart like a vice.

I clutched Stephen's hand in mine, and reached down inside myself to pluck at the connection that lived there, the bond that grounded me.

Darja looked up, her eyes dark and unreadable in the shifting flames. I held out my hand, and she slipped hers through mine, an invisible icy touch.

"*Üheskoos*," I whispered.

"*Üheskoos*," she repeated, her gaze steady on mine.

Together.

CHAPTER 46

DARJA

"How could one person have so many teacups?" I shook my head and smiled, and though it felt genuine, it took some effort. Sofi and Stephen were going through the wagon, gathering up Mirtel's things and packing them carefully away in the few cardboard boxes we'd brought from Stephen's parents' house.

"She loves a good cup of tea," I said, and felt a sting when I realized I was still using the present tense when speaking about her.

Sofi either didn't notice, or wisely chose to ignore the slip. "I'd like to keep a few," she said, gently tracing a delicate rose-patterned china cup with one fingertip. "And maybe one of the teapots."

"She'd like that," Stephen said, putting a hand on Sofi's shoulder. She looked up at him and they shared a soft smile. I was happy for them, seeing whatever was blossoming between them, but it hurt, too. I wished I could let my consciousness evaporate, so I wouldn't have to feel this ache anymore.

I looked away from Sofi and Stephen, letting them have their moment without my prying eyes playing third wheel, and flicked my fingers toward a stack of papers and notebooks piled on the small table. The papers rustled and the top one floated into the air. I waved it toward me and glanced at the small print. It was an electric bill. I hadn't imagined Mirtel doing anything so mundane as paying bills, but I supposed she would have had to.

I curled my hand into a fist, and the paper crumpled, and then I waved it into the trash bag we'd put in the middle of the wagon. We were going to leave the items we didn't want, but we also didn't want to leave personal information just lying about for some Vaikesti Council member to find.

I sorted through the stack almost lazily, my mind wandering to places and times I wasn't sure I was ready to revisit. Places like the river's edge, where I'd traced my fingers along Aggie's cheek under a moody sky. Places like the house she'd grown up in, where I'd seen her in memories, vibrant and alive and so, so beautiful. And the time we'd spent at Stephen's house, poring over spells, practicing our magic.

Was that where it'd happened? Had Mirtel stumbled across the spell of sacrifice there? Had she snuck it into the pocket of one of her oversized cardigans? Had she known then how this would all play out, or had she hoped she'd never have to use it?

The surge of magic rushed through me before I even knew what was happening, and the stack of bills and letters rose from the table and spun in a whirlwind of paper. Startled, I quickly closed my hand in a tight fist, and the papers all dropped, scattering across the floor.

"Uh, Darja?" Sofi said, looking at the mess with a concerned furrow in her brow. "You okay?"

I nodded, not trusting my voice enough to speak. I stared

down at the pile and made a gathering motion with my hands, sweeping the debris together. It was then that I noticed the small book that had fallen out from amongst the sheets. I waved it toward me and looked closely at the cover. It was deep emerald green, maybe leather or some other soft material, and had the word *Journal* embossed in gold at the top.

"Sofi," I said, nodding my head toward the notebook, which was hovering in the air between us.

"What's—" she began, but then she stopped short as she came around and saw the cover.

We looked at each other, an unspoken question between us.

"Should we?" she said finally, and I shrugged. "I mean," she went on, "I don't think Mirtel would mind, but doesn't it feel like an invasion of privacy?'

"What if..." I swallowed back a rush of emotion. "What if she wrote about all this? About everything that's happened? We can't let something like that get into the wrong hands. I think we should...I think we should check."

Sofi nodded, but her gaze was worried. "Are you sure you can—?"

"I'm sure."

She didn't question me. Slowly, almost reverently, I flipped my hand toward the journal and opened the cover, skimming through the pages until we reached the end. Sofi was still and silent behind me; I wasn't even sure she was breathing.

Mirtel's cramped, messy scrawl filled every page. Most of it seemed mundane: a chicken refusing to lay, the kids she saw playing at the *koolis*—ordinary events from what turned out to be an extraordinary life.

On the last page, the writing was different. Still messy,

but broader strokes, as if she'd been writing in a hurry and couldn't be bothered to keep the words within the lines.

> *My heart keeps going back to the island,* it read. *The old country. The home of our ancestors.*
>
> *A place I have never been, but seems so clear in my mind. I can see the forests. Smell the sea air.*
>
> *I think that's where I will go, if it is up to me to choose. To the place where the magic is alive, where it is pure and unfettered. To the place where I know I can rest.*
>
> *Home.*
>
> *They will not understand, not now, but I hope one day they will.*
>
> *I hope, one day, a very long time from now, they will join me. Where the magic lives, like a beating heart, inside us all. Where it is eternal and infinite and free.*
>
> *I will wait. I will wait for them to come home.*

Sofi sucked in a shuddering breath behind me, and I knew she had reached the end. She moved her hand over my shoulder, and I leaned into the touch-that-wasn't-a-touch.

"What does it mean?" she whispered.

I shook my head. "I don't know. But I think she wanted us to find this."

I turned around and Sofi nodded. "I think you're right." She looked at Stephen, who was watching us with unabashed curiosity, but saying nothing.

She took a breath, then plucked the journal from the air and offered it to him.

He took it, and she smiled up at him. "I think I know where we have to go."

CHAPTER 47

SOFI

We left Vaikesti in the middle of the night. As Stephen drove slowly through the silent streets of the town, I wondered if it would be the last time I would ever see this place. This town I'd practically never set foot beyond in my eighteen years of life, and might never see again.

The moon ducked in and out of scudding clouds, the streetlights casting yellow pools of light on the pavement as we moved like wraiths through the dark, still night air. Unwilling to leave Mirtel's chickens to scrabble at soil that could no longer nourish them, we'd asked Ms. Kross to come gather them up and take them back to the *koolis*. I wondered what would become of them, what would become of the girls who lived there as well. Would there be more Spring Day sacrifices? Would any of our traditions continue? Who were the Vaikesti without their magic?

Darja was silent in the back seat, staring out the window as the town drifted by. Stephen was watching the road as he drove, though periodically his gaze would drift to me. His brow was furrowed, his knuckles tight on the steering wheel, and I knew he was worried. But I didn't have any words of reassurance.

"Turn here," I said suddenly, ducking to look out the window as my old neighborhood drew near on the left.

"Are you sure?" Stephen asked, his concerned gaze seeking me out again.

I nodded. "Just...just drive by. One last time."

He didn't seem convinced, but he made the turn, the darkened storefronts of the main road replaced by rows of quiet houses. My chest constricted as I took in the scene. The carefully manicured lawns were nothing but endless expanses of gray dirt, shining pale and dull under the streetlights. Flowerbeds were withered and dead, houses framed by desiccated bushes and skeletal trees.

"What's that?" Darja's voice drifted from the back seat, and Stephen slowed the car as we all turned to stare. It was the coroner's hearse, parked in the driveway of a nondescript blue house with white shutters. The lights were on in the house and I could see bodies moving around, a shroud-covered figure laid out in the front room, shadows dancing on the walls behind them.

"Who...who is that?" Stephen asked, his voice a little shaky.

I met Darja's eyes.

"That's...Henri and Marleen Luts' house," I answered in barely more than a whisper. "They performed the first spell together at the town meeting."

Stephen didn't answer.

"So, it's started," Darja said flatly.

I swallowed hard. I knew she believed those who had used the magic deserved their fate, and while I understood where she was coming from, I couldn't quite bring myself to feel the same. They hadn't known. They'd been just as blind as I had been, once.

The car rolled into motion again.

My parents' house was only a few blocks away, and Stephen slowed the car again as we drew near, rolling to a stop across the street. The house I'd grown up in was dark, the inhabitants thankfully asleep.

I wished I didn't feel any emotions at the sight of the house. The coroner wasn't here for my father yet, but he would be soon. I wished I didn't feel sympathy for my mother, who would have to deal with the aftermath of his death. I wished I didn't miss my sisters, didn't feel a sense of loss at the closeness we'd once had.

But it didn't matter. It was too late. There was nothing left for me here.

Mirtel's scrawled words chased themselves through my memory. *My heart keeps going back to the island.*

My future lay far away, across the oceans in a place I couldn't even imagine, where maybe I could find answers to questions I didn't even know how to ask. Not here. Not anymore.

I looked up at the dark house one last time.

"Bye, Sprat," I whispered, then turned to Stephen.

"Let's go."

―――

Thank you for reading *Season of Embers*. The story continues in *Season of Ashes: The Bonded Book 2*. If you enjoyed the book, please consider leaving a review.

ALSO BY THE AUTHORS

To view the complete catalogue of books by Rachael Vaughn,
please visit https://books2read.com/ap/R5mw12/Rachael-Vaughn

To view the complete catalogue of books by Wendi Williams,
please visit https://books2read.com/ap/nkqoPb/Wendi-Williams

CONNECT WITH THE AUTHORS

Rachael Vaughn

Sign up for my email reader group:
https://www.rachaelvaughn.com/signup

Visit my website:
www.rachaelvaughn.com

Visit my Facebook page:
www.facebook.com/rachaelvaughnauthor

Find me on Instagram:
@rachaelvaughnauthor

Send me an email:
rachaelvaughnauthor@gmail.com

Wendi Williams

Visit my Facebook page:
www.facebook.com/wendiwilliamswrites

Find me on TikTok:
https://www.tiktok.com/@wendiwilliams_author

ACKNOWLEDGMENTS

Wendi Williams

I am thankful to so many amazing people who assisted in the genesis of this book. But I have to begin by expressing my deep gratitude to the inimitable Rachael Vaughn, without whom there would be no book, no story, no Vaikesti, and no Sofi or Darja. From her creative spark, a whole world burst into being. She has been so much more than a co-author. Throughout the process, she has acted as builder of worlds, composer of words, unpaid therapist and giver of encouraging (but, thankfully, firm) motivation. Thank you for bringing me along for this wild ride, and helping me achieve a lifelong dream in the process.

To all of the supporters we've had along the way, thank you. To our beta readers, Bekah and Jordan, for giving us insights that pushed us to try harder, and helped make the book you're reading now better than it was before. To our editor, August, whose comments were just perfectly (and sometimes painfully) so *spot on*. And to the many friends and family members who have been our cheerleaders and biggest fans, and hopefully will continue to be, even after all the murder-y stuff.

And finally, thank you, Erik, for providing the foundation upon which we build all these crazy dreams together. You believed I could when I didn't. You told me to keep going when I wanted to quit. You took this "hobby" of mine seriously when I wanted to undermine it. And you were there, every step of the way. You, and our beautiful boys, mean the world to me. And that world is so much bigger and brighter, and full of greater possibility, with you in it.

ABOUT THE AUTHORS

Wendi Williams is a professional writer from outside Indianapolis, Indiana, where she resides with her husband, two sons, and pet lizard. Her career spans a vast world of words, from writing for broadcast news to blogs on choosing the right toilet. She has worked as a marketing copywriter for more than a decade, half of that devoted to starting her own business as a freelancer. In her spare time, she enjoys starting craft projects she will never finish, misses acting in community theatre, and watches Scandinavian crime dramas with her husband, a real-life Scandinavian. This is her first novel, but she's pretty set on making sure it's not her last.

Rachael Vaughn is the creative brainchild of a husband-and-wife writing duo. Rachael is the wordsmith of the pair. Her interests encompass all things creative, from mosaics to wood carving, and when she isn't writing she stays busy as a full-time tattoo artist. Vaughn acts as the bookends of the writing process. He serves as the team's world-builder on the front end, and acts as an editor and proofreader (plus the ultimate voice of reason) on the backside. The couple lives outside of Indianapolis with their daughter and cat, as well as more books than they could possibly read.

This is a work of fiction. Names, characters, places, and incidents either are the product of the author's imagination or are used fictitiously. Any resemblance to actual persons, living or dead, events, or locales is entirely coincidental.

Copyright © 2021 by Rachael Vaughn and Wendi Williams

All rights reserved. No part of this book may be reproduced or used in any manner without written permission of the copyright owner except for the use of quotations in a book review. For more information, address: rachaelvaughnauthor@gmail.com

First paperback edition November 2021

Cover image by Dane of Ebook Launch

ISBN 978-1-7362838-9-9 (paperback)
ISBN 978-1-7362838-6-8 (ebook)

www.glasswingpress.com

CPSIA information can be obtained
at www.ICGtesting.com
Printed in the USA
BVHW082350161121
621782BV00004B/490